W9-CFE-685

MODELS FOR WRITERS
SHORT ESSAYS FOR COMPOSITION
Third Edition

MODELS FOR WRITERS

SHORT ESSAYS FOR COMPOSITION
Third Edition

Editors

Alfred Rosa
Paul Eschholz
University of Vermont

ST. MARTIN'S PRESS   NEW YORK

Editor: Mark Gallaher
Project Editor: Elise Bauman
Production Supervisor: Julie Power
Graphics: G&H Soho
Cover Design: Darby Downey
Cover Art: Weaving by Cynthia Schira

Library of Congress Catalog Number: 88-60541
Copyright © 1989 by St. Martin's Press, Inc.
All rights reserved. No part of this publication may be reproduced, stored in a retrieval system, or transmitted by any form or by any means, electronic, mechanical, photocopying, recording, or otherwise, except as may be expressly permitted by the 1976 Copyright Act or in writing by the Publisher.
Manufactured in the United States of America.
3210
f

For information, write:
St. Martin's Press, Inc.
175 Fifth Avenue
New York, NY 10010

ISBN: 0-312-01227-6

Acknowledgments

I. The Elements of an Essay

1. Thesis

Page 22, "Give Us Jobs, Not Admiration" by Eric Bigler. From *Newsweek*, April 1987. © 1987, Newsweek Inc. All rights reserved. Printed by permission.

Page 27, "Anxiety: Challenge by Another Name" by James Lincoln Collier. Reprinted by permission of the author and *Reader's Digest* from the December 1986 *Reader's Digest*. Copyright © 1986 by The Reader's Digest Assn., Inc.

Acknowledgments and copyrights are continued at the back of the book on pages 408–411, which constitute an extension of the copyright page.

Preface

Models for Writers offers sixty-six short, lively essays that represent particularly appropriate models for use by beginning college writers. Most of our selections are comparable in length to the essays students will write themselves, and each clearly illustrates a basic rhetorical element, principle, or pattern. Just as important, the essays deal with subjects that we know from our own classroom experience will spark the interest of most college students. In making our selections, we have sought a level of readability that is neither so easy as to be condescending nor so difficult as to distract the reader's attention from the rhetorical issue under study. And, although we have included a few older classics, most of the essays have been written in the last ten years. Drawn from a wide range of sources, they represent a variety of contemporary prose styles.

This third edition of *Models for Writers* has been revised in a manner that is based on our own experiences as well as on the many suggestions made by instructors who adopted and liked the first two editions. We have added a second student essay to the introduction which explains the purpose of the text and shows students how it can be used to improve their writing. The new student essay, an explanation of the main reasons for the cockroach's durability, is expository and exemplifies the traditional five-paragraph format. This expository essay and the second student essay, which argues against the use of Astroturf, demonstrate the types of writing students will be doing at the beginning of the semester as well as later in the term. In addition, we have increased the number of study questions following each reading to an average of six per selection; the new questions generally focus on content and nicely complement the rhetorical emphasis for which the text has become known. Finally, well over one-third of the essays in this edition are new, many of them written in the last two or three years. At the suggestion of past users and reviewers, we have replaced selections with ones that we believe will prove even more workable, being careful in every case that the new essays meet the essential qualifications of brevity, clarity, and suitability for student writers.

As in the second edition, the essays in *Models for Writers, Third Edition*, are grouped into eighteen chapters, each devoted to a particular element or pattern. Chapters 1–7 focus on the concepts of thesis, unity, organization, beginnings and endings, paragraphs, transitions, and effective sentences. Next, Chapters 8 and 9 illustrate some aspects of language: the effects of diction and tone and the uses of figurative language. Finally, Chapters 10–18 explore the various types of writing most often required of college students: illustration, narration, description, process analysis, definition, division and classification, comparison and contrast, cause and effect, and argument. The arrangement of the chapters suggests a logical teaching sequence, moving from the elements of the essay to its language to the different types of essays. An alternative teaching strategy might be to structure the course around Chapters 10–18, bringing in earlier chapters as necessary to illustrate various individual elements. Each chapter is self-contained, so that instructors may easily devise their own sequences, omitting or emphasizing certain chapters according to the needs of a particular group of students. Whatever sequence is followed, thematic comparisons among the selections will be facilitated by the alternate *Thematic Table of Contents* at the beginning of the book.

The chapters all follow a similar pattern. Each opens with an explanation of the element or principle to be considered, many including paragraph–length examples. We then present three or four essays, each of which has its own brief introduction providing information about the author and directing the student's attention to specific rhetorical features. Every essay is followed by study materials in three parts: *Questions for Study and Discussion*, *Vocabulary*, and *Suggested Writing Assignments*.

The *Questions for Study and Discussion* focus on the content, the author's purpose, and the rhetorical strategy used to achieve that purpose. Some questions allow brief answers, but most are designed to stimulate more searching analysis and to promote lively classroom discussion. In order to reinforce the lessons of other chapters and remind students that good writing is never one-dimensional, at least one question at the end of each series focuses on a writing concern other than the one highlighted in the chapter at hand. Whenever it seemed helpful, we have referred students to the *Glossary of Useful Terms*, which provides concise definitions of rhetorical and other terms. The *Vocabulary* exercise draws from each reading several words that students will find worth adding to their vocabularies. The exercise asks them to define each word as it is used in the context of the selection and then to use the word in a new sentence of their own.

The *Suggested Writing Assignments* provide two writing assignments for each essay. The first calls for an essay closely related to the content and style of the essay it follows, in effect encouraging the use of the reading selection as a direct model. The second writing assignment, while ranging a little further afield in subject, gives the student yet another opportunity to practice the particular rhetorical element or principle being illustrated.

We are indebted to many people for their criticism and advice as we prepared this third edition of *Models for Writers*. We are especially grateful to:

Terence Aamodt, Walla Walla College; Charlotte Alexander, College of Staten Island; Susan Aylworth, Butte Community College; Diana H. Balogh, Glendale Community College; Lillian Bateman, Butte Community College; Rebecca Bennett, Broome Community College; Robin Betram, Evergreen Valley College; Marguerite Blackman, Montclair State College; Pearl J. Brandwein, Pace University—Pace Plaza; Christopher A. Bray, University of Vermont; Neville Britto, Delta Community College; Jean Clark, Butte Community College; Stan Coberly, Parkersburg Community College; Karen Conrath, Montcalm Community College; Ellen A. Cottrell, Armstrong State College; David Crosby, Alcorn State University; Judith Dan, Boston University; Ken DeLong, Montcalm Community College; Martha Edmonds, University of Richmond; Byron Fountain, Butte College; Carol Franks, Portland State University; Sylvia H. Gamboa, College of Charleston; Samuel B. Garren, North Carolina A&T State University; Hesterly B. Goodson, University of Vermont—Burlington; Kathleen B. Graham, Saginaw Valley State College; Hannah S. Gray, Holyoke Community College; Mary Y. Hallab, Central Missouri State University; Brigit

Hans, University of Arizona; Robert Henderson, Southeastern Oklahoma State University; Dora M. Houston, Southeastern Oklahoma State University; Norma R. Jones, Alcorn State University; Phyllis Katz, University of Hartford and Ward College of Technology; Joyce B. Kessel, Villa Maria College; Rosemarie Kistler, El Camino College; Patricia Kulata, Burlington County College; Mary S. Lauberg, Florissant Valley Community College; Elva Lauter, Glendale Community College; Denise Lynch, Central Connecticut State University; Joyce Marks, Indian Valley College; Shirley Morrell, Portland State University; Renate Muendel, West Chester University; Alan Natali, California University of Penn; Kenneth E. Newman, Diablo Valley College; Larry O'Kelley, Pierce Community College; John V. Pastoor, Montcalm Community College; Betty Pex, College of San Mateo; Jerry Lynn Piper, California State University—Sacramento; Raymond F. Pike, San Joaquin Delta College; Katherine Pluta, Bakersfield College; Ruth Ray, Wayne State University; Karyn Riedell, College of Southern Idaho; Betsy Rodriguez-Bachiller, Kean College of New Jersey; Elisabeth Rosenberg, Normandale Community College; Ilene Rubenstein, Moorpark College; Elizabeth Ann Sachs, Western Connecticut State University; Douglas Salerno, Washtenaw Community College; Richard Sanzenbacher, Embry-Riddle University; Diane Scharper, Towson State University; Wayne B. Scheer, Atlanta Junior College; Walter Schlager, Butte College; Julie Segedy, Chabot College; Alice Snelgrove, College of DuPage; Lee W. Speer, College of San Mateo; T. Ella Strother, Madison Area Technical College; Pamela Thomas, Fresno City College; Margaret Tritle, El Camino College; June Verbillion, Northeastern Illinois University; Leon Ward, Grayson College; Tryna Zeedyk, Waubonsee Community College; Mary E. Zeman, Adelphi University; Janet Zito, Thames Valley Technical College.

It was once again our good fortune to have the editorial guidance of Mark Gallaher of St. Martin's Press as we worked on this new edition. Our greatest debt, as always, is to our students, for all that they have taught us.

Alfred Rosa
Paul Eschholz

Contents

II. *The Language of the Essay* 145

8. **Diction and Tone** 147

9. **Figurative Language** 172

III. *Types of Essays* 185

10. **Illustration** 187

Thematic Contents

Practical Advice

Education

Health and Medicine

INTRODUCTION

Models for Writers is designed to help you learn to write by providing you with a collection of model essays, essays that are examples of good writing. We know that one of the best ways to learn to write and to improve our writing is to read. By reading we can begin to see how other writers have communicated their experiences, ideas, thoughts, and feelings. We can study how they have used the various elements of the essay—words, sentences, paragraphs, organizational patterns, transitions, examples, evidence, and so forth—and thus learn how we might effectively do the same. When we see, for example, how a writer like James Lincoln Collier develops an essay from a strong thesis statement, we can better appreciate the importance of having a clear thesis statement in our writing. When we see the way Russell Baker uses transitions to link key phrases and important ideas so that readers can recognize clearly how the parts of his essay are meant to fit together, we have a better idea of how to achieve such clarity in our own writing.

But we do not learn only by observing, by reading. We also learn by doing, by writing, and in the best of all situations we engage in these two activities in conjunction with one another. *Models for Writers* encourages you, therefore, to write your essays, to practice what you are learning, as you are actually reading and analyzing the model essays in the text.

The kind of composition that you will be asked to write for your college writing instructor is most often referred to as an essay—a relatively short piece of nonfiction in which a writer attempts to develop one or more closely related points or ideas. An effective essay has a clear purpose, often provides useful information, has an effect on the reader's thoughts and feelings, and is usually a pleasure to read.

All well-written essays also share a number of structural and stylistic features that are illustrated by the various essays in

1

Models for Writers. One good way to learn what these features are and how you can involve them in your own writing is to look at each of them in isolation. For this reason we have divided *Models for Writers* first into three major sections and, within these sections, into eighteen chapters, each with its own particular focus and emphasis.

"The Elements of an Essay," the first section, includes chapters on the following subjects: thesis, unity, organization, beginnings and endings, paragraphs, transitions, and effective sentences. All these elements are essential to a well-written essay, but the concepts of thesis, unity, and organization underlie all the others and so come first in our sequence.

Briefly, "Thesis" shows how authors put forth or state the main ideas of their essays and how they use such statements to develop and control content; "Unity," how authors achieve a sense of wholeness in their essays; and "Organization," some important patterns that authors use to organize their thinking and writing. "Beginnings and Endings" offers advice and models of ways to begin and conclude essays, while "Paragraphs" concentrates on the importance of well-developed paragraphs and what is necessary to achieve them. "Transitions" concerns the various devices that writers use to move from one idea or section of an essay to the next. Finally, "Effective Sentences" focuses on techniques to make sentences powerful and create stylistic variety.

"The Language of the Essay," the second major section of the text, includes a chapter on diction and tone and one on figurative language. "Diction and Tone" shows how carefully writers choose words either to convey exact meanings or to be purposefully suggestive. In addition, this chapter shows how the words a writer uses can create a particular tone or relationship between the writer and the reader—one of irony, for example, or humor or great seriousness. "Figurative Language" concentrates on the usefulness of the special devices of language—such as simile, metaphor, and analogy—that add richness and depth to one's writing.

The final section of *Models for Writers*, "Types of Essays," includes chapters on the various types of writing most often required of college writing students: "Illustration" (how to use examples to illustrate a point or idea); "Narration" (how to tell a story or give an account of an event); "Description" (how to present a verbal picture); "Process Analysis" (how to explain how something is done or happens); "Definition" (how to explain what something is); "Division and Classification" (how to divide a subject into its parts and place items into appropriate categories); "Comparison and Contrast" (how to demonstrate likenesses and differences); "Cause and Effect" (how to explain the causes of an event or the effects of an action); and, finally, "Argument" (how to use reason and logic to persuade someone to your way of thinking).

All of the chapters follow a similar pattern. Each opens with an explanation of the element or principle under consideration. These introductions are intended to be brief, clear, and memorable. Here you will also usually find one or more short examples of the feature or principle being studied. Following the introduction, we present three or four model essays, each with a brief introduction of its own providing information about the author and directing your attention to the highlighted rhetorical features. Every essay is followed by study materials in three parts: *Questions for Study and Discussion, Vocabulary,* and *Suggested Writing Assignments.*

Models for Writers, then, provides information, instruction, and practice in writing essays. By reading carefully and thoughtfully and by applying what you learn, you can begin to have more and more control over your own writing. Courtney Smith and Andy Pellett, two of our own writing students at the University of Vermont, found this to be true, and their work is a good example of what can be achieved from studying models.

Two Model Student Essays

For an assignment following one of the readings in the chapter on unity, Courtney Smith was inspired by a television commercial to choose an unusual topic: cockroaches. In order to develop a thesis about these creatures, Courtney did some preliminary reading in the library, spoke to her biology professor who had some interesting exhibits to show her, and surveyed the roach control products available at her local supermarket. In sorting through the information she gathered, she was particularly surprised by the ability of cockroaches to survive under almost any circumstances. This ability seemed to her to provide a suitably narrow focus for a short, unified essay, so she began to analyze the various reasons for the insect's resiliency. By first making lists of the points she wanted to include in her essay, Courtney discovered that she could cluster the reasons into three groups. She was then able to formulate the following thesis: "Cockroaches are remarkably resilient creatures for three basic reasons." This thesis, in turn, helped Courtney to map her organization; she decided that her essay would have three major paragraphs to discuss each of the basic reasons cockroaches are so durable and that she would also need an introductory paragraph and a concluding paragraph. This five-paragraph pattern provided the basis for her first draft.

What follows is the final draft of Courtney's essay, incorporating a number of changes she made based on a critical evaluation of her first draft.

Cockroaches

Courtney Smith

BEGINNING: captures readers' attention

Have you ever tried to get rid of cockroaches? Those stupid little bugs refuse to go. You can chase them, starve them, spray them, and even try to squash them. But no matter what you do, they always come back. I have heard they are the only creatures that can survive a nuclear explosion. What do cockroaches have that enables them to be such extremely resilient insects? The answer is

THESIS

simple. Cockroaches have survived in even the most hostile environments because they possess several unique physical features, an amazing reproductive process, and an immune system that has frustrated even the best efforts of exterminators to get rid of them.

Cockroaches are thin, torpedo-shaped insects. Their body shape allows them to squeeze into small cracks or holes in walls and ceilings or dart into drains, thus avoiding all dangers. Their outer shell is extremely hard, making them almost impossible to crush. Cockroaches have sticky pads on their claws that enable them to climb walls or crawl upside down on ceilings. They also have two little tails called "cerci" to alert them to danger. These cerci are covered wth tiny hairs that, like antennae, are sensitive to things as small as a speck of dust or as seemingly innocent as a puff of air. Finally, if cockroaches can't find food, they can sustain themselves for up to a month without food, as long as they have water. Combined with their other physical features, this ability to go for long periods without food has made the cockroach almost invincible.

Cockroaches give credence to the old adage that there is safety in numbers. They reproduce at a truly amazing rate. About two months after mating, a new generation of cockroaches is born. One cockroach can produce about two dozen offspring each time it mates. To get some idea of their reproductive power, imagine that you start with three pairs of cockroaches that mate. Approximately three weeks after mating the females lay their eggs, which hatch some forty-five days later. If we assume two dozen eggs from each female, the first generation would number seventy-two offspring. These

FIRST POINT:
"physical features"

DESCRIPTION

TOPIC SENTENCE:
PARAGRAPH UNITY

SECOND POINT:
"reproductive process"

ILLUSTRATION:
hypothetical example

roaches would continue to multiply
geometrically so that by year's end the
colony's population would total more than
10,000 cockroaches. Stopping this process is
almost impossible because, even if we were
successful in annihilating the adult
population, it is more than likely that a new
generation would already be on the way.

**THIRD POINT:
"immune
system"**

Finally, cockroaches have frustrated
scientists with their ability to immunize
themselves against drugs, poison, and bomb
gases. The cockroaches then pass this new
immunity on to the next generation quicker
than a new poison can be made. Although
scientists have studied the cockroach for a
long time, they have not discovered the
biological mechanism that enables them to
develop immunity quickly. It is only
natural, therefore, that many scientists
have been at work on a "birth control"
solution for cockroaches. By rendering at
least some portion of the adult population
sterile, scientists hope to gain a measure of
control over the pesty creatures.

**ENDING:
prediction for
the future**

Today there are 3,500 different species
of cockroaches. They have survived on this
planet since the time of the dinosaurs some
350 million years ago. Whether or not
scientists are successful in their latest
efforts to rid us of cockroaches is yet to be
determined. Odds are that they won't
succeed. Given the cockroach's amazing
record of survivability, it is not likely to
turn up on the world's list of endangered
species.

Andy Pellet's paper grew out of his reading of essays in Chapter 18. He was assigned to write an argument and, like Courtney, he was free to choose his own topic. He knew from past experience that in order to write a good essay he would have to write on a topic he cared about. He also knew that he should allow himself a reasonable amount of time to find such a topic and to gather his ideas. An avid sports fan, Andy immediately decided to write about some aspect of sports. After considering and rejecting several possible topics within that subject area—including professional salaries, Olympic basketball teams, and sports heroes in advertisements—he decided that his strong feelings concerning artificial playing surfaces provided a good basis for an argumentative essay. Because of what he had read in the popular press and what he himself had seen, Andy had developed a longstanding dislike of artificial playing surfaces, and he determined that his major argument, the thesis of his essay, would be that such surfaces were bad for athletes and for sports.

Andy began by brainstorming about the topic. He made lists of all the ideas, facts, issues, arguments, and counterarguments that came to mind and that he thought he might want to include in his essay. Once he was confident that he had amassed enough information to begin writing, he made a rough outline of an organizational pattern that he felt would work well for him: first point out the weakness of the arguments put forth in favor of artificial turf, then conclude with his own strong arguments against. Keeping that organizational pattern in mind, Andy next wrote a first draft of his essay and proceeded to examine it carefully, assessing what still needed to be done to improve it.

Andy was writing this particular essay in the second half of the semester, after he had read a good number of essays and had learned the importance of such matters as good paragraphing, unity, and transitions. In rereading his first draft, he discovered that he could still do several things to improve his essay. First, he had failed to mention an important objection to artificial turf when he was writing the first draft (the high cost of installation and replacement), so he now included it. He also found places where phrases and even sentences could be added to make his meaning clearer. He changed the order of the sentences in his sixth paragraph, and he even improved his original organizational pattern by deciding to wait until just before his conclusion to bring up his argument about injuries. In addition, he inserted transitions (for example, in paragraph 5) and changed a number of words, as in paragraph 8, to create a more forceful effect.

The final draft of Andy's paper illustrates how well he has learned how the parts of a well-written essay fit together, and how to make revisions based on what his reading and study of model essays has taught him. The following is the final draft of Andy's essay.

The Perils of AstroTurf

Andy Pellett

BEGINNING: establishes author's viewpoint and purpose

As a purist sports fan, I am suspicious of changes that occur in my favorite pastimes, namely, baseball and football. In the past two decades, there have been many new developments--some good and some bad.

THESIS

But the most disturbing change has been the introduction of artificial turf as a playing surface.

DICTION: "artificial turf" vs. "fake grass"

This fake grass first appeared on the sporting scene in 1966. The grass in the Houston Astrodome was dying, so in a desperation move, it was replaced by

PARAGRAPH UNITY: chronology/ repeated words (grass, turf, etc.)

artificial turf. This new surface, manufactured by the Monsanto Company, was appropriately called AstroTurf.

Since then, the living grass in stadiums and playing fields everywhere has been replaced with one form of artificial turf or another, usually made up of green nylon fibers stitched over a cushioned polyester mat. AstroTurf is still the most common.

What's so great about artificial turf? If real grass was good enough for the sports heroes of yesteryear, why shouldn't it be good enough for those of today? The proponents of artificial turf have at least two basic arguments.

RHETORICAL QUESTIONS

The first argument uses a familiar line of reasoning: artificial turf saves money. The field needs less maintenance, and rain water drains easily through small holes in the mat. Also, the field can be used for more than one sport. A football game won't tear up the turf, thereby making it possible to play a baseball game on the same field a day later.

ORGANIZATION: proponents' first argument

This argument, however, overlooks several important problems. The cost of laying down a new synthetic field is very high--close to a million dollars. In addition, artificial turf deteriorates in appearance and condition. Tobacco juice spit onto the ground will soak in; on AstroTurf it makes an ugly stain that gives grounds-keepers fits. In 1971, the artificial turf in Miami's Orange Bowl was decoratively painted for the Super Bowl. After the game, the paint couldn't be removed and remained on the field for months. For these and other reasons, older fields may have to be resurfaced. Such resurfacing increases, not decreases, the cost of field maintenance.

TRANSITION: "however" sets up refutation

ILLUSTRATION: examples used as evidence

The second argument proponents of AstroTurf make is that traction is increased by artificial turf, thereby making it easier to play in inclement weather. But why should we make it easier to play in bad weather? A

ORGANIZATION: proponents' second argument

game like football is a tough sport, and
playing in horrible conditions personifies
that toughness. Most fans enjoy watching two
football teams battle it out, with mud
covering every part of their uniforms.
Baseball, like football, was meant to be
played outside on grass, and, if we take the
natural element out of sport, we lose a sense
of drama.

TRANSITIONAL PARAGRAPH: introduces opposing arguments

It is evident that arguments in favor of
artificial turf tend to ignore some important
facts. Furthermore, these arguments appear
even weaker when compared to the arguments
put forth by the detractors of AstroTurf.
Opponents of artificial turf make essentially two arguments: artificial turf causes
the ball to hop unnaturally, which affects
team statistics and strategy, and artificial
turf causes more injuries to players.

ORGANIZATION: first opposing argument

FIGURATIVE LANGUAGE

In the major leagues the baseball
diamond has been turned into a basketball
court by the hard surface. The ball rockets
off the turf as if being fired from a cannon.
It rolls faster and farther than on natural
grass, thus allowing for more extra-base
hits.

"Great," some fans will say; "we like
to see more offense." But a baseball
player's performance is measured by
statistics. So it really isn't fair for a
weak hitter to acquire more extra-base hits
just because he plays on artificial turf.

Strategy is also affected. An
outfielder must play back to prevent the ball
from caroming over his head. This allows

cheap bloop singles that ordinarily would be caught. And what about when the batter grounds the ball into the turf in front of home plate? Normally this should be an out; but by the time the ball comes down, the batter is standing on first base with a "Monsanto single."

DEFINITION: "Monsanto single"

EFFECTIVE SENTENCE

The other topic of debate has been injuries. Athletes have complained that artificial turf is responsible for everything from friction burns to broken bones. Because of the hard surface, athletes must make adaptations in their running style, which can often result in painful foot ailments. Also, the greatly improved traction of AstroTurf means that, when a player plants his foot, it won't slide at all. Therefore, if a player is in an awkward position with his feet planted, and he gets hit, serious knee injuries can result. Earlier this year, Billy Sims of the Detroit Lions blamed his season-ending knee injury on the artificial turf. Years ago, Gale Sayers blamed artificial turf for delaying his comeback from knee surgery.

ORGANIZATION: second opposing argument

CAUSE AND EFFECT

EVIDENCE OF AUTHORITIES

My fervent, yet probably unrealistic, hope is that artificial turf be banned. There was never any controversy when real grass was the only surface on which outdoor games were played. If we stick with natural substances, we can't go wrong. Trying to improve on nature only causes trouble. Richie Allen, former baseball player, probably said it best: "If my horse can't eat it, I don't want to play on it."

ENDING: argument enforced by appropriate quotation

I

THE ELEMENTS OF AN ESSAY

1

THESIS

The *thesis* of an essay is its main idea, the point it is trying to make. The thesis is often expressed in a one- or two-sentence statement, although sometimes it is implied or suggested rather than stated directly. The thesis statement controls and directs the content of the essay: everything that the writer says must be logically related to the thesis statement.

Usually the thesis is presented early in an essay, sometimes in the first sentence. Here are some thesis statements that begin essays:

> New York is a city of things unnoticed.
>
> Gay Talese

> Most Americans are in terrible shape.
>
> James F. Fixx

> One of the most potent elements in body language is eye behavior.
>
> Flora Davis

Each of these sentences does what a good thesis statement should do—it identifies the topic and makes an assertion about it.

Often writers prepare readers for a thesis statement with one or several sentences that establish a context. Notice, in the following example, how the author eases the reader into his thesis about television instead of presenting it abruptly in the first sentence:

> With the advent of television, for the first time in history, all aspects of animal and human life and death, of societal and individual behavior have been condensed on the average to a 19 inch diagonal screen and a 30 minute time slot. Television, a unique medium, claiming to be neither a reality nor art, has become reality for many of us, particularly for our children who are growing up in front of it.
>
> Jerzy Kosinski

On occasion a writer may even purposefully delay the presentation of a thesis until the middle or end of an essay. If the thesis is controversial or needs extended discussion and illustration, the writer might present it later to make it easier for the reader to understand and accept it. Appearing near or at the end of an essay, a thesis also gains prominence.

Some kinds of writing do not need thesis statements. These include descriptions, narratives, and personal writing such as letters and diaries. But any essay that seeks to explain or prove a point has a thesis that is usually set forth in a thesis statement.

THE MOST IMPORTANT DAY

Helen Keller

Helen Keller (1880–1968) was afflicted by a disease that left her blind and deaf at the age of eighteen months. With the aid of her teacher, Anne Sullivan, she was able to overcome her severe handicaps, to graduate from Radcliffe College, and to lead a productive and challenging adult life. In the following selection from her autobiography, The Story of My Life *(1902), Keller tells of the day she first met Anne Sullivan, a day she regarded as the most important in her life. Notice that Keller states her thesis in the first paragraph and that it serves to focus and unify the remaining paragraphs.*

The most important day I remember in all my life is the one on which my teacher, Anne Mansfield Sullivan, came to me. I am filled with wonder when I consider the immeasurable contrast between the two lives which it connects. It was the third of March, 1887, three months before I was seven years old.

On the afternoon of that eventful day, I stood on the porch, dumb, expectant. I guessed vaguely from my mother's signs and from the hurrying to and fro in the house that something unusual was about to happen, so I went to the door and waited on the steps. The afternoon sun penetrated the mass of honeysuckle that covered the porch and fell on my upturned face. My fingers lingered almost unconsciously on the familiar leaves and blossoms which had just come forth to greet the sweet southern spring. I did not know what the future held of marvel or surprise for me. Anger and bitterness had preyed upon me continually for weeks and a deep languor had succeeded this passionate struggle.

Have you ever been at sea in a dense fog, when it seemed as if   3
a tangible white darkness shut you in, and the great ship, tense
and anxious, groped her way toward the shore with plummet
and sounding-line, and you waited with beating heart for something to happen? I was like that ship before my education began, only I was without compass or sounding-line, and had no
way of knowing how near the harbor was. "Light! give me
light!" was the wordless cry of my soul, and the light of love
shone on me in that very hour.

I felt approaching footsteps. I stretched out my hand as I sup-   4
posed to my mother. Someone took it, and I was caught up and
held close in the arms of her who had come to reveal all things
to me, and, more than all things else, to love me.

The morning after my teacher came she led me into her room   5
and gave me a doll. The little blind children at the Perkins Institution had sent it and Laura Bridgman had dressed it; but I did
not know this until afterward. When I had played with it a little
while, Miss Sullivan slowly spelled into my hand the word
"d-o-l-l." I was at once interested in this finger play and tried to
imitate it. When I finally succeeded in making the letters cor-
rectly I was flushed with childish pleasure and pride. Running
downstairs to my mother I held up my hand and made the letters for doll. I did not know that I was spelling a word or even
that words existed; I was simply making my fingers go in
monkeylike imitation. In the days that followed I learned to
spell in this uncomprehending way a great many words, among
them *pin, hat, cup* and a few verbs like *sit, stand* and *walk*. But
my teacher had been with me several weeks before I under-
stood that everything has a name.

One day, while I was playing with my new doll, Miss Sullivan   6
put my big rag doll into my lap also, spelled "d-o-l-l" and tried
to make me understand that "d-o-l-l" applied to both. Earlier
in the day we had had a tussle over the words "m-u-g" and
"w-a-t-e-r." Miss Sullivan had tried to impress it upon me that
"m-u-g" is *mug* and that "w-a-t-e-r" is *water*, but I persisted in
confounding the two. In despair she had dropped the subject
for the time, only to renew it at the first opportunity. I became
impatient at her repeated attempts and, seizing the new doll, I
dashed it upon the floor. I was keenly delighted when I felt the

fragments of the broken doll at my feet. Neither sorrow nor regret followed my passionate outburst. I had not loved the doll. In the still, dark world in which I lived there was no strong sentiment or tenderness. I felt my teacher sweep the fragments to one side of the hearth, and I had a sense of satisfaction that the cause of my discomfort was removed. She brought me my hat, and I knew I was going out into the warm sunshine. This thought, if a wordless sensation may be called a thought, made me hop and skip with pleasure.

We walked down the path to the well-house, attracted by the 7 fragrance of the honeysuckle with which it was covered. Some one was drawing water and my teacher placed my hand under the spout. As the cool stream gushed over one hand she spelled into the other the word *water*, first slowly, then rapidly. I stood still, my whole attention fixed upon the motions of her fingers. Suddenly I felt a misty consciousness as of something forgotten—a thrill of returning thought; and somehow the mystery of language was revealed to me. I knew then that "w-a-t-e-r" meant the wonderful cool something that was flowing over my hand. The living word awakened my soul, gave it light, hope, joy, set it free! There were barriers still, it is true, but barriers that could in time be swept away.

I left the well-house eager to learn. Everything had a name, 8 and each name gave birth to a new thought. As we returned to the house every object which I touched seemed to quiver with life. That was because I saw everything with the strange, new sight that had come to me. On entering the door I remembered the doll I had broken. I felt my way to the hearth and picked up the pieces. I tried vainly to put them together. Then my eyes filled with tears; for I realized what I had done, and for the first time I felt repentance and sorrow.

I learned a great many new words that day. I do not remem- 9 ber what they all were; but I do know that *mother, father, sister, teacher* were among them—words that were to make the world blossom for me, "like Aaron's rod, with flowers." It would have been difficult to find a happier child than I was as I lay in my crib at the close of that eventful day and lived over the joys it had brought me, and for the first time longed for a new day to come.

Questions for Study and Discussion

1. What is Helen Keller's thesis in this essay?
2. What is Helen Keller's purpose in this essay? (Glossary: *Purpose*)
3. What was Helen Keller's state of mind before Anne Sullivan arrived to help her? To what does she compare herself?
4. Why was the realization that everything has a name important to Helen Keller?
5. How was the "mystery of language" (7) revealed to Helen Keller? What were the consequences of this new understanding of the nature of language for her?
6. Helen Keller narrates the events of the day Anne Sullivan arrived (2–4), the morning after she arrived (5), and one day several weeks after her arrival (6–9). Describe what happens on each day, and explain how these separate incidents support her thesis.

Vocabulary

Refer to your dictionary to define the following words as they are used in this selection. Then use each word in a sentence of your own.

dumb (2)	plummet (3)
preyed (2)	tussle (6)
languor (2)	vainly (8)
passionate (2)	

Suggested Writing Assignments

1. Think about an important day in your own life. Using the thesis statement "The most important day of my life was _____," write an essay in which you show the significance of that day by recounting and explaining the events that took place.
2. For many people around the world, the life of Helen Keller stands as the symbol of what can be achieved by an individual despite seemingly insurmountable handicaps. Her

achievements have also had a tremendous impact upon those who are not afflicted with handicaps, leading them to believe that they can accomplish more than they ever thought possible. Consider the role of handicapped people in our society, develop an appropriate thesis, and write an essay on the topic.

GIVE US JOBS, NOT ADMIRATION

Eric Bigler

Eric Bigler was born in Powhatan Point, Ohio, in 1958. Despite a diving accident while he was in high school that left him paralyzed from the chest down, Bigler went on to earn his bachelor's degree in social work and his master's degree in business and industrial counseling management at Wright State University in Dayton, Ohio. Eric now works part-time in the Augmentative Communications Research Laboratory at Wright State, where he does research on using state-of-the-art computer technology to help the disabled work with computers. At this writing, however, he is still looking for full-time employment, still waiting to hear the words, "You're hired."

Tuesday I have another job interview. Like most I have had so far, it will probably end with the all-too-familiar words, "We'll let you know of our decision in a few days."

Many college graduates searching for their first career job might simply accept that response as, "Sorry, we're not interested in you," and blame the rejection on inexperience or bad chemistry. For myself and other disabled people, however, this response often seems to indicate something more worrisome: a reluctance to hire the handicapped even when they're qualified. I have been confined to a wheelchair since 1974, when a high-school diving accident left me paralyzed from the chest down. But that didn't prevent me from earning a bachelor's in social work in 1983, and I am now finishing up a master's degree in business and industrial management, specializing in employee relations and human-resource development.

Our government spends a great deal of money to help the handicapped, but it does not necessarily spend it all wisely. For example, in 1985 Ohio's Bureau of Vocational Rehabilitation (BVR) spent more than $4 million in tuition and other expenses

22

so that disabled students could obtain a college education. BVR's philosophy is that the amount of money spent educating students will be repaid in disabled employees' taxes. The agency assists graduates by offering workshops on résumé writing and interviewing techniques, skills many already learned in college. BVR also maintains files of résumés that are matched with help-wanted notices from local companies and employs placement specialists to work directly with graduates during their job search.

Even with all this assistance, however, graduates still have   4
trouble getting hired. Such programs might do better if they concentrated on the perceptions of employers as well as the skills of applicants. More important, improving contacts with prospective employers might encourage them to actively recruit the disabled.

Often, projects that *do* show promise don't get the chance to   5
thrive. I was both a client and an informal consultant to one program, Careers for the Disabled in Dayton, which asked local executives to make a commitment to hire disabled applicants whenever possible. I found this strategy to be on target, since support for a project is more likely when it is ordered from the top. The program also offered free training seminars to corporations on how they can work effectively with the disabled candidate. In April of 1986—less than a year after it was started and after only three disabled people were placed—the program was discontinued because, according to the director, they had "no luck at getting [enough] corporations to join the program."

Corporations need to take a more independent and active   6
part in hiring qualified handicapped persons. Today's companies try to show a willingness to innovate, and hiring people like myself would enhance that image. Madison Avenue has finally recognized that the disabled are also consumers; more and more often, commercials include them. But advertisers could break down even more stereotypes. I would like to see one of those Hewlett-Packard commercials, for instance, show an employee racing down the sidewalk in his wheelchair, pulling alongside a pay phone and calling a colleague to ask "What if . . .?"

Corporate recruiters also need to be better prepared for   7
meeting with disabled applicants. They should be ready to an-

swer queries about any barriers that their building's design may pose, and they should be forthright about asking their own questions. It's understandable that employers are afraid to mention matters that are highly personal and may prove embarassing—or, even worse, discriminatory. There's nothing wrong, however, with an employer reassuring him or herself about whether an applicant will be able to reach files, operate computers or even get into the bathroom. Until interviewers change their style, disabled applicants need to initiate discussion of disability-related issues.

Cosmetic acts: Government has tried to improve hiring for the disabled through Affirmative Action programs. The Rehabilitation Act of 1973 says institutions or programs receiving substantial amounts of federal money can't discriminate on the basis of handicap. Yet I was saddened and surprised to discover how many companies spend much time and money writing great affirmative-action and equal-opportunity guidelines but little time following them. Then there are the cosmetic acts, such as the annual National Employ the Handicapped Week every October. If President Reagan (or anyone else) wants to help the disabled with proclamations, more media exposure is necessary. I found out about the last occasion in 1985 from a brief article on the back of a campus newspaper—a week after it had happened. 8

As if other problems were not enough, the disabled who search unsuccessfully for employment often face a loss of self-esteem and worth. In college, many disabled people I have talked to worked hard toward a degree so they would be prepared for jobs after graduation. Now they look back on their four or more years as wasted time. For these individuals, the days of earning good grades and accomplishing tough tasks fade away, leaving only frustrating memories. Today's job market is competitive enough without prejudice adding more "handicaps." 9

About that interview . . . five minutes into it, I could feel the atmosphere chill. The interviewer gave me general information instead of trying to find out if I was right for the job. I've been there before. Then the session closed with a handshake, and those same old words: "We'll let you know." They said I should be so proud of myself for doing what I am doing. That's what they always say. I'm tired of hearing how courageous I am. So 10

are other disabled people. We need jobs, and we want to work
like anyone else.

But still, I remain an optimist. I know someday soon a company will be smart enough to realize how much I have to offer
them in both my head and my heart.

Maybe then I'll hear the words so many of us really want to   12
hear: "You're hired."

Questions for Study and Discussion

1. What does Bigler feel is wrong with government programs
   aimed at helping the disabled? What does he suggest be
   done to improve the situation?
2. What is Bigler's thesis in this essay? Where in the essay is
   his thesis most clearly presented?
3. Does Bigler give his readers any reasons why the disabled
   are not being hired as often as they should be? Does the
   success of his thesis depend upon his providing such reasons? Explain.
4. Bigler frames his essay with references to a particular job
   interview. Discuss the way Bigler connects the beginning
   and ending of his essay. Has he employed an effective strategy in this regard? Explain.
5. What are the "cosmetic acts" that Bigler refers to in paragraph 8? Why does he use this particular term? (Glossary:
   Diction)
6. What audience(s) would seem to be most interested in what
   Bigler has to say in his essay? Explain.

Vocabulary

Refer to your dictionary to define the following words as they
are used in this selection. Then use each word in a sentence of
your own.

worrisome (2)	forthright (7)
seminars (5)	proclamations (8)
enhance (6)	self-esteem (9)

Suggested Writing Assignments

1. Write an essay in which you use as your thesis the formula "Give us _____, not _____." You may use one of the following topics or create one of your own:

   Give us peace, not more arms.

   Give us results, not more red tape.

   Give us action, not talk.

   Give us jobs, not welfare.

   Give us choices, not rules.

   Give us answers, not excuses.

   Give us opportunities, not promises.

   Give us better government, not more taxes.

2. One year after Eric Bigler's essay was published, he was still not employed in a full-time position. Develop a thesis and write an essay of your own as to why the disabled have a difficult time gaining employment despite their personal talents and educational backgrounds.

ANXIETY: CHALLENGE BY ANOTHER NAME

James Lincoln Collier

James Lincoln Collier is a free-lance writer with over six hundred articles to his credit. He was born in New York in 1928 and graduated from Hamilton College in 1950. Among his many books are Rock Star *(1970),* It's Murder at St. Basket's *(1972),* My Brother Sam Is Dead *(1974),* Rich and Famous *(1975),* Give Dad My Best *(1976), and* Duke Ellington *(1987). Collier's best-known book is* The Making of Jazz: A Comprehensive History *(1978), still regarded as the best general history of the subject. As you read the following essay, pay particular attention to Collier's thesis, where it is placed in the essay, and how well he supports it.*

Between my sophomore and junior years at college, a chance came up for me to spend the summer vacation working on a ranch in Argentina. My roommate's father was in the cattle business, and he wanted Ted to see something of it. Ted said he would go if he could take a friend, and he chose me.

The idea of spending two months on the fabled Argentine Pampas was exciting. Then I began having second thoughts. I had never been very far from New England, and I had been homesick my first few weeks at college. What would it be like in a strange country? What about the language? And besides, I had promised to teach my younger brother to sail that summer. The more I thought about it, the more the prospect daunted me. I began waking up nights in a sweat.

In the end I turned down the proposition. As soon as Ted asked somebody else to go, I began kicking myself. A couple of weeks later I went home to my old summer job, unpacking cartons at the local supermarket, feeling very low. I had turned down something I wanted to do because I was scared, and had ended up feeling depressed. I stayed that way for a long time. And it didn't help when I went back to college in the fall to discover that Ted and his friend had had a terrific time.

In the long run that unhappy summer taught me a valuable lesson out of which I developed a rule for myself: *do what makes you anxious; don't do what makes you depressed.*   4

I am not, of course, talking about severe states of anxiety or depression, which require medical attention. What I mean is that kind of anxiety we call stage fright, butterflies in the stomach, a case of nerves—the feelings we have at a job interview, when we're giving a big party, when we have to make an important presentation at the office. And the kind of depression I am referring to is that downhearted feeling of the blues, when we don't seem to be interested in anything, when we can't get going and seem to have no energy.   5

I was confronted by this sort of situation toward the end of my senior year. As graduation approached, I began to think about taking a crack at making my living as a writer. But one of my professors was urging me to apply to graduate school and aim at a teaching career.   6

I wavered. The idea of trying to live by writing was scary—a lot more scary than spending a summer on the Pampas, I thought. Back and forth I went, making my decision, unmaking it. Suddenly, I realized that every time I gave up the idea of writing, that sinking feeling went through me; it gave me the blues.   7

The thought of graduate school wasn't what depressed me. It was giving up on what deep in my gut I really wanted to do. Right then I learned another lesson. To avoid that kind of depression meant, inevitably, having to endure a certain amount of worry and concern.   8

The great Danish philosopher Søren Kierkegaard believed that anxiety always arises when we confront the possibility of our own development. It seems to be a rule of life that you can't advance without getting that old, familiar, jittery feeling.   9

Even as children we discover this when we try to expand ourselves by, say, learning to ride a bike or going out for the school play. Later in life we get butterflies when we think about having that first child, or uprooting the family from the old home-   10 town to find a better opportunity halfway across the country. Any time, it seems, that we set out aggressively to get something we want, we meet up with anxiety. And it's going to be our traveling companion, at least part of the way, into any new venture.

When I first began writing magazine articles, I was fre- 11 quently required to interview big names—people like Richard Burton, Joan Rivers, sex authority William Masters, baseball-great Dizzy Dean. Before each interview I would get butterflies and my hands would shake.

At the time, I was doing some writing about music. And one 12 person I particularly admired was the great composer Duke Ellington. Onstage and on television, he seemed the very model of the confident, sophisticated man of the world. Then I learned that Ellington still got stage fright. If the highly honored Duke Ellington, who had appeared on the bandstand some 10,000 times over 30 years, had anxiety attacks, who was I to think I could avoid them?

I went on doing those frightening interviews, and one day, as 13 I was getting onto a plane for Washington to interview columnist Joseph Alsop, I suddenly realized to my astonishment that I was looking forward to the meeting. What had happened to those butterflies?

Well, in truth, they were still there, but there were fewer of 14 them. I had benefited, I discovered, from a process psychologists call "extinction." If you put an individual in an anxiety-provoking situation often enough, he will eventually learn that there isn't anything to be worried about.

Which brings us to a corollary to my basic rule: *you'll never 15 eliminate anxiety by avoiding the things that caused it.* I remember how my son Jeff was when I first began to teach him to swim at the lake cottage where we spent our summer vacations. He resisted, and when I got him into the water he sank and sputtered and wanted to quit. But I was insistent. And by summer's end he was splashing around like a puppy. He had "extinguished" his anxiety the only way he could—by confronting it.

The problem, of course, is that it is one thing to urge some- 16 body else to take on those anxiety-producing challenges; it is quite another to get ourselves to do it.

Some years ago I was offered a writing assignment that 　17
would require three months of travel through Europe. I had
been abroad a couple of times on the usual "If it's Tuesday this
must be Belgium" trips, but I hardly could claim to know my
way around the continent. Moreover, my knowledge of foreign
languages was limited to a little college French.

I hesitated. How would I, unable to speak the language, to- 　18
tally unfamiliar with local geography or transportation systems, set up interviews and do research? It seemed impossible,
and with considerable regret I sat down to write a letter begging off. Halfway through, a thought—which I subsequently
made into another corollary to my basic rule—ran through my
mind: *you can't learn if you don't try.* So I accepted the assignment.

There were some bad moments. But by the time I had fin- 　19
ished the trip I was an experienced traveler. And ever since, I
have never hesitated to head for even the most exotic of places,
without guides or even advanced bookings, confident that
somehow I will manage.

The point is that the new, the different, is almost by defini- 　20
tion scary. But each time you try something, you learn, and as
the learning piles up, the world opens to you.

I've made parachute jumps, learned to ski at 40, flown up the 　21
Rhine in a balloon. And I know I'm going to go on doing such
things. It's not because I'm braver or more daring than others.
I'm not. But I don't let the butterflies stop me from doing what
I want. Accept anxiety as another name for challenge and you
can accomplish wonders.

Questions for Study and Discussion

1. What is Collier's thesis in this essay? Based on your own
   experiences, do you think that Collier's thesis is a valid one?
   Explain.
2. What is the process known to psychologists as "extinction"?
3. Collier provides some rules for himself. What are these
   rules? He says that his second and third rules are corollar-

ies to a basic rule. What does Collier mean? (Glossary: *Definition*)

4. What do you think Collier's purpose was in writing this essay? (Glossary: *Purpose*) Explain.

5. Identify the figure of speech that Collier uses toward the end of paragraph 10. (Glossary: *Figures of Speech*)

6. Explain how paragraphs 17–19 function within the context of Collier's essay. (Glossary: *Illustration*)

Vocabulary

Refer to your dictionary to define the following words as they are used in this selection. Then use each word in a sentence of your own.

daunted (2)   butterflies (5)
proposition (3)   crack (6)
anxiety (5)   venture (10)
depression (5)   corollary (15)

Suggested Writing Assignments

1. Building on your own experiences and the reading you have done, write an essay in which you use as your thesis either Collier's basic rule or one of his corollaries to that basic rule.

2. Write an essay in which you use any of the following as your thesis:

Good manners are a thing of the past.

We need rituals in our lives.

To tell a joke well is an art.

We are a drug-dependent society.

Losing weight is a breeze.

2

UNITY

A well-written essay should be unified; that is, everything in it should be related to its thesis, or main idea. The first requirement for unity is that the thesis itself be clear, either through a direct statement, called the *thesis statement*, or by implication. The second requirement is that there be no digressions, no discussion or information that is not shown to be logically related to the thesis. A unified essay stays within the limits of its thesis.

Here, for example, is a short essay called "Over-Generalizing" about the dangers of making generalizations. As you read, notice how carefully author Stuart Chase sticks to his point.

One swallow does not make a summer, nor can two or three cases often support a dependable generalization. Yet all of us, including the most polished eggheads, are constantly falling into this mental mantrap. It is the commonest, probably the most seductive, and potentially the most dangerous, of all the fallacies. 1

You drive through a town and see a drunken man on the sidewalk. A few blocks further on you see another. You turn to your companion: "Nothing but drunks in this town!" Soon you are out in the country, bowling along at fifty. A car passes you as if you were parked. On a curve a second whizzes by. Your companion turns to you: "All the drivers in this state are crazy!" Two thumping generalizations, each built on two cases. If we stop to think, we usually recognize the exaggeration and the unfairness of such generalizations. Trouble comes when we do not stop to think—or when we build them on a prejudice. 2

This kind of reasoning has been around for a long time. Aristotle was aware of its dangers and called it "reasoning by example," meaning too few examples. What it boils down to is failing to count your swallows before announcing that summer is here. Driving from my home to New Haven the other day, a distance of about forty miles, I caught 3

myself saying: "Every time I look around I see a new
ranch-type house going up." So on the return trip I counted
them; there were exactly five under construction. And how
many times had I "looked around"? I suppose I had
glanced to right and left—as one must at side roads and so
forth in driving—several hundred times.

In this fallacy we do not make the error of neglecting   4
facts altogether and rushing immediately to the level of
opinion. We start at the fact level properly enough, but *we
do not stay there.* A case of two and up we go to a rousing
over-simplification about drunks, speeders, ranch-style
houses—or, more seriously, about foreigners, Negroes, labor leaders, teen-agers.

Why do we over-generalize so often and sometimes so di-   5
sastrously? One reason is that the human mind is a generalizing machine. We would not be men without this power.
The old academic crack: "All generalizations are false, including this one," is only a play on words. We *must* gener-
alize to communicate and to live. But we should beware of
beating the gun; of not waiting until enough facts are in to
say something useful. Meanwhile it is a plain waste of time
to listen to arguments based on a few hand-picked examples.

Everything in the essay relates to Chase's thesis statement,
which is included in the essay's first sentence: ". . . nor can two
or three cases often support a dependable generalization." Paragraphs 2 and 3 document the thesis with examples; paragraph
4 explains how over-generalizing occurs; paragraph 5 analyzes
why people over-generalize; and, for a conclusion, Chase re-
states his thesis in different words. An essay may be longer,
more complex, and more wide-ranging than this one, but to be
effective it must also avoid digressions and remain close to the
author's main idea.

MODERN COURTESY

Lore Segal

Lore Segal is an author of both adult and children's books. She was born in Vienna, Austria, in 1928 and graduated from Bedford College, London, in 1948. She lives in New York City. Her books include Other People's Houses *(1964),* Tell Me a Mitzi *(1970),* Tell Me a Trudy *(1977), and* Her First American *(1985). She has also contributed short stories to* The New Yorker, Saturday Evening Post, The New Republic, Epoch, Commentary, *and other periodicals. As you read the essay, notice how Segal uses an argument with her son to unify her essay, so that every paragraph is related to her thesis about courtesy.*

My son and I were having one of our rare quarrels. Jacob is a formidable person and our difference was on a matter of substance—modern manners versus the old courtesies. Signor Giuseppe, and elderly neighbor from the Old World, had complained that Jacob didn't say good morning when he got on the elevator and that he answered Signor Giuseppe's questions reluctantly.

My son said Signor Giuseppe's questions were phonies. Signor Giuseppe did not give a hoot about how many inches my son had grown and couldn't care less what subjects he was taking in school. My son said these were questions that didn't deserve answers.

I argued that it is the business of courtesy to cover up the terrible truth that we don't give a hoot about the other person in the elevator.

"Why is that terrible and why cover it up?" my son asked sensibly.

Jacob belongs to the generation that says "Me and Joe are going out," and whichever walks through the door first trusts the other to take care its back swing doesn't catch him in the head.

My generation says "Signor Giuseppe and I are going out," and Signor Giuseppe opens the door and holds it for me.

Jacob said: "Why? You can open it for yourself." 6

This is true. It is also true that "me and Joe" is the formula- 7 tion that corresponds to my experience. It's my own passage through the door that occupies my mind. It's because Signor Giuseppe might, in the press of the things on *his* mind, forget that I'm coming behind, that courtesy tells him to let me go ahead. Courtesy makes me pass him the cookies, keeping me artificially aware of his hunger, which I don't experience. My own appetite can be trusted to take care of *my* cookies.

Signor Giuseppe and I reach the corner. His anachronistic 8 hand under my forearm presumes that a lady cannot step off the curb without a supporting gentleman—a presumption for which modern men have been hit across the head with umbrellas. That is why my graduate student, who chats amusingly as we walk down the corridor, does *not* open the door for me.

"Why should he?" Jacob asked. 9

"Because I'm carrying two packages in my right hand, my 10 books in my left, and my handbag and umbrella under my armpit," I said.

If my son or my graduate student were boors, we would not 11 be addressing this matter. A boor is a boor and was always a boor. But I can tell that the muscles of my graduate student's back are readying to bend and pick up the book and umbrella I have dropped. He struggles between his natural courtesy and the learned inhibition that *I* have taught him: My being a woman is no reason for him to pick my things up for me. I crawl on the floor retrieving my property. He remains standing.

My son is not only formidable, he is a person of good will. He 12 said: "That's stupid! If you see someone is in trouble you go and help them out. What's it got to do with courtesy?"

This is what it has to do with it: Having thrown out the old, 13 dead, hypocritical rules about napkins, knives, and how to address the ladies, it is Jacob's and it is my graduate student's business to recover the essential baby that went down the drain as well. They must invent their own rules for eating so they don't look and sound nasty, and my student must count my packages to see if I need his help. When Jacob enters the elevator, he is required to perform a complex act of the imagination: Is Signor Giuseppe a plain pain in the neck or does he have trouble?

"His trouble is he's a pain in the neck," Jacob said.   14

"And your business is to keep him from finding it out."   15

"Why?" Jacob shouted.   16

"Because once Signor Giuseppe understands that he's too   17
great a pain to chat with for the time the elevator takes to descend from the 12th to the ground floor, he will understand that he will die alone."

My son guffawed. He is not required to join me in this leap: 18
The old courtesy was in the essential business of the cover-up. It was the contract by which I agreed to pretend to find your concerns of paramount interest, in return for which you took care not to let on that you did not care a hoot about mine.

Jacob said he still thought one should say what one meant   19
and talk to the people one liked. But he said next time he got in the elevator with Signor Giuseppe, he was going to tell him good morning.

Questions for Study and Discussion

1. Segal writes that "it is the business of courtesy to cover up the terrible truth that we don't give a hoot about the other person in the elevator"(3). What exactly does she mean?

2. Summarize the two views of courtesy represented by Segal and her son Jacob in this essay. Is there a right and wrong way to view the problem that Segal raises, or is this question just another one of life's impossible dilemmas? With whom do you agree, Segal or her son? Explain.

3. One of the basic requirements of a unified essay is that it have a clear thesis. What is Segal's thesis? Where is it stated? Is it clear to you? Explain. (Glossary: *Thesis*)

4. Segal uses examples to illustrate her thesis. (Glossary: *Example*) Choose three examples that she uses and explain their relationship to her thesis.

5. Transitional devices indicate relationships between paragraphs and thus help to unify the essay. Identify three transitions in this essay. Explain how they help to unify the essay. (Glossary: *Transitions*)
6. Discuss Segal's ending. Is she suggesting that Jacob is now convinced by her arguments? Explain. (Glossary: *Beginnings and Endings*)

Vocabulary

formidable (1)	boors (11)
substance (1)	inhibition (11)
formulation (7)	guffawed (18)
anachronistic (8)	contract (18)

Suggested Writing Assignments

1. Lore Segal believes that a "cover-up" is inherent in the idea of courtesy. Do you believe as she does, or do you have a different sense of what courtesy is all about? Write a well-unified essay in which you attempt to define the concept of courtesy, making sure that your examples and discussion of them are related to your thesis.
2. Make a generalization about a topic and write an essay in which you use multiple examples to support it. Make sure that your essay is unified; choose your examples carefully and relate them to your thesis. Choose a generalization of your own, or consider one of the following:

   Dishonesty is sometimes the best policy.
   First impressions are lasting.
   Most conversation is gossip.
   The best party is one where _____.
   Talent and ability are nothing without hard work.

BE KIND TO COMMUTERS

Christopher M. Bellitto

*Christopher M. Bellitto was born in the Bronx,
New York, in 1965. Admitted to New York University as a University Scholar, he graduated Phi
Beta Kappa with a degree in journalism and politics. Among his other honors are scholarships in
journalism from Gannett and from Scripps-
Howard, and the prestigious Time Inc. College
Achievement Award for being one of the twenty
top college students in the country. After graduation, he worked for* Newsweek On Campus. *He
currently teaches at a New York City high
school. As you read his essay, notice the way Bellitto has ensured that all of his information relates to his thesis that college students who com-
mute don't have it as easy as you might think.
This essay first appeared in the October 1986 issue of* Newsweek on Campus.

You may think that those of us who live at home and com- 1
mute to school have it easy. There's a washing machine
with no wait, a new tube of toothpaste in the medicine cabinet
and, most important, a fridge stocked with food someone else
has paid for. Not only that, but the phone bill is usually taken
care of and dinner's sitting in the microwave even late at night.
That's not college, you sneer—that's permanent adolescence.

So maybe we look like pampered kids, but it's not that sim- 2
ple. The college student living at home leads a paradoxical life.
Like you, we came to college to learn about ourselves; self-
exploration is as much a part of our education as organic chem.
Yet it's hard to maintain our independence when Mom or Dad
can't shake the parental instincts for surveillance. Nor can
family obligations be avoided easily. What do I do, for example,
when my parents' anniversary falls the day before my finals?
The truth is, being a student who hasn't left the nest can be just

as difficult as trying to get along with a roommate you don't like.

Dear Abby: Our problems can be complex. To some extent,   3
we're second-class citizens in the social world: it's tough to enjoy clubs, frat parties and dances when you have to drive back
home or catch the last bus. Ditto when you realize you can't
make the only review class for business law because it ends
late. But that's not the critical issue: after all, everybody's got
standing invites to crash with friends in the dorm. The real
problem is that we lose out on the results of those activities: a
sense of camaraderie that springs from nights spent cramming
for industrial psychology, gossiping about who's sleeping with
whom and, after most of the favorite topics of both George Will
and Dear Abby are exhausted, sharing the heart-to-heart realization that graduation is closer than we think. True, we commuters can join in every now and again, but we can't fall into
the day-and-night rhythm of collegial introspection. There's a
whole group of us who'll never be able to appreciate the lifetime bonds of "The Big Chill" as much as our dorming peers.

Then there's the issue of budgeting time. Commuters have   4
much more structured days than dormers; we have to. Many of
us live as we do to save money, and we devote a lot of hours to
jobs that can help defray tuition. Of course, working out our
convoluted schedules may teach more about efficiency than all
the freshman workshops on note-taking. Who else but a commuter could perfect the art of plotting discreet-probability dis-
tribution on a train hurtling through a dark tunnel while some
sleaze with Mick Belker breath hulks down over your textbook? And sharing one bathroom with parents preparing for
work, little brothers late for school and a sister rinsing stockings in the sink makes the three-minute shower sprint a useful
skill that rivals almost anything gleaned from a class. True, all
this planning becomes moot when the 40-minute trip takes two
hours because of a track fire and a wino who gets caught in the
door.

Leftover lasagna: There's a myth that commuters are lucky   5
because they can leave the jungle of school and go home. Actually, you dormers may have it easier here: at least you can get
away with screaming out of the window and working off tension at a party that's never hard to find. When we have a bad

stretch, there's no escape; the end of a frustrating day is just the beginning. First there's the long ride home where, on public transportation, the heaters and air conditioners seem to operate on Argentina's schedule of seasons. Then there are the reminders from parents which, however well intentioned, are still nagging. How can we feel "on our own" when we're constantly told: *"Call* if you'll be late"? And of course there's Grandma, who starts heating up the leftovers when we're three blocks away, sits to watch us eat them and then clucks that we're too skinny and not getting enough sleep. Even if the lasagna is major league, it might be even nicer just to be left ALONE sometimes.

And when the breakaway point does come, leave-taking is   6
more painful for those of us who've never really left. Students who move out of the house for college can enjoy a separate peace; they build another base of operations on campus. True, all families have a hard time saying goodbye to the child who goes off to school at 18, but by graduation they've gotten over it and come to view you as an adult with your own life. Commuters are not nearly so detached. There are some family situations we can't ignore. It's the difference between returning for Thanksgiving to discover how old Grandpa has gotten and living with him, watching him die a little more each day. That makes the parting at graduation even more poignant—for both families *and* students.

The living arrangement is hard on our elders, too, since   7
they're torn between stepping back to allow us autonomy and jumping in where they always have before. When school is miles away, parents can't *see* their kids staying up until 6 a.m. to type a paper or letting loose with a keg—though I'm sure both situations are vividly imagined during many a late night's insomnia. Naturally, at home your movement is watched. I can appreciate that my mother worries if I don't make it home by a certain hour, but I build up some tense moments myself if I can't stay late at the library doing research for tomorrow's oral presentation. "I don't even know you anymore," is a frustrated parent's response to a student who, of necessity, sometimes uses home like a boarding house. But we're supposed to get to know our profs, make new friends and be exposed to new

fields—and that can only be accomplished when we're on our own.

We are a special breed: young adults who are enthusiastic 8 about the independence of being in college yet remain to some degree children in our family's eyes—and to some extent, perhaps, in our own. I still believe that I'm receiving a top-notch education, though I'll be the first to admit—and lament—that I'm also missing out on some of the traditional collegiate experiences. So don't think of commuters as lesser beings or as softies who are taking the easy way out. We're just caught between the rock of academia and the sometimes hard place of home, struggling with the age-old problem of serving two masters.

Questions for Study and Discussion

1. What is Bellitto's thesis? (Glossary: *Thesis*) Where is it stated? What relationship does Bellitto's title have to his thesis?

2. According to Bellitto, what are some of the problems that commuters face while at school? While at home? What, if anything, does he want from us as readers of his essay?

3. One student who has read this essay thought that the examples Bellitto uses are very practical and good ones. What is your assessment of his examples? If you, too, find them effective, explain why. (Glossary: *Examples*)

4. How effective is Bellitto's use of transitions to link paragraphs? (Glossary: *Transitions*)

5. Bellitto's style in this essay is informal. It is smooth, easy to read, but nevertheless controlled and detailed. What is there about the author's choice of words that contributes to his informal style? (Glossary: *Diction*)

6. Explain in your own words the meaning of the following phrases from this selection:

   a. permanent adolescence (1)
   b. parental instincts for surveillance (2)

c. standing invites to crash (3)
d. collegial introspection (3)
e. convoluted schedules (4)
f. Argentina's schedule of seasons (5)
g. letting loose with a keg (7)
h. the rock of academia and the sometimes hard place of home (8)

Vocabulary

Refer to your dictionary to define the following words as they are used in this selection. Then use each word in a sentence of your own.

sneer (1)	defray (4)
pampered (2)	sleaze (4)
ditto (3)	moot (4)
camaraderie (3)	autonomy (7)

Suggested Writing Assignments

1. What general impression do you think most students have of commuters? If you are a commuter yourself, what do you feel is the general impression that other students have of you? What relationship do these impressions have to reality? Are commuters "second-class citizens in the social world," as Bellitto claims? Write a unified essay that relies on your experiences as well as the experiences of your friends in exploring this topic.

2. Bellitto says that "being a student who hasn't left the nest can be just as difficult as trying to get along with the roommate you don't like" (2). How difficult is it to get along with a roommate? What concessions have to be made? What kind of communication is necessary for one to live in the confines of a dorm room? What lessons have to be learned? Write an essay that is well unified on living with a roommate. Be sure that your examples are well chosen and illustrate the thesis you establish.

Don't Let Stereotypes Warp Your Judgments

Robert L. Heilbroner

*The economist Robert L. Heilbroner was edu-
cated at Harvard and at the New School for Social Research, where he has been the Norman
Thomas Professor of Economics since 1972. He
has written* The Future as History *(1960),* A
Primer of Government Spending: Between Capitalism and Socialism *(1970), and* An Inquiry into
the Human Prospect *(1974). "Don't Let Stereotypes Warp Your Judgments" first appeared in*
Reader's Digest. *As you read this essay, pay particular attention to its unity—the relationships
of the paragraphs to the thesis.*

Is a girl called Gloria apt to be better-looking than one called   1
Bertha? Are criminals more likely to be dark than blond?
Can you tell a good deal about someone's personality from
hearing his voice briefly over the phone? Can a person's nation-
ality be pretty accurately guessed from his photograph? Does
the fact that someone wears glasses imply that he is intelligent?

The answer to all these questions is obviously, "No."   2

Yet, from all the evidence at hand, most of us believe these   3
things. Ask any college boy if he'd rather take his chances with
a Gloria or a Bertha, or ask a college girl if she'd rather blind-
date a Richard or a Cuthbert. In fact, you don't have to ask:
college students in questionnaires have revealed that names
conjure up the same images in their minds as they do in
yours—and for as little reason.

Look into the favorite suspects of persons who report "suspi-   4
cious characters" and you will find a large percentage of them
to be "swarthy" or "dark and foreign-looking"—despite the testimony of criminologists that criminals do *not* tend to be dark,

43

foreign or "wild-eyed." Delve into the main asset of a telephone stock swindler and you will find it to be a marvelously confidence-inspiring telephone "personality." And whereas we all think we know what an Italian or a Swede looks like, it is the sad fact that when a group of Nebraska students sought to match faces and nationalities of 15 European countries, they were scored wrong in 93 percent of their identifications. Finally, for all the fact that horn-rimmed glasses have now become the standard television sign of an "intellectual," optometrists know that the main thing that distinguishes people with glasses is just bad eyes.

Stereotypes are a kind of gossip about the world, a gossip that makes us prejudge people before we ever lay eyes on them. Hence it is not surprising that stereotypes have something to do with the dark world of prejudice. Explore most prejudices (note that the word means prejudgment) and you will find a cruel stereotype at the core of each one.

For it is the extraordinary fact that once we have typecast the world, we tend to see people in terms of our standardized pictures. In another demonstration of the power of stereotypes to affect our vision, a number of Columbia and Barnard students were shown 30 photographs of pretty but unidentified girls, and asked to rate each in terms of "general liking," "intelligence," "beauty" and so on. Two months later, the same group were shown the same photographs, this time with fictitious Irish, Italian, Jewish and "American" names attached to the pictures. Right away the ratings changed. Faces which were now seen as representing a national group went down in looks and still farther down in likability, while the "American" girls suddenly looked decidedly prettier and nicer.

Why is it that we stereotype the world in such irrational and harmful fashion? In part, we begin to type-cast people in our childhood years. Early in life, as every parent whose child has watched a TV Western knows, we learn to spot the Good Guys from the Bad Guys. Some years ago, a social psychologist showed very clearly how powerful these stereotypes of childhood vision are. He secretly asked the most popular youngsters in an elementary school to make errors in their morning gym exercises. Afterwards, he asked the class if anyone had noticed any mistakes during gym period. Oh, yes, said the children. But

it was the *unpopular* members of the class—the "bad guys"—
they remembered as being out of step.

We not only grow up with standardized pictures forming in-   8
side of us, but as grown-ups we are constantly having them
thrust upon us. Some of them, like the half-joking, half-serious
stereotypes of mothers-in-law, or country yokels, or psychiatrists, are dinned into us by the stock jokes we hear and repeat.
In fact, without such stereotypes, there would be a lot fewer
jokes. Still other stereotypes are perpetuated by the advertisements we read, the movies we see, the books we read.

And finally, we tend to stereotype because it helps us make   9
sense out of a highly confusing world, a world which William
James once described as "one great, blooming, buzzing confusion." It is a curious fact that if we don't *know* what we're looking at, we are often quite literally unable to *see* what we're
looking at. People who recover their sight after a lifetime of
blindness actually cannot at first tell a triangle from a square.
A visitor to a factory sees only noisy chaos where the superin-
tendent sees a perfectly synchronized flow of work. As Walter
Lippmann has said, "For the most part we do not first see, and
then define; we define first, and then we see."

Stereotypes are one way in which we "define" the world in   10
order to see it. They classify the infinite variety of human beings into a convenient handful of "types" towards whom we
learn to act in stereotyped fashion. Life would be a wearing
process if we had to start from scratch with each and every human contact. Stereotypes economize on our mental effort by
covering up the blooming, buzzing confusion with big recogniz-
able cut-outs. They save us the "trouble" of finding out what
the world is like—they give it its accustomed look.

Thus the trouble is that stereotypes make us mentally lazy.   11
As S. I. Hayakawa, the authority on semantics, has written:
"The danger of stereotypes lies not in their existence, but in the
fact that they become for all people some of the time, and for
some people all the time, *substitutes for observation*." Worse
yet, stereotypes get in the way of our judgment, even when we
do observe the world. Someone who has formed rigid precon-
ceptions of all Latins as "excitable," or all teenagers as "wild,"
doesn't alter his point of view when he meets a calm and deliberate Genoese, or a serious-minded high school student. He

brushes them aside as "exceptions that prove the rule." And, of course, if he meets someone true to type, he stands triumphantly vindicated. "They're all like that," he proclaims, having encountered an excited Latin, an ill-behaved adolescent.

Hence, quite aside from the injustice which stereotypes do to others, they impoverish ourselves. A person who lumps the world into simple categories, who type-casts all labor leaders as "racketeers," all businessmen as "reactionaries," all Harvard men as "snobs," and all Frenchmen as "sexy," is in danger of becoming a stereotype himself. He loses his capacity to be himself—which is to say, to see the world in his own absolutely unique, inimitable and independent fashion.   12

Instead, he votes for the man who fits his standardized picture of what a candidate "should" look like or sound like, buys the goods that someone in his "situation" in life "should" own, lives the life that others define for him. The mark of the stereotype person is that he never surprises us, that we do indeed have him "typed." And no one fits this strait-jacket so perfectly as someone whose opinions about *other people* are fixed and inflexible.   13

Impoverishing as they are, stereotypes are not easy to get rid of. The world we type-cast may be no better than a Grade B movie, but at least we know what to expect of our stock characters. When we let them act for themselves in the strangely unpredictable way that people do act, who knows but that many of our fondest convictions will be proved wrong?   14

Nor do we suddenly drop our standardized pictures for a blinding vision of the Truth. Sharp swings of ideas about people often just substitute one stereotype for another. The true process of change is a slow one that adds bits and pieces of reality to the pictures in our heads, until gradually they take on some of the blurriness of life itself. Little by little, we learn not that Jews and Negroes and Catholics and Puerto Ricans are "just like everybody else"—for that, too, is a stereotype—but that each and every one of them is unique, special, different and individual. Often we do not even know that we have let a stereotype lapse until we hear someone saying, "all so-and-so's are like such-and-such," and we hear ourselves saying, "Well— maybe."   15

Can we speed the process along? Of course we can.   16

First, we can become *aware* of the standardized pictures in   17
our heads, in other people's heads, in the world around us.

Second, we can become suspicious of all judgments that we   18
allow exceptions to "prove." There is no more chastening
thought than that in the vast intellectual adventure of science,
it takes but one tiny exception to topple a whole edifice of
ideas.

Third, we can learn to be chary of generalizations about peo-   19
ple. As F. Scott Fitzgerald once wrote: "Begin with an individual, and before you know it you have created a type; begin with
a type, and you find you have created—nothing."

Most of the time, when we type-cast the world, we are not in   20
fact generalizing about people at all. We are only revealing the
embarrassing facts about the pictures that hang in the gallery
of stereotypes in our own heads.

Questions for Study and Discussion

1. What is Heilbroner's main point, or thesis, in this essay?
   (Glossary: *Thesis*)
2. Study paragraphs 6, 8, and 15. Each paragraph illustrates
   Heilbroner's thesis. How? What does each paragraph contribute to support the thesis?
3. Transitional devices indicate relationships between paragraphs and thus help to unify the essay. Identify three transitions in this essay. Explain how they help to unify the essay. (Glossary: *Transitions*)
4. What are the reasons Heilbroner gives for why we stereotype individuals? What are some of the dangers of stereotypes, according to Heilbroner? How does he say can we rid
   ourselves of stereotypes?
5. Heilbroner uses the word *picture* in his discussion of stereotypes. Why is this an appropriate word in this discussion?
   (Glossary: *Diction*)

Vocabulary

Refer to your dictionary to define the following words as they are used in this selection. Then use each word in a sentence of your own.

irrational (7)	impoverish (12)
perpetuated (8)	chastening (18)
infinite (10)	edifice (18)
preconceptions (11)	chary (19)
vindicated (11)	

Suggested Writing Assignments

1. Write an essay in which you attempt to convince your readers that it is not in their best interests to perform a particular act—for example, smoke, take stimulants to stay awake, go on a crash diet, or make snap judgments. In writing your essay, follow Heilbroner's lead: first identify the issue; then explain why it is a problem; and, finally, offer a solution or some advice. Remember to unify the various parts of your essay.

2. Have you ever been considered as a stereotype—a student, or a member of a particular sex, class, ethnic, national, or racial group? Write a unified essay that examines how stereotyping has affected you, how it has perhaps changed you, and how you regard the process.

3

ORGANIZATION

In an essay, ideas and information cannot be presented all at once; they have to be arranged in some order. That order is the essay's organization.

The pattern of organization in an essay should be suited to the writer's subject and purpose. For example, if you are writing about your experience working in a fast-food restaurant, and your purpose is to tell about the activities of a typical day, you might present those activities in chronological order. If, on the other hand, you wish to argue that working in a bank is an ideal summer job, you might proceed from the least rewarding to the most rewarding aspect of this job; this is called "climactic" order.

Some often-used patterns of organization are time order, space order, and logical order. Time order, or chronological order, is used to present events as they occurred. A personal narrative, a report of a campus incident, or an account of a historical event can be most naturally and easily related in chronological order. The description of a process, such as the refinishing of a table, the building of a stone wall, or the way to serve a tennis ball, almost always calls for a chronological organization. Of course, the order of events can sometimes be rearranged for special effect. For example, an account of an auto accident may begin with the collision itself and then go back in time to tell about the events leading up to it. One essay that is a model of chronological order is Dick Gregory's "Shame" (pp. 212–16).

Space order is used when describing a person, place, or thing. This organizational pattern begins at a particular point and moves in some direction, such as left to right, top to bottom, east to west, outside to inside, front to back, near to far, around, or over. In describing a house, for example, a writer could move from top to bottom, from outside to inside, or in a circle around the outside. Gilbert Highet's "Subway Station"

(p. 238–40) is an essay in which space is used as the organizing principle.

Logical order can take many forms depending on the writer's purpose. These include: general to specific, most familiar to least familiar, and smallest to biggest. Perhaps the most common type of logical order is order of importance. Notice how the writer uses this order in the following paragraph:

> The Egyptians have taught us many things. They were excellent farmers. They knew all about irrigation. They built temples which were afterwards copied by the Greeks and which served as the earliest models for the churches in which we worship nowadays. They invented a calendar which proved such a useful instrument for the purpose of measuring time that it has survived with a few changes until today. But most important of all, the Egyptians learned how to preserve speech for the benefit of future generations. They invented the art of writing.

By organizing the material according to the order of increasing importance, the writer places special emphasis on the final sentence. In writing a descriptive essay you can move from the least striking to the most striking detail, so as to keep your reader interested and involved in the description. In an explanatory essay you can start with the point that readers will find least difficult to understand and move on to the most difficult; that's how teachers organize many courses. Or, in writing an argumentative essay, you can move from your least controversial point to the most controversial, preparing your reader gradually to accept your argument.

REACH OUT AND WRITE SOMEONE

Lynn Wenzel

Lynn Wenzel has been published in many major newspapers and magazines, including Newsweek, The New York Times, Newsday, *and* Down East: The Magazine of Maine. *She is currently music reviewer for* New Directions for Women. *Her book* Just a Song at Twilight: The Story of American Popular Sheet Music *will be published in 1989. Wenzel was graduated magna cum laude from William Paterson College and makes her home in Maywood, New Jersey. As you read her essay, pay particular attention to the way she has organized her examples to illustrate the importance of letter writing.*

Everyone is talking about the breakup of the telephone company. Some say it will be a disaster for poor people and a bonanza for large companies while others fear a personal phone bill so exorbitant that—horror of horrors—we will all have to start writing letters again.

It's about time. One of the many talents lost in this increasingly technological age is that of putting pen to paper in order to communicate with family, friends and lovers.

Reading, and enjoying it, may not be the strong suit of our young but writing has truly become a lost art. I am not talking about creative writing because this country still has its full share of fine fiction and poetry writers. There will always be those special few who need to transform experiences into short stories or poetry.

No, the skill we have lost is that of letter writing. When was the last time the mailbox contained anything more than bills, political and fund-raising appeals, advertisements, catalogs, magazines or junk mail?

Keepsake: Once upon a time, the only way to communicate from a distance was through the written word. As the country

51

expanded and people moved west, they knew that when they left mother, father, sister, brother, it was very probably the last time they would see them again. So daughters, pioneering in Indiana or Michigan, wrote home with the news that their first son had been born dead, but the second child was healthy and growing and they also had a house and barn. By the time the letter reached east, another child might have been born, yet it was read over and again, then smoothed out and slipped into the family Bible or keepsake box.

Letters were essential then. Imagine John Adams fomenting revolution and forming a new government without Abigail's letters to sustain him. Think of Elizabeth Barrett and Robert Browning without their written declarations of love; of all the lovers who, parted against their will, kept hope alive through letters often passed by hand or mailed in secret. 6

And what of history? Much of our knowledge of events and of the people who lived them is based on such commonplace communication. Harry Truman's letters to Bess, Mamie and Ike's correspondence and Eleanor Roosevelt's letters to some of her friends all illuminate actions and hint at intent. F. Scott Fitzgerald's letters to his daughter, Scottie, which were filled with melancholy over his wife's mental illness, suggest in part the reason why his last years were so frustratingly uncreative. Without letters we would have history—dry facts and dates of wars, treaties, elections, revolutions. But the causes and effects might be left unclear. 7

We would also know little about women's lives. History, until recently, neglected women's contributions to events. Much of what we now know about women in history comes from letters found, more often than not, in great-grandmother's trunk in the attic, carefully tied with ribbon, or stored, yellowed and boxed, in a carton in the archives of a "women's college." These letters have helped immensely over the past ten years to create a verifiable women's history which is now taking its rightful place alongside weighty tomes about men's contributions to the changing world. 8

The story of immigration often begins with a letter. Millions of brave souls, carrying their worldly possessions in one bag, stepped off a ship and into American life on the strength of a note saying, "Come. It's better here." 9

To know how important the "art" of letter writing was, we   10
have only to look at the accouterments our ancestors treasured
and considered necessary: inkstands of silver, gold or glass,
crafted to occupy a prominent place on the writing table; hot
wax for a personal seal; the seals themselves, sometimes or-
nately carved in silver; quills, and then fountain pens. These
were not luxuries but necessities.

Polish: Perhaps most important of all, letter writing required   11
thinking before putting pen to paper. No hurried telephone call
can ever replace the thoughtful, intelligent correspondence between two people, the patching up of a friendship, the formal
request for the pleasure of someone's company, or a personal
apology. Once written and sent, the writer can never declare,
"But I never said that." Serious letter writing demands
thought, logic, organization and sincerity because words, once
written, cannot be taken back. These are qualities we must not
lose, but ones we should polish and bring to luster.

What, after all, will we lose: our lover's letters tied with an   12
old hair ribbon, written from somewhere far away; our children's first scribbled note from summer camp; the letters
friends sent us as we scattered after college; letters we sent our
parents telling them how much they meant to us? Without letters, what will we save, laugh about, read out loud to each
other 20 years from now on a snowy afternoon in front of a
fire?

Telephone bills.   13

And that is the saddest note of all.   14

Questions for Study and Discussion

1. What is Wenzel's thesis in this essay? Where is it stated?
   (Glossary: *Thesis*)
2. Why does Wenzel concentrate on letter writing in her essay
   and not on other kinds of writing?
3. What role has letter writing played in our understanding of
   history, according to Wenzel?
4. In what ways is writing a letter different from making a
   phone call? What can letter writing do to help us develop as
   human beings?

5. Which of the three patterns of organization has Wenzel used in presenting her examples of the importance of letter writing? Support your answer with examples.
6. How effective do you find the beginning and ending of Wenzel's essay? Explain. (Glossary: *Beginnings and Endings*)

Vocabulary

Refer to your dictionary to define the following words as they are used in this selection. Then use each word in a sentence of your own.

exorbitant (1)   accouterments (10)
fomenting (6)   seal (10)
tomes (8)

Suggested Writing Assignments

1. Write a personal letter to a friend or relative with whom you haven't been in contact for some while. Draft and redraft the letter carefully, making it as thoughtful and interesting as you can. Send the letter and report back to your class or instructor on the response that the letter elicited.
2. Think of a commonplace subject that people might take for granted but that you find interesting. Write an essay on that subject, using one of the following types of logical order:

least important to most important
most familiar to least familiar
smallest to biggest
oldest to newest
easiest to understand to most difficult to understand
good news to bad news
general to specific

PERMANENT RECORD

Bob Greene

*Bob Greene was born in 1947 in Columbus, Ohio.
He is a syndicated columnist for the* Chicago
Tribune, *and his column appears in over 150
newspapers throughout the United States.
Greene has written eight books, the most recent
being* Cheeseburgers: The Best of Bob Greene
*(1985). In 1984 he published his best-selling
chronicle of his daughter's first year of life,* Good
Morning, Merry Sunshine. *"Permanent Record,"
Greene's discussion of the disappearance
(maybe) of that most dreaded of educational
myths, is taken from* Cheeseburgers.

There are thousands of theories about what's gone wrong 1
with the world, but I think it comes down to one simple
thing: The death of the Permanent Record.

You remember the Permanent Record. When you were in ele- 2
mentary school, junior high school, and high school, you were
constantly being told that if you screwed up, news of that
screw-up would be sent down to the principal's office, and
would be placed in your Permanent Record.

Nothing more needed to be said. No one had ever seen a Per- 3
manent Record; that didn't matter. We knew they were there.
We all imagined a steel filing cabinet, crammed full of Permanent Records—one for each kid in the school. I think we always
assumed that when we graduated our Permanent Record was
sent on to college with us, and then when we got out of college
our Permanent Record was sent to our employer—probably
with a duplicate copy sent to the U.S. Government.

I don't know if students are still threatened with the promise 4
of unpleasant things included in their Permanent Record, but I
doubt it. I have a terrible feeling that mine was the last generation to know what a Permanent Record was—and that not only
has it disappeared from the schools of the land, but it has disappeared as a concept in society as a whole.

There once was a time when people really stopped before 5
they did something they knew was deceitful, immoral, or
unethical—no matter how much fun it might sound. They
didn't stop because they were such holy folks. They stopped
because—no matter how old they were—they had a nagging
fear that if they did it, it would end up on their Permanent
Record.

At some point in the last few decades, I'm afraid, people 6
wised up to something that amazed them: There is no Permanent Record. There probably never was.

They discovered that regardless of how badly you fouled up 7
your life or the lives of others, there was nothing permanent
about it on your record. You would always be forgiven, no matter what; no matter what you did, other people would shrug it
off.

So pretty soon men and women—instead of fearing the Per- 8
manent Record—started laughing at the idea of the Permanent
Record. The kinds of things that they used to be ashamed of—
the kinds of things that they used to secretly cringe at when
they thought about them—now became "interesting" aspects
of their personalities.

If those "interesting" aspects were weird enough—if they 9
were the kinds of things that would have really jazzed up the
Permanent Record—the people sometimes wrote books con-
fessing those things, and the books became best-sellers. And
the people found out that other people—far from scorning
them—would line up in the bookstores to get their autographs
on the inside covers of the books.

The people started going on talk shows to discuss the things 10
that, in decades past, would have been included in their Permanent Records. The talk-show hosts would say, "Thank you for
being so honest with us; I'm sure the people in our audience
can understand how much guts it must take for you to tell us

these things." The Permanent Records were being opened up for the whole world to see—and the sky did not fall in.

If celebrities had dips in their careers, all they had to do to   11 guarantee a new injection of fame was to admit the worst things about themselves—the Permanent Record things—and the celebrity magazines would print those things, and the celebrities would be applauded for their candor and courage. And they would become even bigger celebrities.

As Americans began to realize that there was no Permanent   12 Record, and probably never had been, they deduced for themselves that any kind of behavior was permissible. After all, it wasn't as if anyone was keeping track; all you would have to do—just like the men and women with best-sellers and on the talk shows and in the celebrity magazines—was to say, "That was a real crazy period in my life." All would be forgiven; all would be erased from the Permanent Record, which, of course, was no longer permanent.

And that is where we are today. Without really thinking   13 about it, we have accepted the notion that no one is, indeed, keeping track. No one is even *allowed* to keep track. I doubt that you can scare a school kid today by telling him the principal is going to inscribe something on his Permanent Record; the kid would probably file a suit under the Freedom of Information Act, and gain possession of his Permanent Record by recess. Either that, or the kid would call up his Permanent Record on his computer terminal, and purge any information he didn't want to be there.

As for us adults—it has been so long since we have believed   14 in the Permanent Record that the very mention of it today probably brings a nostalgic smile to our faces. We feel naive for ever having believed that a Permanent Record was really down there in the principal's office, anyway.

And who really knows if our smiles may freeze on some dis-   15 tant day—the day it is our turn to check out of this earthly world, and we are confronted with a heavenly presence greeting us at the gates of our new eternal home—a heavenly presence sitting there casually leafing through a dusty, battered volume of our Permanent Record as we come jauntily into view.

Questions for Study and Discussion

1. What is Greene's purpose in this essay? Why does he choose to write about the Permanent Record? (Glossary: *Purpose*)
2. What is Greene's attitude toward the Permanent Record? (Glossary: *Attitude*) What in particular in the essay reveals his attitude?
3. Has Greene used the principle of space, time, or logic to organize his essay? Explain your answer.
4. It might be argued that for Greene the Permanent Record has almost symbolic significance, that the Permanent Record stands for something more important than might be supposed at first. What do you think its meaning might be? (Glossary: *Symbol*)
5. How might Greene have begun his essay differently? What would be gained or lost with a different beginning? (Glossary: *Beginnings and Endings*)
6. In all fifteen paragraphs of his essay Greene uses the words *permanent* and *record*. In fourteen of those paragraphs he uses the actual phrase *permanent record*. Does Greene's repetition of the words and phrase become annoying for you? Does the repetition serve a useful function? Explain.

Vocabulary

Refer to your dictionary to define the following words as they are used in this selection. Then use each word in a sentence of your own.

unethical (5)	purge (13)
nagging (5)	naive (14)
candor (11)	jauntily (15)
deduced (12)	

Suggested Writing Assignments

1. Bob Greene's "Permanent Record" might be seen as another label, or even as a symbol, for what we call "con-

science" or "morality." Write an essay in which you attempt to define either term and to explain what it means to you. Be careful to offer as many examples as is appropriate in order to make the term you choose clear and understandable. Also, be sure to choose a clear, appropriate pattern of organization.

2. Reflect on your elementary- and high-school experiences. Did a commonly used concept or phrase like "Permanent Record" take on emotional dimensions for you? Was the school principal someone whose title evoked fear, deep respect, or love? Was the coach, the band leader, or Latin or math teacher such a figure? Were the college board examinations more frightening than seemed natural? Using Bob Greene's essay as a starting point or even a model, write a well-organized essay in which you discuss the importance of such a concept, event, or person in your life.

THE CORNER STORE

Eudora Welty

*Eudora Welty is perhaps one of the most hon-
ored and respected writers at work today. She
was born in 1909 in Jackson, Mississippi, where
she has lived most of her life. Her published
works include many short stories, now available
as her* Collected Stories *(1980); five novels; a collection of her essays,* The Eye of the Story *(1975);
and a memoir,* One Writer's Beginnings *(1987).
In 1973 her novel* The Optimist's Daughter *won
the Pulitizer prize for fiction. Welty's description
of the corner store, taken from an essay about
growing up in Jackson, will recall for many readers the neighborhood store where they grew up.*

Our Little Store rose right up from the sidewalk; standing
in a street of family houses, it alone hadn't any yard in
front, any tree or flower bed. It was a plain frame building covered over with brick. Above the door, a little railed porch ran
across on an upstairs level and four windows with shades were
looking out. But I didn't catch on to those.

Running in out of the sun, you met what seemed total obscu-
rity inside. There were almost tangible smells—licorice recently sucked in a child's cheek, dill pickle brine that had
leaked through a paper sack in a fresh trail across the wooden
floor, ammonia-loaded ice that had been hoisted from wet cro-
ker sacks and slammed into the icebox with its sweet butter at
the door, and perhaps the smell of still untrapped mice.

Then through the motes of cracker dust, cornmeal dust, the
Gold Dust of the Gold Dust Twins that the floor had been swept
out with, the realities emerged. Shelves climbed to high reach
all the way around, set out with not too much of any one thing
but a lot of things—lard, molasses, vinegar, starch, matches,
kerosene, Octagon soap (about a year's worth of octagon-
shaped coupons cut out and saved brought a signet ring ad-

dressed to you in the mail). It was up to you to remember what you came for, while your eye traveled from cans of sardines to tin whistles to ice cream salt to harmonicas to flypaper (over your head, batting around on a thread beneath the blades of the ceiling fan, stuck with its testimonial catch).

Its confusion may have been in the eye of its beholder. En- 4 chantment is cast upon you by all those things you weren't supposed to have need for, to lure you close to wooden tops you'd outgrown, boys' marbles and agates in little net pouches, small rubber balls that wouldn't bounce straight, frail, frazzly kite string, clay bubble pipes that would snap off in your teeth, the stiffest scissors. You could contemplate those long narrow boxes of sparklers gathering dust while you waited for it to be the Fourth of July or Christmas, and noisemakers in the shape of tin frogs for somebody's birthday party you hadn't been invited to yet, and see that they were all marvelous.

You might not have even looked for Mr. Sessions when he 5 came around his store cheese (as big as a doll's house) and in front of the counter looking for you. When you'd finally asked him for, and received from him in its paper bag, whatever single thing it was that you had been sent for, the nickel that was left over was yours to spend.

Down at a child's eye level, inside those glass jars with 6 mouths in their sides through which the grocer could run his scoop or a child's hand might be invited to reach for a choice, were wineballs, all-day suckers, gumdrops, peppermints. Making a row under the glass of a counter were the Tootsie Rolls, Hershey bars, Goo Goo Clusters, Baby Ruths. And whatever was the name of those pastilles that came stacked in a cardboard cylinder with a cardboard lid? They were thin and dry, about the size of tiddledy-winks, and in the shape of twisted rosettes. A kind of chocolate dust came out with them when you shook them out in your hand. Were they chocolate? I'd say, rather, they were brown. They didn't taste of anything at all, unless it was wood. Their attraction was the number you got for a nickel.

Making up your mind, you circled the store around and 7 around, around the pickle barrel, around the tower of Crackerjack boxes; Mr. Sessions had built it for us himself on top of a packing case like a house of cards.

If it seemed too hot for Crackerjacks, I might get a cold   8
drink. Mr. Sessions might have already stationed himself by
the cold-drinks barrel, like a mind reader. Deep in ice water
that looked black as ink, murky shapes—that would come up as
Coca-Colas, Orange Crushes, and various flavors of pop—were
all swimming around together. When you gave the word, Mr.
Sessions plunged his bare arm in to the elbow and fished out
your choice, first try. I favored a locally bottled concoction
called Lake's Celery. (What else could it be called? It was made
by a Mr. Lake out of celery. It was a popular drink here for
years but was not known universally, as I found out when I arrived in New York and ordered one in the Astor bar.) You drank
on the premises, with feet set wide apart to miss the drip, and
gave him back his bottle and your nickel.

But he didn't hurry you off. A standing scales was by the   9
door, with a stack of iron weights and a brass slide on the balance arm, that would weigh you up to three hundred pounds.
Mr. Sessions, whose hands were gentle and smelled of carbolic,
would lift you up and set your feet on the platform, hold your
loaf of bread for you, and taking his time while you stood still
for him, he would make certain of what you weighed today. He
could even remember what you weighed the last time, so you
could subtract and announce how much you'd gained. That was
goodbye.

Questions for Study and Discussion

1. Which of the three patterns of organization has Welty used
   in this essay: chronological, spatial, or logical? If she has
   used more than one, where precisely has she used each
   type?

2. What is the dominant impression that Welty creates in her
   description of the corner store? (Glossary: *Dominant Impression*) How does Welty create this dominant impression?

3. What does Welty mean when she writes that the store's
   "confusion may have been in the eye of its beholder"(4)?
   What factors might lead one to become confused?

4. What impression of Mr. Sessions does Welty create? What details contribute to this impression?

5. Welty places certain pieces of information in parentheses in this essay. Why are they in parentheses? What, if anything, does this information add to our understanding of the corner store? Might this information be left out? Explain.

6. Comment on Welty's ending. Is it too abrupt? Why or why not? (Glossary: *Beginnings and Endings*)

Vocabulary

Refer to your dictionary to define the following words as they are used in this selection. Then use each word in a sentence of your own.

frame (1)	signet (3)
tangible (2)	agates (4)
brine (2)	concoction (8)
motes (3)	scales (9)

Suggested Writing Assignments

1. Describe your neighborhood store or supermarket. Gather a large quantity of detailed information from memory and from an actual visit to the store if that is still possible. Once you have gathered your information, try to select those details that will help you create a dominant impression of the store. Finally, organize your examples and illustrations according to some clear organizational pattern.

2. Write an essay on one of the following topics:

   local restaurants
   reading materials
   television shows
   ways of financing a college education
   types of summer employment

   Be sure to use an organizational pattern that is well thought out and suited to both your material and your purpose.

4

Beginnings and Endings

"Begin at the beginning and go on till you come to the end: then stop," advised the King of Hearts in *Alice in Wonderland*. "Good advice, but more easily said than done," you might be tempted to reply. Certainly, no part of writing essays can be more daunting than coming up with effective beginnings and endings. In fact, many writers feel these are the most important parts of any piece of writing regardless of its length. Even before coming to your introduction proper, your readers will usually know something about your intentions from your title. Titles like "The Case Against Euthanasia," "How to Buy a Used Car," or "What Is a Migraine Headache?" indicate both your subject and approach and prepare your readers for what is to follow.

But what makes for an effective beginning? Not unlike a personal greeting, a good beginning should catch a reader's interest and then hold it. The experienced writer realizes that most readers would rather do almost anything than make a commitment to read, so the opening or "lead," as journalists refer to it, requires a lot of thought and much revising to make it right and to keep the reader's attention from straying. The inexperienced writer knows that the beginning is important but tries to write it first and to perfect it before moving on to the rest of the essay. Although there are no "rules" for writing introductions, we can offer one bit of general advice: wait until the writing process is well underway or almost completed before focusing on your lead. Following this advice will keep you from spending too much time on an introduction that you will probably revise. More importantly, once you actually see how your essay develops, you will know better how to introduce it to your reader.

In addition to capturing your reader's attention, a good beginning frequently introduces your thesis and either suggests or actually reveals the structure of the composition. Keep in mind that the best beginning is not necessarily the most catchy or the most shocking but the one most appropriate for the job you are trying to do.

Beginnings

The following examples from published essays show you some effective beginnings:

Short Generalization

> It is a miracle that New York works at all.
>
> E. B. White

Startling Claim

> It is possible to stop most drug addiction in the United States within a very short time.
>
> Gore Vidal

Questions

> Just how interconnected *is* the animal world? Is it true that if we change any part of that world we risk unduly damaging life in other, larger parts of it?
>
> Matthew Douglas

Humor/Apt Quotation

> The right to pursue happiness is issued to Americans with their birth certificates, but no one seems quite sure which way it ran. It may be we are issued a hunting license but offered no game. Jonathan Swift seemed to think so when he attacked the idea of happiness as "the possession of being well-deceived," the felicity of being "a fool among knaves." For Swift saw society as Vanity Fair, the land of false goals.
>
> John Ciardi

Startling Fact

> Charles Darwin and Abraham Lincoln were born on the same day—February 12, 1809. They are also linked in another curious way—for both must simultaneously play, and for similar reasons, the role of man and legend.
>
> Stephen Jay Gould

Dialogue

"This would be excellent, to go in the ocean with this thing," says Dave Gembutis, fifteen.

He is looking at a $170 Sea Cruiser raft.

"Great," says his companion, Dan Holmes, also fifteen.

This is at Herman's World of Sporting Goods, in the middle of the Woodfield Mall in Schaumburg, Illinois.

Bob Greene

Statistics/Question

In the 40 years from 1939 to 1979 white women who work full time have with monotonous regularity made slightly less than 60 percent as much as white men. Why?

Lester C. Thurow

Irony

In Moulmein, in lower Burma, I was hated by large numbers of people—the only time in my life that I have been important enough for this to happen to me.

George Orwell

There are many more excellent ways to begin an essay, but there are also some ways of beginning that should be avoided. Some of these follow:

Apology

I am a college student and do not consider myself an expert on the computer industry, but I think that many computer companies make false claims about just how easy it is to learn to use a computer.

Complaint

I'd rather write about a topic of my own choice than the one that is assigned, but here goes.

Webster's Dictionary

Webster's New Collegiate Dictionary defines the verb *to snore* as follows: "to breathe during sleep with a rough hoarse noise due to vibration of the soft palate."

Platitude

> America is the land of opportunity and no one knows it better than Lee Iacocca.

Reference to Title

> As you can see from my title, this essay is about why we should continue to experiment with human heart transplants.

Endings

An effective ending does more than simply indicate where the writer stopped writing. A conclusion may summarize; may inspire the reader to further thought or even action; may return to the beginning by repeating key words, phrases, or ideas; or may surprise the reader by providing a particularly convincing example to support a thesis. Indeed, there are, as with beginnings, many ways to write a conclusion, but the effectiveness of any choice really must be measured by how appropriately it fits what has gone before it. In the following conclusion to a long chapter on weasel words, a form of deceptive advertising language, writer Paul Stevens summarizes the points that he has made:

> A weasel word is a word that's used to imply a meaning that cannot be truthfully stated. Some weasels imply meanings that are not the same as their actual definition, such as "help," "like," or "fortified." They can act as qualifiers and/or comparatives. Other weasels, such as "taste" and "flavor," have no definite meanings, and are simply subjective opinions offered by the manufacturer. A weasel of omission is one that implies a claim so strongly that it forces you to supply the bogus fact. Adjectives are weasels used to convey feelings and emotions to a greater extent than the product itself can.
>
> In dealing with weasels, you must strip away the innuendos and try to ascertain the facts, if any. To do this, you need to ask questions such as: How? Why? How many? How much? Stick to basic definitions of words. Look them up if you have to. Then, apply the strict definition to the text of the advertisement or commercial. "Like" means

similar to, but not the same as. "Virtually" means the same in essence, but not in fact.

Above all, never underestimate the devious qualities of a weasel. Weasels twist and turn and hide in dark shadows. You must come to grips with them, or advertising will rule you forever.

My advice to you is: Beware of weasels. They are nasty and untrainable, and they attack pocketbooks.

If you are having trouble with your conclusion—and this is not an uncommon problem—it may be because of problems with your essay itself. Frequently, writers do not know when to end because they are not sure about their overall purpose in the first place. For example, if you are taking a trip and your purpose is to go to Chicago, you'll know when you get there and will stop. But if you don't really know where you are going, it's very difficult to know when to stop.

It's usually a good idea in your conclusion to avoid such over-worked expressions as "In conclusion," "In summary," "I hope I have shown," or "Finally." Your conclusion should also do more than simply repeat what you've said in your opening paragraph. The most satisfying essays are those in which the conclusion provides an interesting way of wrapping up ideas introduced in the beginning and developed throughout.

WHAT IS FREEDOM?

Jerald M. Jellison and John H. Harvey

*Jerald M. Jellison, professor of psychology at the
University of Southern California, specializes in
theories of human social behavior. John H. Harvey, professor of social psychology at Vanderbilt
University, recently coedited a collection of studies in social behavior. In this selection from* Psychology Today, *Jellison and Harvey begin with
an illustrative story to help them define the elusive concept of freedom.*

The pipe under your kitchen sink springs a leak and you   1
call in a plumber. A few days later you get a bill for $40. At
the bottom is a note saying that if you don't pay within 30 days,
there'll be a 10 percent service charge of $4. You feel trapped,
with no desirable alternative. You pay $40 now or $44 later.

Now make two small changes in the script. The plumber   2
sends you a bill for $44, but the note says that if you pay within
30 days you'll get a special $4 discount. Now you feel pretty
good. You have two alternatives, one of which will save you $4.

In fact, your choices are the same in both cases—pay $40 now   3
or $44 later—but your feelings about them are different. This
illustrates a subject we've been studying for several years:
What makes people feel free and why does feeling free make
them happy? One factor we've studied is that individuals feel
freer when they can choose between positive alternatives (delaying payment or saving $4) rather than between negative ones
(paying immediately or paying $4 more).

Choosing between negative alternatives often seems like no   4
choice at all. Take the case of a woman trying to decide
whether to stay married to her inconsiderate, incompetent husband, or get a divorce. She doesn't want to stay with him, but
she feels divorce is a sign of failure and will stigmatize her socially. Or think of the decision faced by many young men a few

years ago, when they were forced to choose between leaving
their country and family or being sent to Vietnam.

When we face decisions involving only alternatives we see as   5
negatives, we feel so little freedom that we twist and turn
searching for another choice with some positive characteristics.

Freedom is a popular word. Individuals talk about how they   6
feel free with one person and not with another, or how their
bosses encourage or discourage freedom on the job. We hear
about civil wars and revolutions being fought for greater freedom, with both sides righteously making the claim. The feeling
of freedom is so important that people say they're ready to die
for it, and supposedly have.

Still, most people have trouble coming up with a precise defi-   7
nition of freedom. They give answers describing specific
situations—"Freedom means doing what I want to do, not what
the Government wants me to do," or "Freedom means not having my mother tell me when to come home from a party"—
rather than a general definition covering many situations. The
idea they seem to be expressing is that freedom is associated
with making decisions, and that other people sometimes limit
the number of alternatives from which they can select.

Questions for Study and Discussion

1. The first three paragraphs serve as the beginning of Jellison
   and Harvey's essay. What point are the authors trying to
   make? Is the beginning effective? Why or why not?

2. What general definition of *freedom* do Jellison and Harvey
   present? Where in the essay is that definition given?

3. When, according to Jellison and Harvey, do individuals feel
   free?

4. Explain how Jellison and Harvey use examples to develop
   their definition of *freedom*. (You may find it helpful to outline the essay paragraph by paragraph.)

5. Paragraph 5 is pivotal in this essay. Explain why it is so
   important. (It might be helpful to consider the essay without paragraph 5.)

6. The authors' tone in this essay is informal, almost conversational. Cite examples of diction and sentence structure to show how they establish and maintain this tone. (Glossary: *Tone*)

Vocabulary

Refer to your dictionary to define the following words as they are used in this selection. Then use each word in a sentence of your own.

script (2)	stigmatize (4)
incompetent (4)	righteously (6)

Suggested Writing Assignments

1. Write an essay of your own defining freedom. You may wish to consult the work of others—writers and philosophers, for example—or draw exclusively on personal observations and experiences.

2. Write a short essay in which you define one of the following abstract terms. Begin your essay with an illustrative example as Jellison and Harvey do in their essay.

charm
friendship
hatred
leadership
trust
commitment
religion
love

YOU ARE HOW YOU EAT

Enid Nemy

*Born in Winnipeg, Canada, Enid Nemy has had
an active career in journalism. She worked as a
reporter and an editor for Canadian newspapers
before joining* The New York Times *in 1963. At
the* Times *she writes "New Yorkers, Etc.," an
award-winning column devoted to New York
City's people and events. Notice how Nemy's beginning establishes her thesis and sets up her examples and how her ending reverberates back
through the essay.*

There's nothing peculiar about a person walking along a
Manhattan street, or any other street for that matter, eating an ice cream cone. It's the approach that's sometimes a little strange—ice-cream-cone-eating is not a cut-and-dried,
standardized, routine matter. It is an accomplishment with infinite variety, ranging from methodical and workmanlike procedures to methods that are visions of delicacy and grace.

The infinite variety displayed in eating ice cream isn't by any
means unique; it applies to all kinds of food. The fact is that although a lot of research has been done on what people eat and
where they eat it, serious studies on the way food is eaten have
been sadly neglected.

Back to ice cream, as an example. If five people leave an ice
cream store with cones, five different methods of eating will
likely be on view. There are people who stick out their tongues
on top of a scoop, but don't actually eat the ice cream. They
push it down into the cone—push, push, push—then take an in-
termission to circle the perimeter, lapping up possible drips.

After this, it's again back to pushing the ice cream farther
into the cone. When the ice cream has virtually disappeared
into the crackly cone, they begin eating. These people obviously
don't live for the moment; they plan for the future, even if the
future is only two minutes away. Gobble up all the ice cream on

top and be left with a hollow cone? Forget it. Better to forgo immediate temptation and then enjoy the cone right to the end.

On the other hand, there are the "now" types who take great gobby bites of the ice cream. Eventually, of course, they get down to an empty cone, which they might eat and, then again, they might throw away (if the latter, one wonders why they don't buy cups rather than cones, but no point in asking).

The most irritating of all ice cream eaters are the elegant creatures who manage to devour a whole cone with delicate little nibbles and no dribble. The thermometer might soar, the pavement might melt, but their ice cream stays as firm and as rounded as it was in the scoop. No drips, no minor calamities— and it's absolutely not fair, but what can you do about it?

Some of the strangest ice cream fans can be seen devouring sundaes and banana splits. They are known as "layer by layer" types. First they eat the nuts and coconut and whatever else is sprinkled on top. Then they eat the sauce; then the banana, and finally the ice cream, flavor by flavor. Some might feel that they are eating ingredients and not a sundae or a split, but what do they care?

As for chocolate eaters, there are three main varieties, at least among those who like the small individual chocolates. A certain percentage pop the whole chocolate into their mouths, crunch once or twice and down it goes. Others pop the whole chocolate into their mouths and let it slowly melt. A smaller number hold the chocolate in hand while taking dainty little bites.

Peanuts and popcorn are a completely different matter. Of course, there are always one or two souls who actually pick up single peanuts and popcorn kernels, but the usual procedure is to scoop up a handful. But even these can be subdivided into those who feed them in one at a time and those who sort of throw the handful into the open mouth, then keep on throwing in handfuls until the plate, bag or box is empty. The feeders-in-one-at-a-time are, needless to say, a rare breed with such iron discipline that they probably exercise every morning and love it.

Candies like M & M's are treated by most people in much the same way as peanuts or popcorn. But there are exceptions, among them those who don't start eating until they have separated the colors. Then they eat one color at a time, or one of each color in rotation. Honestly.

A sandwich cookie is a sandwich cookie, and you take bites of it, and so what? So what if you're the kind who doesn't take bites until it's pulled apart into two sections. And if you're this kind of person, and an amazing number are, the likelihood is that the plain part will be eaten first, and the one with icing saved for last. Watch Oreo eaters. 11

A woman who seems quite normal in other respects said that although she considers her eating habits quite run-of-the-mill, she has been told that they are, in fact, peculiar. 12

"If I have meat or chicken and a couple of vegetables on a plate, I go absolutely crazy if they don't come out even," she said. "I like to take a piece of meat and a little bit of each vegetable together. If, as I'm eating I end up with no meat and a lot of broccoli, or no potatoes and a piece of chicken, it drives me mad." 13

A man listening to all this rolled his eyes in disbelief. Peculiar is putting it mildly, he said. He would never eat like that. 14

How does he eat? 15

"One thing at a time," he said. "First I eat the meat, then one of the vegetables, then the other. How else would you eat?" 16

Questions for Study and Discussion

1. Study the beginning of Nemy's essay. How does it serve Nemy's purpose? (Glossary: *Purpose*)

2. What is Nemy's thesis in this essay? (Glossary: *Thesis*)

3. Nemy has written as essay of classification. (Glossary: *Division and Classification*) How does classification serve her purpose?

4. What connection does Nemy make between paragraphs 7 and 8? Where in the essay does Nemy prepare you for the change in subject from ice cream to chocolate?

5. Is this essay merely an attempt to be humorous, or is there something more to its subject than we might suspect? You

might wish to reconsider the title in determining your response to this question. (Glossary: *Title*)

6. How fitting is Nemy's conclusion for the essay she has written? Would it have been better if the essay ended with a different paragraph—say, paragraph 11 or 13? Explain.

Vocabulary

Refer to your dictionary to define the following words as they are used in this selection. Then use each word in a sentence of your own.

infinite (1)	irritating (6)
methodical (1)	dainty (8)
unique (2)	iron (9)
perimeter (3)	icing (11)

Suggested Writing Assignments

1. Enid Nemy's discussion of the various ways people eat is by no means exhaustive. Much remains to observe and report. Write an essay modeled on hers in which you report on what you have observed of people's eating habits. Try, as Nemy has done, to suggest the importance of what you have observed, perhaps even spending more time in your essay developing a theory on the relationship between eating and behavior or personality.

2. How we say "Hello" and "Goodbye" can be extremely important in interpersonal relationships. Write an essay using your own experiences to examine the importance of the various kinds of greetings and farewells. Your essay should have an effective opening and a fitting conclusion.

How to Take a Job Interview

Kirby W. Stanat

*A former personnel recruiter and placement offi-
cer at the University of Wisconsin—Milwaukee,
Kirby W. Stanat has helped thousands of people
get jobs. His book* Job Hunting Secrets and Tac-
tics *(1977) tells readers what they need to know
in order to get the jobs they want. In this selection Stanat analyzes the campus interview, a
process that hundreds of thousands of college
students undergo each year as they seek to enter
the job market. Notice how Stanat begins and
how the "snap" of his ending echoes back
through his essay.*

To succeed in campus job interviews, you have to know
where that recruiter is coming from. The simple answer is
that he is coming from corporate headquarters.

That may sound obvious, but it is a significant point that too
many students do not consider. The recruiter is not a free spirit
as he flies from Berkeley to New Haven, from Chapel Hill to
Boulder. He's on an invisible leash to the office, and if he is
worth his salary, he is mentally in corporate headquarters all
the time he's on the road.

If you can fix that in your mind—that when you walk into
that bare-walled cubicle in the placement center you are walking into a branch office of Sears, Bendix or General Motors—
you can avoid a lot of little mistakes and maybe some big ones.

If, for example, you assume that because the interview is on
campus the recruiter expects you to look and act like a student,
you're in for a shock. A student is somebody who drinks beer,
wears blue jeans and throws a Frisbee. No recruiter has jobs
for student Frisbee whizzes.

A cool spring day in late March, Sam Davis, a good recruiter
who has been on the college circuit for years, is on my campus

talking to candidates. He comes out to the waiting area to meet the student who signed up for an 11 o'clock interview. I'm standing in the doorway of my office taking in the scene. Sam calls the candidate: "Sidney Student." There sits Sidney. He's at a 45 degree angle, his feet are in the aisle, and he's almost lying down. He's wearing well-polished brown shoes, a tasteful pair of brown pants, a light brown shirt, and a good looking tie. Unfortunately, he tops off this well-coordinated outfit with his Joe's Tavern Class A Softball Championship jacket, which has a big woven emblem over the heart.   6

If that isn't bad enough, in his left hand is a cigarette and in his right hand is a half-eaten apple.   7

When Sam calls his name, the kid is caught off guard. He ditches the cigarette in an ashtray, struggles to his feet, and transfers the apple from the right to the left hand. Apple juice is everywhere, so Sid wipes his hand on the seat of his pants and shakes hands with Sam.   8

Sam, who by now is close to having a stroke, gives me that what-do-I-have-here look and has the young man follow him into the interviewing room.   9

The situation deteriorates even further—into pure Laurel and Hardy. The kid is stuck with the half-eaten apple, doesn't know what to do with it, and obviously is suffering some discomfort. He carries the apple into the interviewing room with him and places it in the ashtray on the desk—right on top of Sam's freshly lit cigarette.   10

The interview lasts five minutes. . . .   11

Let us move in for a closer look at how the campus recruiter operates.   12

Let's say you have a 10 o'clock appointment with the recruiter from the XYZ Corporation. The recruiter gets rid of the candidate in front of you at about 5 minutes to 10, jots down a few notes about what he is going to do with him or her, then picks up your résumé or data sheet (which you have submitted in advance). . . .   13

Although the recruiter is still in the interview room and you are still in the lobby, your interview is under way. You're on. The recruiter will look over your sheet pretty carefully before he goes out to call you. He develops a mental picture of you.   14

He thinks, "I'm going to enjoy talking with this kid," or "This 15
one's going to be a turkey." The recruiter has already begun to
make a screening decision about you.

His first impression of you, from reading the sheet, could 16
come from your grade point. It could come from misspelled
words. It could come from poor erasures or from the fact that
necessary information is missing. By the time the recruiter has
finished reading your sheet, you've already hit the plus or minus column.

Let's assume the recruiter got a fairly good impression from 17
your sheet.

Now the recruiter goes out to the lobby to meet you. He al- 18
most shuffles along, and his mind is somewhere else. Then he
calls your name, and at that instant he visibly clicks into gear.
He just went to work.

As he calls your name he looks quickly around the room, 19
waiting for somebody to move. If you are sitting on the middle
of your back, with a book open and a cigarette going, and if you
have to rebuild yourself to stand up, the interest will run right
out of the recruiter's face. You, not the recruiter, made the appointment for 10 o'clock, and the recruiter expects to see a
young professional come popping out of that chair like today is
a good day and you're anxious to meet him.

At this point, the recruiter does something rude. He doesn't 20
walk across the room to meet you halfway. He waits for you to
come to him. Something very important is happening. He
wants to see you move. He wants to get an impression about
your posture, your stride, and your briskness.

If you slouch over him, sidewinderlike, he is not going to be 21
impressed. He'll figure you would probably slouch your way
through your workdays. He wants you to come at him with lots
of good things going for you. If you watch the recruiter's eyes,
you can see the inspection. He glances quickly at shoes, pants,
coat, shirt; dress, blouse, hose—the whole works.

After introducing himself, the recruiter will probably say, 22
"Okay, please follow me," and he'll lead you into his interviewing room.

When you get to the room, you may find that the recruiter 23
will open the door and gesture you in—with him blocking part

of the doorway. There's enough room for you to get past him, but it's a near thing.

As you scrape past, he gives you a closeup inspection. He   24
looks at your hair; if it's greasy, that will bother him. He looks at your collar; if it's dirty, that will bother him. He looks at your shoulders; if they're covered with dandruff, that will bother him. If you're a man, he looks at your chin. If you didn't get a close shave, that will irritate him. If you're a woman, he checks your makeup. If it's too heavy, he won't like it.

Then he smells you. An amazing number of people smell bad.   25
Occasionally a recruiter meets a student who smells like a canal horse. That student can expect an interview of about four or five minutes.

Next the recruiter inspects the back side of you. He checks   26
your hair (is it combed in front but not in back?), he checks your heels (are they run down?), your pants (are they baggy?), your slip (is it showing?), your stockings (do they have runs?).

Then he invites you to sit down.   27

At this point, I submit, the recruiter's decision on you is 75 to   28
80 percent made.

Think about it. The recruiter has read your résumé. He   29
knows who you are and where you are from. He knows your marital status, your major and your grade point. And he knows what you have done with your summers. He has inspected you, exchanged greetings with you and smelled you. There is very little additional hard information that he must gather on you. From now on it's mostly body chemistry.

Many recruiters have argued strenuously with me that they   30
don't make such hasty decisions. So I tried an experiment. I told several recruiters that I would hang around in the hall outside the interview room when they took candidates in.

I told them that as soon as they had definitely decided not to   31
recommend (to department managers in their companies) the candidate they were interviewing, they should snap their fingers loud enough for me to hear. It went like this.

First candidate: 38 seconds after the candidate sat down: 32
Snap!

Second candidate: 1 minute, 42 seconds: Snap!   33

Third candidate: 45 seconds: Snap!   34

One recruiter was particularly adamant, insisting that he   35
didn't rush to judgment on candidates. I asked him to participate in the snapping experiment. He went out in the lobby,
picked up his first candidate of the day, and headed for an interview room.

As he passed me in the hall, he glared at me. And his fingers   36
went "Snap!"

Questions for Study and Discussion

1. Explain the appropriateness of the beginning and ending of
   Stanat's essay.
2. What are Stanat's purpose and thesis in telling the reader
   how the recruitment process works? (Glossary: *Purpose* and
   Thesis)
3. In paragraphs 12–29 Stanat explains how the campus recruiter works. Make a list of the steps in that process.
4. Why do recruiters pay so much attention to body language
   when they interview job candidates?
5. What specifically have you learned from reading Stanat's
   essay? Do you feel that the essay is useful in preparing
   someone for a job interview? Explain.
6. Stanat's tone—his attitude toward his subject and
   audience—in this essay is informal. What in his sentence
   structure and diction creates this informality? Cite examples. How might the tone be made more formal for a different audience?

Vocabulary

Refer to your dictionary to define the following words as they
are used in this selection. Then use each word in a sentence of
your own.

cubicle (3)   résumé (13)
deteriorates (10)   adamant (35)

Suggested Writing Assignments

1. Stanat's purpose is to offer practical advice to students interviewing for jobs. Determine a subject about which you could offer advice to a specific audience. Present your advice in the form of an essay, being careful to provide an attention-grabbing beginning and a convincing conclusion.

2. Stanat gives us an account of the interview process from the viewpoint of the interviewer. If you have ever been interviewed and remember the experience well, write an essay on your feelings and thoughts as the interview took place. What were the circumstances of the interview? What questions were asked of you, how did you feel about them, and how comfortable was the process? How did the interview turn out? What precisely, if anything, did you learn from the experience? What advice would you give anyone about to be interviewed?

HUGH TROY: PRACTICAL JOKER

Alfred Rosa and Paul Eschholz

Alfred Rosa and Paul Eschholz are both profes-
sors of English at the University of Vermont,
where they teach courses in composition, the En-
glish language, and American literature. In the
following article, which first appeared in The
People's Almanac #2 *in 1978, Rosa and Eschholz*
draw a portrait of a man who believed that in
the hands of an expert a practical joke was more
than just a good laugh. As you read, notice how
the opening serves to build interest and how the
conclusion works to reflect the point of the
essay.

Nothing seemed unusual. In fact, it was a rather common   1
occurrence in New York City. Five men dressed in over-
alls roped off a section of busy Fifth Avenue in front of the old
Rockefeller residence, hung out MEN WORKING signs, and began
ripping up the pavement. By the time they stopped for lunch,
they had dug quite a hole in the street. This crew was different,
however, from all the others that had descended upon the
streets of the city. It was led by Hugh Troy—the world's greatest practical joker.

For lunch, Troy led his tired and dirty crew into the dining   2
room of a fashionable Fifth Avenue hotel that was nearby.
When the headwaiter protested, Troy took him into his confidence. "It's a little gag the manager wants to put over," he told
the waiter. The men ate heartily and seemed not to notice that
indignant diners were leaving the premises. After lunch Troy
and his men returned to their digging, and by late afternoon
they had greatly enlarged the hole in the avenue. When quitting
time arrived, they dutifully hung out their red lanterns, left the
scene, and never returned. City officials discovered the hoax
the next day, but they never learned who the pranksters were.

Hugh Troy was born in Ithaca, N.Y., where his father was a   3 professor at Cornell University. After graduating from Cornell, Troy left for New York City, where he became a successful illustrator of children's books. When W.W. II broke out, he went into the army and eventually became a captain in the 21st Bomber Command, 20th Air Force, under Gen. Curtis LeMay. After the war he made his home in Garrison, N.Y., for a short while before finally settling in Washington, D.C., where he lived until his death.

As a youngster Troy became a friend of the painter Louis   4
Agassiz Fuertes, who encouraged Troy to become an artist and may have encouraged the boy to become a practical joker as well. While Fuertes and Troy were out driving one day, Fuertes saw a JESUS SAVES sign and swiped it. Many a good laugh was had when several days later people saw the sign firmly planted in front of the Ithaca Savings Bank. The boy put up a few signs of his own. Fascinated by the word *pinking*, he posted a sign in front of his house: PINKING DONE. No one needed pinking done, but curiosity got the best of some, who stopped to ask what pinking was. "It's a trade secret," Troy quipped. The boy was also a member of a skating club, and when he needed some pocket money, he tacked an old cigar box near the entrance of the clubhouse, along with a PLEASE HELP sign. People naturally began dropping change into the box, change which Troy routinely pocketed.

The fun for Troy really began when he entered Cornell. Some   5
of his celebrated antics involved a phony plane crash, reports on the campus radio station of an enemy invasion, an apparent ceiling collapse, and a cherry tree which one year miraculously bore apples. Troy's most successful stunt at Cornell concerned a rhinoceros. Using a wastebasket made from the foot of a rhinoceros, which he borrowed from his friend Fuertes, Troy made tracks across the campus and onto the frozen reservoir, stopping at the brink of a large hole in the ice. Nobody knew what to make of the whole thing until campus zoologists confirmed the authenticity of the tracks. Townspeople then began to complain that their tap water tasted of rhinoceros. Not until the truth surfaced did the complaints subside.

Troy's antics did not stop when he graduated from Cornell.   6
Shortly after moving to New York, he purchased a park bench, an exact duplicate of those used by the city. With the help of a

friend, he hauled it into Central Park. As soon as Hugh and his cohort spied a policeman coming down the path, they picked up the bench and started off with it. In no time the mischievous pair were in the local hoosegow. At that point the clever Troy produced his bill of sale, forcing the embarrassed police to release him and his pal. The two men repeated the caper several times before the entire force finally caught on.

Often Troy's pranks were conceived on the spur of the moment. For example, on a whim Troy bought a dozen copies of the 1932 election-night extra announcing Roosevelt's victory. The papers remained in mothballs until New Year's Eve, 1935, when Hugh and a group of merrymakers rode the city's subways, each with a copy of the newspaper. Other passengers, most of whom were feeling no pain, did a double take at the bold headline: ROOSEVELT ELECTED. 7

When the Museum of Modern Art sponsored the first American showing of Van Gogh's work in 1935, Hugh was on the scene again. The exhibit attracted large crowds of people who Troy suspected were more interested in the sensational aspects of the artist's life than in his paintings. To test his theory, Troy fashioned a replica of an ear out of chipped beef and had it neatly mounted in a blue velvet display case. A small card telling the grisly story was attached: "This was the ear which Vincent Van Gogh cut off and sent to his mistress, a French prostitute, Dec. 24, 1888." The "chipped beef ear" was then placed on a table in the gallery where Van Gogh's paintings were displayed. Troy got immediate results. New York's "art lovers" flocked to the ear, which, as Troy suspected, was what they really wanted to see after all. 8

Hugh Troy's pranks were never vindictive, but once, when irked by the operator of a Greenwich Village movie theater, he got the last laugh. One evening he took a jar full of moths into the theater and released them during the show. The moths flew directly for the light from the projector and made it impossible for anyone to see the picture. While the manager tried to appease the angry moviegoers, Hugh looked on with satisfaction. 9

To protest the tremendous amount of paperwork in the army during W.W. II, Troy invented the special "flypaper report." Each day he sent this report to Washington to account for the number of flies trapped on the variously coded flypaper ribbons hanging in the company's mess hall. Soon the Pentagon, 10 as might be expected, was asking other units for their flypaper reports. Troy was also responsible for "Operation Folklore." While stationed in the South Pacific, he and two other intelligence officers coached an island youngster in fantastic Troy-devised folktales, which the child then told to a gullible visiting anthropologist.

While some of his practical jokes were pure fun, many were designed to expose the smugness and gullibility of the American public. Annoyed by a recently announced course in ghostwriting at American University, Troy placed the following ad in the *Washington Post:* "Too Busy to Paint? Call on The Ghost Artists. We Paint It—You Sign It!! Why Not Give an Exhibition?" The response was more than he had bargained for. The hundreds of letters and phone calls only highlighted the fact that Americans' pretentiousness about art and their attempts to buy their way into "arty circles" had not waned since the Van Gogh escapade.

Whether questioning the values of American society or simply relieving the monotony of daily life, Hugh Troy always managed to put a little bit of himself into each of his stunts. One day he attached a plaster hand to his shirt sleeve and took a trip through the Holland Tunnel. As he approached the toll-booth, with his toll ticket between the fingers of the artificial hand, Troy left both ticket and hand in the grasp of the stunned tollbooth attendant and sped away.

Questions for Study and Discussion

1. Reread the first two paragraphs of this essay. Are they a fitting introduction to the essay? Why, or why not? What would be gained or lost if the essay began with paragraph 3?

2. Reread the last paragraph of the essay. Is this paragraph a fitting conclusion? Why, or why not?

3. What in particular made Hugh Troy the world's greatest practical joker; that is, what put him in a different league than the ordinary prankster?

4. Briefly describe the organization of Rosa and Eschholz's essay. Would the essay be as effective if the paragraphs

were rearranged in a different order? Explain. (Glossary: *Organization*)

5. Rosa and Eschholz write that many of Troy's jokes "were designed to expose the smugness and gullibility of the American public" (11). What do they mean by that statement? Choose several of Troy's jokes and explain how they accomplished this particular purpose.

6. Are people today as smug and gullible as they used to be or less or more so? Explain.

Vocabulary

Refer to your dictionary to define the following words as they are used in this selection. Then use each word in a sentence of your own.

hoax (2)	vindictive (9)
pinking (4)	irked (9)
hoosegow (6)	appease (9)
caper (6)	smugness (11)
whim (7)	waned (11)

Suggested Writing Assignments

1. If you yourself are a practical joker, or if you have ever known one, write an essay modeled after Rosa and Eschholz's "Hugh Troy." Try to recount in detail the pranks that have been carried out and, most importantly, try to assess their significance. Give extra time and attention to the opening and concluding portions of your essay, making sure they do their jobs well.

2. Write an essay in which you discuss the need for humor in our lives. Draw upon your experiences, as well as those of classmates, to recount humorous situations, events, and statements in order to analyze how they have served to ease tensions, tone down aggressive behavior, or lighten an otherwise dark moment. Be sure that the beginning of your essay grabs and holds the reader's attention and that the ending provides a conclusion rather than just a stopping point.

5

PARAGRAPHS

Within an essay, the paragraph is the most important unit of thought. Like the essay, it has its own main idea, often stated directly in a topic sentence. Like a good essay, a good paragraph is unified: it avoids digressions and develops its main idea. Paragraphs use many of the rhetorical techniques that essays use, techniques such as classification, comparison and contrast, and cause and effect. In fact, many writers find it helpful to think of the paragraph as a very small, compact essay.

Here is a paragraph from an essay on testing:

> Multiple-choice questions distort the purposes of education. Picking one answer among four is very different from thinking a question through to an answer of one's own, and far less useful in life. Recognition of vocabulary and isolated facts makes the best kind of multiple-choice questions, so these dominate the tests, rather than questions that test the use of knowledge. Because schools want their children to perform well, they are often tempted to teach the limited sorts of knowledge most useful on the tests.

This paragraph, like all well-written paragraphs, has several distinguishing characteristics: it is unified, coherent, and adequately developed. It is unified in that every sentence and every idea relate to the main idea, stated in the topic sentence, "Multiple-choice questions distort the purposes of education." It is coherent in that the sentences and ideas are arranged logically and the relationships among them are made clear by the use of effective transitions. Finally, the paragraph is adequately developed in that it presents a short but persuasive argument supporting its main idea.

How much development is "adequate" development? The answer depends on many things: how complicated or controversial the main idea is; what readers already know and believe;

how much space the writer is permitted. Everyone, or nearly everyone, agrees that the earth circles around the sun; a single sentence would be enough to make that point. A writer trying to prove that the earth does *not* circle the sun, however, would need many sentences, indeed many paragraphs, to develop that idea convincingly.

Here is another model of an effective paragraph. As you read this paragraph about the resourcefulness of pigeons in evading attempts to control them, pay particular attention to its controlling idea, unity, development, and coherence.

> Pigeons [and their human friends] have proved remarkably resourceful in evading nearly all the controls, from birth-control pellets to carbide shells to pigeon apartment complexes, that pigeon-haters have devised. One of New York's leading museums once put large black rubber owls on its wide ledges to discourage the large number of pigeons that roosted there. Within the day the pigeons had gotten over their fear of owls and were back perched on the owls' heads. A few years ago San Francisco put a sticky coating on the ledges of some public buildings, but the pigeons got used to the goop and came back to roost. The city then tried trapping, using electric owls, and periodically exploding carbide shells outside a city building, hoping the noise would scare the pigeons away. It did, but not for long, and the program was abandoned. More frequent explosions probably would have distressed the humans in the area more than the birds. Philadelphia tried a feed that makes pigeons vomit, and then, they hoped, go away. A New York firm claimed it had a feed that made a pigeon's nervous system send "danger signals" to the other members of its flock.

The controlling idea is stated at the beginning in a topic sentence. Other sentences in the paragraph support the controlling idea with examples. Since all the separate examples illustrate how pigeons have evaded attempts to control them, the paragraph is unified. Since there are enough examples to convince the reader of the truth of the topic statement, the paragraph is adequately developed. Finally, the regular use of transitional words and phrases such as *once, within the day, a few years ago,* and *then,* lends the paragraph coherence.

How long should a paragraph be? In modern essays most paragraphs range from 50 to 250 words, but some run a full page or more and others may be only a few words long. The best answer is that a paragraph should be long enough to develop its main idea adequately. Some authors, when they find a paragraph running very long, may break it into two or more paragraphs so that readers can pause and catch their breath. Other writers forge ahead, relying on the unity and coherence of their paragraph to keep their readers from getting lost.

Articles and essays that appear in magazines and newspapers often have relatively short paragraphs, some of only one or two sentences. The reason is that they are printed in very narrow columns, which make paragraphs of average length appear very long. But often you will find that these journalistic "paragraphs" could be joined together into a few longer, more normal paragraphs. Longer, more normal paragraphs are the kind you should use in all but journalistic writing.

CLAUDE FETRIDGE'S INFURIATING LAW

H. Allen Smith

*H. Allen Smith (1907–1976) wrote many humor-
ous books, among them* Low Man on the Totem
Pole *(1941),* Life in a Putty Knife Factory *(1943),
and* Larks in the Popcorn *(1948). As can be seen
in the following selection, Smith perceived the
humor in everyday life and captured this humor
in his writing. Notice the way in which Smith's
topic sentences serve to control and focus the
material in each of the essay's five paragraphs.*

Fetridge's Law, in simple language, states that important   1
things that are supposed to happen do not happen, especially when people are looking; or, conversely, things that are
supposed not to happen do happen, especially when people are
looking. Thus a dog that will jump through a hoop a thousand
times a day for his owner will not jump through a hoop when a
neighbor is called in to watch; and a baby that will say "Dada"
in the presence of its proud parents will, when friends are sum-
moned, either clam up or screech like a jaybird.

Fetridge's Law takes its name from a onetime radio engineer   2
named Claude Fetridge. Back in 1936, Mr. Fetridge thought up
the idea of broadcasting the flight of the famous swallows from
San Juan de Capistrano mission in Southern California. As is
well known, the swallows depart from the mission each year on
St. John's Day, October 23, and return on March 19, St. Joseph's Day. Claude Fetridge conceived the idea of broadcasting
the flutter of wings of the departing swallows on October 23.
His company went to considerable expense to set up its equipment at the mission; then, with the whole nation waiting anxiously for the soul-stirring event, it was discovered that this
year the swallows, out of sheer orneriness, had departed a day
ahead of schedule. Thus did a flock of birds lend immortality to
Claude Fetridge.

Television sets, of course, are often subject to the workings   3
of Fetridge's Law. If a friend tells me he is going to appear on a

television show and asks me to watch it, I groan inwardly, knowing this is going to cost me money. The moment his show comes on the air, my screen will snow up or acquire the look of an old-school-tie pattern. I turn it off and call the repairman. He travels three miles to my house and turns the set on. The picture emerges bright and clear, the contrast exactly right, a better picture than I've ever had before. It's that way always and forever, days without end.

An attractive woman neighbor of mine drives her husband to the railroad station every morning. On rare occasions she has been late getting her backfield in motion, and hasn't had time to get dressed. These times she has thrown a coat over her nightgown and, wearing bedroom slippers, headed for the depot. Fetridge's Law always seems to give her trouble. Once she clashed fenders with another car on the highway and had to go to the police station in her night shift. Twice she has had motor trouble in the depot plaza, requiring that she get out of her car in robe and slippers and pincurlers. The last I heard, she was considering sleeping in her street clothes.

Fetridge's Law operates fiercely in the realm of dentistry. In my own case, I have often noted that whenever I develop a raging toothache it is a Sunday and the dentists are all on the golf course. Not long ago, my toothache hung on through the weekend, and Monday morning it was still throbbing and pulsating like a diesel locomotive, I called my dentist, proclaimed an emergency, and drove to his office. As I was going up the stairway, the ache suddenly vanished. By the time I got into his chair, I was confused and embarrassed and unable to tell him with certainty which tooth it was that had been killing me. The X ray showed no shady spots, though it would have several if he had pointed the thing at my brain. Claude Fetridge's law clearly has its good points; it can exasperate, but it can also cure toothaches.

Questions for Study and Discussion

1. How does Fetridge's Law work?
2. For whom was Fetridge's Law named? For what reason?
3. Have you ever encountered Fetridge's Law? Explain.

4. Identify the topic sentences in paragraphs 1, 3, and 5. (Glossary: *Topic Sentence*) How, specifically, do the other sentences in each paragraph support and/or develop the topic sentence?

5. Explain how Smith achieves coherence in paragraph 2. (Glossary: *Coherence*)

6. Briefly describe the organization of the essay. Would the essay be as effective if the paragraphs were arranged in a different order? Explain. (Glossary: *Organization*)

7. Do you think that the last sentence is an effective ending for the essay? Why or why not? (Glossary: *Beginnings and Endings*)

Vocabulary

Refer to your dictionary to define the following words as they are used in this selection. Then use each word in a sentence of your own.

conversely (1)   pulsating (5)
orneriness (2)   exasperate (5)

Suggested Writing Assignments

1. Using several examples from your own experience, write a short essay illustrating the validity of Fetridge's Law. Make sure that each of your paragraphs has a clearly identifiable topic sentence.

2. Fetridge's Law describes events that show remarkable consistency in the way they occur or fail to occur. If you have observed similarly consistent patterns of behavior in the people around you or in the events of everyday life, formulate a law of your own. For example, do your favorite sports teams lose when you personally attend the games? Do your friends ask you to go out only on the nights when you have an important exam the next day? Do you always do well on exams when you wear your favorite old sweatshirt? Write an essay in which you give examples of how your law works. Be sure your paragraphs are well developed.

SIMPLICITY

William Zinsser

*William Zinsser was born in New York City in
1922. After graduating from Princeton University, he worked for the* New York Herald Tribune, *first as a feature writer and later as its
drama editor and film critic. Currently the exec-
utive editor of the Book-of-the-Month Club, Zinsser has written a number of books, including*
Pop Goes America *(1966),* The Lunacy Boom
(1970), Writing with a Word Processor *(1983),
and* Willie and Dwike: An American Profile
*(1984), as well as other social and cultural com-
mentaries. In this selection from his popular
book* On Writing Well, *Zinsser, reminding us of
Thoreau before him, exhorts the writer to "Simplify, simplify." Notice that Zinsser's paragraphs
are unified and logically developed, and consequently work well together to support his thesis.*

Clutter is the disease of American writing. We are a society   1
strangling in unnecessary words, circular constructions,
pompous frills and meaningless jargon.

Who can understand the viscous language of everyday Amer-   2
ican commerce and enterprise: the business letter, the interof-
fice memo, the corporation report, the notice from the bank explaining its latest "simplified" statement? What member of an
insurance or medical plan can decipher the brochure that tells
him what his costs and benefits are? What father or mother can
put together a child's toy—on Christmas Eve or any other eve—
from the instructions on the box? Our national tendency is to
inflate and thereby sound important. The airline pilot who an-
nounces that he is presently anticipating experiencing considerable precipitation wouldn't dream of saying that it may rain.
The sentence is too simple—there must be something wrong
with it.

But the secret of good writing is to strip every sentence to its 3
cleanest components. Every word that serves no function,
every long word that could be a short word, every adverb that
carries the same meaning that's already in the verb, every passive construction that leaves the reader unsure of who is doing
what—these are the thousand and one adulterants that weaken
the strength of a sentence. And they usually occur, ironically,
in proportion to education and rank.

During the late 1960s, the president of a major university 4
wrote a letter to mollify the alumni after a spell of campus un-
rest. "You are probably aware," he began, "that we have been
experiencing very considerable potentially explosive expressions of dissatisfaction on issues only partially related." He
meant that the students had been hassling them about different
things. I was far more upset by the president's English than by
the students' potentially explosive expressions of dissatisfaction. I would have preferred the presidential approach taken by
Franklin D. Roosevelt when he tried to convert into English his
own government's memos, such as this blackout order of 1942:

> Such preparations shall be made as will completely ob-
> scure all Federal buildings and non-Federal buildings oc-
> cupied by the Federal government during an air raid for
> any period of time from visibility by reason of internal or
> external illumination.

"Tell them," Roosevelt said, "that in buildings where they 5
have to keep the work going to put something across the windows."

Simplify, simplify. Thoreau said it, as we are so often re- 6
minded, and no American writer more consistently practiced
what he preached. Open *Walden* to any page and you will find a
man saying in a plain and orderly way what is on his mind:

> I love to be alone. I never found the companion that was
> so companionable as solitude. We are for the most part
> more lonely when we go abroad among men than when we
> stay in our chambers. A man thinking or working is always
> alone, let him be where he will. Solitude is not measured
> by the miles of space that intervene between a man and his
> fellows. The really diligent student in one of the crowded
> hives of Cambridge College is as solitary as a dervish in the
> desert.

How can the rest of us achieve such enviable freedom from clutter? The answer is to clear our heads of clutter. Clear thinking becomes clear writing: one can't exist without the other. It is impossible for a muddy thinker to write good English. He may get away with it for a paragraph or two, but soon the reader will be lost, and there is no sin so grave, for he will not easily be lured back.

Who is this elusive creature the reader? He is a person with an attention span of about twenty seconds. He is assailed on every side by forces competing for his time: by newspapers and magazines, by television and radio, by his stereo and videocassettes, by his wife and children and pets, by his house and his yard and all the gadgets that he has bought to keep them spruce, and by that most potent of competitors, sleep. The man snoozing in his chair with an unfinished magazine open on his lap is a man who was being given too much unnecessary trouble by the writer.

It won't do to say that the snoozing reader is too dumb or too lazy to keep pace with the train of thought. My sympathies are with him. If the reader is lost, it is generally because the writer has not been careful enough to keep him on the path.

This carelessness can take any number of forms. Perhaps a sentence is so excessively cluttered that the reader, hacking his way through the verbiage, simply doesn't know what it means. Perhaps a sentence has been so shoddily constructed that the reader could read it in any of several ways. Perhaps the writer has switched pronouns in mid-sentence, or has switched tenses, so the reader loses track of who is talking or when the action took place. Perhaps Sentence B is not a logical sequel to Sentence A—the writer, in whose head the connection is clear, has not bothered to provide the missing link. Perhaps the writer has used an important word incorrectly by not taking the trouble to look it up. He may think that "sanguine" and "sanguinary" mean the same thing, but the difference is a bloody big one. The reader can only infer (speaking of big differences) what the writer is trying to imply.

Faced with these obstacles, the reader is at first a remarkably tenacious bird. He blames himself—he obviously missed something, and he goes back over the mystifying sentence, or over the whole paragraph, piecing it out like an ancient rune, making guesses and moving on. But he won't do this for long. The writer is making him work too hard, and the reader will look for one who is better at his craft.

The writer must therefore constantly ask himself: What am I trying to say? Surprisingly often, he doesn't know. Then he must look at what he has written and ask: Have I said it? Is it clear to someone encountering the subject for the first time? If it's not, it is because some fuzz has worked its way into the machinery. The clear writer is a person clear-headed enough to see this stuff for what it is: fuzz. 12

I don't mean that some people are born clear-headed and are therefore natural writers, whereas others are naturally fuzzy and will never write well. Thinking clearly is a conscious act that the writer must force upon himself, just as if he were embarking on any other project that requires logic: adding up a laundry list or doing an algebra problem. Good writing doesn't come naturally, though most people obviously think it does. The professional writer is forever being bearded by strangers who say that they'd like to "try a little writing sometime" when they retire from their real profession. Or they say, "I could write a book about that." I doubt it. 13

Writing is hard work. A clear sentence is no accident. Very few sentences come out right the first time, or even the third time. Remember this as a consolation in moments of despair. If you find that writing is hard, it's because it *is* hard. It's one of the hardest things that people do. 14

Questions for Study and Discussion

1. What exactly does Zinsser mean by clutter? How does Zinsser feel that we can free ourselves of clutter?

2. In paragraph 3 Zinsser lists a number of "adulterants" that weaken English sentences and claims that "they usually occur, ironically, in proportion to education and rank." Why do you suppose this is true?

3. What is the relationship between thinking and writing for Zinsser?

4. In paragraph 12, Zinsser says that writers must constantly ask themselves some questions. What are these and why are they important?

5. How do Zinsser's first and last paragraphs serve to introduce and conclude his essay? (Glossary: *Beginnings and Endings*.)

6. What is the function of paragraphs 4–6 in the context of the essay?

7. How do the questions in paragraph 2 further Zinsser's purpose? (Glossary: *Rhetorical Question*)

Vocabulary

Refer to your dictionary to define the following words as they are used in this selection. Then use each word in a sentence of your own.

pompous (1)	enviable (7)
decipher (2)	tenacious (11)
adulterants (3)	bearded (13)
mollify (4)	

Suggested Writing Assignments

1. The following pages show a passage from the final manuscript for Zinsser's essay. Carefully study the manuscript and Zinsser's changes, and then write several well-developed paragraphs analyzing the ways he has eliminated clutter.

```
is too dumb or too lazy to keep pace with the w̶r̶i̶t̶e̶r̶'̶s̶ train

of thought.  My sympathics are e̶n̶t̶i̶r̶e̶l̶y̶ with him. H̶e̶'̶s̶ ̶n̶o̶t̶.

s̶o̶ ̶d̶u̶m̶b̶. If the reader is lost, it is generally because the

writer o̶f̶ ̶t̶h̶e̶ ̶a̶r̶t̶i̶c̶l̶e̶ has not been careful enough to keep

him on the p̶r̶o̶p̶e̶r̶ path.

     This carelessness can take any number of d̶i̶f̶f̶e̶r̶e̶n̶t̶ forms.

Perhaps a sentence is so excessively l̶o̶n̶g̶ ̶a̶n̶d̶ cluttered that
```

the reader, hacking his way through ~~all~~ the verbiage, simply
doesn't know what ~~the writer~~ [it] means. Perhaps a sentence has
been so shoddily constructed that the reader could read it in
any of [several] ~~two or three different~~ ways. ~~He thinks he knows what~~
~~the writer is trying to say, but he's not sure.~~ Perhaps the
writer has switched pronouns in mid-sentence, or ~~perhaps he~~
has switched tenses, so the reader loses track of who is
talking ~~to whom,~~ or ~~exactly~~ when the action took place. Perhaps Sentence B is not a logical sequel to Sentence A -- the
writer, in whose head the connection is ~~perfectly~~ clear, has
not [bothered to provide] ~~given enough thought to providing~~ the missing link. Perhaps the writer has used an important word incorrectly by not
taking the trouble to look it up ~~and make sure.~~ He may think
that "sanguine" and "sanguinary" mean the same thing, but
~~I can assure you that~~ the difference is a bloody big one ~~to the~~
~~reader.~~ [The reader] ~~He~~ can only ~~try to~~ infer ~~xxxx~~ (speaking of big differences) what the writer is trying to imply.

Faced with [these] ~~such a variety of~~ obstacles, the reader
is at first a remarkably tenacious bird. He ~~tends to~~ blame[s]
himself ~~He~~ obviously missed something, ~~he thinks,~~ and he goes
back over the mystifying sentence, or over the whole paragraph,
piecing it out like an ancient rune, making guesses and moving
on. But he won't do this for long. ~~He will soon run out of~~
~~patience.~~ The writer is making him work too hard ~~→ harder~~
~~than he should have to work --~~ and the reader will look for
[one] ~~a writer~~ who is better at his craft.

The writer must therefore constantly ask himself: What am
I trying to say? ~~in this sentence?~~ Surprisingly often, he
doesn't know. ~~And~~ Then he must look at what he has ~~just~~
written and ask: Have I said it? Is it clear to someone
[encountering] ~~who is coming upon~~ the subject for the first time? If it's

not, ~~clear,~~ it is because some fuzz has worked its way into the machinery. The clear writer is a person ~~who is~~ clear-headed enough to see this stuff for what it is: fuzz.

I don't mean ~~to suggest~~ that some people are born clear-headed and are therefore natural writers, whereas *others* ~~other people~~ are naturally fuzzy and will ~~therefore~~ never write well. Thinking clearly is ~~an entirely~~ conscious act that the writer must *force* ~~keep forcing~~ upon himself, just as if he were *embarking* ~~starting out~~ on any other ~~kind of~~ project that *requires* ~~calls for~~ logic: adding up a laundry list or doing an algebra problem ~~or playing chess.~~ Good writing doesn't ~~just~~ come naturally, though most people obviously think *it does.* ~~it's as easy as walking.~~ The professional

2. If what Zinsser writes about clutter is an accurate assessment, we should easily find numerous examples of clutter all around us. During the next few days, make a point of looking for clutter in the written materials you come across. Choose one example that you find—an article, an essay, a form letter, or a chapter from a textbook, for example—and write an extended analysis explaining how it might have been written more simply. Develop your paragraphs well, make sure they are coherent, and try not to "clutter" your own writing.

OLD AT SEVENTEEN

David Vecsey

David Vecsey was born in Port Washington, New York, in 1969. When the following essay was published in the "About Men" column of The New York Times Magazine, David Vecsey was an eighteen-year-old freshman at Bradley University in Peoria, Illinois. Vecsey loves all sports, but out of his particular interest in baseball he is writing a novel that is, he says, "half fiction and half fact interweaving events in the narrator's life with those of a baseball team's season from opening day to the World Series." Vecsey says that the theme of "Old at Seventeen" is very important and has enduring interest for him. As you read his account of the many signs of his "aging," pay particular attention to the way he composes his paragraphs.

There are signs that say you're getting older. Getting a driver's license, needing a shave every morning, going to college and reading the front page of a paper before the sports section—these all say a person is getting older. Any man who says getting older comes later, that it's a matter of balding and middle-aged spread, just can't remember, I say.

The most major signal up to now that I was getting old happened late last winter when Richie and Micah appeared at my front door early in the morning. School had been canceled because of a foot of snow. They asked me if I wanted to go on the golf course for a little while. I actually asked them, "For what?"

In the summer, the Plandome Country Club golf course is a haven for doctors and lawyers who like to wear plaid pants and hit a defenseless white ball. It's also good for catching some rays. But in the winter, it has traditionally been a haven for children who soar down "Old Glory" hill as fast as they can on a flimsy piece of wood or plastic. When I was younger, friends and I spent every waking moment out on the golf course, sledding. Now I was asking them why they wanted to go out there. Soon I'll be calling pants "trousers" and reading the *Reader's Digest* on a regular basis.

I agreed to go with them, and I put on jeans and a sweatshirt, as opposed to the snowsuit my mother used to bundle me up in when I was 8 or 9. I wisely decided to wear boots instead of sneakers. Old Glory is the most popular hill on the course, and is literally 50 yards from my house, so we were there in no time. I helped Richie carry the toboggan; I no longer own a sled.   4

When we reached the top of Old Glory, my first thought was that it must have shrunk, because it is no longer the mountain it used to be. It looked more like a fairway with snow on it. I watched the little kids zooming down the hill at top speeds, and I noticed something: they no longer ride Flexible Flyers or Yankee Clippers. They own sleds of the 1980's, plastic structures that look like bikes and cars and boats and things. I think some even have power steering and shocks.   5

Richie dropped the toboggan, and we figured out the best route to take down to the bottom. I suggested that we take a side way, so we wouldn't hit the bumps in the middle. I was greeted with sour looks of disgust. Hitting all the bumps was the idea. I was berated into going first—taking the middle path. My knees cracked and my back ached as I crouched into a sitting position on the toboggan. Micah pushed me off, and I slowly started to descend the hill. "This isn't so bad," I said, "I used to do this all the time."   6

Then I picked up speed. The nightmare began. Snow flew into my face as I hit about 60 miles an hour. I screamed at the top of my lungs, only to be greeted by a mouthful of snow. Out of control, I screamed at people to get out of the way. Bodies jumped and dodged aside. Up ahead, a snow bank headed right toward me. I was engulfed in it. Snow was everywhere—down my shoes, down my pants, about a gallon of it down my throat.   7

I ached and was freezing to death. There's no way, I thought, that I used to do this every day, all day. That was another little kid, a masochist, not me. I stood up and turned around to see two sleds, each containing a small child of about 12. They were   8 going too fast, and they collided. The two children lay there motionless. I ran to help, and I noticed that the reason they were motionless was because they were laughing too hard to move. "That was awesome, Jimmy. Let's do it again," one yelled, and they grabbed their sleds and ran up the hill.

I decided to do the same, and headed up the hill. That is when 9
it finally looked like the massive mountain I remembered. Each step I took became heavier and heavier. I dragged the toboggan of death behind me as I trudged up the hill. I reached the top, where Richie and Micah anxiously awaited their turns. They wanted to try it standing up.

I told them that, from then on, I'd prefer to observe. More 10
sour looks. They disappeared into the crowd, and I looked around. One father was yelling at his son for going too fast, and another scolded his son for not beating his friend in a race. A crowd of mothers huddled together over a steaming thermos, talking about what idiots their husbands were, always excited about last week's football game. "Who are they playing in the Super Bowl?" one woman asked. "I think they already played it," her friend said. "Who won?" "CBS, I think." Their conversation rolled on, and I walked away.

A group of children formed a train by hanging onto one an- 11
other's ankles. it reminded me of when we used to play "hijack the sled." We'd all start within five feet of one another at the top of the hill, but once we picked up speed, the object was to crash into the other players, knock them off, and take their empty sleds down the hill. The man who got to the bottom first won. Ah, those were the days. But I'm civilized now. I'd rather play "negotiation," in which we sit on the sleds at the top of the hill and discuss life.

A boy of about 11 sat on his sled, holding snow up to his 12
bloody nose. His friends called him a wimp because he wouldn't go down again. A little girl punched out a little boy for touching her sled, and he went crying to his mom, who was busy listening to her other son complain about the cold. The mom's face turned red, partially because of the cold, but mostly because of her wrath. She grabbed both kids' wrists and dragged them to the car. Their day is history now. Never complain to a cold mother, it's bad news.

I came to the conclusion that leaving the golf course wasn't 13
such a bad idea. I'm no longer the weatherproof tot I used to be.
Instead, I'm a teen-ager who would rather read or watch a
movie than wrap my body around a tree while sledding. If the
me of my Old Glory days met the me of my teen-age years, he
would call me a lame-o and find someone else to sled with. He
would be right, too, but sledding is for the younger crowd, not
for us ancient 17-year-olds.

I miss that wiry little kid who used to daredevil on sleds to 14
impress his friends. Fear was no object then. But today the
thought of coasting down ice and snow isn't my idea of Eden.
I'll watch, thanks, with the other old people.

Questions for Study and Discussion

1. Vecsey realized that he was getting old when he went sledding. What in particular made him realize that he was not
   as young as he used to be?
2. Identify the topic sentences in paragraphs 1, 2, and 7. (Glossary: *Topic Sentence*) How does Vecsey develop these topic
   sentences?
3. What transitions, if any, has Vecsey used between paragraphs 10 and 11 and between paragraphs 11 and 12? (Glossary: *Transitions*)
4. In the context of the whole essay what is the function of
   paragraph 10? Of paragraph 12?
5. Much of Vecsey's essay is a narrative. (Glossary: *Narration*)
   Where does the narrative proper begin? What is the nature
   of the material that precedes the narrative proper?
6. What is Vecsey's tone in this essay? (Glossary: *Tone*) What
   in particular leads you to your assessment?

Vocabulary

Refer to your dictionary to define the following words as they
are used in this selection. Then use each word in a sentence of
your own.

haven (3)   trudged (9)
berated (6)   wimp (12)
engulfed (7)   wiry (14)
masochist (8)

Suggested Writing Assignments

1. Write an essay modeled on Vecsey's in which you consider signs that you, too, are growing older. Support your thesis with small, insightful examples and then with one more detailed extended example. Pay particular attention to the way in which your topic sentences are established and positioned within the paragraphs as well as the way the paragraphs themselves are developed.

2. Select one of the following statements as the thesis for a short essay. Make sure that each paragraph of your essay is unified, coherent, and adequately developed.

   Car pooling is beneficial but makes demands of people.

   Social activities for first-year college students are limited.

   A college should be a community not merely a collection of people.

   College is expensive.

6

TRANSITIONS

Transitions are words and phrases that are used to signal the relationships between ideas in an essay and to join the various parts of an essay together. Writers use transitions to relate ideas within sentences, between sentences, and between paragraphs. Perhaps the most common type of transition is the so-called transitional expression. Following is a list of transitional expressions categorized according to their functions.

ADDITION: and, again, too, also, in addition, further, furthermore, moreover, besides

CAUSE AND EFFECT: therefore, consequently, thus, accordingly, as a result, hence, then, so

COMPARISON: similarly, likewise, by comparison

CONCESSION: to be sure, granted, of course, it is true, to tell the truth, certainly, with the exception of, although this may be true, even though, naturally

CONTRAST: but, however, in contrast, on the contrary, on the other hand, yet, nevertheless, after all, in spite of

EXAMPLE: for example, for instance

PLACE: elsewhere, here, above, below, farther on, there, beyond, nearby, opposite to, around

RESTATEMENT: that is, as I have said, in other words, in simpler terms, to put it differently, simply stated

SEQUENCE: first, second, third, next, finally

SUMMARY: in conclusion, to conclude, to summarize, in brief, in short

TIME: afterward, later, earlier, subsequently, at the same time, simultaneously, immediately, this time, until now, before, meanwhile, shortly, soon, currently, when, lately, in the meantime, formerly

Besides transitional expressions, there are two other important ways to make transitions: by using pronoun reference and by repeating key words and phrases. This paragraph begins with the phrase "Besides transitional expressions": the phrase contains the transitional word *besides* and also repeats an earlier idea. Thus the reader knows that this discussion is moving toward a new but related idea. Repetition can also give a word or idea emphasis: "Foreigners look to America as a land of freedom. Freedom, however, is not something all Americans enjoy."

Pronoun reference avoids monotonous repetition of nouns and phrases. Without pronouns, these two sentences are wordy and tiring to read: "Jim went to the concert, where he heard some of Beethoven's music. Afterwards, Jim bought a recording of some of Beethoven's music." A more graceful and readable passage results if two pronouns are substituted in the second sentence: "Afterwards, he bought a recording of it." The second version has another advantage in that it is now more tightly related to the first sentence. The transition between the two sentences is smoother.

In the following example, notice how Rachel Carson uses transitional expressions, repetition of words and ideas, and pronoun reference:

> Under primitive agricultural conditions the farmer had few insect problems. *These* arose   *pronoun reference* with the intensification of agriculture—the devotion of immense acreages to a single crop. *Such a system* set the stage for explosive increases in specific insect populations. Single-crop farming does not take advantage of the principles by which nature works; *it* is agriculture as an engineer might conceive it to be. Nature has introduced great variety into the landscape, but man has displayed a passion for

repeated key idea

pronoun reference

pronoun reference
repeated key word

simplifying *it*. *Thus he* undoes the built-in checks and balances by which nature holds the species within bounds. One important natural *check* is a limit on the amount of suitable habitat for each species. *Obviously then,* an insect that lives on wheat can build up its population to much higher levels on a farm devoted to wheat than on one in which wheat is intermingled with other crops to which the insect is not adapted.

transitional expression; pronoun reference

transitional expression

repeated key idea

The same thing happens in other situations. A generation or more ago, the towns of large areas of the United States lined their streets with the noble elm tree. *Now* the beauty *they* hopefully created is threatened with complete destruction as disease sweeps through the elms, carried by a beetle that would have only limited chance to build up large populations and to spread from tree to tree if the elms were only occasional trees in a richly diversified planting.

transitional expression; pronoun reference

Carson's transitions in this passage enhance its *coherence—* that quality of good writing that results when all sentences, paragraphs, and longer divisions of an essay are effectively and naturally connected.

WHY I WANT TO HAVE A FAMILY

Lisa Brown

When she wrote the following essay, Lisa Brown was a junior majoring in American Studies at the University of Texas. In her essay, which was published as a "My Turn" column in the October 1984 issue of Newsweek on Campus, *she uses a variety of transitional devices to put together a coherent argument that many women in their drive to success have overlooked the potential for fulfillment inherent in good relationships and family life.*

For years the theory of higher education operated something like this: men went to college to get rich, and women went to college to marry rich men. It was a wonderful little setup, almost mathematical in its precision. To disturb it would have been to rock an American institution.

During the '60s, though, this theory lost much of its luster. As the nation began to recognize the idiocy of relegating women to a secondary role, women soon joined men in what once were male-only pursuits. This rebellious decade pushed women toward independence, showed them their potential and compelled them to take charge of their lives. Many women took the opportunity and ran with it. Since then feminine autonomy has been the rule, not the exception, at least among college women.

That's the good news. The bad news is that the invisible push has turned into a shove. Some women are downright obsessive about success, to the point of becoming insular monuments to selfishness and fierce bravado, the condescending sort that hawks: "I don't need *anybody*. So there." These women dismiss children and marriage as unbearably outdated and potentially harmful to their up-and-coming careers. This notion of independence smacks of egocentrism. What do these women fear? Why can't they slow down long enough to remember that relationships and a family life are not inherently awful things?

Granted that for centuries women were on the receiving end   4
of some shabby treatment. Now, in an attempt to liberate college women from the constraints that forced them almost exclusively into teaching or nursing as a career outside the
home—always subject to the primary career of motherhood—
some women have gone too far. Any notion of motherhood
seems to be regarded as an unpleasant reminder of the past,
when homemakers were imprisoned by husbands, tots and
household chores. In short, many women consider motherhood
a time-consuming obstacle to the great joy of working outside
the home.

The rise of feminism isn't the only answer. Growing up has   5
something to do with it, too. Most people find themselves in a
bind as they hit their late 20s: they consider the ideals they
grew up with and find that these don't necessarily mix with the
ones they've acquired. The easiest thing to do, it sometimes
seems, is to throw out the precepts their parents taught. Growing up, my friends and I were enchanted by the idea of starting
new traditions. We didn't want self-worth to be contingent
upon whether there was a man or child around the house to
make us feel wanted.

I began to reconsider my values after my sister and a friend   6
had babies. I was entertained by their pregnancies and fascinated by the births; I was also thankful that I wasn't the one
who had to change the diapers every day. I was a doting aunt
only when I wanted to be. As my sister's and friend's lives
changed, though, my attitude changed. I saw their days flip-
flop between frustration and joy. Though these two women lost
the freedom to run off to the beach or to a bar, they gained
something else—an abstract happiness that reveals itself when
they talk about Jessica's or Amanda's latest escapade or vocabulary addition. Still in their 20s, they shuffle work and motherhood with the skill of poker players. I admire them, and I marvel at their kids. Spending time with the Jessicas and Amandas
of the world teaches us patience and sensitivity and gives us a
clue into our own pasts. Children are also reminders that there
is a future and that we must work to ensure its quality.

Now I feel challenged by the idea of becoming a parent. I   7
want to decorate a nursery and design Halloween costumes; I
want to answer my children's questions and help them learn to

read. I want to be unselfish. But I've spent most of my life working in the opposite direction: toward independence, no emotional or financial strings attached. When I told a friend—one who likes kids but never, ever wants them—that I'd decided to accommodate motherhood, she accused me of undermining my career, my future, my life. "If that's all you want, then why are you even in college?" she asked.

The answer's simple: I want to be a smart mommy. I have 8 solid career plans and look forward to working. I make a distinction between wanting kids and wanting nothing but kids. And I've accepted that I'll have to give up a few years of full-time work to allow time for being pregnant and buying Pampers. As for undermining my life, I'm proud of my decision because I think it's evidence that the women's movement is working. While liberating women from the traditional child-bearing role, the movement has given respectability to motherhood by recognizing that it's not a brainless task like dishwashing. At the same time, women who choose not to have children are not treated as oddities. That certainly wasn't the case even 15 years ago. While the graying, middle-aged bachelor was respected, the female equivalent—tagged a spinster—was automatically suspect.

Today, women have choices: about careers, their bodies, chil- 9 dren. I am grateful that women are no longer forced into motherhood as a function of their biology; it's senseless to assume that having a uterus qualifies anyone to be a good parent. By the same token, it is ridiculous for women to abandon all maternal desire because it might jeopardize personal success. Some women make the decision to go childless without ever analyzing their true needs or desires. They forget that motherhood can add to personal fulfillment.

I wish those fiercely independent women wouldn't look down 10 upon those of us who, for whatever reason, choose to forgo much of the excitement that runs in tandem with being single, liberated and educated. Excitement also fills a family life; it just comes in different ways.

I'm not in college because I'll learn how to make tastier pot 11 roast. I'm a student because I want to make sense of the world and of myself. By doing so, I think I'll be better prepared to be a mother to the new lives that I might bring into the world. I'll also be a better me. It's a package deal I don't want to turn down.

Questions for Study and Discussion

1. What is Brown arguing for in this essay? What does she say prompted a change in her attitude? (Glossary: *Attitude*)
2. Against what group is Brown arguing? What does she find wrong with the beliefs of that group?
3. What reasons does she provide for wanting to have a family?
4. Identify Brown's use of transitions in paragraphs 2, 3, 4, 6, 8, and 9. How do these help you as a reader to follow her point?
5. What are the implications for you of Brown's last two sentences in paragraph 6: "Spending time with the Jessicas and Amandas of the world teaches us patience and sensitivity and gives us a clue into our pasts. Children are also the reminders that there is a future and that we must work to ensure its quality"?
6. For what audience do you think this essay is intended? Do you think men would be as interested as women in the author's viewpoint? Explain. (Glossary: *Audience*)

Vocabulary

Refer to your dictionary to define the following words as they are used in this selection. Then use each word in a sentence of your own.

relegating (2)   precepts (5)
autonomy (2)   contingent (5)
insular (3)   doting (6)
bravado (3)   tandem (10)

Suggested Writing Assignments

1. Write an essay in which you argue any one of the following positions with regard to the women's movement: it has gone too far; it is out of control; it is misdirected; it hasn't gone far enough or done enough; it needs to reach more women and men; it should lower its sights; a position of your own different from the above. Whichever position you argue, be sure that you provide sufficient evidence to support your point of view.

2. Fill in the following statement and write an argument in support of it:

   The purpose of a college education is to _____

   _____.

Auto Suggestion

Russell Baker

After graduating from Johns Hopkins University in 1947, Russell Baker joined the staff of the Baltimore Sun *and later worked in the Washington bureau of* The New York Times. *Since 1962 he has written a syndicated column for the* Times *for which he was awarded a Pulitzer Prize in 1979. Baker won a second Pulitzer Prize for his autobiography* Growing Up *(1982). "Auto Suggestion," first published in the* Times *on April 1, 1979, presents Baker's techniques for not buying a car. As you read, notice how the author's transitions give coherence to the essay.*

M any persons have written asking the secret of my technique for not buying a new car. Aware that it could destroy the American economy and reduce the sheiks of OPEC to prowling the streets with pleas for baksheesh, I divulge it here with the greatest reluctance.

In extenuation, let me explain that my power to resist buying a new car does not derive from a resentment of new cars. In fact, I bought a new car 10 years ago and would buy another at any moment if the right new car came along.

When seized by new-car passion, however, I do not deal with it as most people do. To conquer the lust and escape without a new car, you must have a program. The first step is to face the philosophical question: Is a new car really going to give you less trouble than your old car?

In most cases the notion that a new car will free its owner of auto headache will not hold water. Common experience shows that all cars, old or new, are trouble. The belief that a change of vintage will relieve the headache is a mental exercise in willful self-deception.

A new car simply presents a new set of troubles, which may be more disturbing than the beloved, familiar old troubles the old car presented. With your old car, strange troubles do not take you by surprise, but a new car's troubles are invariably terrifying for being strange and unexpected.

Before entering the new-car bazaar, I always remind myself   6
that I am about to acquire an entirely new set of troubles and that it is going to take me months, maybe years, to learn to live happily with them.

Step Two is to place a sensible limit on the amount you will   7
pay for a new car. As a guide to value, I use the price my parents paid for the house in which I grew up. To own a car that costs more than a house is vulgar and reflects an alarming disproportion in one's sense of values. Wheels may be splendid but they should not be valued more highly than four bedrooms, dining room, bath and cellar.

The price of my parents' house, purchased in 1940, was   8
$5,900. This becomes my limit, effectively ruling out the kind of new car you have to drive to get to a business appointment in Los Angeles, as well as most other new cars on the market today.

After setting a price limit, the next step is to study the car's   9
capacity to perform its duties. For this purpose I always go to the car dealer's place with two large children, a wife, a grandmother, two cats, six suitcases, an ice chest and a large club suitable for subduing quarrelsome children on the turnpike.

Loading all the paraphernalia and people into the car under   10
study, I then ask myself whether I could drive 400 miles in this environment without suffering mental breakdown.

Since most cars within the $5,900 price limit nowadays are   11
scarcely commodious enough to transport two persons and a strand of spaghetti, I am now approaching very close to the goal I despise, which is to avoid buying a new car.

Suppose, however, that you pack everything inside—chil-   12
dren, wife, cats, club and grandmother—and it seems just barely possible that you might cover 400 miles despite the knees from the back seat grinding into your kidneys. Now is the time to take out your checkoff list.

Can you slide in behind the wheel without denting the skull   13
against the door, frame? Will you be able to do it at night when you have had a drink and aren't thinking about it?

If the car passes this test, which is unlikely unless you're get-   14

ting an incredible deal on a pickup truck—and cats and grand-
mothers, remember, don't much like riding in the open beds of
pickup trucks, especially when it rains—if the car passes this
test, you must give it the cascading rainwater test.

For this purpose I take a garden hose to the car lot, spray the   15
top of the car heavily and then, upon opening the door, try to
slide in without being drenched in a cascade of water pouring
into the driver's seat. If the car soaks you with hose water,
imagine what it will do with a heavy dose of rain.

If the car passes this examination, the final test is to slip a   16
fingernail under the plastic sheathing on the dashboard and
see if the entire piece peels away easily. If it does not, I buy the
new car immediately. The last time I had to do so was in 1969.

Questions for Study and Discussion

1. What are the steps in Baker's program for not buying a car?
   Give examples of transitions he uses to move from one step
   to the next.
2. In explaining how not to buy a new car, Baker pokes fun at
   the economy and at the auto industry. What aspects of each
   does he criticize?
3. Do you find Baker's essay amusing? If you do, explain how
   you think he achieves this quality in his writing. Are there
   any lessons for you as a writer in understanding how Baker
   achieves his brand of humor? Explain.
4. What transitional device does Baker use to link paragraphs
   7, 8, and 9?
5. Baker's essay provides an interesting combination of diction. It is colloquial as well as sophisticated. Cite several
   examples of each type of diction. (Glossary: *Diction*)

Vocabulary

Refer to your dictionary to define the following words as they
are used in this selection. Then use each word in a sentence of
your own.

divulge (1)   vulgar (7)
extenuation (2)   paraphernalia (10)
lust (3)   commodious (11)
vintage (4)   cascading (14)

Suggested Writing Assignments

1. Baker's essay is a spoof on how not to buy an automobile.
   But how should a person really buy a new (or used) car?
   Write an essay in which you explain the process to follow to
   ensure getting the car you want at a price you can afford. Be
   sure that you use transitions effectively to link the steps in
   the selection process you prescribe.

2. Write a short essay in which you describe the steps a person
   ought to take when making a major decision, such as determining where to go to school. Be sure to use transitions
   wherever necessary, both to make the sequence of your
   ideas clear and to give your essay coherence.

How I Got Smart

Steve Brody

*Steve Brody is a retired high-school English
teacher who enjoys writing about the lighter side
of teaching. He was born in Chicago in 1915 and
received his bachelor's degree in English from
Columbia University. In addition to his articles
in educational publications, Brody has published many newspaper articles on travel and a
humorous book about golf,* How to Break
Ninety Before You Reach It *(1979). As you read
his account of how love made him smart, notice
the way he uses transitional words and expressions to unify his essay and make it a seamless
whole.*

A common misconception among youngsters attending
school is that their teachers were child prodigies. Who
else but a bookworm, prowling the libraries and disdaining the
normal youngster's propensity for play rather than study,
would grow up to be a teacher anyway?

I tried desperately to explain to my students that the image
they had of me as an ardent devotee of books and homework
during my adolescence was a bit out of focus. Au contraire! I
hated compulsory education with a passion. I could never quite
accept the notion of having to go to school while the fish were
biting.

Consequently, my grades were somewhat bearish. That's
how my father, who dabbled in the stock market, described
them. Presenting my report card for my father to sign was like
serving him a subpoena. At midterm and other sensitive periods, my father kept a low profile.

But in my sophomore year, something beautiful and exciting
happened. Cupid aimed his arrow and struck me squarely in
the heart. All at once, I enjoyed going to school, if only to gaze
at the lovely face beneath the raven tresses in English II. My

117

princess sat near the pencil sharpener, and that year I ground up enough pencils to fuel a campfire.

Alas, Debbie was far beyond my wildest dreams. We were separated not only by five rows of desks, but by about 50 I.Q. points. She was the top student in English II, the apple of Mrs. Larrivee's eye. I envisioned how eagerly Debbie's father awaited her report card.

Occasionally, Debbie would catch me staring at her, and she would flash a smile—an angelic smile that radiated enlightenment and quickened my heartbeat. It was a smile that signaled hope and made me temporarily forget the intellectual gulf that separated us.

I schemed desperately to bridge that gulf. And one day, as I was passing the supermarket, an idea came to me.

A sign in the window announced that the store was offering the first volume of a set of encyclopedias at the introductory price of 29 cents. The remaining volumes would cost $2.49 each, but it was no time to be cynical.

I purchased Volume I—Aardvark to Asteroid—and began my venture into the world of knowledge. I would henceforth become a seeker of facts. I would become chief egghead in English II and sweep the princess off her feet with a surge of erudition. I had it all planned.

My first opportunity came one day in the cafeteria line. I looked behind me and there she was.

"Hi," she said.

After a pause, I wet my lips and said, "Know where anchovies come from?"

She seemed surprised. "No, I don't."

I breathed a sigh of relief. "The anchovy lives in salt water and is rarely found in fresh water." I had to talk fast, so that I could get all the facts in before we reached the cash register. "Fishermen catch anchovies in the Mediterranean Sea and along the Atlantic coast near Spain and Portugal."

"How fascinating," said Debbie.

"The anchovy is closely related to the herring. It is thin and silvery in color. It has a long snout and a very large mouth."

"Incredible."

"Anchovies are good in salads, mixed with eggs, and are often used as appetizers before dinner, but they are salty and cannot be digested too rapidly."

Debbie shook her head in disbelief. It was obvious that I had   19
made quite an impression.

A few days later, during a fire drill, I sidled up to her and   20
asked, "Ever been to the Aleutian Islands?"

"Never have," she replied.   21

"Might be a nice place to visit, but I certainly wouldn't want   22
to live there," I said.

"Why not?" said Debbie, playing right into my hands.   23

"Well, the climate is forbidding. There are no trees on any of   24
the 100 or more islands in the group. The ground is rocky and
very little plant life can grow on it."

"I don't think I'd even care to visit," she said.   25

The fire drill was over and we began to file into the building,   26
so I had to step it up to get the natives in. "The Aleuts are short
and sturdy and have dark skin and black hair. They subsist on
fish, and they trap blue fox, seal and otter for their valuable
fur."

Debbie's hazel eyes widened in amazement. She was un-   27
doubtedly beginning to realize that she wasn't dealing with an
ordinary lunkhead. She was gaining new and valuable insights
instead of engaging in the routine small talk one would expect
from most sophomores.

Luck was on my side, too. One day I was browsing through   28
the library during my study period. I spotted Debbie sitting at a
table, absorbed in a crossword puzzle. She was frowning, apparently stumped on a word. I leaned over and asked if I could
help.

"Four-letter word for Oriental female servant," Debbie said.   29

"Try *amah*," I said, quick as a flash.   30

Debbie filled in the blanks, then turned to stare at me in   31
amazement. "I don't believe it," she said. "I just don't believe
it."

And so it went, that glorious, amorous, joyous sophomore   32
year. Debbie seemed to relish our little conversations and hung
on my every word. Naturally, the more I read, the more my confidence grew. I expatiated freely on such topics as adenoids, air
brakes, and arthritis.

In the classroom, too, I was gradually making my presence   33
felt. Among my classmates, I was developing a reputation as a
wheeler-dealer in data. One day, during a discussion of Coleridge's "The Ancient Mariner," we came across the word *albatross.*

"Can anyone tell us what an albatross is?" asked Mrs. Lar-   34
rivee.

My hand shot up. "The albatross is a large bird that lives   35
mostly in the ocean regions below the equator, but may be
found in the north Pacific as well. The albatross measures as
long as four feet and has the greatest wingspread of any bird. It
feeds on the surface of the ocean, where it catches shellfish.
The albatross is a very voracious eater. When it is full it has
trouble getting into the air again."

There was a long silence in the room. Mrs. Larrivee couldn't   36
quite believe what she had just heard. I sneaked a peek at Debbie and gave her a big wink. She beamed proudly and winked
back.

It was a great feeling, having Debbie and Mrs. Larrivee and   37
my peers according me respect and paying attention when I
spoke.

My grades edged upward and my father no longer tried to   38
avoid me when I brought home my report card. I continued
reading the encyclopedia diligently, packing more and more
into my brain.

What I failed to perceive was that Debbie all this while was   39
going steady with a junior from a neighboring school—a
hockey player with a C+ average. The revelation hit me hard,
and for a while I felt like disgorging and forgetting everything I
had learned. I had saved enough money to buy Volume II—
Asthma to Bullfinch—but was strongly tempted to invest in a
hockey stick instead.

How could she lead me on like that—smiling and concurring   40
and giving me the impression that I was important?

I felt not only hurt, but betrayed. Like Agamemnon, but with   41
less dire consequences, thank God.

In time I recovered from my wounds. The next year Debbie   42
moved from the neighborhood and transferred to another
school. Soon she became no more than a fleeting memory.

Although the original incentive was gone, I continued pour- 43
ing over the encyclopedias, as well as an increasing number of
other books. Having savored the heady wine of knowledge, I
could not now alter my course. For:

> "A little knowledge is a dangerous thing:
> Drink deep, or taste not the Pierian spring."

So wrote Alexander Pope, Volume XIV, Paprika to Ptero- 44
dactyl.

Questions for Study and Discussion

1. Why didn't Brody stop reading the volumes of the encyclopedias when he discovered that Debbie had a steady boy-
   friend?
2. If you find Brody's narrative humorous, try to explain the
   sources of his humor. For example, what humor resides in
   the choice of examples Brody uses?
3. How are paragraphs 2 and 3, 3 and 4, 5 and 6, 31 and 32, and
   43 and 44 linked? Identify the transitions that Brody uses in
   paragraph 35.
4. Brody refers to Coleridge's "The Ancient Mariner" in paragraph 33 and Agamemnon in paragraph 41, and he quotes
   Alexander Pope in paragraph 43. Use an encyclopedia to
   explain Brody's allusions. (Glossary: *Allusion*)
5. Comment on the effectiveness of the beginning and ending
   of Brody's essay. (Glossary: *Beginnings and Endings*)
6. Brody could have told his story using far less dialogue than
   he did. What, in your opinion, would have been gained or
   lost had he done so? (Glossary: *Dialogue*)

Vocabulary

Refer to your dictionary to define the following words as they
are used in this selection. Then use each word in a sentence of
your own.

misconception (1)	forbidding (24)
prodigies (1)	subsist (26)
devotee (2)	amorous (32)
bearish (3)	expatiated (32)
dabbled (3)	adenoids (32)
surge (9)	voracious (35)
erudition (9)	disgorging (39)
snout (16)	savored (43)
sidled (20)	

Suggested Writing Assignments

1. One serious thought that arises as a result of reading Brody's essay is that perhaps we learn best when we are sufficiently motivated to do so. And once motivated, the desire to learn seems to feed on itself: "Having savored the heady wine of knowledge, I could not now alter my course" (43). Write an essay in which you explore this same subject using your own experiences.

2. In *The New York Times Complete Manual of Home Repair,* Bernard Gladstone gives directions for applying blacktop sealer to a driveway. His directions appear below in scrambled order. First, carefully read all of Gladstone's sentences. Next, arrange the sentences in what seems to you the correct sequence, paying attention to transitional devices. Be prepared to explain the reasons for your particular arrangement of the sentences.

   1. A long-handled pushbroom or roofing brush is used to spread the coating evenly over the entire area.
   2. Care should be taken to make certain the entire surface is uniformly wet, though puddles should be swept away if water collects in low spots.
   3. Greasy areas and oil slicks should be scraped up, then scrubbed thoroughly with a detergent solution.
   4. With most brands there are just three steps to follow.
   5. In most cases one coat of sealer will be sufficient.
   6. The application of blacktop sealer is best done on a day when the weather is dry and warm, preferably while the sun is shining on the surface.

7. This should not be applied until the first coat is completely dry.
8. First sweep the surface absolutely clean to remove all dust, dirt and foreign material.
9. To simplify spreading and to assure a good bond, the surface of the driveway should be wet down thoroughly by sprinkling with a hose.
10. However, for surfaces in poor condition a second coat may be required.
11. The blacktop sealer is next stirred thoroughly and poured on while the surface is still damp.
12. The sealer should be allowed to dry overnight (or longer if recommended by the manufacturer) before normal traffic is resumed.

7

EFFECTIVE SENTENCES

Each of the following paragraphs describes the city of Vancouver. Although the content of both paragraphs is essentially the same, the first paragraph is written in sentences of nearly the same length and pattern and the second paragraph in sentences of varying length and pattern.

Water surrounds Vancouver on three sides. The snow-crowned Coast Mountains ring the city on the northeast. Vancouver has a floating quality of natural loveliness. There is a curved beach at English Bay. This beach is in the shape of a half moon. Residential high rises stand behind the beach. They are in pale tones of beige, blue, and ice-cream pink. Turn-of-the-century houses of painted wood frown upward at the glitter of office towers. Any urban glare is softened by folds of green lawns, flowers, fountains, and trees. Such landscaping appears to be unplanned. It links Vancouver to her ultimate treasure of greenness. That treasure is thousand-acre Stanley Park. Surrounding stretches of water dominate. They have image-evoking names like False Creek and Lost Lagoon. Sailboats and pleasure craft skim blithely across Burrard Inlet. Foreign freighters are out in English Bay. They await their turn to take on cargoes of grain.

Surrounded by water on three sides and ringed to the northeast by the snow-crowned Coast Mountains, Vancouver has a floating quality of natural loveliness. At English Bay, the half-moon curve of beach is backed by high rises in pale tones of beige, blue, and ice-cream pink. Turn-of-the-century houses of painted wood frown upward at the glitter of office towers. Yet any urban glare is quickly softened by folds of green lawns, flowers, fountains, and trees that in a seemingly unplanned fashion link Vancouver to her ultimate treasure of greenness—thousand-acre Stanley Park. And always it is the surrounding stretches of water that dominate, with their image-evoking names like False Creek and Lost Lagoon. Sailboats and pleasure craft skim blithely across Burrard Inlet, while out in English Bay foreign freighters await their turn to take on cargoes of grain.

The difference between these two paragraphs is dramatic. The first is monotonous because of the sameness of the sentences and because the ideas are not related to one another in a meaningful way. The second paragraph is much more interesting and readable; its sentences vary in length and are structured to clarify the relationships among the ideas. Sentence variety, an important aspect of all good writing, should not be used for its own sake, but rather to express ideas precisely and to emphasize the most important ideas within each sentence. Sentence variety includes the use of subordination, the periodic and loose sentence, the dramatically short sentence, the active and passive voice, and coordination.

Subordination, the process of giving one idea less emphasis than another in a sentence, is one of the most important characteristics of an effective sentence and a mature prose style. Writers subordinate ideas by introducing them either with subordinating conjunctions (*because, if, as though, while, when, after, in order that*) or with relative pronouns (*that, which, who, whomever, what*). Subordination not only deemphasizes some ideas, but also highlights others that the writer feels are more important.

Of course, there is nothing about an idea—*any* idea—that automatically makes it primary or secondary in importance. The writer decides what to emphasize, and he or she may choose to emphasize the less profound or noteworthy of two ideas. Consider, for example, the following sentence: "Jane was reading a novel the day that Mount St. Helens erupted." Everyone, including the author of the sentence, knows that the Mount St. Helens eruption is a more noteworthy event than Jane's reading a novel. But the sentence concerns Jane, not the volcano, and so her reading is stated in the main clause, while the eruption is subordinated in a dependent clause.

Generally, writers place the ideas they consider important in main clauses, and other ideas go into dependent clauses. For example:

> When she was thirty years old, she made her first solo flight across the Atlantic.
>
> When she made her first solo flight across the Atlantic, she was thirty years old.

The first sentence emphasizes the solo flight; in the second, the emphasis is on the pilot's age.

Another way to achieve emphasis is to place the most important words, phrases, and clauses at the beginning or end of a sentence. The ending is the most emphatic part of a sentence; the beginning is less emphatic; and the middle is the least emphatic of all. The two sentences about the pilot put the main clause at the end, achieving special emphasis. The same thing occurs in a much longer kind of sentence, called a *periodic sentence*. Here is an example from John Updike:

> On the afternoon of the first day of spring, when the gutters were still heaped high with Monday's snow but the sky itself had been swept clean, we put on our galoshes and walked up the sunny side of Fifth Avenue to Central Park.

By holding the main clause back, Updike keeps his readers in suspense and so puts the most emphasis possible on his main idea.

A *loose sentence*, on the other hand, states its main idea at the beginning and then adds details in subsequent phrases and clauses. Rewritten as a loose sentence, Updike's sentence might read like this:

> We put on our galoshes and walked up the sunny side of Fifth Avenue to Central Park on the afternoon of the first day of spring, when the gutters were still heaped high with Monday's snow but the sky itself had been swept clean.

The main idea still gets plenty of emphasis, since it is contained in a main clause at the beginning of the sentence. Yet a loose sentence resembles the way people talk: it flows naturally and is easy to understand.

Another way to create emphasis is to use a *dramatically short sentence*. Especially following a long and involved sentence, a short declarative sentence helps drive a point home. Here are two examples, the first from Edwin Newman and the second from David Wise:

> Meaning no disrespect, I suppose there is, if not general rejoicing, at least some sense of relief when the football season ends. It's a long season.

> The executive suite on the thirty-fifth floor of the Columbia Broadcasting System skyscraper in Manhattan is a tasteful blend of dark wood paneling, expensive abstract paintings, thick carpets, and pleasing colors. It has the quiet look of power.

Finally, since the subject of a sentence is automatically emphasized, writers may choose to use the *active voice* when they want to emphasize the doer of an action and the *passive voice* when they want to downplay or omit the doer completely. Here are two examples:

> High winds pushed our sailboat onto the rocks, where the force of the waves tore it to pieces.

> Our sailboat was pushed by high winds onto the rocks, where it was torn to pieces by the force of the waves.

The first sentence emphasizes the natural forces that destroyed the boat, while the second sentence focuses attention on the boat itself. The passive voice may be useful in placing emphasis, but it has important disadvantages. As the examples show, and as the terms suggest, active-voice verbs are more vigorous and vivid than the same verbs in the passive voice. Then, too, some writers use the passive voice to hide or evade responsibility. "It has been decided" conceals who did the deciding, whereas "I have decided" makes all clear. So the passive voice should be used only when necessary—as it is in this sentence.

Often, a writer wants to place equal emphasis on several facts or ideas. One way to do this is to give each its own sentence. For example:

> Tom Watson selected his club. He lined up his shot. He chipped the ball to within a foot of the pin.

But a long series of short, simple sentences quickly becomes tedious. Many writers would combine these three sentences by using *coordination*. The coordinating conjunctions *and, but, or, nor, for, so,* and *yet* connect words, phrases, and clauses of equal importance:

> Tom Watson selected his club, lined up his shot, *and* chipped the ball to within a foot of the pin.

By coordinating three sentences into one, the writer not only makes the same words easier to read, but also shows that Watson's three actions are equally important parts of a single process.

When parts of a sentence are not only coordinated but also grammatically the same, they are *parallel*. Parallelism in a sentence is created by balancing a word with a word, a phrase with a phrase, or a clause with a clause. Parallelism is often used in speeches—for example, in the last sentence of Lincoln's *Gettysburg Address* ("government of the people, by the people, for the people, shall not perish from the . . ."). Here is another example, from the beginning of Mark Twain's *The Adventures of Huckleberry Finn:*

> Persons attempting to find a motive in this narrative will be prosecuted; persons attempting to find a moral in it will be banished; persons attempting to find a plot in it will be shot.

An Eye-Witness Account of the San Francisco Earthquake

Jack London

Jack London (1876–1916) was born in San Francisco and attended school only until the age of fourteen. A prolific and popular fiction writer, he is perhaps best remembered for his novels The Call of the Wild *(1903),* The Sea Wolf *(1904), and* White Fang *(1906). London was working near San Francisco when the great earthquake hit that city in the early morning of April 16, 1906. Notice how, in this account of the quake's aftermath, London uses a variety of sentence structures to capture the feelings that this disaster evoked in him.*

The earthquake shook down in San Francisco hundreds of thousands of dollars' worth of walls and chimneys. But the conflagration that followed burned up hundreds of millions of dollars' worth of property. There is no estimating within hundreds of millions the actual damage wrought. Not in history has a modern imperial city been so completely destroyed. San Francisco is gone! Nothing remains of it but memories and a fringe of dwelling houses on its outskirts. Its industrial section is wiped out. Its social and residential section is wiped out. The factories and warehouses, the great stores and newspaper buildings, the hotels and the palaces of the nabobs, are all gone. Remains only the fringe of dwelling houses on the outskirts of what was once San Francisco.

Within an hour after the earthquake shock the smoke of San Francisco's burning was a lurid tower visible a hundred miles away. And for three days and nights this lurid tower swayed in the sky, reddening the sun, darkening the day, and filling the land with smoke.

On Wednesday morning at a quarter past five came the earthquake. A minute later the flames were leaping upward. In a dozen different quarters south of Market Street, in the working-class ghetto, and in the factories, fires started. There was no opposing the flames. There was no organization, no communication. All the cunning adjustments of a twentieth-century city had been smashed by the earthquake. The streets were humped into ridges and depressions and piled with debris of fallen walls. The steel rails were twisted into perpendicular and horizontal angles. The telephone and telegraph systems were disrupted. And the great water mains had burst. All the shrewd contrivances and safeguards of man had been thrown out of gear by thirty seconds' twitching of the earth's crust.

By Wednesday afternoon, inside of twelve hours, half the heart of the city was gone. At that time I watched the vast conflagration from out on the bay. It was dead calm. Not a flicker of wind stirred. Yet from every side wind was pouring in upon the city. East, west, north, and south, strong winds were blowing upon the doomed city. The heated air rising made an enormous suck. Thus did the fire of itself build its own colossal chimney through the atmosphere. Day and night, this dead calm continued, and yet, near to the flames, the wind was often half a gale, so mighty was the suck. . . .

Wednesday night saw the destruction of the very heart of the city. Dynamite was lavishly used, and many of San Francisco's proudest structures were crumbled by man himself into ruins, but there was no withstanding the onrush of the flames. Time and again successful stands were made by the fire fighters, and every time the flames flanked around on either side, or came up from the rear, and turned to defeat the hard-won victory.

An enumeration of the buildings destroyed would be a directory of San Francisco. An enumeration of the buildings undestroyed would be a line and several addresses. An enumeration of the deeds of heroism would stock a library and bankrupt the Carnegie medal fund.* An enumeration of the dead—will never be made. All vestiges of them were destroyed by the flames. The number of the victims of the earthquake will never be known.

---

*Fund established by the philanthropist Andrew Carnegie in 1905 for the recognition of heroic deeds.

Questions for Study and Discussion

1. In this short passage London draws contrasts between the forces of nature and those of humans. Why do you think London draws these contrasts? What is their effect?
2. In paragraph 4 London says that "the fire of itself [built] its own colossal chimney through the atmosphere." What does he mean?
3. From what vantage point does London describe the destruction of the city? Where does he tell us where he is?
4. What is the effect of the short sentences "San Francisco is gone!" and "It was dead calm" in paragraphs 1 and 4?
5. Why do you suppose London uses the passive voice instead of the active voice in paragraph 3? (Glossary: *Voice*)
6. Point out examples of parallelism in paragraphs 1, 2, and 6. How does London add emphasis through the use of this rhetorical device? (Glossary: *Parallelism*)

Vocabulary

Refer to your dictionary to define the following words as they are used in this selection. Then use each word in a sentence of your own.

conflagration (1) contrivances (3)
nabobs (1) vestiges (6)
lurid (2)

Suggested Writing Assignments

1. If you have ever been an eyewitness to a disaster, either natural or man-made, write an account similar to London's of its consequences. Give special attention to the variety of your sentences according to the advice provided in the introduction to "Effective Sentences."
2. Write a brief essay using one of the following sentences to focus and control the descriptive details you select. Place

the sentence in the essay wherever it will have the greatest emphasis.

It was a strange party.
He was nervous.
I was shocked.
Music filled the air.
Dirt was everywhere.

TERROR AT TINKER CREEK

Annie Dillard

Annie Dillard was born in Pittsburgh, and now makes her home in the Pacific Northwest. A poet, journalist, and contributing editor to Harper's *magazine, Dillard has written* Tickets for a Prayer Wheel *(1975),* Holy the Firm *(1977),* Living by Fiction *(1982),* Encounters with Chinese Winters *(1984), and* An American Childhood *(1987). In 1974 she published* Pilgrim at Tinker Creek, *a fascinating collection of natural observations for which she was awarded the Pulitzer Prize for nonfiction. As you read the following selection from that work, notice how the varied structures of Dillard's sentences enhance her descriptions of her experience.*

A couple of summers ago I was walking along the edge of the island to see what I could see in the water, and mainly to scare frogs. Frogs have an inelegant way of taking off from invisible positions on the bank just ahead of your feet, in dire panic, emitting a froggy "Yike!" and splashing into the water. Incredibly, this amused me, and incredibly, it amuses me still. As I walked along the grassy edge of the island, I got better and better at seeing frogs both in and out of the water. I learned to recognize, slowing down, the difference in texture of the light reflected from mudbank, water, grass, or frog. Frogs were flying all around me. At the end of the island I noticed a small green frog. He was exactly half in and half out of the water, looking like a schematic diagram of an amphibian, and he didn't jump.

He didn't jump; I crept closer. At last I knelt on the island's winterkilled grass, lost, dumbstruck, staring at the frog in the creek just four feet away. He was a very small frog with wide, dull eyes. And just as I looked at him, he slowly crumpled and began to sag. The spirit vanished from his eyes as if snuffed.

His skin emptied and drooped; his very skull seemed to collapse and settle like a kicked tent. He was shrinking before my eyes like a deflating football. I watched the taut, glistening skin on his shoulders ruck, and rumple, and fall. Soon, part of his skin, formless as a pricked balloon, lay in floating folds like bright scum on top of the water: it was a monstrous and terrifying thing. I gaped bewildered, appalled. An oval shadow hung in the water behind the drained frog; then the shadow glided away. The frog skin bag started to sink.

I had read about the giant water bug, but never seen one. "Giant water bug" is really the name of the creature, which is an enormous, heavy-bodied brown beetle. It eats insects, tadpoles, fish, and frogs. Its grasping forelegs are mighty and hooked inward. It seizes a victim with these legs, hugs it tight, and paralyzes it with enzymes injected during a vicious bite. That one bite is the only bite it ever takes. Through the puncture shoot the poisons that dissolve the victim's muscles and bones and organs—all but the skin—and through it the giant water bug sucks out the victim's body, reduced to a juice. This event is quite common in warm fresh water. The frog I saw was being sucked by a giant water bug. I had been kneeling on the island grass; when the unrecognizable flap of frog skin settled on the creek bottom, swaying, I stood up and brushed the knees of my pants. I couldn't catch my breath. 3

Questions for Study and Discussion

1. Why do you think Dillard chooses to describe the scene that she does? If there is a message here, what do you think it might be?

2. Why do you suppose that Dillard could not catch her breath after the experience she describes?

3. Why do you think Dillard waits until nearly the end of the passage to make it clear that a giant water bug was responsible for the frog's death?

4. Paragraph 1 contains sentences that are varied in both length and structure, including loose sentences as well as

periodic sentences, long ones as well as short. Identify two loose sentences and two periodic sentences, and compare the effects each one has on the narrative.

5. Can you recognize a relationship between kinds of sentences and the content they contain? In other words, does Dillard use loose sentences for certain kinds of information and periodic sentences for other kinds? Support your answer with examples from the selection.

6. The first sentence in paragraph 2 contains a semicolon. Would the sentence have a different sense if the two clauses were instead joined with a coordinating conjunction—for example, *and* or *so*? Would they be different if punctuated with a period? How?

Vocabulary

Refer to your dictionary to define the following words as they are used in this selection. Then use each word in a sentence of your own.

dire (1)   taut (2)
schematic (1)   appalled (2)
dumbstruck (2)   enzymes (3)

Suggested Writing Assignments

1. After watching the attack on the frog by the water bug, Annie Dillard says, in her last sentence, "I couldn't catch my breath." If you have ever had a similar response to an event, not necessarily tied to an event in nature, describe it in such a way that the reader understands it. At each stage of the writing process—writing a first draft, revising, and editing—you should pay particular attention to the variety of your sentences, making sure that they add emphasis and interest to your writing.

2. Without changing the meaning, rewrite the following paragraph using a variety of sentence structures to add interest and emphasis.

The hunter crept through the leaves. The leaves had fallen. The leaves were dry. The hunter was tired. The hunter had a gun. The gun was new. The hunter saw a deer. The deer had antlers. A tree partly hid the antlers. The deer was beautiful. The hunter shot at the deer. The hunter missed. The shot frightened the deer. The deer bounded away.

BOY MEETS BEAR

Stephen W. Hyde

Stephen W. Hyde was born in Naugatuck, Connecticut, in 1951 and now makes his home in Maine. He studied English literature as an undergraduate at the University of Connecticut and as a graduate student at McGill University. Having worked as a naturalist and an environmental educator in Maine, Hyde is now working as a free-lance writer producing essays and newspaper articles. In the following selection, Hyde tells us of an encounter he and his son had with a bear. Reflecting on why he wrote the essay, Hyde said, "This incident occurred during a year in which I had many interactions with bears. Bears kept reappearing in my life. It seemed like more than mere coincidence, as if some invitation was being extended to look more closely at the subject of bears."

W e slid the canoe into the water. Behind us, somewhere   1
high in the red pines, a great horned owl hooted. The
earth was white with frost. A low mist hung over the river. I
whispered a last reminder to my son that if we hoped to see any
wildlife it was very important to be quiet.

This early morning paddle on the river was new to him.   2
Though he had traveled through its rapids before he could walk
and like the young Achilles had been dipped in its frigid,
spring-fed waters, the river was always new to him. It was always new to me.

I slipped the paddle into the water, gave two gentle thrusts,   3
and we were gone, swallowed up by the mist, carried off by the
current, severed, by the first bend in the river, from our camp
and all things familiar. We glided by a muskrat seated on a log.
It seemed not to notice us. A good sign, I thought, for a four-
year-old boy not used to being still for very long.

The quiet of the autumn morning made ordinary sounds   4
stand out. My son's eyes grew big at the scolding of a red squir-
rel and when a blue jay, disturbed by our approach, screamed
at us from shore. He was not sure what to make of it all. The
cold mist tumbled and swirled over the water, half suggesting
shapes of things that did not exist and half concealing shapes of
things that did.

Except for an occasional whisper, no words passed between   5
us, though I could sense that the silence was beginning to wear
on him. It was then that I heard a rustling in the woods, like a
sparrow scuffling in the leaf litter.

My son spotted some forget-me-nots growing against the   6
bank. He signaled to me to paddle him closer. I eased the bow
of the canoe into the alders overhanging the bank so he could
reach the flowers. As I did, I heard a second slight crack and
turned toward the sound. Not 20 feet away, looking back at me,
was a large black bear. Neither the bear nor I moved; the little
boy was stretching for the flowers.

Everything seemed to stop: mist, river, sun, falling leaves, lit-   7
tle boy. But in the next instant he reached the flowers, pulled
them away in his hand, sat up, and saw the bear, dark and huge,
rising out of the bushes before him. The little boy said nothing,
uttered no cry, not even a gasp.

We were trapped in a shallow channel between the shore and   8
a sandbar. There was nowhere to flee, nor was there any way to
graciously give ground. We sat still and waited. The bear
waited, too. A solitary mosquito hovered about his head, caus-
ing him to twitch one black ear.

I glanced behind me to check our position in the river, and   9
when I looked back, the bear had vanished, leaving no trace: no
twigs snapping, no outcry from the birds, nothing to indicate
where he had gone.

We drifted with the current for a while, both a little thrilled,   10
both a little terrified. Within moments, however, the little boy
returned to voice with a thousand new questions about bears.
His questions did not stop until we reached camp, where he
leaped from the canoe and ran to tell his mother the story, forgetting in his haste the bright blue flowers he had struggled so
hard to reach.

Questions for Study and Discussion

1. What role do the forget-me-nots play in Hyde's narrative?
2. What indications does Hyde provide that this trip might be revealing of deeper meanings? How do the creatures with which they share the environment respond to the presence of Hyde and his son?
3. Why doesn't Hyde simply flee the scene so that he and his son are not in danger of being attacked by the black bear?
4. What, in your opinion, is the point of Hyde's story?
5. Hyde mixes short dramatic sentences with sentences that are longer and more complicated. Choose several instances where he does this and comment on the possible reason(s) for writing in this manner. (Glossary *Emphasis*)
6. Paragraph 10 begins with the following sentence: "We drifted with the current for a while, both a little thrilled, both a little terrified." What effect does the parallelism in this sentence have on you as a reader? Why, in your opinion, has Hyde used the parallelism? (Glossary: *Parallelism*)

Vocabulary

Refer to your dictionary to define the following words as they are used in this selection. Then use each word in a sentence of your own.

muskrat (3)   alders (6)
scuffling (5)   graciously (8)
litter (5)

Suggested Writing Assignments

1. Read or reread Annie Dillard's essay, "Terror at Tinker Creek" (pp. 133–34). Write an essay in which you compare and contrast Hyde's essay with Dillard's.
2. In a number of ways, Hyde's essay is very much like a poem. Its point is understated, left unsaid. Its imagery, use of a variety of sentence patterns, and tone all add to its poetic

quality. Try turning the essay into a poem that is shorter in length than Hyde's essay. This is a difficult assignment because you will have to compress as many of the essential details as you possibly can, perhaps even leaving out some unnecessary details without losing the story line. You may find it necessary to change some of the circumstances in the process of converting the essay into a poem, but make sure that the new work you create has an equally valid point to make to the reader.

SALVATION

Langston Hughes

Born in Joplin, Missouri, Langston Hughes (1902–1967), an important figure in the black cultural movement of the 1920s known as the Harlem Renaissance, wrote poetry, fiction, and plays, and contributed a column to the New York Post. *He is best known for* The Weary Blues *(1926) and other books of poetry that express his racial pride, his familiarity with black traditions, and his understanding of jazz rhythms. As you read the following selection from his autobiography* The Big Sea *(1940), notice how Hughes varies the lengths and types of sentences he uses for the sake of emphasis.*

I was saved from sin when I was going on thirteen. But not really saved. It happened like this. There was a big revival at my Auntie Reed's church. Every night for weeks there had been much preaching, singing, praying, and shouting, and some very hardened sinners had been brought to Christ, and the membership of the church had grown by leaps and bounds. Then just before the revival ended, they held a special meeting for children, "to bring the young lambs to the fold." My aunt spoke of it for days ahead. That night I was escorted to the front row and placed on the mourners' bench with all the other young sinners, who had not yet been brought to Jesus.

My aunt told me that when you were saved you saw a light, and something happened to you inside! And Jesus came into your life! And God was with you from then on! She said you could see and hear and feel Jesus in your soul. I believed her. I have heard a great many old people say the same thing and it seemed to me they ought to know. So I sat there calmly in the hot, crowded church, waiting for Jesus to come to me.

The preacher preached a wonderful rhythmical sermon, all moans and shouts and lonely cries and dire pictures of hell, and then he sang a song about the ninety and nine safe in the fold, but one little lamb was left out in the cold. Then he said: "Won't you come? Won't you come to Jesus? Young lambs, won't you come?" And he held out his arms to all us young sinners there on the mourners' bench. And the little girls cried. And some of them jumped up and went to Jesus right away. But most of us just sat there.

A great many old people came and knelt around us and   4
prayed, old women with jet-black faces and braided hair, old men with work-gnarled hands. And the church sang a song about the lower lights are burning, some poor sinners to be saved. And the whole building rocked with prayer and song.

Still I kept waiting to *see* Jesus.   5

Finally all the young people had gone to the altar and were   6
saved, but one boy and me. He was a rounder's son named Westley. Westley and I were surrounded by sisters and deacons praying. It was very hot in the church, and getting late now. Finally Westley said to me in a whisper: "God damn! I'm tired o' sitting here. Let's get up and be saved." So he got up and was saved.

Then I was left all alone on the mourners' bench. My aunt   7
came and knelt at my knees and cried, while prayers and songs swirled all around me in the little church. The whole congregation prayed for me alone, in a mighty wail of moans and voices. And I kept waiting serenely for Jesus, waiting, waiting—but he didn't come. I wanted to see him, but nothing happened to me. Nothing! I wanted something to happen to me, but nothing happened.

I heard the songs and the minister saying: "Why don't you   8
come? My dear child, why don't you come to Jesus? Jesus is waiting for you. He wants you. Why don't you come? Sister Reed, what is this child's name?"

"Langston," my aunt sobbed.   9

"Langston, why don't you come? Why don't you come and be   10
saved? Oh, Lamb of God! Why don't you come?"

Now it was really getting late. I began to be ashamed of my-   11
self, holding everything up so long. I began to wonder what God thought about Westley, who certainly hadn't seen Jesus either, but who was now sitting proudly on the platform, swinging his knickerbockered legs and grinning down at me, surrounded by

deacons and old women on their knees praying. God had not struck Westley dead for taking his name in vain or for lying in the temple. So I decided that maybe to save further trouble, I'd better lie, too, and say that Jesus had come, and get up and be saved.

So I got up. 12

Suddenly the whole room broke into a sea of shouting, as 13 they saw me rise. Waves of rejoicing swept the place. Women leaped in the air. My aunt threw her arms around me. The minister took me by the hand and led me to the platform.

When things quieted down, in a hushed silence, punctuated 14 by a few ecstatic "Amens," all the new young lambs were blessed in the name of God. Then joyous singing filled the room.

That night, for the last time in my life but one—for I was a 15 big boy twelve years old—I cried. I cried, in bed alone, and couldn't stop. I buried my head under the quilts, but my aunt heard me. She woke up and told my uncle I was crying because the Holy Ghost had come into my life, and because I had seen Jesus. But I was really crying because I couldn't bear to tell her that I had lied, that I had deceived everybody in the church, that I hadn't seen Jesus, and that now I didn't believe there was a Jesus any more, since he didn't come to help me.

Questions for Study and Discussion

1. What is salvation? Is it important to young Langston Hughes that he be saved? Why is it important to Langston's aunt that he be saved?

2. Why does young Langston expect to be saved at the revival meeting? Once the children are in church, what appeals are made to them to encourage them to seek salvation?

3. Why does young Langston cry on the night of his being "saved"? Why is the story of his being saved so ironic? (Glossary: *Irony*)

4. What would be gained or lost if the essay began with the first two sentences combined as follows: "I was saved from

sin when I was going on thirteen, but I was not really saved''?

5. Identify the coordinating conjunctions in paragraph 3. Rewrite the paragraph without them. Compare your paragraph with the original, and explain what Hughes gains by using coordinating conjunctions. (Glossary: *Coordination*)

6. Identify the subordinating conjunctions in paragraph 15. What is it about the ideas in this last paragraph that makes it necessary for Hughes to use these subordinating conjunctions?

7. How does Hughes's choice of words, or diction, help to establish a realistic atmosphere for a religious revival meeting? (Glossary: *Diction*)

Vocabulary

Refer to your dictionary to define the following words as they are used in this selection. Then use each word in a sentence of your own.

dire (3)	punctuated (14)
gnarled (4)	ecstatic (14)
vain (11)	

Suggested Writing Assignments

1. Like the young Langston Hughes, we sometimes find ourselves in situations in which, for the sake of conformity, we do things we do not believe in. Consider one such experience you have had, and write an essay about it. What is it about human nature that makes us occasionally act in ways that contradict our inner feelings? As you write, pay particular attention to your sentence variety.

2. Reread the introduction to this chapter. Then review one of the essays that you have written, paying particular attention to sentence structure. Recast sentences as necessary in order to make your writing more interesting and effective.

II

THE LANGUAGE OF THE ESSAY

8

DICTION AND TONE

DICTION

Diction refers to a writer's choice and use of words. Good diction is precise and appropriate—the words mean exactly what the writer intends, and the words are well suited to the writer's subject, purpose, and intended audience.

For careful writers it is not enough merely to come close to saying what they want to say; they select words that convey their exact meaning. Perhaps Mark Twain put this best when he said, "The difference between the right word and the almost right word is the difference between lightning and the lightning bug." Inaccurate, imprecise, or inappropriate diction not only fails to convey the writer's intended meaning but also may cause confusion and misunderstanding for the reader.

Connotation and Denotation

Both connotation and denotation refer to the meanings of words. Denotation is the dictionary meaning of a word, the literal meaning. Connotative meanings are the associations or emotional overtones that words have acquired gradually. For example, the word *home* denotes a place where someone lives, but it connotes warmth, security, family, comfort, affection, and other more private thoughts and images. The word *residence* also denotes a place where someone lives, but its connotations are colder and more formal.

Many words in English have synonyms, words with very similar denotations—for example, *mob, crowd, multitude,* and *bunch*. Deciding which to use depends largely on the connotations that each synonym has and the context in which the word is to be used. For example, you might say, "There was a crowd at the lecture," but not "There was a mob at the lecture." Good

147

writers are sensitive to both the denotations and the connotations of words.

Abstract and Concrete Words

Abstract words name ideas, conditions, emotions—things nobody can touch, see, or hear. Some abstract words are *love, wisdom, cowardice, beauty, fear,* and *liberty*. People often disagree about abstract things. You may find a forest beautiful, while someone else might find it frightening, and neither of you would be wrong. Beauty and fear are abstract ideas; they exist in your mind, not in the forest along with the trees and the owls. Concrete words refer to things we can touch, see, hear, smell, and taste, such as *sandpaper, soda, birch trees, smog, cow, sailboat, rocking chair,* and *pancake*. If you disagree with someone on a concrete issue—say, you claim that the forest is mostly birch trees, while the other person says it is mostly pine—only one of you can be right, and both of you can be wrong; what kinds of trees grow in the forest is a concrete fact, not an abstract idea.

Good writing balances ideas and facts, and it also balances abstract and concrete diction. If the writing is too abstract, with too few concrete facts and details, it will be unconvincing and tiresome. If the writing is too concrete, devoid of ideas and emotions, it can seem pointless and dry.

General and Specific Words

General and *specific* do not necessarily refer to opposites. The same word can often be either general or specific, depending on the context: *Dessert* is more specific than *food*, but more general than *chocolate cream pie*. Being very specific is like being concrete: *chocolate cream pie* is something you can see and taste. Being general, on the other hand, is like being abstract. *Food, dessert,* and even *pie* are general classes of things that bring no particular taste or image to mind.

Good writing moves back and forth from the general to the specific. Without specific words, generalities can be unconvincing and even confusing: the writer's idea of "good food" may be very different from the reader's. But writing that does not relate specifics to each other by generalization often lacks focus and direction.

Clichés

Some words, phrases, and expressions have become trite through overuse. Let's assume your roommate has just returned from an evening out. You ask her "How was the concert?" She responds, "The concert was okay, but they had us *packed in* there *like sardines.* How was your evening?" And you reply, "Well, I finished my term paper, but the noise here is enough to *drive me crazy.* The dorm is a real *zoo.*" At one time the italicized expressions were vivid and colorful, but through constant use they have grown stale and ineffective. The experienced writer always tries to avoid such clichés as *believe it or not, doomed to failure, hit the spot, let's face it, sneaking suspicion, step in the right direction,* and *went to great lengths.*

Jargon

Jargon, or technical language, is the special vocabulary of a trade or profession. Writers who use jargon do so with an awareness of their audience. If their audience is a group of coworkers or professionals, jargon may be used freely. If the audience is a more general one, jargon should be used sparingly and carefully so that readers can understand it. Jargon becomes inappropriate when it is overused, used out of context, or used pretentiously. For example, computer terms such as *input, output,* and *feedback* are sometimes used in place of *contribution, result,* and *response* in other fields, especially in business. If you think about it, the terms suggest that people are machines, receiving and processing information according to a program imposed by someone else.

Formal and Informal Diction

Diction is appropriate when it suits the occasion for which it is intended. If the situation is informal—a friendly letter, for example—the writing may be colloquial; that is, its words may be chosen to suggest the way people talk with each other. If, on the other hand, the situation is formal—a term paper or a research report, for example—then the words should reflect this formality. Informal writing tends to be characterized by slang, contractions, references to the reader, and concrete nouns. Formal writing tends to be impersonal, abstract, and free of contractions and references to the reader. Formal writing and informal writing are, of course, the extremes. Most writing falls between these two extremes and is a blend of those formal and informal elements that best fit the context.

TONE

Tone is the attitude a writer takes toward the subject and the audience. The tone may be friendly or hostile, serious or humorous, intimate or distant, enthusiastic or skeptical.

As you read the following paragraphs, notice how each writer has created a different tone and how that tone is supported by the diction—the writer's particular choice and use of words.

Nostalgic

My generation is special because of what we missed rather than what we got, because in a certain sense we are the first and the last. The first to take technology for granted. (What was a space shot to us, except an hour cut from Social Studies to gather before a TV in the gym as Cape Canaveral counted down?) The first to grow up with TV. My sister was 8 when we got our set, so to her it seemed magic and always somewhat foreign. She had known books already and would never really replace them. But for me, the TV set was, like the kitchen sink and the telephone, a fact of life.

Joyce Maynard, "An 18-Year-Old Looks Back on Life"

Angry

Cans. Beer cans. Glinting on the verges of a million miles of roadways, lying in scrub, grass, dirt, leaves, sand, mud, but never hidden. Piels, Rheingold, Ballantine, Schaefer, Schlitz, shining in the sun or picked by moon or the beams of headlights at night; washed by rain or flattened by wheels, but never dulled, never buried, never destroyed. Here is the mark of savages, the testament of wasters, the stain of prosperity.

Marya Mannes, "Wasteland"

Humorous

In perpetrating a revolution, there are two requirements: someone or something to revolt against and someone to actually show up and do the revolting. Dress is usually casual and both parties may be flexible about time and
place but if either faction fails to attend the whole enterprise is likely to come off badly. In the Chinese Revolution
of 1650 neither party showed up and the deposit on the hall
was forfeited.

Woody Allen, "A Brief, Yet Helpful Guide to Civil Disobedience"

Resigned

I make my living humping cargo for Seaboard World
Airlines, one of the big international airlines at Kennedy
Airport. They handle strictly all cargo. I was once told that
one of the Rockefellers is the major stockholder for the airline, but I don't really think about that too much. I don't
get paid to think. The big thing is to beat that race with the
time clock every morning of your life so the airline will be
happy. The worst thing a man could ever do is to make suggestions about building a better airline. They pay people
$40,000 a year to come up with better ideas. It doesn't mat-
ter that these ideas never work; it's just that they get nervous when a guy from South Brooklyn or Ozone Park acts
like he has a brain.

Patrick Fenton, "Confessions of a Working Stiff"

Ironic

Once upon a time there was a small, beautiful, green and
graceful country called Vietnam. It needed to be saved. (In
later years no one could remember exactly what it needed
to be saved from, but that is another story.) For many years
Vietnam was in the process of being saved by France, but
the French eventually tired of their labors and left. Then
America took on the job. America was well equipped for
country-saving. It was the richest and most powerful nation on earth. It had, for example, nuclear explosives on
hand and ready to use equal to six tons of TNT for every
man, woman, and child in the world. It had huge and very
efficient factories, brilliant and dedicated scientists, and
most (but not everybody) would agree, it had good inten-

tions. Sadly, America had one fatal flaw—its inhabitants were in love with technology and thought it could do no wrong. A visitor to America during the time of this story would probably have guessed its outcome after seeing how its inhabitants were treating their own country. The air was mostly foul, the water putrid, and most of the land was either covered with concrete or garbage. But Americans were never much on introspection, and they didn't foresee the result of their loving embrace on the small country. They set out to save Vietnam with the same enthusiasm and determination their forefathers had displayed in conquering the frontier.

The Sierra Club, "A Fable for Our Times"

ON BEING 17, BRIGHT, AND UNABLE TO READ

David Raymond

When the following article appeared in The New York Times *in 1976, David Raymond was a high-school student in Connecticut. In his essay he poignantly discusses his great difficulty in reading because of dyslexia and the many problems he experienced in school as a result. As you read, pay attention to the naturalness of the author's diction.*

One day a substitute teacher picked me to read aloud from the textbook. When I told her "No, thank you," she came unhinged. She thought I was acting smart, and told me so. I kept calm, and that got her madder and madder. We must have spent 10 minutes trying to solve the problem, and finally she got so red in the face I thought she'd blow up. She told me she'd see me after class.

Maybe someone like me was a new thing for that teacher. But she wasn't new to me. I've been through scenes like that all my life. You see, even though I'm 17 and a junior in high school, I can't read because I have dyslexia. I'm told I read "at a fourth-grade level," but from where I sit, that's not reading. You can't know what that means unless you've been there. It's not easy to tell how it feels when you can't read your homework assignments or the newspaper or a menu in a restaurant or even notes from your own friends.

My family began to suspect I was having problems almost from the first day I started school. My father says my early years in school were the worst years of his life. They weren't so good for me, either. As I look back on it now, I can't find the words to express how bad it really was. I wanted to die. I'd come home from school screaming, "I'm dumb. I'm dumb—I wish I were dead!"

I guess I couldn't read anything at all then—not even my own   4
name—and they tell me I didn't talk as good as other kids. But
what I remember about those days is that I couldn't throw a
ball where it was supposed to go, I couldn't learn to swim, and I
wouldn't learn to ride a bike, because no matter what anyone
told me, I knew I'd fail.

Sometimes my teachers would try to be encouraging. When I   5
couldn't read the words on the board they'd say, "Come on,
David, you know that word." Only I didn't. And it was embarrassing. I just felt dumb. And dumb was how the kids treated
me. They'd make fun of me every chance they got, asking me to
spell "cat" or something like that. Even if I knew how to spell
it, I wouldn't; they'd only give me another word. Anyway, it was
awful, because more than anything I wanted friends. On my
birthday when I blew out the candles I didn't wish I could learn
to read; what I wished for was that the kids would like me.

With the bad reports coming from school, and with me moan-   6
ing about wanting to die and how everybody hated me, my parents began looking for help. That's when the testing started.
The school tested me, the child-guidance center tested me, private psychiatrists tested me. Everybody knew something was
wrong—especially me.

It didn't help much when they stuck a fancy name onto it. I   7
couldn't pronounce it then—I was only in second grade—and I
was ashamed to talk about it. Now it rolls off my tongue, because I've been living with it for a lot of years—dyslexia.

All through elementary school it wasn't easy. I was always   8
having to do things that were "different," things the other kids
didn't have to do. I had to go to a child psychiatrist, for instance.

One summer my family forced me to go to a camp for chil-   9
dren with reading problems. I hated the idea, but the camp
turned out pretty good, and I had a good time. I met a lot of
kids who couldn't read and somehow that helped. The director
of the camp said I had a higher I.Q. than 90 percent of the population. I didn't believe him.

About the worst thing I had to do in fifth and sixth grade was   10
go to a special education class in another school in our town. A
bus picked me up, and I didn't like that at all. The bus also

picked up emotionally disturbed kids and retarded kids. It was like going to a school for the retarded. I always worried that someone I knew would see me on that bus. It was a relief to go to the regular junior high school.

Life began to change a little for me then, because I began to 11 feel better about myself. I found the teachers cared; they had meetings about me and I worked harder for them for a while. I began to work on the potter's wheel, making vases and pots that the teachers said were pretty good. Also, I got a letter for being on the track team. I could always run pretty fast.

At high school the teachers are good and everyone is trying to 12 help me. I've gotten honors some marking periods and I've won a letter on the cross-country team. Next quarter I think the school might hold a show of my pottery. I've got some friends. But there are still some embarrassing times. For instance, every time there is writing in the class, I get up and go to the special education room. Kids ask me where I go all the time. Sometimes I say, "to Mars."

Homework is a real problem. During free periods in school I 13 go into the special ed room and staff members read assignments to me. When I get home my mother reads to me. Sometimes she reads an assignment into a tape recorder, and then I go into my room and listen to it. If we have a novel or something like that to read, she reads it out loud to me. Then I sit down with her and we do the assignment. She'll write, while I talk my answers to her. Lately I've taken to dictating into a tape recorder, and then someone—my father, a private tutor or my mother—types up what I've dictated. Whatever homework I do takes someone else's time, too. That makes me feel bad.

We had a big meeting in school the other day—eight of us, 14 four from the guidance department, my private tutor, my parents and me. The subject was me. I said I wanted to go to college, and they told me about colleges that have facilities and staff to handle people like me. That's nice to hear.

As for what happens after college, I don't know and I'm worried about that. How can I make a living if I can't read? Who will hire me? How will I fill out the application form? The only thing that gives me any courage is the fact that I've learned about well-known people who couldn't read or had other problems and still made it. Like Albert Einstein, who didn't talk until he was 4 and flunked math. Like Leonardo da Vinci, who everyone seems to think had dyslexia.

I've told this story because maybe some teacher will read it   16
and go easy on a kid in the classroom who has what I've got. Or, maybe some parent will stop nagging his kid, and stop calling him lazy. Maybe he's not lazy or dumb. Maybe he just can't read and doesn't know what's wrong. Maybe he's scared, like I was.

Questions for Study and Discussion

1. What is dyslexia? Is it essential for an understanding of the essay that we know more about dyslexia than Raymond tells us? Explain.

2. What does Raymond say his purpose is in telling his story?

3. What does Raymond's story tell us about the importance of our early childhood experiences, especially within our educational system?

4. Raymond uses many colloquial and idiomatic expressions, such as "she got so red in the face I thought she'd blow up" and "she came unhinged" (1). Identify other examples of such diction and tell how they affect the essay.

5. In the context of the essay, comment on the appropriateness of each of the following possible choices of diction. Which word is better in each case? Why?
   a. *selected* for *picked* (1)
   b. *experience* for *thing* (2)
   c. *speak as well* for *talk as good* (4)
   d. *negative* for *bad* (6)
   e. *important* for *big* (14)
   f. *failed* for *flunked* (15)
   g. *frightened* for *scared* (16)

6. How would you describe Raymond's tone in this essay?

Vocabulary

Refer to your dictionary to define the following words as they are used in this selection. Then use each word in a sentence of your own.

dyslexia (2)   psychiatrists (6)

Suggested Writing Assignments

1. Imagine that you are away at school. Recently you were caught in a radar speed trap—you were going 70 miles per hour in a 55-mile-per-hour zone—and have just lost your license; you will not be able to go home this coming weekend, as you had planned. Write two letters in which you explain why you will not be able to go home, one to your parents and the other to your best friend. Your audience is different in each case, so be sure to choose your diction accordingly.

2. Select an essay you have already completed in this course, and rewrite it in a different tone. If the essay was originally formal or serious, lighten it so that it is now informal and humorous. Pay special attention to diction. Actually think in terms of a different reader as your audience—not your instructor but perhaps your classmates, your clergyman, your sister, or the state environmental protection board. Reshape your essay as necessary.

THE FLIGHT OF THE EAGLES

N. Scott Momaday

N. Scott Momaday, a professor of English at Stanford University, is a Kiowa Indian. He has based much of his writing on his Indian ancestry, particularly on his childhood experiences with his Kiowa grandmother. In 1969 he won the Pulitzer Prize for his novel House Made of Dawn *(1968). His other works include* The Way to Rainy Mountain *(1969),* Angle of Geese and Other Poems *(1974), and* The Gourd Dancer *(1976). In the following selection, taken from* House Made of Dawn, *Momaday closely observes the mating flight of a pair of golden eagles. Notice how his sensitive choice of verbs enables him to capture the beautiful and graceful movements of these birds.*

They were golden eagles, a male and a female, in their mating flight. They were cavorting, spinning and spiraling on the cold, clear columns of air, and they were beautiful. They swooped and hovered, leaning on the air, and swung close together, feinting and screaming with delight. The female was full-grown, and the span of her broad wings was greater than any man's height. There was a fine flourish to her motion; she was deceptively, incredibly fast, and her pivots and wheels were wide and full-blown. But her great weight was streamlined and perfectly controlled. She carried a rattlesnake; it hung shining from her feet, limp and curving out in the trail of her flight. Suddenly her wings and tail fanned, catching full on the wind, and for an instant she was still, widespread and spectral in the blue, while her mate flared past and away, turning around in the distance to look for her. Then she began to beat upward at an angle from the rim until she was small in the sky, and she let go of the snake. It fell slowly, writhing and rolling, floating out like a bit of silver thread against the wide backdrop of the land. She held still above, buoyed up on the cold current, her crop and hackles gleaming like copper in the sun. The male swerved and sailed. He was younger than she and a little more than half as large. He was quicker, tighter in his moves. He let the carrion drift by; then suddenly he gathered himself and stooped, sliding down in a blur of motion to the strike. He hit the snake in the head, with not the slightest deflection of his course or speed, cracking its long body like a whip. Then he rolled and swung upward in a great pendulum arc, riding out his momentum. At the top of his glide he let go of the snake in turn, but the female did not go for it. Instead she soared out over the plain, nearly out of sight, like a mote receding into the haze of the far mountain. The male followed.

Questions for Study and Discussion

1. What are the differences between the two eagles as Momaday describes them?
2. What role does the rattlesnake play in this description?
3. In describing the mating flight of the golden eagles, Momaday has tried to capture their actions accurately. Identify the strong verbs that he uses, and discuss how these verbs enhance his description. (Glossary: *Verb*)
4. Comment on the denotative and connotative meanings of the italicized words and phrases in the following excerpts:
   a. on the *cold, clear* columns of air
   b. feinting and screaming with *delight*
   c. a *fine flourish* to her motion
   d. her *pivots* and *wheels* were wide and full-blown
   e. her *crop* and *hackles* gleaming
5. Identify several examples of Momaday's use of concrete and specific diction. What effect does this diction have on you?
6. Identify the figures of speech that Momaday uses in this selection and tell how you think each one functions in the essay. (Glossary: *Figures of Speech*)

Vocabulary

Refer to your dictionary to define the following words as they are used in this selection. Then use each word in a sentence of your own.

cavorting   spectral
feinting

Suggested Writing Assignments

1. Select one of the following activities as the subject for a brief descriptive essay. Be sure to use strong verbs, as Momaday has done, in order to describe the action accurately and vividly.

   the movements of a dancer
   the actions of a kite
   the antics of a pet
   a traffic jam
   a violent storm

2. Accounts of natural events often rely on scientific data and are frequently presented in the third person. Carefully observe some natural event (fire, hurricane, birth of an animal, bird migration, etc.), and note significant details and facts about that occurrence. Then, using very carefully chosen diction, write an account of the event.

THE POND

Ellen Gilchrist

Ellen Gilchrist is a poet, playwright, novelist, and short story writer. She was born in Vicksburg, Mississippi, in 1935, and graduated from Millsaps College in 1967. She now makes her home in Fayetteville, Arkansas. Gilchrist has published The Land Surveyor's Daughter *(1979),* The Annunciation *(1983), and* Victory Over Japan *(1984). She is perhaps best know for* In the Land of Dreamy Dreams *(1981), a collection of fourteen short stories set in New Orleans about adolescents and their problems. Note the intensity of Gilchrist's tone in this selection taken from* Falling Through Space: The Journals of Ellen Gilchrist *(1987).*

I'm not a bad person. If I see a turtle on the road, I stop and pick it up and return it to the grass. I know the universe is one. I know it's all one reality. So why does it make me so furious, why do I want to kill and kill and kill when the turtles on the pond kill the baby ducks? They killed seven in April and five more in May and they are at it again.

Edmund Wilson once wrote a great short story on this subject, called "The Man Who Hated Snapping Turtles." I could have written that story. I wouldn't have had to invent a character. I could have used myself. One morning I wake up and there are five brand-new beautiful soft fluffy baby ducks following their mother out from behind a grass nest and walking side by side to the water. They enter the water without sound. They glide like angels. The mother looks like my beautiful daughter-in-law Rita. The baby ducks are my grandchildren. A turtle rears its head. Kill, I'm screaming. The neighbors are on their porches. They know what's going on. We have all been sharing the tragedy of the ducks.

Kill, I'm screaming. Doesn't anybody have a gun? I grab an empty Coke bottle and run out onto the pier and throw it at the turtle. Success. It scares him off for the moment. Get those babies back on the land, I'm screaming at the large ducks. Don't you know what's good for you? Can't you protect your young?

I can't stand it. Here we are in the sovereign state of Mississippi and we are helpless to prevent those ducks from getting killed. How am I going to travel and see the world? What's going to happen when I get to Mexico or India? Get back in the bushes, I'm yelling at the ducks. We'll drain the pond. We'll kill all the turtles in the world. What am I supposed to do? I can't stay in the house and never go out on the porch. I can't keep the drapes closed so I'll forget the pond is there. It's there. The baby ducks are on the pond and the turtles are coming to get them. 4

Questions for Study and Discussion

1. In her fourth paragraph Gilchrist wonders how she is going to travel to see the world. What is the difficulty she faces?
2. With whom are the ducks associated for Gilchrist? Does she say what the turtles represent for her? Explain. What do they represent for us the readers?
3. Gilchrist's tone is angry in this essay, but how does she reveal her anger? What other tones does Gilchrist create?
4. In her first paragraph Gilchrist writes, "I know the universe is one. I know it's all one reality." What does she mean by these statements? What do they have to do with the rest of her essay?
5. Comment on the beginning and ending sentences of Gilchrist's essay. (Glossary: *Beginnings and Endings*) Why do you think she begins her essay with the statement that she is "not a bad person."

Vocabulary

Refer to your dictionary to define the following words as they are used in this selection. Then use each word in a sentence of your own.

rears (2)   sovereign (4)

Suggested Writing Assignments

1. Gilchrist's essay conveys a sense of helplessness over a situation that she seems powerless to change. Even if she could drain the pond, kill all the turtles, and let the ducks roam freely, the problem goes deeper: it has to do with the way the strong prey on the weak. Think about this fact of life, and, using another example, express your own feelings about the injustice it illustrates. You may wish to model your essay on Gilchrist's, both as to length and tone.

2. Take a letter or memorandum that you have received from your college administration or some other bureaucratic body, and rewrite it so as to avoid the deadly dull diction and tone of most such correspondence. Your revision should convey all the necessary information contained in the original but should do so in a lively and entertaining way. Be sure, however, that your tone is appropriate for your audience and subject.

NAMELESS, TENNESSEE

William Least Heat Moon

*In 1978 William Least Heat Moon (William
Trogdon before he took on his tribal Osage
name) began a 14,000 mile trip over America's
"blue highways," those back roads that were rendered in blue on old highway maps, and in 1982
he told of his adventures in* Blue Highways, *an
original and authentic American book that became an instant best seller. Shortly after his
book was published Annie Dillard said of William Least Heat Moon that he was "a witty, generous, sophisticated and democratic observer. . . .
His modesty, his subtle, kindly humor, and his
uncanny gift for catching good people at good
moments make* Blue Highways *a joy to read."
Nowhere is her assessment in greater evidence
than in the following excerpt about Nameless,
Tennessee, a small village that Moon has quite
deservedly "put on the map." As you read, notice
the way that Moon captures and preserves the
colorful language of the Watts family.*

Nameless, Tennessee, was a town of maybe ninety people   1
if you pushed it, a dozen houses along the road, a couple
of barns, same number of churches, a general merchandise
store selling Fire Chief gasoline, and a community center with
a lighted volleyball court. Behind the center was an open-roof,
rusting metal privy with PAINT ME on the door; in the hollow of a
nearby oak lay a full pint of Jack Daniel's Black Label. From
the houses, the odor of coal smoke.

Next to a red tobacco barn stood the general merchandise   2
with a poster of Senator Albert Gore, Jr., smiling from the window. I knocked. The door opened partway. A tall, thin man
said, "Closed up. For good," and started to shut the door.

"Don't want to buy anything. Just a question for Mr. Thur- 3
mond Watts."

The man peered through the slight opening. He looked me 4
over. "What question would that be?"

"If this is Nameless, Tennessee, could he tell me how it got 5
that name?"

The man turned back into the store and called out, "Miss 6
Ginny! Somebody here wants to know how Nameless come to
be Nameless."

Miss Ginny edged to the door and looked me and my truck 7
over. Clearly, she didn't approve. She said, "You know as well
as I do, Thurmond. Don't keep him on the stoop in the damp to
tell him." Miss Ginny, I found out, was Mrs. Virginia Watts,
Thurmond's wife.

I stepped in and they both began telling the story, adding a 8
detail here, the other correcting a fact there, both smiling at
the foolishness of it all. It seems the hilltop settlement went for
years without a name. Then one day the Post Office Department told the people if they wanted mail up on the mountain
they would have to give the place a name you could properly
address a letter to. The community met; there were only a
handful, but they commenced debating. Some wanted patriotic
names, some names from nature, one man recommended in all
seriousness his own name. They couldn't agree, and they ran
out of names to argue about. Finally, a fellow tired of the talk;
he didn't like the mail he received anyway. "Forget the durn
Post Office," he said. "This here's a nameless place if I ever
seen one, so leave it be." And that's just what they did.

Watts pointed out the window. "We used to have signs on the 9
road, but the Halloween boys keep tearin' them down."

"You think Nameless is a funny name," Miss Ginny said. "I 10
see it plain in your eyes. Well, you take yourself up north a
piece to Difficult or Defeated or Shake Rag. Now them are silly
names."

The old store, lighted only by three fifty-watt bulbs, smelled 11
of coal oil and baking bread. In the middle of the rectangular
room, where the oak floor sagged a little, stood an iron stove.
To the right was a wooden table with an unfinished game of
checkers and a stool made from an apple-tree stump. On
shelves around the walls sat earthen jugs with corncob stop-

pers, a few canned goods, and some of the two thousand old clocks and clockworks Thurmond Watts owned. Only one was ticking; the others he just looked at. I asked how long he'd been in the store.

"Thirty-five years, but we closed the first day of the year. 12 We're hopin' to sell it to a churchly couple. Upright people. No athians."

"Did you build this store?" 13

"I built this one, but it's the third general store on the 14 ground. I fear it'll be the last. I take no pleasure in that. Once you could come in here for a gallon of paint, a pickle, a pair of shoes, and a can of corn."

"Or horehound candy," Miss Ginny said. "Or corsets and 15 salves. We had cough syrups and all that for the body. In season, we'd buy and sell blackberries and walnuts and chestnuts, before the blight got them. And outside, Thurmond milled corn and sharpened plows. Even shoed a horse sometimes.

"We could fix up a horse or a man or a baby," Watts said. 16

"Thurmond, tell him we had a doctor on the ridge in them 17 days."

"We had a doctor on the ridge in them days. As good as any 18 doctor alivin'. He'd cut a crooked toenail or deliver a woman. Dead these last years."

"I got some bad ham meat one day," Miss Ginny said, "and 19 took to vomitin'. All day, all night. Hangin' on the drop edge of yonder. I said to Thurmond, 'Thurmond, unless you want shut of me, call the doctor.' "

"I studied on it," Watts said. 20

"You never did. You got him right now. He come over and 21 put three drops of iodeen in half a glass of well water. I drank it down and the vomitin' stopped with the last swallow. Would you think iodeen could do that?"

"He put Miss Ginny on one teaspoon of spirits of ammonia in 22 well water for her nerves. Ain't nothin' works better for her to this day."

"Calms me like the hand of the Lord." 23

Hilda, the Wattses' daughter, came out of the backroom. "I 24 remember him," she said. "I was just a baby. Y'all were talkin' to him, and he lifted me up on the counter and gave me a stick of Juicy Fruit and a piece of cheese."

"Knew the old medicines," Watts said. "Only drugstore he   25
needed was a good kitchen cabinet. None of them antee-
beeotics that hit you worsen your ailment. Forgotten lore now,
the old medicines, because they ain't profit in iodeen."

Miss Ginny started back to the side room where she and her   26
sister Marilyn were taking apart a duck-down mattress to
make bolsters. She stopped at the window for another look at
Ghost Dancing.* "How do you sleep in that thing? Ain't you all
cramped and cold?

"How does the clam sleep in his shell?" Watts said in my de-   27
fense.

"Thurmond, get the boy a piece of buttermilk pie afore he   28
goes on."

"Hilda, get him some buttermilk pie." He looked at me. "You   29
like good music?" I said I did. He cranked up an old Edison
phonograph, the kind with the big morning-glory blossom for a
speaker, and put on a wax cylinder. "This will be 'My Mother's
Prayer,'" he said.

While I ate buttermilk pie, Watts served as disc jockey of   30
Nameless, Tennessee. "Here's 'Mountain Rose.'" It was one of
those moments that you know at the time will stay with you to
the grave: the sweet pie, the gaunt man playing the old music,
the coals in the stove glowing orange, the scent of kerosene and
hot bread. "Here's 'Evening Rhapsody.'" The music was so
heavily romantic we both laughed. I thought: It is for this I
have come.

Feathered over and giggling, Miss Ginny stepped from the   31
side room. She knew she was a sight. "Thurmond, give him
some lunch. Still looks hungry."

Hilda pulled food off the woodstove in the backroom: home-   32
butchered and canned whole-hog sausage, home-canned June
apples, turnip greens, cole slaw, potatoes, stuffing, hot corn-
bread. All delicious.

Watts and Hilda sat and talked while I ate. "Wish you would   33
join me."

"We've ate," Watts said. "Cain't beat a woodstove for flavor-   34
ful cookin'."

---

*The name Trogdon gave his van.

He told me he was raised in a one-hundred-fifty-year-old   35
cabin still standing in one of the hollows. "How many's left,"
he said, "that grew up in a log cabin? I ain't the last surely, but
I must be climbin' on the list."

Hilda cleared the table. "You Watts ladies know how to   36
cook."

"She's in nursin' school at Tennessee Tech. I went over for   37
one of them football games last year there at Coevul." To say
Cookeville, you let the word collapse in upon itself so that it
comes out "Coevul."

"Do you like football?" I asked.   38

"Don't know. I was so high up in that stadium, I never opened   39
my eyes."

Watts went to the back and returned with a fat spiral note-   40
book that he set on the table. His expression had changed.
"Miss Ginny's *Deathbook*."

The thing startled me. Was it something I was supposed to   41
sign? He opened it but said nothing. There were scads of names
written in a tidy hand over pages incised to crinkliness by a
ballpoint. Chronologically, the names had piled up: wives,
grandparents, a stillborn infant, relatives, friends close and
distant. Names, names. After each, the date of *the* unknown finally known and transcribed. The last entry bore yesterday's
date.

"She's wrote out twenty years' worth. Ever day she listens to   42
the hospital report on the radio and puts the names in. Folks
come by to check a date. Or they just turn through the books.
Read them like a scrapbook."

Hilda said, "Like Saint Peter at the gates inscribin' the   43
names."

Watts took my arm. "Come along." He led me to the fruit cel-   44
lar under the store. As we went down, he said, "Always take a
newborn baby upstairs afore you take him downstairs, otherwise you'll incline him downwards."

The cellar was dry and full of cobwebs and jar after jar of   45
home-canned food, the bottles organized as a shopkeeper
would: sausage, pumpkin, sweet pickles, tomatoes, corn, relish,
blackberries, peppers, squash, jellies. He held a hand out
toward the dusty bottles. "Our tomorrows."

Upstairs again, he said, "Hope to sell the store to the right   46
folk. I see now, though, it'll be somebody offen the ridge. I've
studied on it, and maybe it's the end of our place." He stirred
the coals. "This store could give a comfortable livin', but not
likely get you rich. But just gettin' by is dice rollin' to people
nowadays. I never did see my day guaranteed."

When it was time to go, Watts said, "If you find anyone along   47
your way wants a good store—on the road to Cordell Hull
Lake—tell them about us."

I said I would. Miss Ginny and Hilda and Marilyn came out to   48
say goodbye. It was cold and drizzling again. "Weather to give a
man the weary dismals," Watts grumbled. "Where you headed
from here?"

"I don't know."   49

"Cain't get lost then."   50

Miss Ginny looked again at my rig. It had worried her from   51
the first as it had my mother. "I hope you don't get yourself kilt
in that durn thing gallivantin' around the country."

"Come back when the hills dry off," Watts said. "We'll go   52
lookin' for some of them round rocks all sparkly inside."

I thought a moment. "Geodes?"   53

"Them's the ones. The county's properly full of them."   54

Questions for Study and Discussion

1. What dominant impression does Moon create in this essay?
   (Glossary: *Dominant Impression*) Would you like to spend
   some time in Nameless? Why or why not?

2. How would you describe Moon's tone in this selection? Is it
   one of distance, friendship, humor, bewilderment, disbelief,
   scorn, joy, neighborliness, or something other than these
   feelings? How do you know?

3. Central to the impact that the essay has on us is the way
   Moon reveals the relationship between Thurmond and Miss
   Ginny. What do we learn about each character and their
   relationship?

4. Experts in dialects tell us that there are three ways to differentiate one dialect from another: the words a person uses, the way the words are pronounced, and the grammar a person uses. Find several examples of each of these characteristics in the speech of the Wattses that tell us they are speaking a dialect of American English.

5. Thurmond adds humor to this essay. What does he say that strikes you as humorous?

6. What is ironic about Miss Ginny's *Deathbook* in light of the name of the village? (Glossary: *Irony*)

Vocabulary

privy (1)
settlement (8)
piece (10)
horehound (15)
salves (15)

lore (25)
bolsters (26)
scads (41)
incised (41)

Suggested Writing Assignments

1. Write an essay modeled on Moon's in which you attempt to capture the flavor of a particular place—the place where you live or a place that you know very well—by accurately rendering the dialect or speech patterns of the local inhabitants. Remember that it is through the special words, the way they are pronounced, and the unusual grammar that people use that they reveal themselves to be speakers of a particular variety of American English. Of course, along with the speech differences you should also try to include other details that indicate what makes the place unique—location, weather, food, smells, and such characteristics as the types of buildings, the work that people do, and in general their everyday preoccupations. Gather your details first and then build a dominant impression from those details.

2. Read another section of William Least Heat Moon's *Blue Highways*, and write an essay comparing or contrasting

Nameless, Tennessee, to that section of the United States that you have chosen. What differences do you notice in the speech of the inhabitants, their worldly concerns and the dominant impression that Moon conveys about the location?

9

FIGURATIVE LANGUAGE

Figurative language is language used in an imaginative rather than a literal sense. Although it is most often associated with poetry, figurative language is used widely in our daily speech and in our writing. Prose writers have long known that figurative language not only brings freshness and color to writing, but also helps to clarify ideas.

Two of the most commonly used figures of speech are the simile and the metaphor. A *simile* is an explicit comparison between two essentially different ideas or things that uses the words *like* or *as* to link them.

> Canada geese sweep across the hills and valleys like a formation of strategic bombers.
>
> Benjamin B. Bachman

> I walked toward her and hailed her as a visitor to the moon might salute a survivor of a previous expedition.
>
> John Updike

A *metaphor*, on the other hand, makes an implicit comparison between dissimilar ideas or things without using *like* or *as*.

> She was very old and small and she walked slowly in the dark pine shadows, moving a little from side to side in her steps, with the balanced heaviness and lightness of a pendulum in a grandfather clock.
>
> Eudora Welty

> Charm is the ultimate weapon, the supreme seduction, against which there are few defenses.
>
> Laurie Lee

In order to take full advantage of the richness of a particular comparison, writers sometimes use several sentences or even a whole paragraph to develop a metaphor. Such a comparison is called an *extended metaphor*.

The point is that you have to strip down your writing before you can build it back up. You must know what the essential tools are and what job they were designed to do. If I may belabor the metaphor on carpentry, it is first necessary to be able to saw wood neatly and to drive nails. Later you can bevel the edges or add elegant finials, if that is your taste. But you can never forget that you are practicing a craft that is based on certain principles. If the nails are weak, your house will collapse. If your verbs are weak and your syntax is rickety, your sentences will fall apart.

William Zinsser

Another frequently used figure of speech is *personification*. In personification the writer attributes human qualities to animals or inanimate objects.

Blond October comes striding over the hills wearing a crimson shirt and faded green trousers.

Hal Borland

Indeed, haste can be the assassin of elegance.

T. H. White

In the preceding examples, the writers have, through the use of figurative language, both livened up their prose and given emphasis to their ideas. Keep in mind that figurative language should never be used merely to "dress up" writing; above all, it should help you to develop your ideas and to clarify your meaning for the reader.

THE MISSISSIPPI RIVER

Mark Twain

Mark Twain (1835–1910), born in Hannibal, Missouri, created Huckleberry Finn *(1884),* Tom Sawyer *(1876),* The Prince and the Pauper *(1882), and* A Connecticut Yankee in King Arthur's Court *(1889), among other classics. One of America's most popular writers, Twain is generally regarded as the most important practitioner of the realistic school of writing, a style that emphasized observable details. As you read the following passage, notice how Twain makes use of figurative language to describe two quite different ways of seeing the great Mississippi River.*

Now when I had mastered the language of this water and had come to know every trifling feature that bordered the great river as familiarly as I knew the letters of the alphabet, I had made a valuable acquisition. But I had lost something, too. I had lost something which could never be restored to me while I lived. All the grace, the beauty, the poetry, had gone out of the majestic river! I still kept in mind a certain wonderful sunset which I witnessed when steamboating was new to me. A broad expanse of the river was turned to blood; in the middle distance the red hue brightened into gold, through which a solitary log came floating, black and conspicuous; in one place a long, slanting mark lay sparkling upon the water; in another the surface was broken by boiling, tumbling rings that were as many-tinted as an opal; where the ruddy flush was faintest was a smooth spot that was covered with graceful circles and radiating lines, ever so delicately traced; the shore on our left was densely wooded, and the somber shadow that fell from this forest was broken in one place by a long, ruffled trail that shone like silver; and high above the forest wall a clean-stemmed dead tree waved a single leafy bough that glowed like a flame in the unobstructed splendor that was flowing from the sun. There were graceful curves, reflected images, woody heights, soft distances, and over the whole scene, far and near, the dissolving lights drifted steadily, enriching it every passing moment with new marvels of coloring.

I stood like one bewitched. I drank it in, in a speechless rapture. The world was new to me and I had never seen anything like this at home. But as I have said, a day came when I began to cease from noting the glories and the charms which the moon and the sun and the twilight wrought upon the river's face; another day came when I ceased altogether to note them. Then, if that sunset scene had been repeated, I should have looked upon it without rapture and should have commented upon it inwardly after this fashion: "This sun means that we are going to have wind to-morrow; that floating log means that the river is rising, small thanks to it; that slanting mark on the water refers to a bluff reef which is going to kill somebody's steamboat one of these nights, if it keeps on stretching out like that; those tumbling 'boils' show a dissolving bar and a changing channel there; the lines and circles in the slick water over yonder are a warning that that troublesome place is shoaling up dangerously; that silver streak in the shadow of the forest is the 'break' from a new snag and he has located himself in the very best place he could have found to fish for steamboats; that tall dead tree, with a single living branch, is not going to last long, and then how is a body ever going to get through this blind place at night without the friendly old landmark?"

No, the romance and beauty were all gone from the river. All the value any feature of it had for me now was the amount of usefulness it could furnish toward compassing the safe piloting of a steamboat. Since those days, I have pitied doctors from my heart. What does the lovely flush in a beauty's cheek mean to a doctor but a "break" that ripples above some deadly disease? Are not all her visible charms sown thick with what are to him the signs and symbols of hidden decay? Does he ever see her beauty at all, or doesn't he simply view her professionally and comment upon her unwholesome condition all to himself? And doesn't he sometimes wonder whether he has gained most or lost most by learning his trade?

Questions for Study and Discussion

1. Twain's essay reveals that he has two attitudes toward the Mississippi River. What are those attitudes, and where are they presented in the essay? (Glossary: *Attitude*)
2. In his conclusion Twain says that since the days when he learned his profession, he has pitied doctors. Why does he say this?
3. Twain uses a number of similes and metaphors in his essay. Identify three of each, and explain what is being compared in each case.
4. What is Twain's tone in this essay? (Glossary: *Tone*)
5. What effect do the italicized words have in each of the following quotations from this selection? How do these words contribute to Twain's description? (Glossary: *Connotation/ Denotation*)

   a. ever so *delicately* traced (1)
   b. shadow that *fell* from this forest (1)
   c. *wrought* upon the river's face (2)
   d. show a *dissolving* bar (2)
   e. to get through this *blind* place at night (2)
   f. lovely *flush* in a beauty's cheek (3)

Vocabulary

Refer to your dictionary to define the following words as they are used in this selection. Then use each word in a sentence of your own.

acquisition (1)	rapture (2)
hue (1)	romance (3)
opal (1)	

Suggested Writing Assignments

1. Write an essay modeled on Twain's in which you offer your two different views of a particular scene, event, or issue. Describe how you once regarded your subject, and then describe how you now view the subject. For example, you

might wish to present the way you once viewed your home town or high school, and the way you now view it. Be sure to use at least one simile and one metaphor in your essay.

2. Write an essay describing one of the places listed below or any other place of your choice. Use at least one simile and one metaphor to clarify and enliven your description.

a factory
a place of worship
a fast-food restaurant
your dormitory
your college library
your favorite place on campus
your home town

BULLISH ON BASEBALL CARDS

Henry Petroski

Henry Petroski was born in 1943 in New York City and studied engineering at Manhattan College, from which he earned his bachelor's degree. He received his doctorate in engineering from the University of Illinois and is currently a professor in the School of Engineering at Duke University. In the following selection, which is taken from Beyond Engineering *(1986) but originally appeared in the Business Day section of* The New York Times, *Petroski compares collecting baseball cards to the world of business.*

My eight-year-old son began collecting baseball cards this 1 season, and it is none too soon. The activity not only provides him with a link to the sport during a players' strike, but it is an initiation into the world of American business. For the lessons a boy learns from managing a shoebox full of baseball cards are as hard and sobering as any gotten over the bargaining table in a complex labor dispute.

Baseball card collecting teaches its participants all the ele- 2 ments of successful business practice. While it is of course not the only introduction to the realities of the business world, it is a traditional one for boys. To collect and trade cards requires a youngster to become comfortable, or at least proficient, in buying, selling, trading, risking, and generally managing his most important and valuable possessions at the time. There must be an awareness of worth and a deliberateness of purpose in trying to decide whether to specialize in getting the entire home team or to diversify by filling out an all-star team of interleague dimensions.

Assembling the capital of a baseball card collection is as in- 3 structive as any other stage of the activity. The boy must make what are usually among his own first purchases that cannot be wholly eaten or drunk. Although the wrapper may be ripped and discarded like that of a candy bar, the baseball cards and not the token bubble gum are the treasure inside. Buying a package of cards is as important to the young boy as purchasing a stock is to his father. But the element of mystery, the joy of the blind gamble of the purchase, is unique to baseball card collectors and venture capitalists. Unwrapping the package is a holiday, and scanning the contents is an adventure.

On the backs of his baseball cards a boy's fascination with numbers begins, preparing him for the Dow Jones industrial average, the Consumer Price Index, and Moody's credit ratings. Besides the heights and weights and birthdates, there are the columns of performance figures that contain as much mathematics and as many subtleties of interpretation as an adult will encounter in reading the market reports.

The young card collector soon learns to scan each new card for his touchstone statistics as naturally as the commuter scans the newspaper to follow his investments. The boy with a baseball card collection knows averages, records, and statistics the way a market analyst knows prices, dividends, and betas.

The seemingly idle hours spent reading the fine print behind the picture of a baseball player are rewarded in eye muscles attuned to the format of the business pages, not to mention in mental skills favorably inclined to mathematical achievement tests.

A boy's trading cards also give him the chronology of a baseball player's record through obscure minor league teams to success in the majors. The repeated reminder that success and celebrity come of humble beginnings is precisely the lesson one needs later to put his foot firmly on the bottom rung of the corporate ladder and begin his climb with deliberation.

Perhaps the greatest lessons of baseball cards are learned on the trading floors of boys' bedrooms. Here hard decisions and value judgments must be made by children alone in a world of cardboard adults. The worth of a card wanted must be weighed against that of a card or cards that might be traded for it. Order must be maintained among piles of cards numbering in the hundreds to the thousands, none of whose provenance or ownership is documented or documentable beyond the agreements of little gentlemen.

My son is now investing virtually all of his modest allowance   9
in baseball cards, and he is bullish on new issues. His present
portfolio consists of about 100 Fleer, 100 Don Russ, 200 Topps
common, and an odd lot of autographed Topps preferred. He
holds his own trading with the older boys, and soon I expect
him to be willing to trade more than just the Yankees for a
share of Telephone.

Not all traders are gentlemen, of course, and stories are told   10
among the eight- and nine-year-olds of eleven- and twelve-year-
olds to be watched. And the younger traders learn quickly that
it is against their interests to give in to unreasonable demands
for a card they want, no matter how badly. Even a Fernando
Valenzuela is not worth the whole Yankee team.

For all of its traditional values, however, there is one aspect   11
of business that baseball card trading does misrepresent. It is a
very sexist thing, and there are no women on the cards. Thus
the hobby is practiced among a network of good young boys
who may grow up thinking the good-old-boy network still excludes women. It does not, of course, but after their team and
position, the hirsute heroes on baseball cards are described by
the vital statistics of height and weight—6 feet 3 inches, 190
pounds—which all the boys want to attain. There are no
models here for girls.

Questions for Discussion

1. In the context of his essay, what does Petroski's title mean?
   Where in the essay is the connection explicitly made?
2. In your own words, explain the analogy that Petroski employs in this essay. (Glossary: *Analogy*) Does your experience tell you the analogy is valid? Why or why not?
3. Petroski uses a figure of speech in paragraph 7. (Glossary:
   Figures of Speech) What is that figure? Explain how it
   works.
4. Petroski's essay was published first in *The New York Times*
   and then in *Beyond Engineering*, two publications with

adult audiences. Adults do not normally collect baseball cards. Is the essay misdirected? Explain.

5. In paragraph 2, Petroski says, "Baseball card collecting teaches its participants all the elements of successful business practice." Yet, in his final paragraph he says, the hobby misrepresents one aspect of business. What is that aspect? Do you agree with Petroski? Is it impossible for girls to gain anything from card collecting?

6. Some of the diction that Petroski uses relates to the world of business. (Glossary: *Diction*) Give three or four examples of this diction. Does this usage hamper or aid him in getting his point across? Explain.

Vocabulary

Refer to your dictionary to define the following words as they appear in this selection. Then use each word in a sentence of your own.

sobering (1)
proficient (2)
venture capitalists (3)
touchstone (5)

attuned (6)
provenance (8)
hirsute (11)

Suggested Writing Assignments

1. Using Petroski's essay as a model, write about your present hobby or a hobby you had as a youngster. What did it teach you about the adult world? What kind of analogy would best explain the nature of the hobby and its role in preparing you for later life experiences?

2. Petroski's essay places a high premium on the value of numbers in the business world. Not all individuals who hold jobs in business place such value on the ability to work with numbers or the need to devote one's life to them. Write an essay in which you challenge or defend the supremacy of numbers in contemporary life.

THE DEATH OF BENNY PARET

Norman Mailer

Norman Mailer, born in Long Branch, New Jersey, in 1923, graduated from Harvard University in 1943 with a degree in engineering. While at Harvard, he made the decision to become a writer and, with the publication of his first novel, The Naked and the Dead *(1948), based on his war experiences in the Pacific during World War II, Mailer established himself as a writer of note. Mailer's literary interests have ranged widely over the years, from novels to nonfiction and journalism; from politics, sports, feminism, and lunar exploration to popular culture, ancient Egyptian culture, and criminality. In this account of the welterweight championship fight between Benny Paret and Emile Griffith, we can experience what Mailer himself felt as he sat at ringside the fateful night of March 25, 1962, the night of Paret's last fight. As you read, notice the way Mailer uses figures of speech to evoke the scene for the reader.*

P aret was a Cuban, a proud club fighter who had become 1 welterweight champion because of his unusual ability to take a punch. His style of fighting was to take three punches to the head in order to give back two. At the end of ten rounds, he would still be bouncing, his opponent would have a headache. But in the last two years, over the fifteen-round fights, he had started to take some bad maulings.

This fight had its turns. Griffith won most of the early 2 rounds, but Paret knocked Griffith down in the sixth. Griffith had trouble getting up, but made it, came alive and was dominating Paret again before the round was over. Then Paret began to wilt. In the middle of the eighth round, after a clubbing punch had turned his back to Griffith, Paret walked three disgusted steps away, showing his hindquarters. For a champion, he took much too long to turn back around. It was the first hint of weakness Paret had ever shown, and it must have inspired a particular shame, because he fought the rest of the fight as if he were seeking to demonstrate that he could take more punishment than any man alive. In the twelfth, Griffith caught him. Paret got trapped in a corner. Trying to duck away, his left arm and his head became tangled on the wrong side of the top rope. Griffith was in like a cat ready to rip the life out of a huge boxed rat. He hit him eighteen right hands in a row, an act which took perhaps three or four seconds, Griffith making a pent-up whimpering sound all the while he attacked, the right hand whipping like a piston rod which has broken through the crankcase, or like a baseball bat demolishing a pumpkin. I was sitting in the second row of that corner—they were not ten feet away from me, and like everybody else, I was hypnotized. I had never seen one man hit another so hard and so many times. Over the referee's face came a look of woe as if some spasm had passed its way through him, and then he leaped on Griffith to pull him away. It was the act of a brave man. Griffith was uncontrollable. His trainer leaped into the ring, his manager, his cut man, there were four people holding Griffith, but he was off on an orgy, he had left the Garden, he was back on a hoodlum's street. If he had been able to break loose from his handlers and the referee, he would have jumped Paret to the floor and whaled on him there.

And Paret? Paret died on his feet. As he took those eighteen 3 punches something happened to everyone who was in psychic range of the event. Some part of his death reached out to us. One felt it hover in the air. He was still standing in the ropes, trapped as he had been before, he gave some little half-smile of regret, as if he were saying, "I didn't know I was going to die just yet," and then, his head leaning back but still erect, his death came to breathe about him. He began to pass away. As he passed, so his limbs descended beneath him, and he sank slowly to the floor. He went down more slowly than any fighter had ever gone down, he went down like a large ship which turns on end and slides second by second into its grave. As he went down, the sound of Griffith's punches echoed in the mind like a heavy ax in the distance chopping into a wet log.

Questions for Study and Discussion

1. What differentiated Paret and Griffith for Mailer? Who was the welterweight champion?
2. What are the implications of Griffith's actions in the twelfth round of the fight for the sport of boxing in general?
3. Identify at least three similes in this essay. Why do you think Mailer felt the need to use figures of speech in describing Paret's death?
4. Mailer starts paragraph 3 with a question. What effect does this question have on you as a reader? (Glossary: *Rhetorical Question*)
5. Does Mailer place the blame for Paret's death on anyone? Explain.
6. Explain how Mailer personifies death in paragraph 3.

Vocabulary

Refer to your dictionary to define the following words as they are used in this selection. Then use each word in a sentence of your own.

wilt (2)   psychic (3)
spasm (2)   hover (3)

Suggested Writing Assignments

1. The death of Benny Paret was neither the first nor the last death to occur in professional boxing. Should boxing, therefore, be banned? Write an essay arguing for or against the continuation of professional boxing. As you write, use several figures of speech to enliven your essay.
2. Sports commentators and critics have pointed to the role fans have played in the promotion of violence in sports. If you feel that fans promote violent behavior, what do you suggest can be done, if anything, to alleviate the negative effect fans have? Using examples from your own experience in attending sporting events, write an essay explaining your position on this subject. Enrich your descriptions with figures of speech.

III

TYPES
OF
ESSAYS

10

ILLUSTRATION

Illustration is the use of examples to make ideas more concrete and to make generalizations more specific and detailed. Examples enable writers not just to tell but to show what they mean. For example, an essay about recently developed alternative sources of energy becomes clear and interesting with the use of some examples—say, solar energy or the heat from the earth's core. The more specific the example, the more effective it is. Along with general statements about solar energy, the writer might offer several examples of how the home building industry is installing solar collectors instead of conventional hot water systems, or building solar greenhouses to replace conventional central heating.

In an essay a writer uses examples to clarify or support the thesis; in a paragraph, to clarify or support the main idea. Sometimes a single striking example suffices; sometimes a whole series of related examples is necessary. The following paragraph presents a single extended example—an anecdote, or story—that illustrates the author's point about cultural differences:

> Whenever there is a great cultural distance between two people, there are bound to be problems arising from differences in behavior and expectations. An example is the American couple who consulted a psychiatrist about their marital problems. The husband was from New England and had been brought up by reserved parents who taught him to control his emotions and to respect the need for privacy. His wife was from an Italian family and had been brought up in close contact with all the members of her large family, who were extremely warm, volatile and demonstrative. When the husband came home after a hard day at the office, dragging his feet and longing for peace and quiet, his wife would rush to him and smother him. Clasping his hands, rubbing his brow, crooning over his

weary head, she never left him alone. But when the wife was upset or anxious about her day, the husband's response was to withdraw completely and leave her alone. No comforting, no affectionate embrace, no attention— just solitude. The woman became convinced her husband didn't love her and, in desperation, she consulted a psychiatrist. Their problem wasn't basically psychological but cultural.

Edward T. Hall

This single example is effective because it is *representative*— that is, essentially similar to other such problems he might have described and familiar to many readers. Hall tells the story with enough detail that readers can understand the couple's feelings and so better understand the point he is trying to make.

In contrast, Edwin Way Teale supports his topic sentence about country superstitions with eleven examples:

In the folklore of the country, numerous superstitions relate to winter weather. Back-country farmers examine their corn husks—the thicker the husk, the colder the winter. They watch the acorn crop—the more acorns, the more severe the season. They observe where white-faced hornets place their paper nests—the higher they are, the deeper will be the snow. They examine the size and shape and color of the spleens of butchered hogs for clues to the severity of the season. They keep track of the blooming of dogwood in the spring—the more abundant the blooms, the more bitter the cold in January. When chipmunks carry their tails high and squirrels have heavier fur and mice come into country houses early in the fall, the superstitious gird themselves for a long, hard winter. Without any scientific basis, a wider-than-usual black band on a woolly-bear caterpillar is accepted as a sign that winter will arrive early and stay late. Even the way a cat sits beside the stove carries its message to the credulous. According to a belief once widely held in the Ozarks, a cat sitting with its tail to the fire indicates very cold weather is on the way.

Edwin Way Teale

Teale uses numerous examples because he is writing about various superstitions. Also, putting all those strange beliefs

Illustration 189

side by side in a kind of catalogue makes the paragraph fun to read as well as informative.

Illustration is often found in effective writing; nearly every essay in this book contains one or more examples. Likewise this introduction has used examples to clarify its points about illustration.

BROTHERHOOD OF THE INEPT

David Binder

David Binder was born in London, England, in 1931. After graduating from Harvard in 1953 and studying at the University of Cologne in Germany, Binder entered the newspaper world as a reporter. He is now assistant news editor in the Washington Bureau of The New York Times. *Binder has written two books on Germany,* Berlin East and West *(1962) and* The Other German: The Life and Times of Willy Brandt *(1975), and his articles have appeared in such magazines as* The New Republic *and* The Nation. *In "Brotherhood of the Inept," Binder uses a series of funny examples to explain a particular pattern of behavior that he has discovered in his family. While the episodes he describes are humorous to us, they are often a source of pain and embarrassment for Binder.*

Probably it runs in the family, this clumsiness, not as a 1 river but at least as a stream enveloping one of us each generation. My father held on to a garage door handle after he had pulled it down. It slammed on his thumb. He fell off a bicycle and broke his arm. Once, when my mother threw a dress-up luncheon party in our backyard for his business colleagues, a tablecloth concealed a large irregularity on the edge of our rustic table. It was at this spot that my father, wearing a white suit, placed his plate of spaghetti with tomato sauce. It toppled into his lap. He changed into another white suit, sat down at the same place and spilled a second plate. Changing again upstairs, he dropped his pocket watch on the tile floor of the bathroom. It stopped.

One wet and icy February, the roof above our living room be- 2 gan to leak. In a business suit, my father mounted a ladder carrying a claw hammer. Losing his footing, he desperately pounded the claw through the asphalt shingles the way an Alpine climber uses an ice ax. He broke through the ceiling, and the leak increased.

These incidents amused the members of our family and gave me a brief and dangerous sense of superiority. Had I not recognized, at the relatively late age of twelve, that I was heir to the clumsy streak? Had the significance of my inability to throw a basketball through a hoop, much less dribble it, escaped me?

One day a friend took me along to a country club to work for him as a caddy. Golf was more alien to me than Albania. My first and last golfer asked for "a wood." I handed him a 5-iron. We reached the first green and he prepared to putt. I held the flag stick firmly in the hole. The ball hit the pole and bounced off. He cursed. "Clumsy!" I have kept my distance from the game these forty-three years.

At this distance, I can observe that what distinguishes the clumsy from the graceful is our total inability to recognize the functions at which we will surely fail—dancing, fancy diving, sanding wood, catching a fly ball or carrying a glass safely to a table. In high school, where sports were compulsory, I volunteered to dive for the swimming team, knowing, at least, that I would be a poor racer. I could never sufficiently coordinate two arm movements with two leg movements. I can still hear the voice through the loudspeaker announcing: "Binder will attempt a one-and-a-half gainer with a half twist." I lifted off the board, went into wild contortions and landed on my back, splashing the onlookers. I stayed for a time at the bottom of the pool, but when I finally surfaced they were still laughing. I retreated to the cross-country team.

In retrospect, it is the not-knowing that is so galling to the clumsy: not knowing when and where we are going to lumber. A modest facility at playing the clarinet or typing or even getting down a hill on skis is liable to seduce us into feeling that we may have overcome terminal awkwardness. Down this path, and not very far down it, lies a branch over which we will trip.

After years of summers paddling canoes and portaging them on narrow trails, I fancied myself handy with this mode of transportation. Not so. With my father in a canoe, I tipped over on a placid stretch of the upper Wisconsin River, prompting him, of all persons, to brand me: "Clumsy!" Recently I capsized a canoe while trying to retrieve a fishing lure that was snagged on a tree limb, dumping an old friend into the drink. Soon after, my friend lost his glasses. He, too, may belong to the brotherhood of the inept, but it is a mark of the clumsy not to be able to discern the trait readily in others.

When two clumsy persons get together, cataclysm is not far away. Once I was teasing my father in the presence of two of my friends. He playfully threw a short, clumsy punch that caught me in the stomach, sending me reeling across the room and slumping to the floor. My father and I were quite surprised at this sudden confluence of our mutual incoordination. My friends thought it was hilarious.   8

There is a blitheness that attends being clumsy. My father, for instance, floored the brake pedal of the family car at a crossroads where there was a conspicuous amount of loose gravel on the asphalt. The car spun completely around and ended up facing in the direction my father wished to go. His passenger, on leave after being wounded in the Africa campaign of World War II, was frightened more, he said, than by anything he had experienced in the desert fighting. Father only smiled and remarked: "Didn't I do that nicely?"   9

With the passage of much time, a degree of awareness may accumulate for the clumsy. Thus, I watched with a kind of eerie contentment as a recent house guest walked straight into our glass porch door twice within ten minutes. I was also able to appreciate the story of Vasil Bilak, the Czechoslovak Communist Politburo member whose proof of proletarian genuineness was displayed a few years ago at an exhibition commemorating the sixtieth anniversary of the founding of his ruling party in Prague. It was his certificate as a journeyman tailor from a town in Moravia, dated 1926. For ten crowns, a museum guard slipped the parchment out of its frame and displayed the reverse side. On it, the master tailor who examined yough Bilak had written: "He is all right on the trousers, but don't let him at the jackets."   10

But awareness has its limits. So I go on determinedly felling trees on power lines, painting windows shut, bumping people on dance floors, sawing crookedly and spilling sugar. Those, at least, are the clumsinesses I remember, but there may be thousands I never even noticed. My wife is plainly sympathetic,   11 maybe even empathetic. After I sharpen the kitchen knives, invariably nicking them, she usually cuts herself.

Perhaps recognition of clumsiness is at the root of my occa- 12
sional dream of having only to take a deep breath to be able to
rise unaided toward the heavens and, with a few deft hand
movements, to fly to an altitude of about five hundred feet. No
one else is up there with me, and those graceful tennis players,
golfers and fly fishermen I can still see below are in awe of my
gracefulness. In that dream I am never clumsy.

Questions for Study and Discussion

1. What does Binder believe distinguishes clumsy people from graceful people? What examples does he use to illustrate this distinction?
2. What for Binder is the most galling thing about being clumsy?
3. In paragraphs 1 and 2 Binder presents a series of examples showing his father's clumsiness. What generalization do they serve to illustrate?
4. What examples of his own clumsiness does Binder give to show that he belongs to the brotherhood of the inept? Did you find some examples more effective than others? Explain.
5. In paragraph 10 Binder says that "With the passage of much time, a degree of awareness may accumulate for the clumsy." How does he illustrate his own growing awareness? Does his awareness have its own limitations? Explain.
6. Do you think Binder has come to terms with his own clumsiness? What are Binder's feelings about his clumsiness? Where are these feelings expressed?

Vocabulary

Refer to your dictionary to define the following words as they
are used in this selection. Then use each word in a sentence of
your own.

rustic (1)   confluence (8)
galling (6)   blitheness (9)
lumber (6)   journeyman (10)
fancied (7)   empathetic (11)
placid (7)   deft (12)

Suggested Writing Assignments

1. Have there been times in your life when you sympathized or even empathized with someone like Binder who is "chronically" clumsy? Write an essay using examples from your own exepriences or observations in which you discuss how it feels to be awkward or clumsy in a variety of situations.

2. Using one of the following sentences as your thesis statement, write an essay giving examples from personal experience or from reading to support your opinion.

   Consumers have more power than they realize.

   Most products do/do not measure up to the claims of their advertisements.

   Religion is/is not alive and well.

   Government works far better than its critics claim.

   Being able to write well is more than a basic skill.

   The seasons for professional sports are too long.

   Today's college students are serious minded when it comes to academics.

ONE ENVIRONMENT, MANY WORLDS

Judith and Herbert Kohl

Herbert Kohl is a teacher and the author of The Open Classroom *(1970);* Thirty-Six Children *(1973);* Reading, How To *(1974); and* On Teaching *(1976). Also a teacher, Judith Kohl is a student of animal behavior and archaeology. In the following selection from their book* The View *from the* Oak *(1977), the Kohls give one extended example as an illustration of their belief that no two creatures view their environment in exactly the same way.*

Our dog Sandy is a golden retriever. He sits in front of our house all day waiting for someone to come by and throw him a stick. Chasing sticks or tennis balls and bringing them back is the major activity in his life. If you pick up a stick or ball to throw, he acts quite strangely. He looks at the way your body is facing and as soon as you throw something, he runs in the direction you seemed to throw it. He doesn't look at what you threw. His head is down and he charges, all ears. If your stick lands in a tree or on a roof, he acts puzzled and confused. He runs to the sound of the falling stick and sometimes gets so carried away that he will crash into a person or tree in the way as he dashes to the place he hears the stick fall. As he gets close, his nose takes over and smells the odor of your hand on the stick.

Once we performed an experiment to see how sensitive Sandy's nose really was. We were on a beach that was full of driftwood. There was one particular pile that must have had hundreds of sticks. We picked up one stick, walked away from the pile and then threw it back into the pile. It was impossible for us to tell with any certainty which stick we had originally chosen. So many of them looked alike to us that the best we could do was pick out seven sticks which resembled the one that had been thrown.

We tried the same thing with Sandy, only before throwing 3
the stick we carved an X on it. Then we threw it, not once but a
dozen times into the pile. Each time he brought back that stick.
Once we pretended to throw the stick and he charged the driftwood pile without noticing that one of us still had the stick. He
circled the pile over and over, dug out sticks, became agitated
but wouldn't bring another stick. It wasn't the shape or the size
or look of the stick that he used to pick it out from all the others. It was the smell we left on the stick.

It is hard to imagine, but for dogs every living creature has 4
its own distinctive smell. Each person can be identified by the
smell left on things. Each of us gives off a particular combination of chemicals. We can detect the smell of sweat, but even
when we are not sweating, we are giving off smells that senses
finer than ours can detect.

The noses of people have about five million cells that sense 5
smell. Dogs' noses have anywhere from 125 to 300 million cells.
Moreover, these cells are closer to the surface than are cells in
our noses, and more active. It has been estimated that dogs
such as Sandy have noses that are a million times more sensitive than ours. Clothes we haven't worn for weeks, places we've
only touched lightly indicate our presence to dogs. Whenever
Sandy is left alone in the house, on our return we find him surrounded by our sweaters, coats, handkerchiefs, shirts. He surrounds himself with our smell as if to convince himself that we
still exist and will return.

His ears are also remarkable. He can hear sounds that hu- 6
mans can't and at distances which are astonishing. It is hard
for us to know and understand that world. Most of us don't realize that no two people's hands smell the same. Our ears are
not the tuned direction finders his are. It takes a major leap of
the imagination to understand and feel the world the way he
does, to construct a complicated way of dealing with reality using such finely tuned smell and hearing. Yet his world is no
more or less real than ours. His world and ours fit together in
some ways and overlap in places. We have the advantage of being able to imagine what his experience is like, though he probably doesn't think too much about how we see the world. From
observing and trying to experience things through his ears and
nose we can learn about hidden worlds around us and understand behavior that otherwise might seem strange or silly.

The environment is the world that all living things share. It is   7
what is—air, fire, wind, water, life, sometimes culture. The environment consists of all the things that act and are acted upon.
Living creatures are born into the environment and are part of
it too. Yet there is no creature who perceives all of what is and
what happens. Sandy perceives things we can't, and we perceive and understand many things beyond his world. For a dog
like Sandy a book isn't much different than a stick, whereas for
us one stick is pretty much like every other stick. There is no
one world experienced by all living creatures. Though we all
live in the same environment, we make many worlds.

Questions for Study and Discussion

1. What point do the Kohls make in this essay, and where is it
   stated? (Glossary: *Thesis*)
2. What do the Kohls learn from the experiment described in
   paragraphs 2 and 3? What advantage do we have over
   animals like Sandy in learning about the hidden worlds
   around us?
3. How have the Kohls organized their essay? (Glossary: *Organization*) You may find it helpful to make a scratch outline
   of the essay to see how the paragraphs are interrelated.
4. What distinction do they make between the words *environment* and *world*?
5. Why do you suppose the authors use illustration to make
   their point?
6. How does the Kohls' use of examples give unity to their
   essay? (Glossary: *Unity*)

Vocabulary

Refer to your dictionary to define the following words as they
are used in this selection. Then use each word in a sentence of
your own.

agitated (3)   perceives (7)

Suggested Writing Assignments

1. Using the Kohls' statement "Though we all live in the same environment, we make many worlds" (7) as your topic sentence, write an essay supporting this thesis with examples from your own experience. For instance, how is your world different from that of your parents, teachers, friends, or roommates?

2. Using one of the following statements as your main idea, write an essay illustrating your thesis with examples from personal experience or from your reading.

   People show their intelligence in many different ways.

   If things can go wrong, they probably will.

   Many toys on the market today promote sexual stereotypes.

   School teaches us as many undesirable things as good things.

   Clothes do/do not make the man/woman.

WHAT MAKES A LEADER?

Michael Korda

*Michael Korda is the author of such best sellers
as* Male Chauvinism *(1979),* Power *(1975),*
Charmed Lives *(1979), and* Queenie *(1985). In this
essay, which first appeared in* Newsweek, *Korda
discusses the qualities that all good leaders have
in common. Notice Korda's use of a variety of
historic and contemporary examples to make his
definition concrete.*

Not every President is a leader, but every time we elect   1
a President we hope for one, especially in times of
doubt and crisis. In easy times we are ambivalent—the leader,
after all, makes demands, challenges the status quo, shakes
things up.

Leadership is as much a question of timing as anything else.   2
The leader must appear on the scene at a moment when people
are looking for leadership, as Churchill did in 1940, as
Roosevelt did in 1933, as Lenin did in 1917. And when he comes,
he must offer a simple, eloquent message.

Great leaders are almost always great simplifiers, who cut   3
through argument, debate and doubt to offer a solution everybody can understand and remember. Churchill warned the
British to expect "blood, toil, tears and sweat"; FDR told Americans that "the only thing we have to fear is fear itself"; Lenin
promised the war-weary Russians peace, land and bread.
Straightforward but potent messages.

We have an image of what a leader ought to be. We even rec-   4
ognize the physical signs: leaders may not necessarily be tall,
but they must have bigger-than-life, commanding features—
LBJ's nose and ear lobes, Ike's broad grin. A trademark also
comes in handy: Lincoln's stovepipe hat, JFK's rocker. We expect our leaders to stand out a little, not to be like ordinary
men. Half of President Ford's trouble lay in the fact that, if you
closed your eyes for a moment, you couldn't remember his

face, figure or clothes. A leader should have an unforgettable identity, instantly and permanently fixed in people's minds.

It also helps for a leader to be able to do something most of us can't: FDR overcame polio; Mao swam the Yangtze River at the age of 72. We don't want our leaders to be "just like us." We want them to be like us but better, special, more so. Yet if they are *too* different, we reject them. Adlai Stevenson was too cerebral. Nelson Rockefeller, too rich.

Even television, which comes in for a lot of knocks as an image-builder that magnifies form over substance, doesn't altogether obscure the qualities of leadership we recognize, or their absence. Television exposed Nixon's insecurity, Humphrey's fatal infatuation with his own voice.

A leader must know how to use power (that's what leadership is about), but he also has to have a way of showing that he does. He has to be able to project firmness—no physical clumsiness (like Ford), no rapid eye movements (like Carter).

A Chinese philosopher once remarked that a leader must have the grace of a good dancer, and there is a great deal of wisdom to this. A leader should know how to appear relaxed and confident. His walk should be firm and purposeful. He should be able, like Lincoln, FDR, Truman, Ike and JFK, to give a good, hearty, belly laugh, instead of the sickly grin that passes for good humor in Nixon or Carter. Ronald Reagan's training as an actor showed to good effect in the debate with Carter, when by his easy manner and apparent affability, he managed to convey the impression that in fact he was the President and Carter the challenger.

If we know what we're looking for, why is it so difficult to find? The answer lies in a very simple truth about leadership. *People can only be led where they want to go.* The leader follows, though a step ahead. Americans *wanted* to climb out of the Depression and needed someone to tell them they could do it, and FDR did. The British believed that they could still win the war after the defeats of 1940, and Churchill told them they were right.

A leader rides the waves, moves with the tides, understands the deepest yearnings of his people. He cannot make a nation that wants peace at any price go to war, or stop a nation determined to fight from doing so. His purpose must match the national mood. His task is to focus the people's energies and desires, to define them in simple terms, to inspire, to make what people already want seem attainable, important, within their grasp.

Above all, he must dignify our desires, convince us that we 11
are taking part in the making of great history, give us a sense of glory about ourselves. Winston Churchill managed, by sheer rhetoric, to turn the British defeat and the evacuation of Dunkirk in 1940 into a major victory. FDR's words turned the sinking of the American fleet at Pearl Harbor into a national rallying cry instead of a humiliating national scandal. A leader must stir our blood, not appeal to our reason. . . .

A great leader must have a certain irrational quality, a stubborn 12
refusal to face facts, infectious optimism, the ability to convince us that all is not lost even when we're afraid it is. Confucius suggested that, while the advisers of a great leader should be as cold as ice, the leader himself should have fire, a spark of divine madness.

He won't come until we're ready for him, for the leader is 13
like a mirror, reflecting back to us our own sense of purpose, putting into words our own dreams and hopes, transforming our needs and fears into coherent policies and programs.

Our strength makes him strong; our determination makes 14
him determined; our courage makes him a hero; he is, in the final analysis, the symbol of the best in us, shaped by our own spirit and will. And when these qualities are lacking in us, we can't produce him; and even with all our skill at image-building, we can't fake him. He is, after all, merely the sum of us.

Questions for Study and Discussion

1. What is Korda's thesis in this essay and where is it stated? Why do you suppose he states his thesis where he does instead of elsewhere in the essay? (Glossary: *Thesis*)
2. What, for Korda, are the major characteristics of a leader?

3. Identify the topic sentence in paragraph 4. What would be gained or lost if the topic sentence were placed elsewhere in the paragraph?

4. Korda's knowledge of history and great leaders is reflected in the examples he uses to support his topic sentences. Using paragraphs 2, 4, 8, and 11 explain how Korda's examples develop his topic sentences. (Glossary: *Example*)

5. What does Korda gain by using a series of short examples to support each point instead of a single extended example?

6. What does Korda mean when he says that "a great leader must have a certain irrational quality" (12)?

7. What would be gained or lost if paragraphs 13 and 14 were combined?

8. At the beginning of paragraph 9 Korda asks a rhetorical question, one that requires no answer and that is often used for emphasis. What is the purpose of this question in the context of his essay?

Vocabulary

Refer to your dictionary to define the following words as they are used in this selection. Then use each word in a sentence of your own.

ambivalent (1)	cerebral (5)
status quo (1)	affability (8)
eloquent (2)	infectious (12)

Suggested Writing Assignments

1. In his essay, Michael Korda presents his views on what makes a great leader. Most people would agree, however, that for a leader to lead there must be those who are willing to be led, to be good team players. Write an essay in which you explain what it takes to be a willing and productive participant in a group effort, whether the group be as small as a class or a basketball team or as large as a major corporation. While writing be especially conscious of selecting examples that clearly illustrate your thesis.

2. Select one of the following topics for a short essay:

What makes a good teacher?
What makes a good student?
What makes a good team captain?
What makes a good parent?

Make sure that your essay contains well-chosen examples.

LET'S HEAR IT FOR LOSERS!

Michael J. O'Neill

Michael J. O'Neill was born in Detroit, Michigan, in 1922. He interrupted his studies at the University of Detroit to serve in the U.S. Army during World War II and was awarded the Bronze Star. He graduated from Detroit in 1946 and studied for a year at Fordham University. In 1947 he joined United Press International as the syndicate's New York City and Washington correspondent. In 1956 O'Neill was hired by the New York Daily News *in the same capacity. During the next two decades he moved up in editorial rank, eventually becoming editor-in-chief, a post he held from 1975 until retirement in 1982. In his farewell speech to the American Society of Newspaper Editors, O'Neill spoke out against what he called "negative journalism": "What we need most of all in our profession is a generous spirit, infused with human warmth, as ready to see good as to suspect wrong, to find hope as well as cynicism, to have a clear but uncrabbed view of the world." It was in this spirit that O'Neill wrote "Let's Hear It for Losers!" for* Newsweek *in 1987. As you read his essay, watch how he uses examples to make each of his points about losers clear and understandable for his readers.*

Let me state my argument immediately: it's high time we show some appreciation for the losers of this world. They do more for the human race than most of the winners they create. But we are so steeped in the brine of success in this country we rarely give them a break. This is unfair. Losers provide an essential public service for a simple reason: without them, there would be no winners. Lee Iacocca became the star of TV commercials, a potential presidential candidate, a model for millions—while everyone forgets the name of the previous CEO who actually began the bailout at Chrysler.

Our heroes are the people on top of the heap, lionized and glamorized and turned into media icons. But as Andrew Carnegie once preached and Gore Vidal later observed: "It is not enough to succeed. Others must fail." Fame came to Donna Rice only when Gary Hart's bid for the presidency ran aground on the Monkey Business.

Losers are, therefore, a vital force in our capitalist system. By failing in business, politics and other walks of life, they screen out the weak in favor of the strong and the ambitious, the A-types who claw their way to power, wealth and appearances on "Nightline." It is the Darwinian process by which we choose our leaders and build a better America.

In its purest form, losing is one of mankind's highest callings. It is the primal element of progress. Failures precede the great discoveries. Lost battles are as important as military victories. Centuries of error pave the way to advances in civilization.

Socrates, who took hemlock to carry out his own death sentence, did more good for the world with his outlawed ideas than a million ancient winners. George III and the British Parliament fashioned failure out of folly but performed a noble service nonetheless—the blunders which cost them their American Colonies gave us a nation.

Columbus failed to find the East Indies but discovered America instead. Trial and error marked the long trail to stunning medical achievements, from decoding DNA to open-heart surgery and organ transplants. Dismissed as "moon mad" by the American military, Robert H. Goddard pioneered the missiles that revolutionized warfare and put the United States into space.

Defeat is the raw material from which champions are made. The Alamo gave us the state of Texas and the legend of Davy Crockett. And as the naval historian, Samuel Eliot Morison, said when describing the bitter battles for the Solomon Islands during World War II, "One learns more from defeat than from victory." Maybe so, but as John Kennedy mused after the Bay of Pigs, "There's an old saying that victory has a hundred fathers and defeat is an orphan."

Which I suppose is why we have so many of them. It's the   8
same with the poor, losers who are supposed to inherit the
earth but never do. They stay poor in large quantities so that a
few people can be millionaires, embodying the equation that
conservatives support but never endorse and liberals denounce
but never change. And the rich don't even leave big tips. So the
winners keep on winning, to loud applause, while the losers
keep on losing, without public credit.

Of course, some kinds of failure make a smaller contribution   9
to civilization than others. I'm forever misplacing my Ford in
those huge parking mazes, and after searching through acres of
cars, on seven different levels, my wife gasps in wonder at my
stupidity. This gives her a sense of smug satisfaction and is
clearly a losing proposition for me. There is no broader social
benefit. The same was true for the 1962 New York Mets. Although it contributed a colossal 120 victories to opponents, the
team was a doormat; its losses had little redeeming value. The
winners never felt a sense of accomplishment.

Clowns and comedians: The Mets did provide a lot of laughs,   10
though, which brings us to professional failures: clowns and
comedians. One of the oddest truths about human nature is
that we like to laugh at losers. A pratfall draws a guffaw every
time; it is an assertion of one person's superiority over another
or, perhaps, an example of Aristotle's "catharsis of such emotions." Kings have had their jesters while we have our Emmett
Kellys and Danny Kayes. Losers like Charlie Chaplin's Little
Tramp and Jackie Gleasons's Ralph Kramden. They made millions laugh, but their real-life creators failed at failure and became wealthy instead.

Among contemporary losers, one immediately thinks of   11
those antic actors in the Iran-contra farce. Like Lt. Col. Oliver
North. His zealous blundering produced a tumbrel of losers, including his commander in chief, and improved the nation by ex-
posing that secret foreign office in the White House. Ollie hurt
his loser status when he departed from the script to play a TV
hero instead of a villain in the congressional hearings. But
sales of Ollie videos and books have now collapsed. And the
special prosecutor's investigation could put enough new tar-
nish on his medals to reconfirm his eligibility for a losers' hall
of fame.

High honors can also be claimed for Elizabeth Dole. She sur-   12
rendered her cabinet position and put her career on hold in order to help her husband campaign for president. This selfless
decision may have deprived the nation of a great woman president, but it bolstered the sagging self-esteem of husbands.
More important, it was a noble sacrifice by one person for another; and it put Mrs. Dole in the company of heroes such as
Sydney Carton who, in "A Tale of Two Cities," went to the guil-
lotine to save his friend.

These kinds of sacrifices ennoble the loser's role in society;   13
they have civic value. Like the millions of sincere, hard-
working Americans who are losing honorably every day so that
others might succeed. They are unseen sources of our country's
greatness, silent patriots rejected by a society that glorifies
only success. Let us redress the wrong we have done them. Let
us make outstanding losers as eligible as winners for our Pulit-
zers and our Oscars. Let us proclaim April 1 National Losers
Day. Let us dedicate a monument to all who have failed for
their country and engrave on it this simple motto:

"They also serve who only stand and lose."   14

Questions for Study and Discussion

1. What is O'Neill's thesis, and where is it stated? (Glossary:
   Thesis)
2. What does O'Neill see as the importance of losers? Why
   does he believe Americans don't appreciate losers?
3. In paragraphs 5 and 6 O'Neill cites the stories of Socrates,
   George III, Columbus, modern medical achievements, and
   Goddard's missile research. What generalization do these
   examples illustrate?
4. What is O'Neill's point about the poor in paragraph 8? What
   does he mean when he says, "They stay poor in large quantities so that a few people can be millionaires, embodying the
   equation that conservatives support but never endorse and
   liberals denounce but never change"?
5. Are there some kinds of failure that have no societal value?
   Explain. What examples does O'Neill give?

6. The examples of Elizabeth Dole and Oliver North and his Iran-contra cohorts are current to the time O'Neill was writing. What general point do they illustrate?

7. What is the tone of O'Neill's essay? (Glossary *Tone*) Why do you suppose he suggests that April 1 be proclaimed "National Losers Day"?

Vocabulary

Refer to your dictionary to define the following words as they are used in this selection. Then use each word in a sentence of your own.

brine (1)   pratfall (10)
lionized (2)   guffaw (10)
icons (2)   catharsis (10)
folly (5)   tumbrel (11)
proposition (9)

Suggested Writing Assignments

1. Write an essay using the following statement as your thesis: "Americans are too concerned with winning." Use examples from your own experiences and observations to illustrate your points.

2. Each of us has been a "loser" at one time or another: we were on the losing baseball team, we didn't get the summer job we wanted, we failed a test in school, or we were ignored by people we wanted to get to know socially. Think of one or more such experiences that you have had, and write an essay in which you explain what you learned from being a "loser."

11

NARRATION

To *narrate* is to tell a story or to tell what happened. Whenever you relate an incident or use an anecdote to make a point, you use narration. In its broadest sense, narration is any account of an event or series of events. Although most often associated with fiction, narration is effective and useful in all kinds of writing.

Good narration has four essential features: a clear context; well-chosen details; a logical, often chronological organization; and an appropriate and consistent point of view. Consider, for example, the following paragraph from Willie Morris's "On a Commuter Train":

> One afternoon in late August, as the summer's sun streamed into the [railroad] car and made little jumping shadows on the windows, I sat gazing out at the tenement-dwellers, who were themselves looking out of their windows from the gray crumbling buildings along the tracks of upper Manhattan. As we crossed into the Bronx, the train unexpectedly slowed down for a few miles. Suddenly from out of my window I saw a large crowd near the tracks, held back by two policemen. Then, on the other side from my window, I saw a sight I would never be able to forget: a little boy almost severed in halves, lying at an incredible angle near the track. The ground was covered with blood, and the boy's eyes were opened wide, strained and disbelieving in his sudden oblivion. A policeman stood next to him, his arms folded, staring straight ahead at the windows of our train. In the orange glow of late afternoon the policemen, the crowd, the corpse of the boy were for a brief moment immobile, motionless, a small tableau to violence and death in the city. Behind me, in the next row of seats, there was a game of bridge. I heard one of the four men say as he looked out at the sight, "God, that's horrible." Another said, in a whisper, "Terrible, terrible." There was a momentary silence, punctuated only by the clicking

of the wheels on the track. Then, after the pause, I heard the first man say: "Two hearts."

Willie Morris

This paragraph contains all the elements of good narration. At the beginning Morris establishes a clear context for his narrative, telling when, where, and to whom the action happened. He has chosen details well, including enough detail so that we know what is happening but not so much that we become overwhelmed, confused, or bored. Morris organizes his narration logically, with a beginning that sets the scene, a middle that paints the picture, and an end that makes his point, all arranged chronologically. Finally, he tells the story from the first-person point of view: We experience the event directly through the writer's eyes and ears, as if we too had been on the scene of the action.

Morris could have told his story from the third-person point of view. In this point of view, the narrator is not a participant in the action, and does not use the pronoun *I.* In the following example, William Allen White narrates his daughter's fatal accident:

The last hour of her life was typical of its happiness. She came home from a day's work at school, topped off by a hard grind with the copy on the High School Annual, and felt that a ride would refresh her. She climbed into her khakis, chattering to her mother about the work she was doing, and hurried to get her horse and be out on the dirt roads for the country air and the radiant green fields of the spring. As she rode through the town on an easy gallop she kept waving at passers-by. She knew everyone in town. For a decade the little figure with the long pig-tail and the red hair ribbon has been familiar on the streets of Emporia, and she got in the way of speaking to those who nodded at her. She passed the Kerrs, walking the horse, in front of the Normal Library, and waved at them; passed another friend a few hundred feet further on, and waved at her. The horse was walking and, as she turned into North Merchant street she took off her cowboy hat, and the horse swung into a lope. She passed the Tripletts and waved her cowboy hat at them, still moving gaily north on Merchant street. A Gazette carrier passed—a High School boy friend—and she waved at him, but with her bridle hand: the horse veered quickly, plunged into the parking area where the low-hanging limb faced her, and, while she still looked back waving, the blow came. But she did not fall from the horse; she slipped off, dazed a bit, staggered and fell in a faint. She never quite recovered consciousness.

William Allen White

SHAME

Dick Gregory

*Dick Gregory, the well-known comedian, has
long been active in the civil rights movement.
During the 1960s Gregory was also an outspoken
critic of America's involvement in Vietnam. In
the following episode from his autobiography*
Nigger *(1964), he narrates the story of a childhood experience that taught him the meaning of
shame. Through his use of authentic dialogue
and vivid details, he dramatically re-creates this
experience for his readers.*

I never learned hate at home, or shame. I had to go to school
for that. I was about seven years old when I got my first big
lesson. I was in love with a little girl named Helene Tucker, a
light-complexioned little girl with pigtails and nice manners.
She was always clean and she was smart in school. I think I
went to school then mostly to look at her. I brushed my hair
and even got me a little old handkerchief. It was a lady's handkerchief, but I didn't want Helene to see me wipe my nose on
my hand. The pipes were frozen again, there was no water in
the house, but I washed my socks and shirt every night. I'd get a
pot, and go over to Mister Ben's grocery store, and stick my pot
down into his soda machine. Scoop out some chopped ice. By
evening the ice melted to water for washing. I got sick a lot that
winter because the fire would go out at night before the clothes
were dry. In the morning I'd put them on, wet or dry, because
they were the only clothes I had.

Everybody's got a Helene Tucker, a symbol of everything you
want. I loved her for her goodness, her cleanness, her popularity. She'd walk down my street and my brothers and sisters
would yell, "Here comes Helene," and I'd rub my tennis sneakers on the back of my pants and wish my hair wasn't so nappy
and the white folks' shirt fit me better. I'd run out on the street.
If I knew my place and didn't come too close, she'd wink at me

and say hello. That was a good feeling. Sometimes I'd follow her all the way home, and shovel the snow off her walk and try to make friends with her Momma and her aunts. I'd drop money on her stoop late at night on my way back from shining shoes in the taverns. And she had a Daddy, and he had a good job. He was a paper hanger.

I guess I would have gotten over Helene by summertime, but something happened in that classroom that made her face hang in front of me for the next twenty-two years. When I played the drums in high school it was for Helene and when I broke track records in college it was for Helene and when I started standing behind microphones and heard applause I wished Helene could hear it, too. It wasn't until I was twenty-nine years old and married and making money that I finally got her out of my system. Helene was sitting in that classroom when I learned to be ashamed of myself.

It was on a Thursday. I was sitting in the back of the room, in a seat with a chalk circle drawn around it. The idiot's seat, the troublemaker's seat.

The teacher thought I was stupid. Couldn't spell, couldn't read, couldn't do arithmetic. Just stupid. Teachers were never interested in finding out that you couldn't concentrate because you were so hungry, because you hadn't had any breakfast. All you could think about was noontime, would it ever come? Maybe you could sneak into the cloakroom and steal a bite of some kid's lunch out of a coat pocket. A bite of something. Paste. You can't really make a meal of paste, or put it on bread for a sandwich, but sometimes I'd scoop a few spoonfuls out of the paste jar in the back of the room. Pregnant people get strange tastes. I was pregnant with poverty. Pregnant with dirt and pregnant with smells that made people turn away, pregnant with cold and pregnant with shoes that were never bought for me, pregnant with five other people in my bed and no Daddy in the next room, and pregnant with hunger. Paste doesn't taste too bad when you're hungry.

The teacher thought I was a troublemaker. All she saw from the front of the room was a little black boy who squirmed in his idiot's seat and made noises and poked the kids around him. I guess she couldn't see a kid who made noises because he wanted someone to know he was there.

It was on a Thursday, the day before the Negro payday. The 7
eagle always flew on Friday. The teacher was asking each student how much his father would give to the Community Chest.
On Friday night, each kid would get the money from his father,
and on Monday he would bring it to the school. I decided I was
going to buy me a Daddy right then. I had money in my pocket
from shining shoes and selling papers, and whatever Helene
Tucker pledged for her Daddy I was going to top it. And I'd
hand the money right in. I wasn't going to wait until Monday to
buy me a Daddy.

I was shaking, scared to death. The teacher opened her book 8
and started calling out names alphabetically.

"Helene Tucker?" 9

"My daddy said he'd give two dollars and fifty cents." 10

"That's very nice, Helene. Very, very nice indeed." 11

That made me feel pretty good. It wouldn't take too much to 12
top that. I had almost three dollars in dimes and quarters in my
pocket. I stuck my hand in my pocket and held onto the money,
waiting for her to call my name. But the teacher closed her
book after she called everybody else in the class.

I stood up and raised my hand. 13

"What is it now?" 14

"You forgot me." 15

She turned toward the blackboard. "I don't have time to be 16
playing with you, Richard."

"My Daddy said he'd . . ." 17

"Sit down, Richard, you're disturbing the class." 18

"My Daddy said he'd give . . . fifteen dollars." 19

She turned around and looked mad. "We are collecting this 20
money for you and your kind, Richard Gregory. If your Daddy
can give fifteen dollars you have no business being on relief."

"I got it right now, I got it right now, my Daddy gave it to me 21
to turn in today, my Daddy said . . ."

"And furthermore," she said, looking right at me, her nos- 22
trils getting big and her lips getting thin and her eyes opening
wide, "we know you don't have a Daddy."

Helene Tucker turned around, her eyes full of tears. She felt 23
sorry for me. Then I couldn't see her too well because I was crying, too.

"Sit down, Richard." 24

And I always thought the teacher kind of liked me. She al- 25
ways picked me to wash the blackboard on Friday, after school.
That was a big thrill, it made me feel important. If I didn't wash
it, come Monday the school might not function right.

"Where are you going, Richard?" 26

I walked out of school that day, and for a long time I didn't go 27
back very often. There was shame there.

Now there was shame everywhere. It seemed like the whole 28
world had been inside that classroom, everyone had heard
what the teacher had said, everyone had turned around and felt
sorry for me. There was shame in going to the Worthy Boys Annual Christmas Dinner for you and your kind, because everybody knew what a worthy boy was. Why couldn't they just call
it the Boys Annual Dinner; why'd they have to give it a name?
There was shame in wearing the brown and orange and white
plaid mackinaw the welfare gave to three thousand boys.
Why'd it have to be the same for everybody so when you walked
down the street the people could see you were on relief? It was
a nice warm mackinaw and it had a hood, and my Momma beat
me and called me a little rat when she found out I stuffed it in
the bottom of a pail full of garbage way over on Cottage Street.
There was shame in running over to Mister Ben's at the end of
the day and asking for his rotten peaches, there was shame in
asking Mrs. Simmons for a spoonful of sugar, there was shame
in running out to meet the relief truck. I hated that truck, full
of food for you and your kind. I ran into the house and hid
when it came. And then I started to sneak through alleys, to
take the long way home so the people going into White's Eat
Shop wouldn't see me. Yeah, the whole world heard the teacher
that day, we all know you don't have a Daddy.

Questions for Study and Discussion

1. What does Gregory mean by "shame"? What precisely was
   he ashamed of, and what in particular did he learn from the
   incident?

2. How do the first three paragraphs of the essay help to establish a context for the narrative that follows?

3. Why do you think Gregory narrates this episode in the first-person point of view? What would be gained or lost if he instead wrote it in the third-person point of view?
4. What is the teacher's attitude toward Gregory? Consider her own words and actions as well as Gregory's opinion in arriving at your answer.
5. What role does money play in Gregory's narrative? How does money relate to his sense of shame?
6. Specific details can enhance the reader's understanding and appreciation of a narrative. Gregory's description of Helene Tucker's manners or the plaid of his mackinaw, for example, makes his account vivid and interesting. Cite several other specific details he gives, and consider how the narrative would be different without them.
7. Consider the diction of this essay. What effect does Gregory's repetition of the word *shame* have on you? Why do you think Gregory uses simple vocabulary to narrate this particular experience? (Glossary: *Diction*)

Vocabulary

Refer to your dictionary to define the following words as they are used in this selection. Then use each word in a sentence of your own.

nappy (2)   mackinaw (28)

Suggested Writing Assignments

1. Using Dick Gregory's essay as a model, write an essay narrating an experience that made you especially afraid, angry, surprised, embarrassed, or proud. Include sufficient detail so that your readers will know exactly what happened.
2. Most of us have had frustrating experiences with mechanical objects that seem to have perverse minds of their own. Write a brief narrative recounting one such experience with a vending machine, typewriter, television set, pay toilet, computer, pay telephone, or any other such machine. Be sure to establish a clear context for your narrative.

38 WHO SAW MURDER DIDN'T CALL POLICE

Martin Gansberg

*Martin Gansberg was born in 1920 in Brooklyn,
New York, and graduated from St. John's University. A long-time reporter, Gansberg wrote the
following article for* The New York Times *two
weeks after the early morning events he so
poignantly narrates. Once you've finished reading the essay, you will understand why it has
been so often reprinted and why the name Kitty
Genovese is still invoked whenever questions of
public apathy arise.*

For more than half an hour 38 respectable, law-abiding citi- 1
zens in Queens watched a killer stalk and stab a woman in
three separate attacks in Kew Gardens.

Twice their chatter and the sudden glow of their bedroom 2
lights interrupted him and frightened him off. Each time he returned, sought her out, and stabbed her again. Not one person
telephoned the police during the assault; one witness called after the woman was dead.

That was two weeks ago today. 3

Still shocked is Assistant Chief Inspector Frederick M. Lus- 4
sen, in charge of the borough's detectives and a veteran of 25
years of homicide investigations. He can give a matter-of-fact
recitation on many murders. But the Kew Gardens slaying baf-
fles him—not because it is a murder, but because the "good
people" failed to call the police.

"As we have reconstructed the crime," he said, "the assailant 5
had three chances to kill this woman during a 35-minute period. He returned twice to complete the job. If we had been
called when he first attacked, the woman might not be dead
now."

This is what the police say happened beginning at 3:20 A.M. in 6
the staid, middle-class, tree-lined Austin Street area:

Twenty-eight-year-old Catherine Genovese, who was called 7
Kitty by almost everyone in the neighborhood, was returning
home from her job as manager of a bar in Hollis. She parked
her red Fiat in a lot adjacent to the Kew Gardens Long Island
Rail Road Station, facing Mowbray Place. Like many residents
of the neighborhood, she had parked there day after day since
her arrival from Connecticut a year ago, although the railroad
frowns on the practice.

She turned off the lights of her car, locked the door, and 8
started to walk the 100 feet to the entrance of her apartment at
82–70 Austin Street, which is in a Tudor building, with stores
in the first floor and apartments on the second.

The entrance to the apartment is in the rear of the building 9
because the front is rented to retail stores. At night the quiet
neighborhood is shrouded in the slumbering darkness that
marks most residential areas.

Miss Genovese noticed a man at the far end of the lot, near a 10
seven-story apartment house at 82–40 Austin Street. She
halted. Then, nervously, she headed up Austin Street toward
Lefferts Boulevard, where there is a call box to the 102nd Police Precinct in nearby Richmond Hill.

She got as far as a street light in front of a bookstore before 11
the man grabbed her. She screamed. Lights went on in the 10-
story apartment house at 82–67 Austin Street, which faces the
bookstore. Windows slid open and voices punctuated the early-
morning stillness.

Miss Genovese screamed: "Oh, my God, he stabbed me! 12
Please help me! Please help me!"

From one of the upper windows in the apartment house, a 13
man called down: "Let that girl alone!"

The assailant looked up at him, shrugged, and walked down 14
Austin Street toward a white sedan parked a short distance
away. Miss Genovese struggled to her feet.

Lights went out. The killer returned to Miss Genovese, now 15
trying to make her way around the side of the building by the
parking lot to get to her apartment. The assailant stabbed her
again.

"I'm dying!" she shrieked. "I'm dying!" 16

Windows were opened again, and lights went on in many 17
apartments. The assailant got into his car and drove away. Miss
Genovese staggered to her feet. A city bus, O–10, the Lefferts
Boulevard line to Kennedy International Airport, passed. It
was 3:35 A.M.

The assailant returned. By then, Miss Genovese had crawled 18
to the back of the building, where the freshly painted brown
doors to the apartment house held out hope for safety. The
killer tried the first door; she wasn't there. At the second door,
82–62 Austin Street, he saw her slumped on the floor at the foot
of the stairs. He stabbed her a third time—fatally.

It was 3:50 by the time the police received their first call, 19
from a man who was a neighbor of Miss Genovese. In two minutes they were at the scene. The neighbor, a 70-year-old
woman, and another woman were the only persons on the
street. Nobody else came forward.

The man explained that he had called the police after much 20
deliberation. He had phoned a friend in Nassau County for advice and then he had crossed the roof of the building to the
apartment of the elderly woman to get her to make the call.

"I didn't want to get involved," he sheepishly told the police. 21

Six days later, the police arrested Winston Moseley, a 29- 22
year-old business-machine operator, and charged him with
homicide. Moseley had no previous record. He is married, has
two children and owns a home at 133–19 Sutter Avenue, South
Ozone Park, Queens. On Wednesday, a court committed him to
Kings County Hospital for psychiatric observation.

When questioned by the police, Moseley also said that he had 23
slain Mrs. Annie May Johnson, 24, of 146–12 133d Avenue, Ja-
maica, on Feb. 29 and Barbara Kralik, 15, of 174–17 140th Avenue, Springfield Gardens, last July. In the Kralik case, the police are holding Alvin L. Mitchell, who is said to have confessed
that slaying.

The police stressed how simple it would have been to have 24
gotten in touch with them. "A phone call," said one of the detectives, "would have done it." The police may be reached by dial-
ing "O" for operator or SPring 7–3100.

Today witnesses from the neighborhood, which is made up of 25 one-family homes in the $35,000 to $60,000 range with the exception of the two apartment houses near the railroad station, find it difficult to explain why they didn't call the police.

A housewife, knowingly if quite casually, said, "We thought it was a lovers' quarrel." A husband and wife both said, "Frankly, we were afraid." They seemed aware of the fact that events might have been different. A distraught woman, wiping her hands in her apron, said, "I didn't want my husband to get involved." 26

One couple, now willing to talk about that night, said they heard the first screams. The husband looked thoughtfully at the bookstore where the killer first grabbed Miss Genovese. 27

"We went to the window to see what was happening," he said, "but the light from our bedroom made it difficult to see the street." The wife, still apprehensive, added: "I put out the light and we were able to see better." 28

Asked why they hadn't called the police, she shrugged and replied: "I don't know." 29

A man peeked out from a slight opening in the doorway to his apartment and rattled off an account of the killer's second attack. Why hadn't he called the police at the time? "I was tired," he said without emotion. "I went back to bed." 30

It was 4:25 A.M. when the ambulance arrived to take the body of Miss Genovese. It drove off. "Then," a solemn police detective said, "the people came out." 31

Questions for Study and Discussion

1. What is the author's purpose in this selection? What are the advantages or disadvantages in using narration to accomplish this purpose? Explain. (Glossary: *Purpose*)

2. Where does the narrative actually begin? What is the function of the material that precedes the beginning of the narrative proper?

3. What reasons did Kitty Genovese's neighbors give for not calling the police when they first heard her calls for help?

What, in your opinion, do their reasons say about contemporary American society? Explain.

4. How would you describe Gansberg's tone? Is the tone appropriate for the story Gansberg narrates? Explain. (Glossary: *Tone*)

5. Gansberg uses dialogue throughout his essay. How many people does he quote? What does he accomplish by using dialogue? (Glossary: *Dialogue*)

6. What do you think Gansberg achieves by giving the addresses of the victims in paragraph 23?

7. Reflect on Gansberg's ending. What would be lost or gained by adding a paragraph that analyzed the meaning of the narrative for the reader? (Glossary: *Beginnings and Endings*)

Vocabulary

Refer to your dictionary to define the following words as they are used in this selection. Then use each word in a sentence of your own.

stalk (1)
recitation (4)
assailant (5)
staid (6)

shrouded (9)
sheepishly (21)
apprehensive (28)

Suggested Writing Assignments

1. Gansberg's essay is about public apathy and fear. What is your own experience with the public? Modeling an essay after Gansberg's, narrate yet another event or series of events that you personally know about. Or, write a narration about public involvement, one that contradicts Gansberg's essay.

2. It is common when using narration to tell about firsthand experience and to tell the story in the first person. It is good practice, however, to try writing a narration about something you don't know about firsthand but must learn about,

much the same as a newspaper reporter must do. For several days, be attentive to events occurring around you—in your neighborhood, school, community, region—events that would be an appropriate basis for a narrative essay. Interview the principal characters involved in your story, take detailed notes, and then write your narration.

THE DARE

Roger Hoffmann

Born in 1948, Roger Hoffmann is a free-lance writer and the author of The Complete Software Marketplace *(1984). Currently, he is at work on a novel about Vietnam. In "The Dare," first published in* The New York Times Magazine *in 1986, Hoffmann recounts how in his youth he accepted a friend's challenge to dive under a moving freight train and to roll out the other side. As an adult, Hoffmann appreciates the act for what it was—a crazy, dangerous childhood stunt. But he also remembers what the episode meant to him as a seventh grader trying to prove himself to his peers.*

The secret to diving under a moving freight train and rolling out the other side with all your parts attached lies in picking the right spot between the tracks to hit with your back. Ideally, you want soft dirt or pea gravel, clear of glass shards and railroad spikes that could cause you instinctively, and fatally, to sit up. Today, at thirty-eight, I couldn't be threatened or baited enough to attempt that dive. But as a seventh grader struggling to make the cut in a tough Atlanta grammar school, all it took was a dare.

I coasted through my first years of school as a fussed-over smart kid, the teacher's pet who finished his work first and then strutted around the room tutoring other students. By the seventh grade, I had more A's than friends. Even my old cronies, Dwayne and O.T., made it clear I'd never be one of the guys in junior high if I didn't dirty up my act. They challenged me to break the rules, and I did. The I-dare-you's escalated: shoplifting, sugaring teachers' gas tanks, dropping lighted matches into public mailboxes. Each guerrilla act won me the approval I never got for just being smart.

Walking home by the railroad tracks after school, we started   3
playing chicken with oncoming trains. O.T., who was failing
that year, always won. One afternoon he charged a boxcar from
the side, stopping just short of throwing himself between the
wheels. I was stunned. After the train disappeared, we debated
whether someone could dive under a moving car, stay put for a
10-count, then scramble out the other side. I thought it could be
done and said so. O.T. immediately stepped in front of me and
smiled. Not by me, I added quickly, I certainly didn't mean that
I could do it. "A smart guy like you," he said, his smile evapo-
rating, "you could figure it out easy." And then, squeezing each
word for effect, "I. . .DARE. . .you." I'd just turned twelve. The
monkey clawing my back was Teacher's Pet. And I'd been
dared.

As an adult, I've been on both ends of life's implicit business   4
and social I-dare-you's, although adults don't use those words.
We provoke with body language, tone of voice, ambiguous
phrases. I dare you to: argue with the boss, tell Fred what you
think of him, send the wine back. Only rarely are the risks
physical. How we respond to dares when we are young may
have something to do with which of the truly hazardous male
inner dares—attacking mountains, tempting bulls at Pamplo-
na—we embrace or ignore as men.

For two weeks, I scouted trains and tracks. I studied moving   5
boxcars close up, memorizing how they squatted on their axles,
never getting used to the squeal or the way the air fell hot from
the sides. I created an imaginary, friendly train and ran next to
it. I mastered a shallow, head-first dive with a simple half-
twist. I'd land on my back, count to ten, imagine wheels and,
locking both hands on the rail to my left, heave myself over and
out. Even under pure sky, though, I had to fight to keep my eyes
open and my shoulders between the rails.

The next Saturday, O.T., Dwayne and three eighth graders   6
met me below the hill that backed up to the lumberyard. The
track followed a slow bend there and opened to a straight,
slightly uphill climb for a solid third of a mile. My run started
two hundred yards after the bend. The train would have its
tongue hanging out.

The other boys huddled off to one side, a circle on another   7
planet, and watched quietly as I double-knotted my shoelaces.

My hands trembled. O.T. broke the circle and came over to me. He kept his hands hidden in the pockets of his jacket. We looked at each other. BB's of sweat appeared beneath his nose. I stuffed my wallet in one of his pockets, rubbing it against his knuckles on the way in, and slid my house key, wired to a red-and-white fishing bobber, into the other. We backed away from each other, and he turned and ran to join the four already climbing up the hill.

I watched them all the way to the top. They clustered together as if I were taking their picture. Their silhouette resembled a round-shouldered tombstone. They waved down to me, and I dropped them from my mind and sat down on the rail. Immediately, I jumped back. The steel was vibrating.

The train sounded like a cow going short of breath. I pulled my shirttail out and looked down at my spot, then up the incline of track ahead of me. Suddenly the air went hot, and the engine was by me. I hadn't pictured it moving that fast. A man's bare head leaned out and stared at me. I waved to him with my left hand and turned into the train, burying my face in the incredible noise. When I looked up, the head was gone.

I started running alongside the boxcars. Quickly, I found their pace, held it, and then eased off, concentrating on each thick wheel that cut past me. I slowed another notch. Over my shoulder, I picked my car as it came off the bend, locking in the image of the white mountain goat painted on its side. I waited, leaning forward like the anchor in a 440-relay, wishing the baton up the track behind me. Then the big goat fired by me, and I was flying and then tucking my shoulder as I dipped under the train.

A heavy blanket of red dust settled over me. I felt bolted to the earth. Sheet-metal bellies thundered and shook above my face. Count to ten, a voice said, watch the axles and look to your left for daylight. But I couldn't count, and I couldn't find left if my life depended on it, which it did. The colors overhead went from brown to red to black to red again. Finally, I ripped my hands free, forced them to the rail, and, in one convulsive jerk, threw myself into the blue light.

I lay there face down until there was no more noise, and I could feel the sun against the back of my neck. I sat up. The last ribbon of train was slipping away in the distance. Across the tracks, O.T. was leading a cavalry charge down the hill, five very small, galloping boys, their fists whirling above them. I pulled my knees to my chest. My corduroy pants puckered wet across my thighs. I didn't care.

Questions for Study and Discussion

1. Why did Hoffmann accept O.T.'s dare when he was twelve years old? Would he accept the same dare today? Why or why not?

2. How does paragraph 4 function in the context of Hoffmann's narrative?

3. How has Hoffmann organized his essay? (Glossary: *Organization*) What period of time is covered in paragraphs 2–5? In paragraphs 6–12? What conclusions about narrative time can you draw from what Hoffmann has done?

4. What were Hoffmann's feelings on the day of his dive under the moving freight train? Do you think he was afraid? How do you know?

5. Identify four figures of speech that Hoffmann uses in his essay. (Glossary: *Figures of Speech*) What does each figure add to his narrative?

6. Hoffmann tells his story in the first person: the narrator is the principal actor. What would have been gained or lost had Hoffmann used the third person, with O.T. or Dwayne telling the story? Explain.

Vocabulary

Refer to your dictionary to define the following words as they are used in this selection. Then use each word in a sentence of your own.

shards (1)	evaporating (3)
baited (1)	implicit (4)
cronies (2)	ambiguous (4)
escalated (2)	convulsive (11)
guerrilla (2)	

Suggested Writing Assignments

1. Can you remember any dares that you made or accepted while growing up? What were the consequences of these dares? Did you and your peers find dares a way to test or prove yourselves? Write a narrative essay about a dare that you made, accepted, or simply witnessed.

2. Each of us can tell of an experience that has been unusually significant for us. Think about your past, identify one experience that has been especially important for you, and write an essay about it. In preparing to write your narrative, you may find it helpful to ask such questions as: Why is the experience important for me? What details are necessary for me to re-create the experience in an interesting and engaging way? How can my narrative of the experience be most effectively organized? Over what period of time did the experience occur? What point of view will work best?

MOMMA, THE DENTIST, AND ME

Maya Angelou

Maya Angelou is perhaps best known as the author of I Know Why the Caged Bird Sings *(1970), the first of four books in the series which constitutes her autobiography. Starting with her beginnings in St. Louis in 1928, Angelou presents a life story of joyful triumph over hardships that tested her courage and threatened her spirit. Trained as a dancer, Angelou has also published three books of poetry, acted in the television series "Roots," and, at the request of Martin Luther King, Jr., served as a coordinator of the Southern Christian Leadership Conference. In the following excerpt from* I Know Why the Caged Bird Sings, *Angelou narrates what happened, and what might have happened, when her grandmother, the "Momma" of the story, takes her to the local dentist.*

The angel of the candy counter had found me out at last, and was exacting excruciating penance for all the stolen Milky Ways, Mounds, Mr. Goodbars and Hersheys with Almonds. I had two cavities that were rotten to the gums. The pain was beyond the bailiwick of crushed aspirins or oil of cloves. Only one thing could help me, so I prayed earnestly that I'd be allowed to sit under the house and have the building collapse on my left jaw. Since there was no Negro dentist in Stamps, nor doctor either, for that matter, Momma had dealt with previous toothaches by pulling them out (a string tied to the tooth with the other end looped over her fist), pain killers and prayer. In this particular instance the medicine had proved ineffective; there wasn't enough enamel left to hook a string on, and the prayers were being ignored because the Balancing Angel was blocking their passage.

1

I lived a few days and nights in blinding pain, not so much   2
toying with as seriously considering the idea of jumping in the
well, and Momma decided I had to be taken to a dentist. The
nearest Negro dentist was in Texarkana, twenty-five miles
away, and I was certain that I'd be dead long before we reached
half the distance. Momma said we'd go to Dr. Lincoln, right in
Stamps, and he'd take care of me. She said he owed her a favor.

I knew there were a number of whitefolks in town that owed   3
her favors. Bailey and I had seen the books which showed how
she had lent money to Blacks and whites alike during the Depression, and most still owed her. But I couldn't aptly remember seeing Dr. Lincoln's name, nor had I ever heard of a Negro's
going to him as a patient. However, Momma said we were going, and put water on the stove for our baths. I had never been
to a doctor, so she told me that after the bath (which would
make my mouth feel better) I had to put on freshly starched
and ironed underclothes from inside out. The ache failed to respond to the bath, and I knew then that the pain was more serious than that which anyone had ever suffered.

Before we left the Store, she ordered me to brush my teeth   4
and then wash my mouth with Listerine. The idea of even opening my clamped jaws increased the pain, but upon her explanation that when you go to a doctor you have to clean yourself all
over, but most especially the part that's to be examined,
I screwed up my courage and unlocked my teeth. The cool
air in my mouth and the jarring of my molars dislodged
what little remained of my reason. I had frozen to the pain,
my family nearly had to tie me down to take the toothbrush
away. It was no small effort to get me started on the road
to the dentist. Momma spoke to all the passers-by, but didn't
stop to chat. She explained over her shoulder that we were
going to the doctor and she'd "pass the time of day" on our way
home.

Until we reached the pond the pain was my world, an aura   5
that haloed me for three feet around. Crossing the bridge into
whitefolks' country, pieces of sanity pushed themselves forward. I had to stop moaning and start walking straight. The
white towel, which was drawn under my chin and tied over my
head, had to be arranged. If one was dying, it had to be done in
style if the dying took place in whitefolks' part of town.

On the other side of the bridge the ache seemed to lessen as if   6
a whitebreeze blew off the whitefolks and cushioned everything in their neighborhood—including my jaw. The gravel
road was smoother, the stones smaller and the tree branches
hung down around the path and nearly covered us. If the pain
didn't diminish then, the familiar yet strange sights hypnotized
me into believing that it had.

But my head continued to throb with the measured insis-   7
tence of a bass drum, and how could a toothache pass the calaboose, hear the songs of the prisoners, their blues and laughter,
and not be changed? How could one or two or even a mouthful
of angry tooth roots meet a wagonload of powhitetrash children, endure their idiotic snobbery and not feel less important?

Behind the building which housed the dentist's office ran a   8
small path used by servants and those tradespeople who ca-
tered to the butcher and Stamps' one restaurant. Momma and I
followed that lane to the backstairs of Dentist Lincoln's office.
The sun was bright and gave the day a hard reality as we
climbed up the steps to the second floor.

Momma knocked on the back door and a young white girl   9
opened it to show surprise at seeing us there. Momma said she
wanted to see Dentist Lincoln and to tell him Annie was there.
The girl closed the door firmly. Now the humiliation of hearing
Momma describe herself as if she had no last name to the
young white girl was equal to the physical pain. It seemed terribly unfair to have a toothache and a headache and have to bear
at the same time the heavy burden of Blackness.

It was always possible that the teeth would quiet down and   10
maybe drop out of their own accord. Momma said we would
wait. We leaned in the harsh sunlight on the shaky railings of
the dentist's back porch for over an hour.

He opened the door and looked at Momma. "Well, Annie,   11
what can I do for you?"

He didn't see the towel around my jaw or notice my swollen   12
face.

Momma said, "Dentist Lincoln. It's my grandbaby here. She   13
got two rotten teeth that's giving her a fit."

She waited for him to acknowledge the truth of her state-   14
ment. He made no comment, orally or facially.

"She had this toothache purt' near four days now, and today 15
I said, 'Young lady, you going to the Dentist.'"

"Annie?" 16

"Yes, sir, Dentist Lincoln." 17

He was choosing words the way people hunt for shells. "An- 18
nie, you know I don't treat nigra, colored people."

"I know, Dentist Lincoln. But this here is just my little grand- 19
baby, and she ain't gone be no trouble to you . . ."

"Annie, everybody has a policy. In this world you have to 20
have a policy. Now, my policy is I don't treat colored people."

The sun had baked the oil out of Momma's skin and melted 21
the Vaseline in her hair. She shone greasily as she leaned out of
the dentist's shadow.

"Seem like to me, Dentist Lincoln, you might look after her, 22
she ain't nothing but a little mite. And seems like maybe you
owe me a favor or two."

He reddened slightly. "Favor or no favor. The money has all 23
been repaid to you and that's the end of it. Sorry, Annie." He
had his hand on the doorknob. "Sorry." His voice was a bit
kinder on the second "Sorry," as if he really was.

Momma said, "I wouldn't press on you like this for myself 24
but I can't take No. Not for my grandbaby. When you come to
borrow my money you didn't have to beg. You asked me, and I
lent it. Now, it wasn't my policy. I ain't no moneylender, but
you stood to lose this building and I tried to help you out."

"It's been paid, and raising your voice won't make me change 25
my mind. My policy . . ." He let go of the door and stepped
nearer Momma. The three of us were crowded on the small
landing. "Annie, my policy is I'd rather stick my hand in a dog's
mouth than in a nigger's."

He had never once looked at me. He turned his back and went 26
through the door into the cool beyond. Momma backed up inside herself for a few minutes. I forgot everything except her
face which was almost a new one to me. She leaned over and
took the doorknob, and in her everyday soft voice she said,
"Sister, go on downstairs. Wait for me. I'll be there directly."

Under the most common of circumstances I knew it did no 27
good to argue with Momma. So I walked down the steep stairs,
afraid to look back and afraid not to do so. I turned as the door
slammed, and she was gone.

Momma walked in that room as if she owned it. She shoved   28
that silly nurse aside with one hand and strode into the dentist's
office. He was sitting in his chair, sharpening his mean instru-
ments and putting extra sting into his medicines. Her eyes were
blazing like live coals and her arms had doubled themselves in
length. He looked up at her just before she caught him by the
collar of his white jacket.

"Stand up when you see a lady, you contemptuous scoundrel."   29
Her tongue had thinned and the words rolled off well enunci-
ated. Enunciated and sharp like little claps of thunder.

The dentist had no choice but to stand at R.O.T.C. attention.   30
His head dropped after a minute and his voice was humble.
"Yes, ma'am, Mrs. Henderson."

"You knave, do you think you acted like a gentleman, speak-   31
ing to me like that in front of my granddaughter?" She didn't
shake him, although she had the power. She simply held him
upright.

"No, ma'am, Mrs. Henderson."   32

"No, ma'am, Mrs. Henderson, what?" Then she did give him   33
the tiniest of shakes, but because of her strength the action set
his head and arms to shaking loose on the ends of his body. He
stuttered much worse than Uncle Willie. "No, ma'am, Mrs. Hen-
derson, I'm sorry."

With just an edge of her disgust showing, Momma slung him   34
back in his dentist's chair. "Sorry is as sorry does, and you're
about the sorriest dentist I ever laid my eyes on." (She could af-
ford to slip into the vernacular because she had such eloquent
command of English.)

"I didn't ask you to apologize in front of Marguerite, because I   35
don't want her to know my power, but I order you, now and
herewith. Leave Stamps by sundown."

"Mrs. Henderson, I can't get my equipment . . ." He was shak-   36
ing terribly now.

"Now, that brings me to my second order. You will never   37
again practice dentistry. Never! When you get settled in your
next place, you will be a vegetarian caring for dogs with the
mange, cats with the cholera and cows with the epizootic. Is
that clear?"

The saliva ran down his chin and his eyes filled with tears.   38
"Yes, ma'am. Thank you for not killing me. Thank you, Mrs.
Henderson."

Momma pulled herself back from being ten feet tall with 39
eight-foot arms and said, "You're welcome for nothing, you var-
let, I wouldn't waste a killing on the likes of you."

On her way out she waved her handkerchief at the nurse and 40
turned her into a crocus sack of chicken feed.

Momma looked tired when she came down the stairs, but 41
who wouldn't be tired if they had gone through what she had.
She came close to me and adjusted the towel under my jaw (I
had forgotten the toothache; I only knew that she made her
hands gentle in order not to awaken the pain). She took my
hand. Her voice never changed. "Come on, Sister."

I reckoned we were going home where she would concoct a 42
brew to eliminate the pain and maybe give me new teeth too.
New teeth that would grow overnight out of my gums. She led
me toward the drugstore, which was in the opposite direction
from the Store. "I'm taking you to Dentist Baker in Texarkana."

I was glad after all that I had bathed and put on Mum and 43
Cashmere Bouquet talcum powder. It was a wonderful surprise. My toothache had quieted to solemn pain, Momma had
obliterated the evil white man, and we were going on a trip to
Texarkana, just the two of us.

On the Greyhound she took an inside seat in the back, and I 44
sat beside her. I was so proud of being her granddaughter and
sure that some of her magic must have come down to me. She
asked if I was scared. I only shook my head and leaned over on
her cool brown upper arm. There was no chance that a dentist,
especially a Negro dentist, would dare hurt me then. Not with
Momma there. The trip was uneventful, except that she put her
arm around me, which was very unusual for Momma to do.

The dentist showed me the medicine and the needle before he 45
deadened my gums, but if he hadn't I wouldn't have worried.
Momma stood right behind him. Her arms were folded and she
checked on everything he did. The teeth were extracted and she
bought me an ice cream cone from the side window of a drug
counter. The trip back to Stamps was quiet, except that I had to
spit into a very small empty snuff can which she had gotten for
me and it was difficult with the bus humping and jerking on
our country roads.

At home, I was given a warm salt solution, and when I 46
washed out my mouth I showed Bailey the empty holes, where

the clotted blood sat like filling in a pie crust. He said I was quite brave, and that was my cue to reveal our confrontation with the peckerwood dentist and Momma's incredible powers.

I had to admit that I didn't hear the conversation, but what   47
else could she have said than what I said she said? What else done? He agreed with my analysis in a lukewarm way, and I happily (after all, I'd been sick) flounced into the Store. Momma was preparing our evening meal and Uncle Willie leaned on the door sill. She gave her version.

"Dentist Lincoln got right uppity. Said he'd rather put his   48
hand in a dog's mouth. And when I reminded him of the favor, he brushed it off like a piece of lint. Well, I sent Sister downstairs and went inside. I hadn't never been in his office before, but I found the door to where he takes out teeth, and him and the nurse was in there thick as thieves. I just stood there till he caught sight of me." Crash bang the pots on the stove. "He jumped just like he was sitting on a pin. He said, 'Annie, I done tole you, I ain't gonna mess around in no niggah's mouth.' I said, 'Somebody's got to do it then,' and he said, 'Take her to Texarkana to the colored dentist' and that's when I said, 'If you paid me my money I could afford to take her.' He said, 'It's all been paid.' I tole him everything but the interest been paid. He said ' 'Twasn't no interest.' I said, ' 'Tis now. I'll take ten dollars as payment in full.' You know, Willie, it wasn't no right thing to do, 'cause I lent that money without thinking about it.

"He tole that little snippity nurse of his'n to give me ten dol-   49
lars and make me sign a 'paid in full' receipt. She gave it to me and I signed the papers. Even though by rights he was paid up before, I figger, he gonna be that kind of nasty, he gonna have to pay for it."

Momma and her son laughed and laughed over the white   50
man's evilness and her retributive sin.

I preferred, much preferred, my version.   51

Questions for Study and Discussion

1. What is Angelou's purpose in narrating the story she tells? (Glossary: *Purpose*)
2. Compare and contrast the content and style of the interaction between Momma and the dentist that is given in italics

with the one given at the end of the narrative. (Glossary: *Comparison and Contrast*)

3. Angelou tells her story chronologically and in the first person. What are the advantages of the first-person narrative?

4. Identify three similes that Angelou uses in her narrative. Explain how each simile serves her purposes. (Glossary: *Figures of Speech*)

5. Why do you suppose Angelou says she prefers her own version of the episode to that of her grandmother?

6. This story is a story of pain and not just the pain of a toothache. How does Angelou describe the pain of the toothache? What other pain does Angelou tell of in this autobiographical narrative?

Vocabulary

Refer to your dictionary to define the following words as they are used in this selection. Then use each word in a sentence of your own.

bailiwick (1)   varlet (39)
calaboose (7)   concoct (42)
mite (22)   snippety (49)
vernacular (34)   retributive (50)

Suggested Writing Assignments

1. One of Angelou's themes in "Momma, the Dentist, and Me" is that cruelty, whether racial, social, professional, or personal, is very difficult to endure and leaves a lasting impression on a person. Think of a situation where an unthinking or insensitive person made you feel inferior for reasons beyond your control. Prewrite by listing the sequence of events in your narrative before you draft it. You may find it helpful to reread the introduction to this section before you begin working.

2. Write a narrative in which, like Angelou, you give two versions of an actual event—one the way you thought or wished it happened and the other the way events actually took place.

12

DESCRIPTION

To describe is to create a verbal picture. A person, a place, a thing—even an idea or a state of mind—can be made vividly concrete through description. Here, for example, is Thomas Mann's brief description of a delicatessen:

> It was a narrow room, with a rather high ceiling, and crowded from floor to ceiling with goodies. There were rows and rows of hams and sausages of all shapes and colors—white, yellow, red, and black; fat and lean and round and long—rows of canned preserves, cocoa and tea, bright translucent glass bottles of honey, marmalade, and jam; round bottles and slender bottles, filled with liqueurs and punch—all these things crowded every inch of the shelves from top to bottom.

Writing any description requires, first of all, that the writer gather many details about a subject, relying not only on what the eyes see but on the other sense impressions—touch, taste, smell, hearing—as well. From this catalogue of details the writer selects those that will most effectively create a *dominant impression*—the single quality, mood, or atmosphere that the writer wishes to emphasize. Consider, for example, the details that Mary McCarthy uses to evoke the dominant impression in the following passage from *Memories of a Catholic Girlhood:*

> Whenever we children came to stay at my grandmother's house, we were put to sleep in the sewing room, a bleak, shabby, utilitarian rectangle, more office than bedroom, more attic than office, that played to the hierarchy of chambers the role of poor relation. It was a room without pride: the old sewing machine, some cast-off chairs, a shadeless lamp, rolls of wrapping paper, piles of cardboard boxes that might someday come in handy, papers of pins, and remnants of a material united with the iron fold-

ing cots put out for our use and the bare floor boards to give an impression of intense and ruthless temporality. Thin white spreads, of the kind used in hospitals and charity institutions, and naked blinds at the windows reminded us of our orphaned condition and of the ephemeral character of our visit; there was nothing here to encourage us to consider this our home.

The dominant impression that McCarthy creates is one of clutter, bleakness, and shabbiness. There is nothing in the sewing room that suggests permanence or warmth.

Writers must also carefully plan the order in which to present their descriptive details. The pattern of organization must fit the subject of the description logically and naturally, and must also be easy to follow. For example, visual details can be arranged spatially—from left to right, top to bottom, near to far, or in any other logical order. Other patterns include smallest to largest, softest to loudest, least significant to most significant, most unusual to least unusual. McCarthy suggests a jumble of junk not only by her choice of details but by the apparently random order in which she presents them.

How much detail is enough? There is no fixed answer. A good description includes enough vivid details to create a dominant impression and to bring a scene to life, but not so many that readers are distracted, confused, or bored. In an essay that is purely descriptive, there is room for much detail. Usually, however, writers use description to create the setting for a story, to illustrate ideas, to help clarify a definition or a comparison, or to make the complexities of a process more understandable. Such descriptions should be kept short, and should include just enough detail to make them clear and helpful.

SUBWAY STATION

Gilbert Highet

*Gilbert Highet (1906–1978) was born in Scotland
and became a naturalized United States citizen
in 1951. A prolific writer and translator, Highet
was for many years a professor of classics at Columbia University. The following selection is
taken from his book* Talents and Geniuses *(1957).
Notice the author's keen eye for detail as he describes the unseemly world of a subway station.*

Standing in a subway station, I began to appreciate the
place—almost to enjoy it. First of all, I looked at the lighting: a row of meager electric bulbs, unscreened, yellow, and
coated with filth, stretched toward the black mouth of the tunnel, as though it were a bolt hole in an abandoned coal mine.
Then I lingered, with zest, on the walls and ceiling: lavatory
tiles which had been white about fifty years ago, and were now
encrusted with soot, coated with the remains of a dirty liquid
which might be either atmospheric humidity mingled with
smog or the result of a perfunctory attempt to clean them with
cold water; and, above them, gloomy vaulting from which
dingy paint was peeling off like scabs from an old wound, sick
black paint leaving a leprous white undersurface. Beneath my
feet, the floor was a nauseating dark brown with black stains
upon it which might be stale oil or dry chewing gum or some
worse defilement; it looked like the hallway of a condemned
slum building. Then my eye traveled to the tracks, where two
lines of glittering steel—the only positively clean objects in the
whole place—ran out of darkness into darkness above an un-
speakable mass of congealed oil, puddles of dubious liquid, and
a mishmash of old cigarette packets, mutilated and filthy newspapers, and the débris that filtered down from the street above
through a barred grating in the roof. As I looked up toward the
sunlight, I could see more débris sifting slowly downward, and
making an abominable pattern in the slanting beam of dirt-

238

laden sunlight. I was going on to relish more features of this unique scene: such as the advertisement posters on the walls—here a text from the Bible, there a half-naked girl, here a woman wearing a hat consisting of a hen sitting on a nest full of eggs, and there a pair of girl's legs walking up the keys of a cash register—all scribbled over with unknown names and well-known obscenities in black crayon and red lipstick; but then my train came in at last, I boarded it, and began to read. The experience was over for the time.

Questions for Study and Discussion

1. What dominant impression of the subway station does Highet create in his description? (Glossary: *Dominant Impression*)
2. To present a clearly focused dominant impression, a writer must be selective in the use of details. Make a list of those details that help create Highet's dominant impression.
3. Highet uses a spatial organization in his essay. Trace the order in which he describes the various elements of the subway station. (Glossary: *Organization*)
4. What similes and metaphors can you find in Highet's description? How do they help to make the description vivid? (Glossary: *Figures of Speech*)
5. Is this a first-time experience for Highet, or do you think he is a regular subway traveler? What in the essay leads you to your conclusion?

Vocabulary

Refer to your dictionary to define the following words as they are used in this selection. Then use each word in a sentence of your own.

meager	congealed
zest	dubious
defilement	unique

Suggested Writing Assignments

1. If you are familar with a subway station, write a lengthy one-paragraph description of it just as Highet has done. Once you have completed your description, compare and contrast your description with Highet's. How does the dominant impression you have created differ from the one Highet has created?

2. Write a short essay in which you describe one of the following places, or another place of your choice. Arrange the details of your description from top to bottom, left to right, near to far, or according to some other spatial organization.

    an airport terminal

    a pizza parlor

    a locker room

    a barbershop or beauty salon

    a bookstore

    a campus dining hall

THE SOUNDS OF THE CITY

James Tuite

James Tuite has had a long career at The New York Times, *where he once served as sports editor. As a free-lance writer he has contributed to all of the major sports magazines and has written* Snowmobiles and Snowmobiling *(1973) and* How to Enjoy Sports on TV *(1976). The following selection is a model of how a place can be described by using a sense other than sight. Tuite describes New York City by its sounds, which for him comprise the very life of the city.*

New York is a city of sounds: muted sounds and shrill sounds; shattering sounds and soothing sounds; urgent sounds and aimless sounds. The cliff dwellers of Manhattan— who would be racked by the silence of the lonely woods—do not hear these sounds because they are constant and eternally urban.

The visitor to the city can hear them, though, just as some animals can hear a high-pitched whistle inaudible to humans. To the casual caller to Manhattan, lying restive and sleepless in a hotel twenty or thirty floors above the street, they tell a story as fascinating as life itself. And back of the sounds broods the silence.

Night in midtown is the noise of tinseled honky-tonk and violence. Thin strains of music, usually the firm beat of rock 'n' roll or the frenzied outbursts of the discotheque, rise from ground level. This is the cacophony, the discordance of youth, and it comes on strongest when nights are hot and young blood restless.

Somewhere in the canyons below there is shrill laughter or raucous shouting. A bottle shatters against concrete. The whine of a police siren slices through the night, moving ever

closer, until an eerie Doppler effect* brings it to a guttural
halt.

There are few sounds so exciting in Manhattan as those of
fire apparatus dashing through the night. At the outset there is
the tentative hint of the first-due company bullying his way
through midtown traffic. Now a fire whistle from the opposite
direction affirms that trouble is, indeed, afoot. In seconds,
other sirens converging from other streets help the skytop listener focus on the scene of excitement.

But he can only hear and not see, and imagination takes
flight. Are the flames and smoke gushing from windows not far
away? Are victims trapped there, crying out for help? Is it a
conflagration, or only a trash-basket fire? Or, perhaps, it is
merely a false alarm.

The questions go unanswered and the urgency of the moment
dissolves. Now the mind and the ear detect the snarling, arro-
gant bickering of automobile horns. People in a hurry. Taxi-
cabs blaring, insisting on their checkered priority.

Even the taxi horns dwindle down to a precocious few in the
gray and pink moments of dawn. Suddenly there is another
sound, a morning sound that taunts the memory for recognition. The growl of a predatory monster? No, just garbage
trucks that have begun a day of scavenging.

Trash cans rattle outside restaurants. Metallic jaws on sani-
tation trucks gulp and masticate the residue of daily living,
then digest it with a satisfied groan of gears. The sounds of the
new day are businesslike. The growl of buses, so scattered and
distant at night, becomes a demanding part of the traffic bed-
lam. An occasional jet or helicopter injects an exclamation
point from an unexpected quarter. When the wind is right, the
vibrant bellow of an ocean liner can be heard.

The sounds of the day are as jarring as the glare of a sun that
outlines the canyons of midtown in drab relief. A pneumatic
drill frays countless nerves with its rat-a-tat-tat, for dig they
must to perpetuate the city's dizzy motion. After each screech

---

*The drop in pitch that occurs as a source of sound quickly passes by a listener.

of brakes there is a moment of suspension, of waiting for the thud or crash that never seems to follow.

The whistles of traffic policemen and hotel doormen chirp from all sides, like birds calling for their mates across a frenzied aviary. And all of these sounds are adult sounds, for childish laughter has no place in these canyons.

Night falls again, the cycle is complete, but there is no surcease from sound. For the beautiful dreamers, perhaps, the "sounds of the rude world heard in the day, lulled by the moonlight have all passed away," but this is not so in the city.

Too many New Yorkers accept the sounds about them as bland parts of everyday existence. They seldom stop to listen to the sounds, to think about them, to be appalled or enchanted by them. In the big city, sounds are life.

Questions for Study and Discussion

1. What is Tuite's purpose in describing the sounds of New York City? (Glossary: *Purpose*)
2. How does Tuite organize his essay? Do you think that the organization is effective? (Glossary: *Organization*)
3. Tuite describes "raucous shouting" and the "screech of brakes." Make a list of the various other sounds that he describes in his essay. How do the varied adjectives and verbs Tuite uses to capture the essence of each sound enhance his description? (Glossary: *Diction*)
4. According to Tuite, why are visitors to New York City more sensitive to or aware of the multitude of sounds than the "cliff dwellers of Manhattan" (1)? What does he believe New Yorkers have missed when they fail to take notice of these sounds?
5. Locate several metaphors and similes in the essay. What picture of the city does each one give you? (Glossary: *Figures of Speech*)
6. What dominant impression of New York City does Tuite create in this essay? (Glossary: *Dominant Impression*)

Vocabulary

Refer to your dictionary to define the following words as they are used in this selection. Then use each word in a sentence of your own.

muted (1)   precocious (8)
inaudible (2)   taunts (8)
restive (2)   vibrant (9)
raucous (4)   perpetuate (10)
tentative (5)

Suggested Writing Assignments

1. In a short composition describe a city or another place that you know well. Try to capture as many sights, sounds, and smells as you can to depict the place you describe. Your goal should be to create a single dominant impression of the place, as Tuite does in his essay.

2. Describe an inanimate object familiar to you so as to bring out its character and make it interesting to a reader. First determine your purpose for describing the object. For example, suppose your family has had a dining table ever since you can remember. Think of what that table has been a part of over the years—the birthday parties, the fights, the holiday meals, the sad times, the intimate times, the long hours of studying and doing homework. Probably such a table would be worth describing for the way it has figured prominently in the history of your family. Next make an exhaustive list of the object's physical features; then write your descriptive essay.

UNFORGETTABLE MISS BESSIE

Carl T. Rowan

*Carl T. Rowan is a former ambassador to Fin-
land and was director of the United States Information Agency. Born in 1925 in Ravenscroft,
Tennessee, he received degrees from Oberlin College and the University of Minnesota. Once a
columnist for the* Minneapolis Tribune *and the*
Chicago Sun-Times, *Rowan is now a syndicated
columnist and a* Reader's Digest *roving editor.
In the following essay, Rowan describes his former high-school teacher whose lessons went far
beyond the subjects she taught.*

She was only about five feet tall and probably never 1
weighed more than 110 pounds, but Miss Bessie was a
towering presence in the classroom. She was the only woman
tough enough to make me read *Beowulf* and think for a few
foolish days that I liked it. From 1938 to 1942, when I attended
Bernard High School in McMinnville, Tenn., she taught me English, history, civics—and a lot more than I realized.

I shall never forget the day she scolded me into reading 2
Beowulf.

"But Miss Bessie," I complained, "I ain't much interested 3
in it."

Her large brown eyes became daggerish slits. "Boy," she 4
said, "how dare you say 'ain't' to me! I've taught you better
than that."

"Miss Bessie," I pleaded, "I'm trying to make first-string end 5
on the football team, and if I go around saying 'it isn't' and
'they aren't,' the guys are gonna laugh me off the squad."

"Boy," she responded, "you'll play football because you have 6
guts. But do you know what *really* takes guts? Refusing to
lower your standards to those of the crowd. It takes guts to say
you've got to live and be somebody fifty years after all the football games are over."

I started saying "it isn't" and "they aren't," and I still made ⁊ first-string end—and class valedictorian—without losing my buddies' respect.

During her remarkable 44-year career, Mrs. Bessie Taylor ⁸ Gwynn taught hundreds of economically deprived black youngsters—including my mother, my brother, my sisters and me. I remember her now with gratitude and affection—especially in this era when Americans are so wrought-up about a "rising tide of mediocrity" in public education and the problems of finding competent, caring teachers. Miss Bessie was an example of an informed, dedicated teacher, a blessing to children and an asset to the nation.

Born in 1895, in poverty, she grew up in Athens, Ala., where ⁹ there was no public school for blacks. She attended Trinity School, a private institution for blacks run by the American Missionary Association, and in 1911 graduated from the Normal School (a "super" high school) at Fisk University in Nashville. Mrs. Gwynn, the essence of pride and privacy, never talked about her years in Athens; only in the months before her death did she reveal that she had never attended Fisk University itself because she could not afford the four-year course.

At Normal School she learned a lot about Shakespeare, but 10 most of all about the profound importance of education—especially, for a people trying to move up from slavery. "What you put in your head, boy," she once said, "can never be pulled out by the Ku Klux Klan, the Congress or anybody."

Miss Bessie's bearing of dignity told anyone who met her 11 that she was "educated" in the best sense of the word. There was never a discipline problem in her classes. We didn't dare mess with a woman who knew about the Battle of Hastings, the Magna Carta and the Bill of Rights—and who could also play the piano.

This frail-looking woman could make sense of Shakespeare, 12 Milton, Voltaire, and bring to life Booker T. Washington and W. E. B. DuBois. Believing that it was important to know who the officials were that spent taxpayers' money and made public policy, she made us memorize the names of everyone on the Supreme Court and in the President's Cabinet. It could be embarrassing to be unprepared when Miss Bessie said, "Get up and tell the class who Frances Perkins is and what you think about her."

Miss Bessie knew that my family, like so many others during the Depression, couldn't afford to subscribe to a newspaper. She knew we didn't even own a radio. Still, she prodded me to "look out for your future and find some way to keep up with what's going on in the world." So I became a delivery boy for the Chattanooga *Times*. I rarely made a dollar a week, but I got to read a newspaper every day.   13

Miss Bessie noticed things that had nothing to do with schoolwork, but were vital to a youngster's development. Once a few classmates made fun of my frayed, hand-me-down overcoat, calling me "Strings." As I was leaving school, Miss Bessie patted me on the back of that old overcoat and said, "Carl, never fret about what you *don't* have. Just make the most of what you *do* have—a brain."   14

Among the things that I did not have was electricity in the little frame house that my father had built for $400 with his World War I bonus. But because of her inspiration, I spent many hours squinting beside a kerosene lamp reading Shakespeare and Thoreau, Samuel Pepys and William Cullen Bryant.   15

No one in my family had ever graduated from high school, so there was no tradition of commitment to learning for me to lean on. Like millions of youngsters in today's ghettos and barrios, I needed the push and stimulation of a teacher who truly cared. Miss Bessie gave plenty of both, as she immersed me in a wonderful world of similes, metaphors and even onomatopoeia. She led me to believe that I could write sonnets as well as Shakespeare, or iambic-pentameter verse to put Alexander Pope to shame.   16

In those days the McMinnville school system was rigidly "Jim Crow," and poor black children had to struggle to put anything in their heads. Our high school was only slightly larger than the once-typical little red schoolhouse, and its library was outrageously inadequate—so small, I like to say, that if two students were in it and one wanted to turn a page, the other one had to step outside.   17

Negroes, as we were called then, were not allowed in the town library, except to mop floors or dust tables. But through   18 one of those secret Old South arrangements between whites of conscience and blacks of stature, Miss Bessie kept getting books smuggled out of the white library. That is how she introduced me to the Brontës, Byron, Coleridge, Keats and Tennyson. "If you don't read, you can't write, and if you can't write, you might as well stop dreaming," Miss Bessie once told me.

So I read whatever Miss Bessie told me to, and tried to remember the things she insisted that I store away. Forty-five years later, I can still recite her "truths to live by," such as Henry Wadsworth Longfellow's lines from "The Ladder of St. Augustine":   19

> The heights by great men reached and kept
> Were not attained by sudden flight.
> But they, while their companions slept,
> Were toiling upward in the night.

Years later, her inspiration, prodding, anger, cajoling and almost osmotic infusion of learning finally led to that lovely day when Miss Bessie dropped me a note saying, "I'm so proud to read your column in the Nashville *Tennessean*."   20

Miss Bessie was a spry 80 when I went back to McMinnville and visited her in a senior citizens' apartment building. Pointing out proudly that her building was racially integrated, she reached for two glasses and a pint of bourbon. I was momentarily shocked, because it would have been scandalous in the 1930s and '40s for word to get out that a teacher drank, and nobody had ever raised a rumor that Miss Bessie did.   21

I felt a new sense of equality as she lifted her glass to mine. Then she revealed a softness and compassion that I had never known as a student.   22

"I've never forgotten that examination day," she said, "when Buster Martin held up seven fingers, obviously asking you for help with question number seven, 'Name a common carrier.' I can still picture you looking at your exam paper and humming a few bars of 'Chattanooga Choo Choo.' I was so tickled, I couldn't punish either of you."   23

Miss Bessie was telling me, with bourbon-laced grace, that I never fooled her for a moment.   24

When Miss Bessie died in 1980, at age 85, hundreds of her former students mourned. They knew the measure of a great   25 teacher: love and motivation. Her wisdom and influence had rippled out across generations.

Some of her students who might normally have been doomed to poverty went on to become doctors, dentists and college professors. Many, guided by Miss Bessie's example, became public-school teachers. 26

"The memory of Miss Bessie and how she conducted her classroom did more for me than anything I learned in college," recalls Gladys Wood of Knoxville, Tenn., a highly respected English teacher who spent 43 years in the state's school system. "So many times, when I faced a difficult classroom problem, I asked myself, *How would Miss Bessie deal with this?* And I'd remember that she would handle it with laughter and love." 27

No child can get all the necessary support at home, and millions of poor children get *no* support at all. This is what makes a wise, educated, warm-hearted teacher like Miss Bessie so vital to the minds, hearts and souls of this country's children. 28

Questions for Study and Discussion

1. Throughout the essay Rowan offers details of Miss Bessie's physical appearance. What specific details does he give, and in what context does he give them? Did Miss Bessie's physical characteristics match the quality of her character? Explain.

2. How would you sum up the character of Miss Bessie? Make a list of the key words that Rowan uses that you feel best describe her.

3. At what point in the essay does Rowan give us the details of Miss Bessie's background? Why do you suppose he delays giving us this important information? (Glossary: *Beginnings and Endings*)

4. How does dialogue serve Rowan's purposes? (Glossary: *Dialogue*)

5. Does Miss Bessie's drinking influence your opinion of her? Explain. Why do you think Rowan included this part of her behavior in his essay?

6. In his opening paragraph Rowan states that Miss Bessie "taught me English, history, civics—and a lot more than I realized." What did she teach her students beyond the traditional public school curriculum?

Vocabulary

Refer to your dictionary to define the following words as they are used in this selection. Then use each word in a sentence of your own.

civics (1)   cajoling (20)
barrios (16)   osmotic (20)
conscience (18)   measure (25)

Suggested Writing Assignments

1. Think of all the teachers you have had, and write a description of the one that has had the greatest influence on you. Remember to give some consideration to the balance you want to achieve between physical attributes and personality traits.

2. In paragraph 18 Rowan writes the following: " 'If you don't read, you can't write, and if you can't write, you might as well stop dreaming,' Miss Bessie once told me." Write an essay in which you explore this theme that, in essence, is also the theme of *Models for Writers*.

My Friend, Albert Einstein

Banesh Hoffmann

A mathematician, Banesh Hoffmann has served on the faculties of the University of Rochester, the Institute for Advanced Study at Princeton University, and Queens College. Hoffmann is the author of The Strange Story of the Quantum *(1959) and* The Tyranny of Testing *(1964) and co-author with Albert Einstein of an article on the theory of relativity. Hoffmann has also collaborated with Helen Dukas, Einstein's personal secretary, on two biographical studies:* Albert Einstein: Creator and Rebel *(1973) and* Albert Einstein: The Human Side *(1979). In the following selection, Hoffmann describes the kind of man he found Einstein to be.*

He was one of the greatest scientists the world has ever [1] known, yet if I had to convey the essence of Albert Einstein in a single word, I would choose *simplicity*. Perhaps an anecdote will help. Once, caught in a downpour, he took off his hat and held it under his coat. Asked why, he explained, with admirable logic, that the rain would damage the hat, but his hair would be none the worse for its wetting. This knack for going instinctively to the heart of a matter was the secret of his major scientific discoveries—this and his extraordinary feeling for beauty.

I first met Albert Einstein in 1935, at the famous Institute for [2] Advanced Study in Princeton, N.J. He had been among the first to be invited to the Institute, and was offered *carte blanche* as to salary. To the director's dismay, Einstein asked for an impossible sum: it was far too *small*. The director had to plead with him to accept a larger salary.

I was in awe of Einstein, and hesitated before approaching [3] him about some ideas I had been working on. When I finally knocked on his door, a gentle voice said, "Come"—with a rising inflection that made the single word both a welcome and a question. I entered his office and found him seated at a table, calculating and smoking his pipe. Dressed in ill-fitting clothes, his hair characteristically awry, he smiled a warm welcome. His utter naturalness at once set me at ease.

As I began to explain my ideas, he asked me to write the equa-   4
tions on the blackboard so he could see how they developed. Then came the staggering—and altogether endearing—request: "Please go slowly. I do not understand things quickly." This from Einstein! He said it gently, and I laughed. From then on, all vestiges of fear were gone.

Einstein was born in 1879 in the German city of Ulm. He had   5
been no infant prodigy; indeed, he was so late in learning to speak that his parents feared he was a dullard. In school, though his teachers saw no special talent in him, the signs were already there. He taught himself calculus, for example, and his teachers seemed a little afraid of him because he asked questions they could not answer. At the age of 16, he asked himself whether a light wave would seem stationary if one ran abreast of it. From that innocent question would arise, ten years later, his theory of relativity.

Einstein failed his entrance examinations at the Swiss Fed-   6
eral Polytechnic School, in Zurich, but was admitted a year later. There he went beyond his regular work to study the masterworks of physics on his own. Rejected when he applied for academic positions, he ultimately found work, in 1902, as a patent examiner in Berne, and there in 1905 his genius burst into fabulous flower.

Among the extraordinary things he produced in that memo-   7
rable year were his theory of relativity, with its famous offshoot, $E = mc^2$ (energy equals mass times the speed of light squared), and his quantum theory of light. These two theories were not only revolutionary, but seemingly contradictory: the former was intimately linked to the theory that light consists of waves, while the latter said it consists somehow of particles. Yet this unknown young man boldly proposed both at once— and he was right in both cases, though how he could have been is far too complex a story to tell here.

Collaborating with Einstein was an unforgettable experi-   8
ence. In 1937, the Polish physicist Leopold Infeld and I asked if

we could work with him. He was pleased with the proposal, since he had an idea about gravitation waiting to be worked out in detail. Thus we got to know not merely the man and the friend, but also the professional.

The intensity and depth of his concentration were fantastic. 9 When battling a recalcitrant problem, he worried it as an animal worries its prey. Often, when we found ourselves up against a seemingly insuperable difficulty, he would stand up, put his pipe on the table, and say in his quaint English, "I will a little tink" (he could not pronounce "th"). Then he would pace up and down, twirling a lock of his long, graying hair around his forefinger.

A dreamy, faraway and yet inward look would come over his 10 face. There was no appearance of concentration, no furrowing of the brow—only a placid inner communion. The minutes would pass, and then suddenly Einstein would stop pacing as his face relaxed into a gentle smile. He had found the solution to the problem. Sometimes it was so simple that Infeld and I could have kicked ourselves for not having thought of it. But the magic had been performed invisibly in the depths of Einstein's mind, by a process we could not fathom.

Although Einstein felt no need for religious ritual and be- 11 longed to no formal religious group, he was the most deeply religious man I have known. He once said to me, "Ideas come from God," and one could hear the capital "G" in the reverence with which he pronounced the word. On the marble fireplace in the mathematics building at Princeton University is carved, in the original German, what one might call his scientific credo: "God is subtle, but he is not malicious." By this Einstein meant that scientists could expect to find their task difficult, but not hopeless: the Universe was a Universe of law, and God was not confusing us with deliberate paradoxes and contradictions.

Einstein was an accomplished amateur musician. We used to 12 play duets, he on the violin, I at the piano. One day he surprised me by saying Mozart was the greatest composer of all. Beethoven "created" his music, but the music of Mozart was of such purity and beauty one felt he had merely "found" it—that it had always existed as part of the inner beauty of the Universe, waiting to be revealed.

It was this very Mozartean simplicity that most character- 13 ized Einstein's methods. His 1905 theory of relativity, for example, was built on just two simple assumptions. One is the so-called principle of relativity, which means, roughly speaking, that we cannot tell whether we are at rest or moving smoothly. The other assumption is that the speed of light is the same no matter what the speed of the object that produces it. You can see how reasonable this is if you think of agitating a stick in a lake to create waves. Whether you wiggle the stick from a stationary pier, or from a rushing speedboat, the waves, once generated, are on their own, and their speed has nothing to do with that of the stick.

Each of these assumptions, by itself, was so plausible as to seem primitively obvious. But together they were in such violent conflict that a lesser man would have dropped one or the other and fled in panic. Einstein daringly kept both—and by so doing he revolutionized physics. For he demonstrated they could, after all, exist peacefully side by side, provided we gave up cherished beliefs about the nature of time.   14

Science is like a house of cards, with concepts like time and space at the lowest level. Tampering with time brought most of the house tumbling down, and it was this that made Einstein's work so important—and controversial. At a conference in Princeton in honor of his 70th birthday, one of the speakers, a Nobel Prize-winner, tried to convey the magical quality of Einstein's achievement. Words failed him, and with a shrug of helplessness he pointed to his wristwatch, and said in tones of awed amazement, "It all came from this." His very ineloquence made this the most eloquent tribute I have heard to Einstein's genius.   15

We think of Einstein as one concerned only with the deepest aspects of science. But he saw scientific principles in everyday things to which most of us would give barely a second thought. He once asked me if I had ever wondered why a man's feet will sink into either dry or completely submerged sand, while sand that is merely damp provides a firm surface. When I could not answer, he offered a simple explanation.   16

It depends, he pointed out, on *surface tension*, the elastic-skin effect of a liquid surface. This is what holds a drop together, or causes two small raindrops on a windowpane to pull into one big drop the moment their surfaces touch.   17

When sand is damp, Einstein explained, there are tiny 18
amounts of water between grains. The surface tensions of these
tiny amounts of water pull all the grains together, and friction
then makes them hard to budge. When the sand is dry, there is
obviously no water between grains. If the sand is fully immersed, there is water between grains, but no water *surface* to
pull them together.

This is not as important as relativity; yet there is no telling 19
what seeming trifle will lead an Einstein to a major discovery.
And the puzzle of the sand does give us an inkling of the power
and elegance of his mind.

Einstein's work, performed quietly with pencil and paper, 20
seemed remote from the turmoil of everyday life. But his ideas
were so revolutionary they caused violent controversy and irrational anger. Indeed, in order to be able to award him a belated
Nobel Prize, the selection committee had to avoid mentioning
relativity, and pretend the prize was awarded primarily for his
work on the quantum theory.

Political events upset the serenity of his life even more. When 21
the Nazis came to power in Germany, his theories were officially declared false because they had been formulated by a
Jew. His property was confiscated, and it is said a price was
put on his head.

When scientists in the United States, fearful that the Nazis 22
might develop an atomic bomb, sought to alert American authorities to the danger, they were scarcely heeded. In desperation, they drafted a letter which Einstein signed and sent directly to President Roosevelt. It was this act that led to the
fateful decision to go all-out on the production of an atomic
bomb—an endeavor in which Einstein took no active part.
When he heard of the agony and destruction that his $E=mc^2$
had wrought, he was dismayed beyond measure, and from then
on there was a look of ineffable sadness in his eyes.

There was something elusively whimsical about Einstein. It 23
is illustrated by my favorite anecdote about him. In his first
year in Princeton, on Christmas Eve, so the story goes, some
children sang carols outside his house. Having finished, they
knocked on his door and explained they were collecting money
to buy Christmas presents. Einstein listened, then said, "Wait a
moment." He put on his scarf and overcoat, and took his violin

from its case. Then, joining the children as they went from door to door, he accompanied their singing of "Silent Night" on his violin.

How shall I sum up what it meant to have known Einstein and his works? Like the Nobel Prize-winner who pointed helplessly at his watch, I can find no adequate words. It was akin to the revelation of great art that lets one see what was formerly hidden. And when, for example, I walk on the sand of a lonely beach, I am reminded of his ceaseless search for cosmic simplicity—and the scene takes on a deeper, sadder beauty.   24

Questions for Study and Discussion

1. Hoffmann feels that the word *simplicity* captures the essence of Albert Einstein. What character traits does Hoffmann describe in order to substantiate this impression of the man?

2. Make a list of the details of Einstein's physical features. From these details, can you tell what Einstein looked like?

3. Hoffmann uses a number of anecdotes to develop his description of Einstein. In what ways are such anecdotes preferable to mere statements regarding Einstein's character? Refer to several examples to illustrate your opinion.

4. Why do you suppose Hoffmann begins his essay where he does instead of the sentence "Einstein was born in 1879 in the German city of Ulm" (5)? (Glossary: *Beginnings and Endings*)

5. What, for Hoffmann, was the secret of Einstein's major scientific discoveries? Explain.

6. In 1905 Einstein produced his theory of relativity and his quantum theory of light. Although both theories are revolutionary, what is remarkable about the fact that they were both advanced by the same man?

7. What are the two assumptions on which Einstein built his theory of relativity? What analogy does Hoffmann use to explain the reasonableness of these assumptions? (Glossary: *Analogy*)

Vocabulary

Refer to your dictionary to define the following words as they are used in this selection. Then use each word in a sentence of your own.

anecdote (1)   fathom (10)
awry (3)   credo (11)
vestiges (4)   trifle (19)
prodigy (5)   ineffable (22)
recalcitrant (9)

Suggested Writing Assignments

1. Write a descriptive essay on a person you know well, perhaps a friend or a relative. Before writing, be sure that you establish a purpose for your description. Remember that your reader will not know that person; therefore, try to show what makes your subject different from other people.

2. In his essay Hoffmann reveals something of himself—his beliefs, his tastes, his intelligence, his values. Write an essay in which you argue that every writer, to a lesser or greater degree, reveals something of himself or herself in writing about any subject. Choose whatever examples you wish to make your point. You might, however, decide to use Carl Rowan and his essay on Miss Bessie as your primary example. Finally, you might wish to emphasize the significance of the self-revealing qualities of writing.

13

PROCESS ANALYSIS

When you give directions for getting to your house, tell how to make ice cream, or explain how a president is elected, you are using *process analysis*.

Process analysis usually arranges a series of events in order and relates them to one another, as narration and cause and effect do, but it has different emphases. Whereas narration tells mainly *what* happens and cause and effect focuses on *why* it happens, process analysis tries to explain—in detail—*how* it happens.

There are two types of process analysis: directional and informational. The *directional* type provides instructions on how to do something. These instructions can be as brief as the directions printed on a label for making instant coffee or as complex as the directions in a manual for building a home computer. The purpose of directional process analysis is simple: to give the reader directions to follow that lead to the desired results.

Consider the directions for constructing an Astro Tube, a cylindrical airfoil made out of a sheet of heavy writing paper, on p. 259.

The *informational* type of process analysis, on the other hand, tells how something works, how something is made, or how something occurred. You would use informational process analysis if you wanted to explain how the human heart functions, how an atomic bomb works, how hailstones are formed, how you selected the college you are attending, or how the polio vaccine was developed. Rather than giving specific directions, informational process analysis explains and informs.

Clarity is crucial for successful process analysis. The most effective way to explain a process is to divide it into steps and to present those steps in a clear (usually chronological) sequence. Transitional words and phrases such as *first, next,* and *in conclusion* help to connect steps to one another. Naturally, you must be sure that no step is omitted or out of order. Also, you may sometimes have to explain *why* a certain step is necessary, especially if it is not obvious. With intricate, abstract, or particularly difficult steps, you might use analogy or comparison to clarify the steps for your reader.

Start with an 8.5-inch by 11-inch sheet of heavy writing paper. (Never use newspaper in making paper models because it isn't strongly bonded and can't hold a crease.) Follow these numbered steps, corresponding to the illustrations.

1. With the long side of the sheet toward you, fold up one third of the paper.
2. Fold the doubled section in half.
3. Fold the section in half once more and crease well.
4. Unfold preceding crease.
5. Curve the ends together to form a tube, as shown in the illustration.

6. Insert the right end inside the left end between the single outer layer and the doubled layers. Overlap the ends about an inch and a half. (This makes a tube for right-handers, to be used with an underhand throw. For an overhand tube, or an underhand version to be thrown by a lefty, reverse the directions, and insert the left end inside the right end at this step.)
7. Hold the tube at the seam with one hand, where shown by the dot in the illustration, and turn the rim inward along the crease made in step 3. Start turning in at the seam and roll the rim under, moving around the circumference in a circular manner. Then

round out the rim.
8. Fold the fin to the left, as shown, then raise it so that it's perpendicular to the tube. Be careful not to tear the paper at the front.
9. Hold the tube from above, near the rim. Hold it between the thumb and fingers.
The rim end should be forward, with the fin on the bottom. Throw the tube underhanded, with a motion like throwing a bowling ball, letting it spin off the fingers as it is released. The tube will float through the air, spinning as it goes. Indoor flights of 30 feet or more are easy. With practice you can achieve remarkable accuracy.

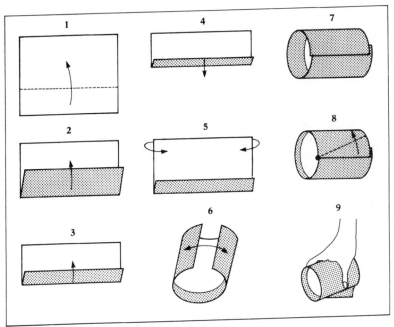

How to Write a Personal Letter

Garrison Keillor

Writer and broadcaster, Garrison Keillor was born in Anoka, Minnesota, in 1942. After graduating from the University of Minnesota, he became a successful writer of humorous stories, many of which appeared in The New Yorker. *He is perhaps best known for his radio program,* Prairie Home Companion, *which was broadcast on National Public Radio Saturday evenings from 1974 until 1987, when Keillor left to devote more of his time to writing. Keillor has written three extremely popular books:* Happy to Be Here *(1982),* Lake Wobegon Days *(1985), and* Leaving Home: A Collection of Lake Wobegon Stories *(1987). In "How to Write a Personal Letter," written as an advertisement for the International Paper Company, the sage of Lake Wobegon offers some wise words on writing letters to friends and special people.*

We shy persons need to write a letter now and then, or else we'll dry up and blow away. It's true. And I speak as one who loves to reach for the phone, dial the number, and talk. I say, "Big Bopper here—what's shakin', babes?" The telephone is to shyness what Hawaii is to February, it's a way out of the woods, *and yet*: a letter is better.

Such a sweet gift—a piece of handmade writing, in an envelope that is not a bill, sitting in our friend's path when she trudges home from a long day spent among wahoos and savages, a day our words will help repair. They don't need to be immortal, just sincere. She can read them twice and again tomorrow: *You're someone I care about, Corinne, and think of often and every time I do you make me smile.*

We need to write, otherwise nobody will know who we are. They will have only a vague impression of us as A Nice Person, because frankly, we don't shine at conversation, we lack the confidence to thrust our faces forward and say, "Hi, I'm Heather Hooten, let me tell you about my week." Mostly we say "Uh-huh" and "Oh really." People smile and look over our shoulder, looking for someone else to talk to.

So a shy person sits down and writes a letter. To be known by another person—to meet and talk freely on the page—to be close despite distance. To escape from anonymity and be our own sweet selves and express the music of our souls.

Same thing that moves a giant rock star to sing his heart out in front of 123,000 people moves us to take ballpoint in hand and write a few lines to our dear Aunt Eleanor. *We want to be known.* We want her to know that we have fallen in love, that we quit our job, and we're moving to New York, and we want to say a few things that might not get said in casual conversation: *thank you for what you've meant to me, I am very happy right now.*

The first step in writing letters is to get over the guilt of *not* writing. You don't "owe" anybody a letter. Letters are a gift. The burning shame you feel when you see unanswered mail makes it harder to pick up a pen and makes for a cheerless letter when you finally do. *I feel bad about not writing, but I've been so busy,* etc. Skip this. Few letters are obligatory, and they are *Thanks for the wonderful gift* and *I am terribly sorry to hear about George's death* and *Yes, you're welcome to stay with us next month,* and not many more than that. Write those promptly if you want to keep your friends. Don't worry about the others, except love letters, of course. When your true love writes *Dear Light of My Life, Joy of My Heart, O Lovely Pulsating Core of My Sensate Life,* some response is called for.

Some of the best letters are tossed off in a burst of inspiration, so keep your writing stuff in one place where you can sit down for a few minutes and *Dear Roy, I am in the middle of an essay for International Paper but thought I'd drop you a line. Hi to your sweetie too* dash off a note to a pal. Envelopes, stamps, address book, everything in a drawer so you can write fast when the pen is hot.

A blank white 8″ × 11″ sheet can look as big as Montana if the pen's not so hot—try a smaller page and write boldly. Or use a note card with a piece of fine art on the front; if your letter ain't good, at least they get the Matisse. Get a pen that makes a sensuous line, get a comfortable typewriter, a friendly word processor—whichever feels easy to the hand.

Sit for a few minutes with the blank sheet in front of you, and   9
meditate on the person you will write to, let your friend come to mind until you can almost see her or him in the room with you. Remember the last time you saw each other and how your friend looked and what you said and what perhaps was unsaid between you, and when your friend becomes real to you, start to write.

Write the salutation— *Dear You*—and take a deep breath and   10
plunge in. A simple declarative sentence will do, followed by another and another and another. Tell us what you're doing and tell it like you were talking to us. Don't think about grammar, don't think about lit'ry style, don't try to write dramatically, just give us your news. Where did you go, who did you see, what did they say, what do you think?

If you don't know where to begin, start with the present mo-   11
ment: *I'm sitting at the kitchen table on a rainy Saturday morning. Everyone is gone and the house is quiet.* Let your simple description of the present moment lead to something else, let the letter drift gently along.

The toughest letter to crank out is one that is meant to im-   12
press, as we all know from writing job applications; if it's hard work to slip off a letter to a friend, maybe you're trying too hard to be terrific. A letter is only a report to someone who already likes you for reasons other than your brilliance. Take it easy.

Don't worry about form. It's not a term paper. When you   13
come to the end of one episode, just start a new paragraph. You can go from a few lines about the sad state of rock 'n roll to the fight with your mother to your fond memories of Mexico to your cat's urinary tract infection to a few thoughts on personal indebtedness to the kitchen sink and what's in it. The more you write, the easier it gets, and when you have a True True Friend to write to, a *compadre*, a soul sibling, then it's like driving a car down a country road, you just get behind the keyboard and press on the gas.

Don't tear up the page and start over when you write a bad   14
line—try to write your way out of it. Make mistakes and plunge

on. Let the letter cook along and let yourself be bold. Outrage, confusion, love—whatever is in your mind, let it find a way to the page. Writing is a means of discovery, always, and when you come to the end and write *Yours ever* or *Hugs and Kisses,* you'll know something you didn't when you wrote *Dear Pal.*

Probably your friend will put your letter away, and it'll be   15 read again a few years from now—and it will improve with age. And forty years from now, your friend's grandkids will dig it out of the attic and read it, a sweet and precious relic of the ancient Eighties that gives them a sudden clear glimpse of you and her and the world we old-timers knew. You will then have created an object of art. Your simple lines about where you went, who you saw, what they said, will speak to those children and they will feel in their hearts the humanity of our times.

You can't pick up a phone and call the future and tell them   16 about our times. You have to pick up a piece of paper.

Questions for Study and Discussion

1. Keillor calls a personal letter a "gift." Why do you suppose he thinks of a letter in this way?

2. What advice does Keillor have for people before they start writing? In what ways is this advice part of his process analysis? Why does he suggest small stationery instead of 8" × 11" sheets of paper?

3. Keillor suggests that before starting to write a friend, you think about that friend for a while until he or she becomes real for you. At that point you're ready to write. What should happen next in the process?

4. What do you think Keillor means when he says, "We need to write, otherwise nobody will know who we are" (3)?

5. Instead of taking us step-by-step through a personal letter in paragraphs 12–14, Keillor anticipates the problems that a letter writer is likely to encounter and offers his own advice. What are the most common problems? What solutions does Keillor offer? How has he organized his advice?

6. By the time you have come to the end of a letter, what, according to Keillor, should have happened? Why?

7. What does Keillor see as the advantages of a letter over a telephone call? Are there times that you believe a telephone call is preferable?

Vocabulary

Refer to your dictionary to define the following words as they are used in this selection. Then use each word in a sentence of your own.

trudges (2)   crank (12)
wahoos (2)   episode (13)
anonymity (4)   relic (15)
sensuous (8)

Suggested Writing Assignments

1. Most do-it-yourself jobs require that you follow a set process in order to achieve the best results. Write a process essay in which you provide direction for doing one of the following household activities:

   paint a room
   clean windows
   repot a plant
   prune shrubbery
   apply driveway sealer
   do laundry
   care for a lawn
   wash a car
   bake bread or chocolate chip cookies
   change a flat tire
   give a home permanent

2. Write an essay in which you give directions or advice for finding a summer job or part-time employment during the school year. In what ways is looking for such jobs different from looking for permanent positions? You can use Keillor's essay as a model for your own.

How to Survive a Hotel Fire

R. H. Kauffman

R. H. Kauffman, born in Portland, Oregon, in 1941, is a captain in the Los Angeles Fire Department. He is best known, however, as the author of a booklet entitled Caution: Hotels Could Be Hazardous to Your Health *(1981), which has over 44 million copies in print. As you read the following selection, an excerpt from his booklet, notice how clearly Kauffman has presented the steps you should follow and those you should avoid if you are caught in a hotel fire.*

A s a firefighter, I have seen many people die in hotel fires. Most could have saved themselves had they been prepared. There are *over 10,000 hotel fires per year* in the United States. In 1979, the latest year for which figures are available, there were 11,500 such fires, resulting in 140 deaths and 1225 injuries.

Contrary to what you have seen in the movies, fire is not likely to chase you down and burn you to death. It's the by-products of fire—smoke and panic—that are almost always the causes of death.

For example, a man wakes up at 2:30 A.M. to the smell of smoke. He pulls on his pants and runs into the hallway—to be greeted by heavy smoke. He has no idea where the exit is, so he runs first to the right. No exit. Where is it? Panic sets in. He's coughing and gagging now; his eyes hurt. He can't see his way back to his room. His chest hurts; he needs oxygen desperately. He runs in the other direction, completely disoriented. At 2:50 A.M. we find him . . . dead of smoke inhalation.

Remember, the presence of smoke doesn't necessarily mean that the hotel will burn down. Air-conditioning and air-exchange systems will sometimes pick up smoke from one room and carry it to other rooms or floors.

Smoke, because it is warmer than air, will start accumulating at the ceiling and work its way down. The fresh air you

265

should breathe is near the floor. What's more, smoke is extremely irritating to the eyes. Your eyes will take only so much irritation, then they will close and you won't be able to open them.

Your other enemy, panic—a contagious, overpowering terror—can make you do things that could kill you. The man in the foregoing example would not have died if he had known what to do. Had he found out beforehand where the exit was—four doors down on the left—he could have gotten down on his hands and knees close to the floor, where the air is fresher. Then, even if he couldn't keep his eyes open, he could have felt the wall as he crawled, counting doors. 6

Here are my rules for surviving hotel fires: 7

Know where the exits are. As soon as you drop your luggage in your room, turn around and go back into the hallway to check for an exit. If two share a room, both should locate the exit. Open the exit door. Are there stairs or another door beyond? As you return to your room, count the doors you pass. Is there anything in the hallway that would be in your way—an ice machine, maybe? This procedure takes very little time and, to be effective, it must become a habit. 8

Become familiar with your room. See if your bathroom has an exhaust fan. In an emergency you can turn it on to help remove smoke. Check the window. If it opens, look outside. Do you see any ledges? How high up are you? 9

Leave the hotel at the first sign of smoke. If something awakens you during the night, investigate it before you go back to sleep. In a hotel fire near Los Angeles airport, one of the guests was awakened by people yelling but went back to bed thinking it was a party. He nearly died in bed. 10

Always take your key. Don't lock yourself out of your room. You may find conditions elsewhere unbearable. Get in the habit of putting the key in the same place. The night stand, close to the bed, is an excellent spot. 11

Stay on your hands and knees. If you do wake up to smoke, grab your key from the night stand, roll off the bed and crawl toward the door. Even if you could tolerate the smoke when standing, don't. Save your eyes and lungs for as long as possible. Five feet up, the air may already be full of carbon monoxide. If the door isn't hot, open it slowly and check the hallway. 12

Should you decide to leave, close the door behind you. Most 13
doors take hours to burn. They are excellent fire shields, so
close every one you go through.

Make your way to the exit. Stay against the wall closest to the 14
exit, counting doors as you pass.

Don't use the elevator. Elevator shafts extend through all 15
floors of a building, and easily fill with smoke and carbon monoxide. Smoke, heat, and fire do odd things to elevator controls.
Several years ago a group of firemen used an elevator in re-
sponding to a fire on a 20th floor. They pushed No. 18, but the
elevator shot past the 18th floor and opened on the 20th—to an
inferno that killed the firemen.

If you can't go down, go up. When you reach the exit stairwell 16
and begin to descend, hang on to the handrail as you go. People
may be running and they could knock you down.

Sometimes smoke gets into the stairwell. If it's a tall build- 17
ing, the smoke may not rise very high before it cools and becomes heavy, or "stacked." You could enter the stairwell on the
23rd floor and find it clear, then as you descend, encounter
smoke. Do not try to run through it; people die that way. Turn
around and walk up.

When you reach the roof, prop open the door. (This is the 18
only time to leave a door open.) Any smoke in the stairwell can
now vent itself. Find the windward side of the building (the side
that the wind is blowing *from*) and wait until the firefighters
reach you. Don't panic if you can't get out onto the roof because
the door is locked. Many people have survived by staying put in
the stairwell until the firefighters arrived. Again, don't try to
run through the smoke.

Look before you leap. If you're on the ground floor, of course, 19
just open the window and climb out. From the next floor you
might make it with only a sprained ankle, but you must jump
out far enough to clear the building. Many people hit window-
sills and ledges on the way down, and cartwheel to the ground.
If you're any higher than the third floor, chances are you won't
survive the fall. You would probably be better off staying inside, and fighting the fire.

If you can't leave your room, fight the fire. If your door is too 20
hot to open or the hallway is completely filled with smoke,
don't panic. First, open the window to help vent any smoke in

your room. (Don't break the window; if there is smoke outside, you may need to close it.)

If your phone is still working, call the fire department. (Do not assume it has been notified. Incredibly enough, some hotels will not call the fire department until they verify whether there is really a fire and try to put it out themselves.)   21

Flip on the bathroom fan. Fill the tub with water. Wet some sheets or towels, and stuff them into the cracks around your door to keep out smoke. Fill your ice bucket or wastebasket with water from the bathtub and douse the door and walls to keep them cool. If possible, put your mattress up against the door and secure it with the dresser. Keep everything wet. A wet towel tied around your nose and mouth can be an effective filter of smoke particles. Swing a wet towel around the room; it will help clear the smoke. If there is fire outside the window, remove the drapes, move away as much combustible material as you can, and throw water around the window. Use your common sense, and keep fighting until help arrives.   22

Questions for Study and Discussion

1. What are the two by-products of fire that Kauffman says are most often the cause of death?

2. What advice does Kauffman offer to handle heavy smoke?

3. What do we learn from Kauffman's opening paragraph? In what ways is such information both appropriate and effective as an introduction to Kauffman's essay? (Glossary: *Beginnings and Endings*)

4. What is the relationship between paragraph 2 and paragraph 3?

5. At what point in the essay does Kauffman begin to give directions or use directional process? Can any steps in this process be reordered? What would be the effect of any suggested changes?

6. What is Kauffman's tone in this essay? How, specifically, has he established his tone? Is the tone appropriate for his material? Explain. (Glossary: *Tone*)

Vocabulary

Refer to your dictionary to define the following words as they are used in this selection. Then use each word in a sentence of your own.

disoriented (3)   inferno (15)
unbearable (11)   incredibly (21)
carbon monoxide (12)

Suggested Writing Assignments

1. Knowing what to do and what not to do in a potentially dangerous situation can be lifesaving information. Frequently such information is process oriented. Write an essay in which you explain the process to follow if you observe one of the following situations:

   a heart attack
   a drowning
   an automobile accident
   a house fire
   a choking episode
   a farm machinery accident
   a mugging
   an accidental poisoning

2. In order to give another person directions about how to do something, you yourself need a thorough understanding of the process. Analyze one of the following activities by listing materials you would need and the steps you would follow in completing it:

   studying for an exam
   determining miles per gallon for an automobile
   getting from where your writing class meets to where you
      normally have lunch
   preparing for a week-long camping trip
   writing an essay

buying a used car

beginning an exercise program

Now write an essay in which you give directions for successfully performing the task.

BEAUTY AND THE BEEF

Joey Green

*A native of Miami, Florida, Joey Green is a grad-
uate of Cornell University. (He was almost suspended for selling fake football programs at the
1979 Cornell–Yale homecoming game.) Editor of
the* Cornell Lunatic, *Green was also president of
the National Association of College Humor Magazines. After college, he served as contributing
editor for* National Lampoon *until he wrote an
article for* Rolling Stone *in which he explained
why* National Lampoon *wasn't funny anymore.
He has worked at the J. Walter Thompson advertising agency, where he wrote a television commercial for Burger King and won the Clio award
for a print ad for Kodak. Editor of* Hellbent on
Insanity—College Humor of the 70s and 80s
*(1982), Green is currently a contributing editor
for* Spy *magazine and is working on a novel. In
the following selection from* Spy, *Green explains
what goes on behind the scenes during the filming of a Burger King commercial.*

When was the last time you opened a carton in a fast-food   1
restaurant to find a hamburger as appetizing as the
ones in the TV commercials? Did you ever look past the
counter help to catch a glimpse of a juicy hamburger patty,
handsomely branded by the grill, sizzling and crackling as it
glides over roaring flames, with tender juices sputtering into
the fire? On television the burger is a magnificent slab of
flame-broiled beef—majestically topped with crisp iceberg lettuce, succulent red tomatoes, tangy onions and plump pickles,
all between two halves of a towering sesame-seed bun. But, of
course, the real-life Whoppers don't quite measure up.

The ingredients of a TV Whopper are, unbelievably, the same   2
as those used in real Whoppers sold to average consumers. But

like other screen personalities, the Whopper needs a little help from makeup.

When making a Burger King commercial, J. Walter Thompson, the company's advertising agency, usually devotes at least one full day to filming "beauty shots" of the food. Burger King supplies the agency with several large boxes of frozen beef patties. But before a patty is sent over the flame broiler, a professionally trained food stylist earning between $500 and $750 a day prepares it for the camera.

The crew typically arrives at 7:00 a.m. and spends two hours setting up lights that will flatter the burger. Then the stylist, aided by two assistants, begins by burning "flame-broiling stripes" into the thawed hamburger patties with a special Madison Avenue branding iron. Because the tool doesn't always leave a rich, charcoal-black impression on the patty, the stylist uses a fine paintbrush to darken the singed crevices with a sauce the color of used motor oil.The stylist also sprinkles salt on the patty so when it passes over the flames, natural juices will be encouraged to rise to the meat's surface.

Thus branded, retouched and juiced, the patties are run back and forth over a conveyor-belt broiler while the director films the little spectacle from a variety of angles. Two dozen people watch from the wings: lighting assistants, prop people, camera assistants, gas specialists, the client and agency people— producers, writers, art directors. Of course, as the meat is broiled blood rises to the surface in small pools. Since, for the purposes of advertising, bubbling blood is not a desirable special effect, the stylist, like a prissy microsurgical nurse, continually dabs at the burger with a Q-Tip.

Before the patty passes over the flame a second time, the food stylist maneuvers a small electric heater an inch or so above the burger to heat up the natural fatty juices until they begin to steam and sizzle. Otherwise puddles of grease will cover the meat. Sometimes patties are dried out on a bed of paper towels. Before they're sent over the flame broiler again, the stylist relubricates them with a drop of corn oil to guarantee picturesque crackling and sizzling.

If you examine any real Whopper at any Burger King closely, you'll discover flame-broiling stripes only on the top side of the beef patty. Hamburgers are sent through the flame broiler

once; they're never flipped over. The commercials imply otherwise. On television a beef patty, fetchingly covered with flame-
broiling stripes, travels over the broiler, indicating that the
burger has been flipped to sear stripes into the other side.

In any case, the camera crew has just five or ten seconds in   8
the life cycle of a TV Whopper to capture good, sizzling brown
beef on film. After that the hamburger starts to shrink rapidly
as the water and grease are cooked from it. Filming lasts anywhere from three to eight hours, depending upon the occurrence of a variety of technical problems—heavy smoke, grease
accumulating on the camera equipment, the gas specialist's
failure to achieve a perfect, preternaturally orange glowing
flame. Out of one day's work, and anywhere between 50 and 75
hamburgers, the agency hopes to get five seconds of usable
footage. Most of the time the patties are either too raw, bloody,
greasy or small.

Of course, the cooked hamburger patty depicted sitting on a   9
sesame-seed bun in the commercial is a different burger from
those towel-dried, steak-sauce-dabbed, corn-oiled specimens
that were filmed sliding over the flames. This presentation
patty hasn't been flame-broiled at all. It's been branded with
the phony flame-broiling marks, retouched with the steak
sauce—and then microwaved.

Truth in advertising, however, is maintained, sort of: when   10
you're shown the final product—a completely built hamburger
topped with sliced vegetables and condiments—you are seeing
the actual quantities of ingredients found on the average real
Whopper. On television, though, you're only seeing half of the
hamburger—the front half. The lettuce, tomatoes, onions and
pickles have all been shoved to the front of the burger. The stylist has carefully nudged and manicured the ingredients so that
they sit just right. The red, ripe tomatoes are flown in fresh
from California the morning of the shoot. You might find such
tomatoes on your hamburger—if you ordered several hundred
Whoppers early in the morning, in Fresno. The lettuce and tomatoes are cut, trimmed and then piled on top of a cold cooked
hamburger patty, and the whole construction is sprayed with a
fine mist of glycerine to glisten and shimmer seductively. Finally the hamburger is capped with a painstakingly hand-
crafted sesame-seed bun. For at least an hour the stylist has

been kneeling over the bun like a lens grinder, positioning each sesame seed. He dips a toothpick in Elmer's glue and, using a pair of tweezers, places as many as 300 seeds, one by one, onto a formerly bald bun.

When it's all over, the crew packs up the equipment, and 75   11
gorgeous-looking hamburgers are dumped in the garbage.

Questions for Study and Discussion

1. What is Green's thesis, and where is it stated? (Glossary: *Thesis*)
2. Green starts his essay with two questions. Did you find this strategy effective as a beginning? (Glossary: *Beginnings and Endings*) Why or why not?
3. In paragraph 1 Green describes the Whopper that we see in Burger King commercials. Explain how he enhances his description of the burger to make it appear special.
4. What process is Green explaining in his essay? Is the process being analyzed here informational or directional?
5. What, according to Green, does a food stylist do to prepare a burger for filming? What problems are encountered while in the process of shooting the commercial? How is each problem handled or solved?
6. What surprised you the most about the filming of a Burger King commercial? Why do you think it surprised you?

Vocabulary

Refer to your dictionary to define the following words as they are used in this selection. Then use each word in a sentence of your own.

sputtering (1)	maneuvers (6)
flatter (4)	fetchingly (7)
singed (4)	preternaturally (8)
prissy (5)	condiments (10)

Suggested Writing Assignments

1. Write an informational process analysis explaining how
   one of the following works:

   a checking account
   cell division
   an automobile engine
   the human eye
   economic supply and demand
   a microwave oven

2. Our world is filled with thousands of natural processes—
   for example, the flowering of a tree, the formation of tides,
   a particular human reflex action, the spawning of salmon,
   the cycle of the moon, and the formation of a hurricane.
   Write an informational process analysis explaining one
   such recurring natural process.

14

DEFINITION

To communicate precisely what you want to say, you will frequently need to *define* key words. Your reader needs to know just what you mean when you use unfamiliar words, such as *accouterment*, or words that are open to various interpretations, such as *liberal*, or words that, while generally familiar, are used in a particular sense. Failure to define important terms, or to define them accurately, confuses readers and hampers communication.

There are three basic ways to define a word; each is useful in its own way. The first method is to give a *synonym*, a word that has nearly the same meaning as the word you wish to define: *face* for *countenance, nervousness* for *anxiety*. No two words ever have *exactly* the same meaning, but you can, nevertheless, pair an unfamiliar word with a familiar one and thereby clarify your meaning.

Another way to define a word quickly, often within a single sentence, is to give a *formal definition*; that is, to place the term to be defined in a general class and then to distinguish it from other members of that class by describing its particular characteristics. For example:

WORD	CLASS	CHARACTERISTICS
A *watch*	is *a mechanical device*	*for telling time* and is usually *carried* or *worn.*
Semantics	is an *area of linguistics*	*concerned with the study of the meaning of words.*

The third method is known as *extended definition*. While some extended definitions require only a single paragraph, more often than not you will need several paragraphs or even an entire essay to define a new or difficult term or to rescue a controversial word from misconceptions and associations that may obscure its meaning.

One controversial term that illustrates the need for extended definition is *obscene*. What is obscene? Books that are banned in one school system are considered perfectly acceptable in another. Movies that are shown in one town cannot be shown in a neighboring town. Clearly, the meaning of *obscene* has been clouded by contrasting personal opinions as well as by conflicting social norms. Therefore, if you use the term *obscene* (and especially if you tackle the issue of obscenity itself), you must be careful to define clearly and thoroughly what you mean by that term—that is, you have to give an extended definition. There are a number of methods you might use to develop such a definition. You could define *obscene* by explaining what it does not mean. You could also make your meaning clear by narrating an experience, by comparing and contrasting it to related terms such as *pornographic* or *exotic*, by citing specific examples, or by classifying the various types of obscenity.

A JERK

Sydney J. Harris

For over forty years Sydney J. Harris wrote a syndicated column for the Chicago Daily News *entitled "Strictly Personal," in which he has considered virtually every aspect of contemporary American life. In the following essay from his book* Last Things First *(1961), Harris defines the term* jerk *by differentiating it from other similar slang terms.*

I don't know whether history repeats itself, but biography 1
certainly does. The other day, Michael came in and asked
me what a "jerk" was—the same question Carolyn put to me a
dozen years ago.

At that time, I fluffed her off with some inane answer, such 2
as "A jerk isn't a very nice person," but both of us knew it was
an unsatisfactory reply. When she went to bed, I began trying
to work up a suitable definition.

It is a marvelously apt word, of course. Until it was coined, 3
not more than 25 years ago, there was really no single word in
English to describe the kind of person who is a jerk—"boob"
and "simp" were too old hat, and besides they really didn't fit,
for they could be lovable, and a jerk never is.

Thinking it over, I decided that a jerk is basically a person 4
without insight. He is not necessarily a fool or a dope, because
some extremely clever persons can be jerks. In fact, it has little
to do with intelligence as we commonly think of it; it is, rather,
a kind of subtle but persuasive aroma emanating from the inner part of the personality.

I know a college president who can be described only as a 5
jerk. He is not an unintelligent man, nor unlearned, nor even
unschooled in the social amenities. Yet he is a jerk *cum laude*,
because of a fatal flaw in his nature—he is totally incapable of
looking into the mirror of his soul and shuddering at what he
sees there.

A jerk, then, is a man (or woman) who is utterly unable to see   6
himself as he appears to others. He has no grace, he is tactless
without meaning to be, he is a bore even to his best friends, he
is an egotist without charm. All of us are egotists to some extent, but most of us—unlike the jerk—are perfectly and horri-
bly aware of it when we make asses of ourselves. The jerk never
knows.

Questions for Study and Discussion

1. What, according to Harris, is a jerk?
2. Jerks, boobs, simps, fools, and dopes are all in the same
   class. How does Harris differentiate a jerk from a boob or a
   simp on the one hand, and a fool or a dope on the other?
3. What does Harris see as the relationship between intelligence and/or cleverness and the idea of a jerk?
4. In paragraph 5 Harris presents the example of the college
   president. How does this example support his definition?
5. In the first two paragraphs Harris tells how both his son
   and daughter asked him what *jerk* was. How does this brief
   anecdote serve to introduce Harris's essay? (Glossary: *Beginnings and Endings*) Do you think it works? Explain.

Vocabulary

Refer to your dictionary to define the following words as they
are used in this selection. Then use each word in a sentence of
your own.

inane (2)	emanating (4)
apt (3)	amenities (5)
coined (3)	tactless (6)

Suggested Writing Assignments

1. Write one or two paragraphs in which you give your own
   definition of *jerk* or another slang term of your choice.

2. Every generation develops its own slang, which generally
   enlivens the speech and writing of those who use it. Ironically, however, no generation can arrive at a consensus definition of even its most popular slang terms—for example,
   nimrod, air-head, flag. Select a slang term that you use frequently, and write an essay in which you define the term.
   Read your definition aloud in class. Do the other members
   of your class agree with your definition?

CHOLESTEROL

Isaac Asimov

Isaac Asimov was born in the Soviet Union in 1920 and came to the United States in 1923. At nineteen he graduated from Columbia University with a major in chemistry. Asimov is a highly prolific writer; he published his three hundredth book in 1984 and is internationally recognized as a great popularizer of science. In addition to his writings on science, he has written much science fiction as well as detective fiction, history, and guides to Shakespeare and the Bible. Whatever kind of writing Asimov undertakes, he is both interesting and lucid, as can be seen in the following selection first published in the Los Angeles Times. *Asimov's subject is cholesterol, a controversial and often misunderstood substance. As you read the essay, notice that Asimov takes much of the mystery away from cholesterol by clearly and simply defining exactly what it is.*

Cholesterol is a dirty word these days, and every report that comes out seems to make it worse. A government study of more than 350,000 American men between 35 and 37 years old was reported last month and 80% of them had cholesterol levels of more than 180 milligrams per 100 milliliters of blood. Anything over the 180 mark indicates an increased probability of an early death from heart disease. The higher the measurement the higher the probability.

And yet this grinning death mask is not the only face that cholesterol bears. Cholesterol happens to be absolutely essential to animal life. Every animal from the amoeba to the whale (including human beings, of course) possesses cholesterol. The human body is about one-third of 1% cholesterol.

The portion of the animal body that is richest in cholesterol   3
is the nervous system. There we encounter masses of nerve
cells which, in bulk, have a grayish appearance and are therefore referred to as "gray matter."

Each nerve cell has fibers extending from it, including a par-   4
ticularly long one called the "axon" along which electrical im-
pulses travel from nerve cell to nerve cell, coordinating the
body and making it possible for us to receive sense-
impressions, to respond appropriately and, above all (for human beings), to think.

The axon is surrounded by a fatty sheath, which presumably   5
acts as an insulating device that enables the electrical impulse
to travel faster and more efficiently. Without its insulating
powers, it is possible that nerve cells would "short-circuit" and
that the nervous system would not function.

The fatty sheath has a whitish appearance so that those por-   6
tions of the nervous system that are made up of masses of ax-
ons are called the "white matter."

As it happens, two out of every five molecules in the fatty   7
sheath are cholesterol. Why that should be, we don't know, but
the cholesterol cannot be dispensed with. Without it, we would
have no nervous system, and without a nervous system, we
could neither think nor live.

So important is cholesterol that the body has the full power   8
to manufacture it from simpler materials. Cholesterol does not
need to be present in the diet at all.

The trouble is, though, that if, for any reason, the body has   9
more cholesterol than it needs, there is a tendency to get rid of
it by storing it on the inner surface of the blood vessels—
especially the coronary vessels that feed the heart. This is "atherosclerosis," and it occurs in men more often than in women.
The cholesterol deposits narrow the blood vessels, stiffen and
roughen them, make internal clotting easier and, in general,
tend to produce heart attacks, strokes and death.

Why is that? Why should such a vital substance, without   10
which we could not live, present such a horrible other face?
Why haven't we evolved in such a way as not to experience such
dangerous cholesterol deposits?

One possible answer is that until the coming of modern medi-   11
cine, human beings did not have a long life span, on the aver-

age. Most people, even in comparatively good times, were dead of violence or infectious disease before they were 40, and by that time atherosclerosis had not had time to become truly dangerous.

It is only since the average human life span has reached 75, in many parts of the world, that atherosclerosis and other "degenerative diseases" have become of overwhelming importance. 12

What to do? There is the matter of diet, for one thing. Apparently, flooding the body with high-cholesterol items of diet (eggs, bacon, butter and other fatty foods of animal origin) encourages a too-high level of cholesterol in the blood and consequently atherosclerosis. 13

As it happens, plants do not contain cholesterol. They have related compounds, but not cholesterol. Therefore, to cut down on fatty animal food in the diet (the cholesterol is in the fat) and to increase plant food lower the chance of atherosclerosis. 14

In fact, since most primates (apes and monkeys) are much more vegetarian in their diet than human beings, can it be that we have not yet had time to fully adapt to the kind of carnivorous diet we have grown accustomed to? This is particularly so in prosperous Western countries. People of the Third World countries eat far less meat than Westerners do. They may have troubles of their own, but atherosclerosis, at least, is a minor problem. 15

We may also develop drugs that interfere with the body's ability to deposit cholesterol in the blood vessels. A new drug called lovastatin has been recently reported to show promising effectiveness in this direction. There is hope. 16

Questions for Study and Discussion

1. What is Asimov's thesis, and where is it presented? (Glossary: *Thesis*)
2. How, according to Asimov, does cholesterol function within the human nervous system?
3. What happens when the human body has more cholesterol than it needs? How does Asimov explain the fact that a sub-

stance that is vital for human existence can cause many potentially fatal problems?

4. In what ways should people adjust their diets to lower their chances of being afflicted with atherosclerosis?

5. What does Asimov mean when he states that "this grinning death mask is not the only face that cholesterol bears" (2)? How is this metaphor related to his definition of cholesterol?

6. In his opening paragraph Asimov cites the findings of a recent government study on cholesterol. Did you find this to be an effective introduction? (Glossary: *Beginnings and Endings*) Why, or why not?

Vocabulary

Refer to your dictionary to define the following words as they are used in this selection. Then use each word in a sentence of your own.

amoeba (2)	strokes (9)
sheath (5)	degenerative diseases (12)
molecules (7)	primates (15)

Suggested Writing Assignments

1. Select one of the following scientific concepts, and write an essay in which you use the strategy of definition to explain what it is.

photosynthesis
osmosis
electricity
wind shear
fission
atom
solar eclipse
cancer
allergy
fog

2. Write a short essay in which you define one of the following abstract terms. You may find it helpful to start your essay with a concrete example that illustrates your point.

charm
friendship
hatred
freedom
leadership
trust
commitment
religion
love

BREAKING THE HUNGRY TEEN CODE

Ellen Goodman

Ellen Goodman was born in Boston in 1941. After graduating from Radcliffe College in 1963, she worked as a reporter and researcher for Newsweek. *In 1967 she began working at the* Boston Globe *and, since 1974, has been a full-time columnist. Her regular column, "At Large," is syndicated and appears in nearly 400 newspapers across the country. In addition, her writing has appeared in* McCall's, Harper's Bazaar, *and* Family Circle, *and her commentaries have been broadcast on radio and television. In 1979 she published* Close to Home, *a collection of her columns; three other collections have appeared since then,* Turning Points *(1979),* At Large *(1981) and* Keeping in Touch *(1985). In "Breaking the Hungry Teen Code," which first appeared in the* Boston Globe *in August 1986, Goodman tackles a definition of the oft-heard cry of American teenagers: "There's Nothing to Eat in This House!"*

As a parent who works with words for a living, I have prided myself over many years for a certain skill in breaking the codes of childspeak. I began by interpreting babytalk, moved to more sophisticated challenges like "chill out" and graduated with "wicked good."

One phrase, however, always stumped me. I was unable to crack the meaning of the common cry echoing through most middle-class American households: "There's Nothing to Eat in This House!"

This exclamation becomes a constant refrain during the summer months when children who have been released from the schoolhouse door grow attached to the refrigerator door. It is during the summer when the average taxpayer realizes the true cost-effectiveness of school: It keeps kids out of the kitchen for roughly seven hours a day. A feat no parent is able to match.

At first, like so many others, I assumed that "NETH!" (as in "Nothing to Eat in This House") was a straightforward description of reality. If there was NETH, it was because the children had eaten it all. After all, an empty larder is something you come to expect when you live through the locust phase of adolescence.

I have one friend with three teenage sons who swears that she doesn't even have to unload her groceries anymore. Her children feed directly from the bags, rather like ponies. I have other friends who only buy ingredients for supper on the way home so that supper doesn't turn into lunch.

Over the years, I have considered color-coding food with red, yellow and green stickers. Green for eat. Yellow for eat only if you are starving. Red for "touch this and you die."

However, I discovered that these same locusts can stand in front of a relatively full refrigerator while bleating the same pathetic choruses of "NETH! NETH!" By carefully observing my research subjects, I discovered that the demand of "NETH!" has little to do with the supply.

What then does the average underage eater mean when he or she bleats "NETH! NETH!" You will be glad to know that I have finally broken the code for the "nothing" in NETH and offer herewith my translation.

NETH includes:

1. Any food that must be cooked, especially in a pan or by convectional heat. This covers boiling, frying or baking. Toasting is acceptable under dire conditions.

2. Any food that is in a frozen state with the single exception of ice cream. A frozen pizza may be considered "something to eat" only if there is a microwave oven on hand.

3. Any food that must be assembled before eaten. This means tuna that is still in a can. It may also mean a banana that has to be peeled, but only in extreme cases. Peanut butter and jelly are exempt from this rule as long as they are on the same shelf beside the bread.

4. Leftovers. Particularly if they must be re-heated. (See 1.)

5. Plain yogurt or anything else that might have been left as a nutrition trap.

6. Food that must be put on a plate, or cut with a knife and fork, as opposed to ripped with teeth while watching videos.

7. Anything that is not stored precisely at eye level. This includes:

8. Any item on a high cupboard shelf, unless it is a box of cookies and:

9. Any edible in the back of the refrigerator, especially on the middle shelf.

While divining the nine meanings of "NETH!" I should also   10
tell you that I developed an anthropological theory about the eating patterns of young Americans. For the most part, I am convinced, Americans below the age of 20 have arrested their development at the food-gathering stage.

They are intrinsically nomadic. Traveling in packs, they en-   11
gage in nothing more sophisticated than hand-to-mouth dining. They are, in effect, strip eaters who devour the ripest food from one home, and move on to another.

Someday, I am sure they will learn about the use of fire, not   12
to mention forks. Someday, they will be cured of the shelf-blindness, the inability to imagine anything hidden behind a large milk carton. But for now, they can only graze. All the rest is NETH-ing.

Questions for Study and Discussion

1. On what basis is Goodman qualified to discuss and define NETH? How did Goodman discover that the demand of NETH had little to do with the amount of food in the refrigerator?

2. What word gave Goodman the most trouble in trying to break the code for the cry "There's Nothing to Eat in This House"? Why?

3. How does Goodman define NETH? Can you add any meanings to her list of nine?

4. Identify several figures of speech that Goodman uses to describe teen-age eaters. (Glossary: *Figures of Speech*) How appropriate did you find them?

5. Goodman's tone in this essay is essentially humorous. Cite several passages that you found humorous, and discuss the ways in which the author achieves her humor.

6. How do the last three paragraphs serve to conclude Goodman's essay? (Glossary: *Beginnings and Endings*) How are these paragraphs related to what she has said before?

Vocabulary

Refer to your dictionary to define the following words as they are used in this selection. Then use each word in a sentence of your own.

chill out (1)	bleats (8)
larder (4)	divining (10)
pathetic (7)	intrinsically (11)

Suggested Writing Assignments

1. It seems that parents at times say things that their children have difficulty understanding. Using Ellen Goodman's essay as a model, write a brief essay in which you define a parent's cry such as "You're Never Home Anymore!" "All You Do Is Play!" or "We Never Had Time To Be Bored When We Were Kids!"

2. Many experiences in our lives are much more meaningful than their formal definitions would ever indicate. The connotations of language can be rich. Think for a moment what it means to have a home or to be a leader; what politics, fear, bravery, and anxiety are really all about; and what constitutes a family or a Thanksgiving dinner. Select one of these topics or choose one of your own, and write an extended definition that captures the essence of your subject.

15

DIVISION AND CLASSIFICATION

To divide is to separate a class of things or ideas into categories, whereas to classify is to group separate things or ideas into those categories. The two processes can operate separately but often go together. Division and classification can be a useful organizational strategy in writing. Here, for example, is a passage about levers in which the writer first discusses generally how levers work and then, in the second paragraph, uses division to establish three categories of levers and classification to group individual levers into those categories:

> Every lever has one fixed point called the "fulcrum" and is acted upon by two forces—the "effort" (exertion of hand muscles) and the "weight" (object's resistance). Levers work according to a simple formula: the effort (how hard you push or pull) multiplied by its distance from the fulcrum (effort arm) equals the weight multiplied by its distance from the fulcrum (weight arm). Thus two pounds of effort exerted at a distance of four feet from the fulcrum will raise eight pounds located one foot from the fulcrum.
>
> There are three types of levers, conventionally called "first kind," "second kind," and "third kind." Levers of the first kind have the fulcrum located between the effort and the weight. Examples are a pump handle, an oar, a crowbar, a weighing balance, a pair of scissors, and a pair of pliers. Levers of the second kind have the weight in the middle and magnify the effort. Examples are the handcar crank and doors. Levers of the third kind, such as a power shovel or a baseball batter's forearm, have the effort in the middle and always magnify the distance.

In writing, division and classification are affected directly by the writer's practical purpose. That purpose—what the writer wants to explain or prove—determines the class of things or ideas being divided and classified. For instance, a writer might divide television programs according to their audiences—adults, families, or children—and then classify individual programs into each of these categories in order to show how much emphasis the television stations place on reaching each audience. A different purpose would require different categories. A writer concerned about the prevalence of violence in television programming would first divide television programs into those which include fights and murders, and those which do not, and would then classify a large sample of programs into those categories. Other writers with different purposes might divide television programs differently—by the day and time of broadcast, for example, or by the number of women featured in prominent roles—and then classify individual programs accordingly.

The following guidelines can help you in using division and classification in your writing:

1. *Identify a clear purpose, and be sure that your principle of division is appropriate to that purpose.* To determine the makeup of a student body, for example, you might consider the following principles of division: college or program, major, class level, sex. It would not be helpful to divide students on the basis of their toothpaste unless you had a purpose and thus a reason for doing so.

2. *Divide your subject into categories that are mutually exclusive.* An item can belong to only one category. For example, it would be unsatisfactory to divide students as men, women, and athletes.

3. *Make your division and classification complete.* Your categories should account for all items in a subject class. In dividing students on the basis of geographic origin, for example, it would be inappropriate to consider only home states, for such a division would not account for foreign students. Then, for your classification to be complete, every student must be placed in one of the established categories.

4. *Be sure to state clearly the conclusion that your division and classification lead you to draw.* For example, a study of the student body might lead to the conclusion that 45 percent of the male athletes with athletic scholarships come from west of the Mississippi.

CHILDREN'S INSULTS

Peter Farb

From his undergraduate years at Vanderbilt University on, Peter Farb (1929–1980) had an intense interest in language and its role in human behavior. Farb was a consultant to the Smithsonian Institute, a curator of the Riverside Museum in New York City, and a visiting lecturer in English at Yale. In this essay, taken from Word Play: What Happens When People Talk *(1973), Farb classifies the names children use to insult one another.*

The insults spoken by adults are usually more subtle than   1
the simple name-calling used by children, but children's insults make obvious some of the verbal strategies people carry into adult life. Most parents engage in wishful thinking when they regard name-calling as good-natured fun which their children will soon grow out of. Name-calling is not good-natured and children do not grow out of it; as adults they merely become more expert in its use. Nor is it true that "sticks and stones may break my bones, but names will never hurt me." Names can hurt very much because children seek out the victim's true weakness, then jab exactly where the skin is thinnest. Name-calling can have major impact on a child's feelings about his identity, and it can sometimes be devastating to his psychological development.

Almost all examples of name-calling by children fall into four   2
categories:

1. Names based on physical peculiarities, such as deformities, use of eyeglasses, racial characteristics, and so forth. A child may be called *Flattop* because he was born with a misshapen skull—or, for obvious reasons, *Fat Lips, Gimpy, Four Eyes, Peanuts, Fatso, Kinky,* and so on.

2. Names based on a pun or parody of the child's own name. Children with last names like Fitts, McClure, and Farb usually find them converted to *Shits, Manure,* and *Fart.*
3. Names based on social relationships. Examples are *Baby* used by a sibling rival or *Chicken Shit* for someone whose courage is questioned by his social group.
4. Names based on mental traits—such as *Clunkhead, Dummy, Jerk,* and *Smartass.*

These four categories were listed in order of decreasing offensiveness to the victims. Children regard names based on physical peculiarities as the most cutting, whereas names based on mental traits are, surprisingly, not usually regarded as very offensive. Most children are very vulnerable to names that play upon the child's rightful name—no doubt because one's name is a precious possession, the mark of a unique identity and one's masculinity or femininity. Those American Indian tribes that had the custom of never revealing true names undoubtedly avoided considerable psychological damage.

Questions for Study and Discussion

1. What is Farb's contention in this selection? Where is it revealed? (Glossary: *Thesis*)
2. For what reason does Farb divide and classify children's insults?
3. Why does Farb feel that name-calling should not be dismissed lightly?
4. Farb states that children "regard names based on physical peculiarities as the most cutting" (2) Why do you suppose this might be true?
5. What principle of division does Farb use to establish his four categories of children's insults? What are the categories, and how does he order them? Be prepared to cite examples from the text.
6. List some insults that you remember from your own childhood or adolescence. Classify the insults according to

Farb's system. Do any items on your list not fit into one of his categories? What new categories can you establish?

Vocabulary

Refer to your dictionary to define the following words as they are used in this selection. Then use each word in a sentence of your own.

subtle (1)	sibling (2)
peculiarities (2)	vulnerable (2)
deformities (2)	unique (2)

Suggested Writing Assignments

1. Using the following sentence as your thesis, write an essay that divides and classifies the students at your college or university:

   There are (number) types of students at (institution).

   Be sure to follow the guidelines for division and classification that appear on page 291.

2. Consider the following classes of items and determine at least two principles of division that can be used for each class. Then write a paragraph or two in which you classify one of the groups of items according to a single principle of division. For example, in discussing crime one could use the seriousness of the crime or the type of crime as principles of division. If the seriousness of the crime were used, this might yield two categories: felonies, or major crimes; and misdemeanors, or minor crimes. If the type of crime were used, this would yield categories such as burglary, murder, assault, larceny, and embezzlement.

   professional sports
   social sciences
   movies
   roommates
   cars
   slang used by college students

HOT BOXES FOR EX-SMOKERS

Franklin E. Zimring

Franklin E. Zimring was born in Los Angeles, California, in 1942. He graduated from Wayne State University in 1963 and went on to the University of Chicago to earn a doctorate in law. He stayed at Chicago as both a professor of law and the director of the Center for Studies in Criminal Justice. A prolific writer, Zimring's books in- clude Deterrence: The Legal Threat in Crime Control *(1973),* Confronting Youth Crime *(1978),* and The Criminal Justice System *(1980). His articles have appeared in both scholarly and popular magazines and newspapers, and he is on the editorial boards of* Law and Behavior, Crime and Delinquency, *and the* Journal of Criminal Justice. *Currently, Zimring is professor of law and director of the Earl Warren Legal Institute at the University of California, Berkeley. In "Hot Boxes for Ex-Smokers," which first appeared in* Newsweek *on April 20, 1987, Zimring classifies former smokers according to the "different emotional states cessation of smoking can cause." A reformed smoker himself, Zimring believes that it is important for us to understand smoking, especially in light of new restrictions and bans around the country.*

A mericans can be divided into three groups—smokers, non-smokers and that expanding pack of us who have quit. Those who have never smoked don't know what they're missing, but former smokers, ex-smokers, reformed smokers can never forget. We are veterans of a personal war, linked by that watershed experience of ceasing to smoke and by the temptation to have just one more cigarette. For almost all of us ex-smokers, smoking continues to play an important part in our lives. And now that it is being restricted in restaurants around the country and will be banned in almost all indoor public places in New York state starting next month, it is vital that everyone understand the different emotional states cessation of smoking can cause. I have observed four of them; and in the interest of science I have classified them as those of the zealot, the evangelist, the elect and the serene. Each day, each category gains new recruits.

Not all antitobacco zealots are former smokers, but a sub- 2 stantial number of fire-and-brimstone opponents do come from the ranks of the reformed. Zealots believe that those who continue to smoke are degenerates who deserve scorn not pity and the penalties that will deter offensive behavior in public as well. Relations between these people and those who continue to smoke are strained.

One explanation for the zealot's fervor in seeking to outlaw 3 tobacco consumption is his own tenuous hold on abstaining from smoking. But I think part of the emotional force arises from sheer envy as he watches and identifies with each lung-filling puff. By making smoking in public a crime, the zealot seeks reassurance that he will not revert to bad habits; give him strong social penalties and he won't become a recidivist.

No systematic survey has been done yet, but anecdotal evi- 4 dence suggests that a disproportionate number of doctors who have quit smoking can be found among the fanatics. Just as the most enthusiastic revolutionary tends to make the most enthusiastic counterrevolutionary, many of today's vitriolic zealots include those who had been deeply committed to tobacco habits.

By contrast, the antismoking evangelist does not condemn 5 smokers. Unlike the zealot, he regards smoking as an easily curable condition, as a social disease, and not a sin. The evangelist spends an enormous amount of time seeking and preaching to the unconverted. He argues that kicking the habit is not *that* difficult. After all, *he* did it; moreover, as he describes it, the benefits of quitting are beyond measure and the disadvantages are nil.

The hallmark of the evangelist is his insistence that he never 6 misses tobacco. Though he is less hostile to smokers than the zealot, he is resented more. Friends and loved ones who have been the targets of his preachments frequently greet the resumption of smoking by the evangelist as an occasion for unmitigated glee.

Among former smokers, the distinctions between the evangelist and the elect are much the same as the differences between proselytizing and nonproselytizing religious sects. While the evangelists preach the ease and desirability of abstinence, the elect do not attempt to convert their friends. They think that virtue is its own reward and subscribe to the Puritan theory of predestination. Since they have proved themselves capable of abstaining from tobacco, they are therefore different from friends and relatives who continue to smoke. They feel superior, secure that their salvation was foreordained. These ex-smokers rarely give personal testimony on their conversion. They rarely speak about their tobacco habits, while evangelists talk about little else. Of course, active smokers find such bluenosed behavior far less offensive than that of the evangelist or the zealot, yet they resent the elect simply because they are smug. Their air of self-satisfaction rarely escapes the notice of those lighting up. For active smokers, life with a member of the ex-smoking elect is less stormy than with a zealot or evangelist, but it is subtly oppressive nonetheless.

Soul of the addict: I have labeled my final category of former smokers the serene. This classification is meant to encourage those who find the other psychic styles of ex-smokers disagreeable. Serenity is quieter than zealotry and evangelism, and those who qualify are not as self-righteous as the elect. The serene ex-smoker accepts himself and also accepts those around him who continue to smoke. This kind of serenity does not come easily nor does it seem to be an immediate option for those who have stopped. Rather it is a goal, an end stage in a process of development during which some former smokers progress through one or more of the less-than-positive psychological points en route. For former smokers, serenity is thus a positive possibility that exists at the end of the rainbow. But all former smokers cannot reach that promised land.

What is it that permits some former smokers to become serene? I think the key is self-acceptance and gratitude. The fully mature former smoker knows he has the soul of an addict and is grateful for the knowledge. He may sit up front in an airplane, but he knows he belongs in the smoking section in back. He doesn't regret that he quit smoking, nor any of his previous adventures with tobacco. As a former smoker, he is grateful for the experience and memory of craving a cigarette.

Serenity comes from accepting the lessons of one's life. And ex-smokers who have reached this point in their world view have much to be grateful for. They have learned about the potential and limits of change. In becoming the right kind of former smoker, they developed a healthy sense of self. This former smoker, for one, believes that it is better to crave (one hopes only occasionally) and not to smoke than never to have craved at all. And by accepting that fact, the reformed smoker does not need to excoriate, envy or disassociate himself from those who continue to smoke.

10

Questions for Study and Discussion

1. Into what three groups does Zimring divide all Americans? Which of the groups is he most interested in? Why?

2. Zimring himself is a former smoker. Do you think this is an advantage or disadvantage in writing this essay? Explain.

3. Into what four categories does Zimring classify former smokers? On what basis does he establish these categories? What distinctions does he draw between his categories? How do people in each group respond to those who continue to smoke?

4. What is Zimring's attitude toward the zealots, the evangelists, the elect, and the serene? In which category do you think Zimring himself belongs? Why?

5. What is it that allows some former smokers to become serene?

6. What seems to be Zimring's purpose in writing this essay? (Glossary: *Purpose*) Is he trying to persuade more people to become ex-smokers, or is he trying to explain the four types of former smokers that he has observed?

Vocabulary

Refer to your dictionary to define the following words as they are used in this selection. Then use each word in a sentence of your own.

watershed (1)   unmitigated (6)
cessation (1)   bluenosed (7)
recidivist (3)   smug (7)
anecdotal (4)   excoriate (10)
vitriolic (4)

Suggested Writing Assignments

1. Using Zimring's essay as a model, write a brief essay in which you classify people who are or have been included in one of the following groups:

   television addicts

   drivers

   dieters

   athletes

   teachers

   fashionable dressers

   sports fans

2. College is a time of stress for many students. In an essay, discuss the specific types of pressure experienced by students at your school.

THE WAYS OF MEETING OPPRESSION

Martin Luther King, Jr.

Martin Luther King, Jr. (1929–1968) was the leading spokesman for the rights of American blacks during the 1950s and 1960s before he was assassinated in 1968. He established the Southern Christian Leadership Conference, organized many civil rights demonstrations, and opposed the Vietnam War and the draft. In 1964 he was awarded the Nobel Prize for Peace. In the following essay, taken from his book Stride Toward Freedom *(1958), King classifies the three ways oppressed people throughout history have reacted to their oppressors.*

Oppressed people deal with their oppression in three characteristic ways. One way is acquiescence: the oppressed resign themselves to their doom. They tacitly adjust themselves to oppression, and thereby become conditioned to it. In every movement toward freedom some of the oppressed prefer to remain oppressed. Almost 2800 years ago Moses set out to lead the children of Israel from the slavery of Egypt to the freedom of the promised land. He soon discovered that slaves do not always welcome their deliverers. They become accustomed to being slaves. They would rather bear those ills they have, as Shakespeare pointed out, than flee to others that they know not of. They prefer the "fleshpots of Egypt" to the ordeals of emancipation.

There is such a thing as the freedom of exhaustion. Some people are so worn down by the yoke of oppression that they give up. A few years ago in the slum areas of Atlanta, a Negro guitarist used to sing almost daily: "Been down so long that down don't bother me." This is the type of negative freedom and resignation that often engulfs the life of the oppressed.

But this is not the way out. To accept passively an unjust system is to cooperate with that system; thereby the oppressed become as evil as the oppressor. Noncooperation with evil is as much a moral obligation as is cooperation with good. The oppressed must never allow the conscience of the oppressor to slumber. Religion reminds every man that he is his brother's keeper. To accept injustice or segregation passively is to say to the oppressor that his actions are morally right. It is a way of allowing his conscience to fall asleep. At this moment the oppressed fails to be his brother's keeper. So acquiescence— while often the easier way—is not the moral way. It is the way of the coward. The Negro cannot win the respect of his oppressor by acquiescing; he merely increases the oppressor's arrogance and contempt. Acquiescence is interpreted as proof of the Negro's inferiority. The Negro cannot win the respect of the white people of the South or the peoples of the world if he is willing to sell the future of his children for his personal and immediate comfort and safety.

A second way that oppressed people sometimes deal with oppression is to resort to physical violence and corroding hatred. Violence often brings about momentary results. Nations have frequently won their independence in battle. But in spite of temporary victories, violence never brings permanent peace. It solves no social problem; it merely creates new and more complicated ones.   4

Violence as a way of achieving racial justice is both impractical and immoral. It is impractical because it is a descending spiral ending in destruction for all. The old law of an eye for an eye leaves everybody blind. It is immoral because it seeks to humiliate the opponent rather than win his understanding; it seeks to annihilate rather than to convert. Violence is immoral because it thrives on hatred rather than love. It destroys community and makes brotherhood impossible. It leaves society in monologue rather than dialogue. Violence ends by defeating itself. It creates bitterness in the survivors and brutality in the destroyers. A voice echoes through time saying to every potential Peter, "Put up your sword."* History is cluttered with the wreckage of nations that failed to follow this command.   5

---

*The apostle Peter had drawn his sword to defend Christ from arrest. The voice was Christ's, who surrendered himself for trial and crucifixion (John 18:11).

If the American Negro and other victims of oppression suc- 6
cumb to the temptation of using violence in the struggle for
freedom, future generations will be the recipients of a desolate
night of bitterness, and our chief legacy to them will be an end-
less reign of meaningless chaos. Violence is not the way.

The third way open to oppressed people in their quest for 7
freedom is the way of nonviolent resistance. Like the synthesis
in Hegelian philosophy, the principle of nonviolent resistance
seeks to reconcile the truths of two opposites—the acquiescence and violence—while avoiding the extremes and immoral-
ities of both. The nonviolent resister agrees with the person
who acquiesces that one should not be physically aggressive
toward his opponent; but he balances the equation by agreeing
with the person of violence that evil must be resisted. He
avoids the nonresistance of the former and the violent resistance of the latter. With nonviolent resistance, no individual or
group need submit to any wrong, nor need anyone resort to violence in order to right a wrong.

It seems to me that this is the method that must guide the 8
actions of the Negro in the present crisis in race relations.
Through nonviolent resistance the Negro will be able to rise to
the noble height of opposing the unjust system while loving the
perpetrators of the system. The Negro must work passionately
and unrelentingly for full stature as a citizen, but he must not
use inferior methods to gain it. He must never come to terms
with falsehood, malice, hate, or destruction.

Nonviolent resistance makes it possible for the Negro to re- 9
main in the South and struggle for his rights. The Negro's problem will not be solved by running away. He cannot listen to the
glib suggestion of those who would urge him to migrate en
masse to other sections of the country. By grasping his great
opportunity in the South he can make a lasting contribution to
the moral strength of the nation and set a sublime example of
courage for generations yet unborn.

By nonviolent resistance, the Negro can also enlist all men of 10
good will in his struggle for equality. The problem is not a
purely racial one, with Negroes set against whites. In the end,
it is not a struggle between people at all, but a tension between
justice and injustice. Nonviolent resistance is not aimed

against oppressors but against oppression. Under its banner consciences, not racial groups, are enlisted.

Questions for Study and Discussion

1. What are the disadvantages that King sees in meeting oppression with acquiescence or with violence?
2. Why, according to King, do slaves not always welcome their deliverers?
3. What does King mean by the "freedom of exhaustion" (2)?
4. What is King's purpose in writing this essay? How does classifying the three types of resistance to oppression serve this purpose? (Glossary: *Purpose*)
5. What principle of division does King use in this essay?
6. Why do you suppose that King discusses acquiescence, violence, and nonviolent resistance in that order? (Glossary: *Organization*)
7. King states that he favors nonviolent resistance over the other two ways of meeting oppression. Look closely at the words he uses to describe nonviolent resistance and those he uses to describe acquiescence and violence. How does his choice of words contribute to his argument? Show examples. (Glossary: *Connotation/Denotation*)

Vocabulary

Refer to your dictionary to define the following words as they are used in this selection. Then use each word in a sentence of your own.

acquiescence (1)   desolate (6)
tacitly (1)   synthesis (7)
corroding (4)   sublime (9)
annihilate (5)

Suggested Writing Assignments

1. Write an essay about a problem of some sort in which you use division and classification to discuss various possible solutions. You might discuss something personal such as the problems of giving up smoking or something that concerns everyone such as the difficulties of coping with limited supplies of oil and gasoline or other natural resources. Whatever your topic, use an appropriate principle of division to establish categories that suit the purpose of your discussion.

2. Consider any one of the following topics for an essay of classification:

   movies
   college courses
   spectators
   life styles
   country music
   newspapers
   pets
   grandparents

Friends, Good Friends
—and Such Good Friends

Judith Viorst

Judith Viorst has written several volumes of light verse as well as many articles that have appeared in popular magazines. The following essay appeared in her regular column in Redbook. *In it she analyzes and classifies the various types of friends that a person can have. As you read the essay, assess its validity by trying to place your friends in Viorst's categories.*

Women are friends, I once would have said, when they totally love and support and trust each other, and bare to each other the secrets of their souls, and run—no questions asked—to help each other, and tell harsh truths to each other (no, you can't wear that dress unless you lose ten pounds first) when harsh truths must be told.

Women are friends, I once would have said, when they share the same affection for Ingmar Bergman, plus train rides, cats, warm rain, charades, Camus, and hate with equal ardor Newark and Brussels sprouts and Lawrence Welk and camping.

In other words, I once would have said that a friend is a friend all the way, but now I believe that's a narrow point of view. For the friendships I have and the friendships I see are conducted at many levels of intensity, serve many different functions, meet different needs and range from those as all-the-way as the friendship of the soul sisters mentioned above to that of the most nonchalant and casual playmates.

Consider these varieties of friendship:

1. Convenience friends. These are women with whom, if our paths weren't crossing all the time, we'd have no particular reason to be friends: a next-door neighbor, a woman in our car pool, the mother of one of our children's closest friends or maybe some mommy with whom we serve juice and cookies each week at the Glenwood Co-op Nursery.

Convenience friends are convenient indeed. They'll lend us
their cups and silverware for a party. They'll drive our kids to
soccer when we're sick. They'll take us to pick up our car when
we need a lift to the garage. They'll even take our cats when we
go on vacation. As we will for them.

But we don't, with convenience friends, ever come too close
or tell too much; we maintain our public face and emotional
distance. "Which means," says Elaine, "that I'll talk about being overweight but not about being depressed. Which means
I'll admit being mad but not blind with rage. Which means that
I might say that we're pinched this month but never that I'm
worried sick over money."

But which doesn't mean that there isn't sufficient value to be
found in these friendships of mutual aid, in convenience
friends.

2. Special-interest friends. These friendships aren't intimate, and they needn't involve kids or silverware or cats. Their
value lies in some interest jointly shared. And so we may have
an office friend or a yoga friend or a tennis friend or a friend
from the Women's Democratic Club.

"I've got one woman friend," says Joyce, "who likes, as I do,
to take psychology courses. Which makes it nice for me—and
nice for her. It's fun to go with someone you know and it's fun
to discuss what you've learned, driving back from the classes."
And for the most part, she says, that's all they discuss.

"I'd say that what we're doing is *doing* together, not being together," Suzanne says of her Tuesday-doubles friends. "It's
mainly a tennis relationship, but we play together well. And I
guess we all need to have a couple of playmates."

I agree.

My playmate is a shopping friend, a woman of marvelous
taste, a woman who knows exactly *where* to buy *what*, and furthermore is a woman who always knows beyond a doubt what
one ought to be buying. I don't have the time to keep up with
what's new in eyeshadow, hemlines and shoes and whether the
smock look is in or finished already. But since (oh, shame!) I
care a lot about eyeshadow, hemlines and shoes, and since I
don't *want* to wear smocks if the smock look is finished, I'm
very glad to have a shopping friend.

3. Historical friends. We all have a friend who knew us when 14
... maybe way back in Miss Meltzer's second grade, when our
family lived in that three-room flat in Brooklyn, when our dad
was out of work for seven months, when our brother Allie got
in that fight where they had to call the police, when our sister
married the endodontist from Yonkers and when, the morning
after we lost our virginity, she was the first, the only, friend we
told.

The years have gone by and we've gone separate ways and 15
we've little in common now, but we're still an intimate part of
each other's past. And so whenever we go to Detroit we always
go to visit this friend of our girlhood. Who knows how we
looked before our teeth were straightened. Who knows how we
talked before our voice got un-Brooklyned. Who knows what
we ate before we learned about artichokes. And who, by her
presence, puts us in touch with an earlier part of ourself, a part
of ourself it's important never to lose.

"What this friend means to me and what I mean to her," says 16
Grace, "is having a sister without sibling rivalry. We know the
texture of each other's lives. She remembers my grandmother's
cabbage soup. I remember the way her uncle played the piano.
There's simply no other friend who remembers those things."

4. Crossroads friends. Like historical friends, our cross- 17
roads friends are important for *what was*—for the friendship
we shared at a crucial, now past, time of life. A time, perhaps,
when we roomed in college together; or worked as eager young
singles in the Big City together; or went together, as my friend
Elizabeth and I did, through pregnancy, birth and that scary
first year of new motherhood.

Crossroads friends forge powerful links, links strong enough 18
to endure with not much more contact than once-a-year letters
at Christmas. And out of respect for those crossroads years, for
those dramas and dreams we once shared, we will always be
friends.

5. Cross-generational friends. Historical friends and cross- 19
roads friends seem to maintain a special kind of intimacy—
dormant but always ready to be revived—and though we may
rarely meet, whenever we do connect, it's personal and intense.
Another kind of intimacy exists in the friendships that form

across generations in what one woman calls her daughter-mother and her mother-daughter relationships.

Evelyn's friend is her mother's age—"but I share so much   20
more than I ever could with my mother"—a woman she talks to of music, of books and of life. "What I get from her is the benefit of her experience. What she gets—and enjoys—from me is a youthful perspective. It's a pleasure for both of us."

I have in my own life a precious friend, a woman of 65 who   21
has lived very hard, who is wise, who listens well; who has been where I am and can help me understand it; and who represents not only an ultimate ideal mother to me but also the person I'd like to be when I grow up.

In our daughter role we tend to do more than our share of   22
self-revelation; in our mother role we tend to receive what's revealed. It's another kind of pleasure—playing wise mother to a questing younger person. It's another very lovely kind of friendship.

6. Part-of-a-couple friends. Some of the women we call our   23
friends we never see alone—we see them as part of a couple at couples' parties. And though we share interests in many things and respect each other's views, we aren't moved to deepen the relationship. Whatever the reason, a lack of time or—and this is more likely—a lack of chemistry, our friendship remains in the context of a group. But the fact that our feeling on seeing each other is always, "I'm *so* glad she's here" and the fact that we spend half the evening talking together says that this too, in its own way, counts as a friendship.

(Other part-of-a-couple friends are the friends that came with   24
the marriage, and some of these are friends we could live without. But sometimes, alas, she married our husband's best friend; and sometimes, alas, she *is* our husband's best friend. And so we find ourself dealing with her, somewhat against our will, in a spirit of what I'll call *reluctant* friendship.)

7. Men who are friends. I wanted to write just of women   25
friends, but the women I've talked to won't let me—they say I must mention man-woman friendships too. For these friendships can be just as close and as dear as those that we form with women. Listen to Lucy's description of one such friendship:

"We've found we have things to talk about that are different 26
from what he talks about with my husband and different from
what I talk about with his wife. So sometimes we call on the
phone or meet for lunch. There are similar intellectual
interests—we always pass on to each other the books that we
love—but there's also something tender and caring too."

In a couple of crises, Lucy says, "he offered himself for talk- 27
ing and for helping. And when someone died in his family he
wanted me there. The sexual, flirty part of our friendship is
very small, but *some*—just enough to make it fun and different." She thinks—and I agree—that the sexual part, though
small, is always *some*, is always there when a man and a
woman are friends.

It's only in the past few years that I've made friends with 28
men, in the sense of a friendship that's *mine*, not just part of
two couples. And achieving with them the ease and the trust
I've found with women friends has value indeed. Under the
dryer at home last week, putting on mascara and rouge, I com-
fortably sat and talked with a fellow named Peter. Peter, I finally decided, could handle the shock of me minus mascara under the dryer. Because we care for each other. Because we're
friends.

8. There are medium friends, and pretty good friends, and 29
very good friends indeed, and these friendships are defined by
their level of intimacy. And what we'll reveal at each of these
levels of intimacy is calibrated with care. We might tell a medium friend, for example, that yesterday we had a fight with
our husband. And we might tell a pretty good friend that this
fight with our husband made us so mad that we slept on the
couch. And we might tell a very good friend that the reason we
got so mad in that fight that we slept on the couch had something to do with that girl who works in his office. But it's only
to our very best friends that we're willing to tell all, to tell
what's going on with that girl in his office.

The best of friends, I still believe, totally love and support 30
and trust each other, and bare to each other the secrets of their
souls, and run—no questions asked—to help each other, and
tell harsh truths to each other when they must be told.

But we needn't agree about everything (only 12-year-old girl 31 friends agree about *everything*) to tolerate each other's point of view. To accept without judgment. To give and to take without ever keeping score. And to *be* there, as I am for them and as they are for me, to comfort our sorrows, to celebrate our joys.

Questions for Study and Discussion

1. In her opening paragraph Viorst explains how she once would have defined friendship. Why does she now think differently?
2. What is Viorst's purpose in this essay? Why is division and classification an appropriate strategy for her to use? (Glossary: *Purpose*)
3. Into what categories does Viorst divide her friends?
4. What principles of division does Viorst use to establish her categories of friends? Where does she state these principles?
5. Discuss the ways in which Viorst makes her categories distinct and memorable.
6. Viorst wrote this essay for *Redbook*, and so her audience was women between the ages of twenty-five and thirty-five. If she had been writing on the same topic for an audience of men of the same age, how might her categories have been different? How might her examples have been different? (Glossary: *Audience*)

Vocabulary

Refer to your dictionary to define the following words as they are used in this selection. Then use each word in a sentence of your own.

ardor (2)	forge (18)
nonchalant (3)	dormant (19)
sibling (16)	perspective (20)

Suggested Writing Assignments

1. If for any reason you dislike or disagree with Viorst's classification of friends, write a classification essay of your own on the same topic. In preparation for writing, you may wish to interview your classmates and dorm members for their ideas on the various types of friends a person can have.

2. The following (p. 312) is a basic exercise in classification. By determining the features that the figures have in common, establish the general class to which they all belong. Next, establish subclasses by determining the distinctive features that distinguish one subclass from another. Finally, place each figure in an appropriate subclass within your classification system. You may wish to compare your classification system with those developed by other members of your class and to discuss any differences that exist.

16

COMPARISON AND CONTRAST

A *comparison* points out the ways that two or more persons, places, or things are alike. A *contrast* points out how they differ. The subjects of a comparison or contrast should be in the same class or general category; if they have nothing in common, there is no good reason for setting them side by side.

The function of any comparison or contrast is to clarify and explain. The writer's purpose may be simply to inform, or to make readers aware of similarities or differences that are interesting and significant in themselves. Or, the writer may explain something unfamiliar by comparing it with something very familiar, perhaps explaining squash by comparing it with tennis. Finally, the writer can point out the superiority of one thing by contrasting it with another—for example, showing that one product is the best by contrasting it with all its competitors.

As a writer, you have two main options for organizing a comparison or contrast: the subject-by-subject pattern or the point-by-point pattern. For a short essay comparing and contrasting the Atlanta Braves and the Los Angeles Dodgers, you would probably follow the *subject-by-subject* pattern of organization. By this pattern you first discuss the points you wish to make about one team, and then go on to discuss the corresponding points for the other team. An outline of your essay might look like this:

    I. Atlanta Braves
       A. Pitching
       B. Fielding
       C. Hitting
   II. Los Angeles Dodgers
       A. Pitching
       B. Fielding
       C. Hitting

The subject-by-subject pattern presents a unified discussion of each team by placing the emphasis on the teams and not on the three points of comparison. Since these points are relatively few, readers should easily remember what was said about the Braves' pitching when you later discuss the Dodgers' pitching and should be able to make the appropriate connections between them.

For a somewhat longer essay comparing and contrasting solar energy and wind energy, however, you should consider the *point-by-point* pattern of organization. With this pattern, your essay is organized according to the various points of comparison. Discussion alternates between solar and wind energy for each point of comparison. An outline of your essay might look like this:

I. Installation Expenses   IV. Convenience
   A. Solar   A. Solar
   B. Wind   B. Wind
II. Efficiency   V. Maintenance
   A. Solar   A. Solar
   B. Wind   B. Wind
III. Operating Costs   VI. Safety
   A. Solar   A. Solar
   B. Wind   B. Wind

The point-by-point pattern allows the writer to make immediate comparisons between solar and wind energy, thus enabling readers to consider each of the similarities and differences separately.

Each organizational pattern has its advantages. In general, the subject-by-subject pattern is useful in short essays where there are few points to be considered, whereas the point-by-point pattern is preferable in long essays where there are numerous points under consideration.

A good essay of comparison and contrast tells readers something significant that they do not already know. That is, it must do more than merely point out the obvious. As a rule, therefore, writers tend to draw contrasts between things that are usually perceived as being similar or comparisons between things usually perceived as different. In fact, comparison and contrast often go together. For example, an essay about Minneapolis and St. Paul might begin by showing how much they are alike, but end with a series of contrasts revealing how much they differ. Or, a consumer magazine might report the contrasting claims made by six car manufacturers, and then go on to demonstrate that the cars all actually do much the same thing in the same way.

THAT LEAN AND HUNGRY LOOK

Suzanne Britt

Suzanne Britt makes her home in Raleigh, North Carolina, where she is a free-lance writer. In 1983 she published Show & Tell, *a collection of her characteristically informal essays. The following essay first appeared in* Newsweek *and became the basis for her book,* Skinny People Are Dull and Crunchy Like Carrots *(1982), titled after a line in the essay. As you read her essay, notice the way that Britt has organized the points of her contrast of fat and thin people.*

Caesar was right. Thin people need watching. I've been watching them for most of my adult life, and I don't like what I see. When these narrow fellows spring at me, I quiver to my toes. Thin people come in all personalities, most of them menacing. You've got your "together" thin person, your mechanical thin person, your condescending thin person, your tsk-tsk thin person, your efficiency-expert thin person. All of them are dangerous.

In the first place, thin people aren't fun. They don't know how to goof off, at least in the best, fat sense of the word. They've always got to be adoing. Give them a coffee break, and they'll jog around the block. Supply them with a quiet evening at home, and they'll fix the screen door and lick S&H green stamps. They say things like "there aren't enough hours in the day." Fat people never say that. Fat people think the day is too damn long already.

Thin people make me tired. They've got speedy little metabolisms that cause them to bustle briskly. They're forever rubbing their bony hands together and eyeing new problems to "tackle." I like to surround myself with sluggish, inert, easygoing fat people, the kind who believe that if you clean it up today, it'll just get dirty again tomorrow.

Some people say the business about the jolly fat person is a myth, that all of us chubbies are neurotic, sick, sad people. I disagree. Fat people may not be chortling all day long, but they're a hell of a lot *nicer* than the wizened and shriveled. Thin people turn surly, mean, and hard at a young age because they never learn the value of a hot-fudge sundae for easing tension. Thin people don't like gooey soft things because they themselves are neither gooey nor soft. They are crunchy and dull, like carrots. They go straight to the heart of the matter while fat people let things stay all blurry and hazy and vague, the way things actually are. Thin people want to face the truth. Fat people know there is no truth. One of my thin friends is always staring at complex, unsolvable problems and saying, "The key thing is. . . ." Fat people never say that. They know there isn't any such thing as the key thing about anything.

Thin people believe in logic. Fat people see all sides. The   5
sides fat people see are rounded blobs, usually gray, always nebulous and truly not worth worrying about. But the thin person persists. "If you consume more calories than you burn," says one of my thin friends, "you will gain weight. It's that simple." Fat people always grin when they hear statements like that. They know better.

Fat people realize that life is illogical and unfair. They know   6
very well that God is not in his heaven and all is not right with the world. If God was up there, fat people could have two doughnuts and a big orange drink anytime they wanted it.

Thin people have a long list of logical things they are always   7
spouting off to me. They hold up one finger at a time as they reel off these things, so I won't lose track. They speak slowly as if to a young child. The list is long and full of holes. It contains tidbits like "get a grip on yourself," "cigarettes kill," "cholesterol clogs," "fit as a fiddle," "ducks in a row," "organize," and "sound fiscal management." Phrases like that.

They think these 2,000-point plans lead to happiness. Fat peo-   8
ple know happiness is elusive at best and even if they could get the kind thin people talk about, they wouldn't want it. Wisely, fat people see that such programs are too dull, too hard, too off the mark. They are never better than a whole cheesecake.

Fat people know all about the mystery of life. They are the   9
ones acquainted with the night, with luck, with fate, with playing it by ear. One thin person I know once suggested that we arrange all the parts of a jigsaw puzzle into groups according to size, shape, and color. He figured this would cut the time

needed to complete the puzzle by at least 50 percent. I said I wouldn't do it. One, I like to muddle through. Two, what good would it do to finish early? Three, the jigsaw puzzle isn't the important thing. The important thing is the fun of four people (one thin person included) sitting around a card table, working a jigsaw puzzle. My thin friend had no use for my list. Instead of joining us, he went outside and mulched the boxwoods. The three remaining fat people finished the puzzle and made chocolate, double-fudged brownies to celebrate.

The main problem with thin people is they oppress. Their   10
good intentions, bony torsos, tight ships, neat corners, cerebral machinations, and pat solutions loom like dark clouds over the loose, comfortable, spread-out, soft world of the fat. Long after fat people have removed their coats and shoes and put their feet up on the coffee table, thin people are still sitting on the edge of the sofa, looking neat as a pin, discussing rutabagas. Fat people are heavily into fits of laughter, slapping their thighs and whooping it up, while thin people are still politely waiting for the punch line.

Thin people are downers. They like math and morality and   11
reasoned evaluation of the limitations of human beings. They have their skinny little acts together. They expound, prognose, probe, and prick.

Fat people are convivial. They will like you even if you're ir-   12
regular and have acne. They will come up with a good reason why you never wrote the great American novel. They will cry in your beer with you. They will put your name in the pot. They will let you off the hook. Fat people will gab, giggle, guffaw, gallumph, gyrate, and gossip. They are generous, giving, and gallant. They are gluttonous and goodly and great. What you want when you're down is soft and jiggly, not muscled and stable. Fat people know this. Fat people have plenty of room. Fat people will take you in.

Questions for Study and Discussion

1. Does Britt use a subject-by-subject or a point-by-point pattern of organization to contrast fat and thin people? Explain. What points of contrast does Britt discuss?

2. How does Britt characterize thin people? Fat people?

3. What does Britt seem to have against thin people? Why does she consider thin "dangerous"? What do you think Britt looks like? How do you know?

4. What is Britt's purpose in this essay? (Glossary: *Purpose*) Is she serious, partially serious, mostly humorous? Are fat and thin people really her subject?

5. Britt makes effective use of the short sentence. Identify examples of sentences with three or fewer words and explain what function they serve.

6. Britt uses many clichés in her essay. Identify at least a dozen examples. What do you suppose is her purpose in using them? (Glossary: *Cliché*)

7. It is somewhat unusual for an essayist to use alliteration (the repetition of initial consonant sounds), a technique more commonly found in poetry. Where has Britt used alliteration and why do you suppose she has used this particular technique?

Vocabulary

Refer to your dictionary to define the following words as they are used in this selection. Then use each word in a sentence of your own.

menacing (1)   nebulous (5)
adoing (2)   rutabagas (10)
metabolism (3) prognose (11)
inert (3)   convivial (12)
chortling (4)   gallant (12)

Suggested Writing Assignments

1. Write a counter-argument in favor of thin people, using comparison and contrast and modeled on Britt's "That Lean and Hungry Look."

2. Reread paragraphs 3–6, and notice how these paragraphs are developed by contrasting the features of thin and fat people. Select two items from the following categories— people, products, events, institutions, places—and make a list of their contrasting features. Then write an essay modeled on Britt's, using the entries on your list.

GRANT AND LEE: A STUDY IN CONTRASTS

Bruce Catton

Bruce Catton (1899–1978) was born in Petoskey, Michigan, and attended Oberlin College. Early in his career, Catton worked as a reporter for various newspapers, among them the Cleveland Plain Dealer. *Having an interest in history, Catton became a leading authority on the Civil War and published a number of books on this subject. These include* Mr. Lincoln's Army *(1951),* Glory Road *(1952),* A Stillness at Appomattox *(1953),* The Hallowed Ground *(1956),* The Coming Fury *(1961),* Never Call Retreat *(1966), and* Gettysburg: The Final Fury *(1974). Catton was awarded both the Pulitzer Prize and the National Book Award in 1954.*

The following selection was included in The American Story, *a collection of historical essays edited by Earl Schenk Miers. In it Catton considers "two great Americans, Grant and Lee— very different, yet under everything very much alike."*

When Ulysses S. Grant and Robert E. Lee met in the parlor of a modest house at Appomattox Court House, Virginia, on April 9, 1865, to work out the terms for the surrender of Lee's Army of Northern Virginia, a great chapter in American life came to a close, and a great new chapter began. 1

These men were bringing the Civil War to its virtual finish. 2 To be sure, other armies had yet to surrender, and for a few days the fugitive Confederate government would struggle desperately and vainly, trying to find some way to go on living now that its chief support was gone. But in effect it was all over when Grant and Lee signed the papers. And the little room where they wrote out the terms was the scene of one of the poignant, dramatic contrasts in American history.

They were two strong men, these oddly different generals, and they represented the strengths of two conflicing currents that, through them, had come into final collision.

Back of Robert E. Lee was the notion that the old aristocratic concept might somehow survive and be dominant in American life.

Lee was tidewater Virginia, and in his background were family, culture, and tradition . . . the age of chivalry transplanted to a New World which was making its own legends and its own myths. He emobodied a way of life that had come down through the age of knighthood and the English country squire. America was a land that was beginning all over again, dedicated to nothing much more complicated than the rather hazy belief that all men had equal rights and should have an equal chance in the world. In such a land Lee stood for the feeling that it was somehow of advantage to human society to have a pronounced inequality in the social structure. There should be a leisure class, backed by ownerhsip of land; in turn, society itself should be keyed to the land as the chief source of wealth and influence. It would bring forth (according to this ideal) a class of men with a strong sense of obligation to the community; men who lived not to gain advantage for themselves, but to meet the solemn obligations which had been laid on them by the very fact that they were privileged. From them the country would get its leadership; to them it could look for the higher values—of thought, of conduct, of personal deportment—to give it strength and virtue.

Lee embodied the noblest elements of this aristocratic ideal. Through him, the landed nobility justified itself. For four years, the Southern states had fought a desperate war to uphold the ideals for which Lee stood. In the end, it almost seemed as if the Confederacy fought for Lee; as if he himself was the Confederacy . . . the best thing that the way of life for which the Confederacy stood could ever have to offer. He had passed into legend before Appomattox. Thousands of tired, underfed, poorly clothed Confederate soldiers, long since past the simple enthusiasm of the early days of the struggle, somehow considered Lee the symbol of everything for which they had been willing to die. But they could not quite put this feeling into words. If the Lost Cause, sanctified by so much heroism and so many deaths, had a living justification, its justification was General Lee.

Grant, the son of a tanner on the Western frontier, was every- 7
thing Lee was not. He had come up the hard way and embodied nothing in particular except the eternal toughness and sinewy fiber of the men who grew up beyond the mountains. He was one of a body of men who owed reverence and obeisance to no one, who were self-reliant to a fault, who cared hardly anything for the past but who had a sharp eye for the future.

These frontier men were the precise opposite of the tidewa- 8
ter aristocrats. Back of them, in the great surge that had taken people over the Alleghenies and into the opening Western country, there was a deep, implicit dissatisfaction with a past that had settled into grooves. They stood for democracy, not from any reasoned conclusion about the proper ordering of human society, but simply because they had grown up in the middle of democracy and knew how it worked. Their society might have privileges, but they would be privileges each man had won for himself. Forms and patterns meant nothing. No man was born to anything, except perhaps to a chance to show how far he could rise. Life was competition.

Yet along with this feeling had come a deep sense of belong- 9
ing to a national community. The Westerner who developed a farm, opened a shop, or set up in business as a trader, could hope to prosper only as his own community prospered—and his community ran from the Atlantic to the Pacific and from Canada down to Mexico. If the land was settled, with towns and highways and accessible markets, he could better himself. He saw his fate in terms of the nation's own destiny. As its horizons expanded, so did his. He had, in other words, an acute dollars-and-cents stake in the continued growth and development of his country.

And that, perhaps, is where the contrast between Grant and 10
Lee becomes most striking. The Virginia aristocrat, inevitably, saw himself in relation to his own region. He lived in a static society which could endure almost anything except change. Instinctively, his first loyalty would go to the locality in which that society existed. He would fight to the limit of endurance to

defend it, because in defending it he was defending everything that gave his own life its deepest meaning.

The Westerner, on the other hand, would fight with an equal tenacity for the broader concept of society. He fought so because everything he lived by was tied to growth, expansion, and a constantly widening horizon. What he lived by would survive or fall with the nation itself. He could not possibly stand by unmoved in the face of an attempt to destroy the Union. He would combat it with everything he had, because he could only see it as an effort to cut the ground out from under his feet. 11

So Grant and Lee were in complete contrast, representing two diametrically opposed elements in American life. Grant was the modern man emerging; beyond him, ready to come on the stage, was the great age of steel and machinery, of crowded cities and a restless burgeoning vitality. Lee might have ridden down from the old age of chivalry, lance in hand, silken banner fluttering over his head. Each man was the perfect champion of his cause, drawing both his strengths and his weaknesses from the people he led. 12

Yet is was not all contrast, after all. Different as they were— in background, in personality, in underlying aspiration—these two great soldiers had much in common. Under everything else, they were marvelous fighters. Furthermore, their fighting qualities were really very much alike. 13

Each man had, to begin with, the great virtue of utter tenacity and fidelity. Grant fought his way down the Mississippi Valley in spite of acute personal discouragement and profound military handicaps. Lee hung on in the trenches at Petersburg after hope itself had died. In each man there was an indomitable quality . . . the born fighter's refusal to give up as long as he can still remain on his feet and lift his two fists. 14

Daring and resourcefulness they had, too; the ability to think faster and move faster than the enemy. These were the qualities which gave Lee the dazzling campaigns of Second Manassas and Chancellorsville and won Vicksburg for Grant. 15

Lastly, and perhaps greatest of all, was the ability, at the end, to turn quickly from war to peace once the fighting was over. Out of the way these two men behaved at Appomattox came the possibility of a peace of reconciliation. It was a 16 possibility not wholly realized, in the years to come, but which did, in the end, help the two sections to become one nation again ... after a war whose bitterness might have seemed to make such a reunion wholly impossible. No part of either man's life became him more than the part he played in their brief meeting in the McLean house at Appomattox. Their behavior there put all succeeding generations of Americans in their debt. Two great Americans, Grant and Lee—very different, yet under everything very much alike. Their encounter at Appomattox was one of the great moments of American history.

Questions for Study and Discussion

1. In paragraphs 10–12 Catton discusses what he considers to be the most striking contrast between Grant and Lee. What is that difference?

2. List the similarities that Catton sees between Grant and Lee. Which similarity does Catton believe is most important? Why?

3. What would have been lost had Catton compared Grant and Lee before contrasting them? Would anything have been gained?

4. How does Catton organize the body of his essay (3–16)? You may find it helpful in answering this question to summarize the point of comparison in each paragraph and label it as being concerned with Lee, Grant, or both.

5. What attitudes and ideas does Catton describe to support the view that tidewater Virginia was a throwback to the "age of chivalry" (5)?

6. Catton says that Grant was "the modern man emerging" (12). How does he support that statement? Do you agree?

7. Catton has carefully made clear transitions between paragraphs. For each paragraph identify the transitional devices he uses. How do they help your reading? (Glossary: *Transitions*)

Vocabulary

Refer to your dictionary to define the following words as they are used in this selection. Then use each word in a sentence of your own.

poignant (2)	obeisance (7)
chivalry (5)	tidewater (8)
sanctified (6)	tenacity (11)
sinewy (7)	aspiration (13)

Suggested Writing Assignments

1. Compare and contrast any two world leaders (or popular singers or singing groups). In selecting a topic, you should consider (1) what your purpose will be, (2) whether you will emphasize similarities or differences, (3) what specific points you will discuss, and (4) what organizational pattern will best suit your purpose.

2. Select one of the following topics for an essay of comparison and contrast:

   two cities

   two friends

   two ways to heat a home

   two restaurants

   two actors or actresses

   two mountains

   two books by the same author

   two sports heroes

   two cars

   two teachers

   two brands of pizza

THE KNIGHT AND THE JESTER

Anna Quindlen

*Anna Quindlen was born in 1952. The oldest of
five children, she attended Barnard before starting work as a reporter for the* New York Post.
Later she moved to The New York Times *where
she wrote its "About New York" column for almost three years and was named deputy metro-
politan editor at the age of thirty-one. Quindlen
has contributed essays to the* Times's *"Hers"
column and currently is writing her own weekly
column, "Life in the 30's," where she explores
the rocky emotional terrain of marriage, parent-
hood, secret desires, and self-doubts, often using
her own family life as material. She's collected
the best of her columns in the book* Living Out
Loud *(1988). In the following essay, first published in 1988, Quindlen compares her own two
sons, Quin and Christopher, to make a point
about parenting and children's personalities.*

Sometimes I think you can tell everything about my two
children by watching them sleep at night. One lies flat on
his back, the quilt tucked neatly under his armpits, his arms at
his side, as though he were a child miming perfect sleep for an
advertisement for cocoa or pajamas. No matter what time it is,
you will find him so.

The other will be sprawled in some corner of the bed, and on
the floor will be his quilt, his sheets, his pillow and, if he's feeling particularly froggy, his pajamas. Sometimes he is at the
head and sometimes he is at the foot, and sometimes half of
him is hanging over the side. For the sake of futile mothering
gestures, I will often cover him up, but if I return 15 minutes
later the quilt will be on the floor again. I look from one bed to
the other and think: the knight and the jester; the gentleman
and the wild man; the parson and the gambler.

I like to think there are no particular value judgments to these assessments, but that is not true. I try to suppress them sometimes, to think in terms of body temperature as I straighten one set of perfectly straight blankets and untangle another from the floor. It is not fair to make two children foils for one another, although it is common and, I suppose, understandable to do so. It can also turn to poison faster than you can say Cain and Abel, for sometimes the unconscious assessments become sharper: the good child and the bad one; the smart one and the stupid one; the success and the failure. And sometimes thinking makes it so.

Perhaps I am overly sensitive on this subject, since I grew up with its shadow. I have a brother barely a year younger than I am, and I suspect that both of us were thoroughly sick, after a while, of the comparisons. Deep down we were not so different, but it was inevitable that in finding his own way around the world, one of the things he wanted was to find a way that was different from mine. By high school, I had become the circle-pin princess of the junior class. My brother, meanwhile, had begun to affect black leather jackets and shoes with pointed toes. If we had had a buck for every teacher who was incredulous that we shared the same parents, we could have started a small business together.

It was not as bad for me as it was for him, since I got the prime position at the starting gate, and he got the "on the other hand." Sometimes I think it turned him into some things he wasn't, just for the sake of living out the contrast.

Now I know how easily it happens, as we play out our liking for prototypes here, in the little bedrooms and the playgrounds and at the kitchen table. At some point after the first child is born, we ditch the books and learn the lessons of eating, sleeping and talking by doing. And in the process what we come to know about children is what the first child teaches us. We use that to measure the progress of the next child. And quietly, subtly, without malice or bad intentions, begins the process of comparison.

Some say that this is in the nature of being second, and that the person a second child becomes has more to do with filling in the spaces that haven't been claimed yet than with some innate difference of temperament. It's easy sometimes for me to believe that. My children are quite different. The eldest had staked out early the territory of being sensitive, sweet, thoughtful and eager to please. There were openings in the areas of independence, confidence, creative craziness and pure moxie, and whether by coincidence or design, the second child has all those things.

Yet when I think of the theory of filling in the family blanks I 8 think, too, of two babies in utero, one slow and languorous and giving no trouble, the other a real pistol, pounding the pavement, dancing the fandango, throwing his sheets on the floor even while floating in amniotic fluid. And I remember that in every knight there is something of the jester; in every wild man, a bit of the gentleman. The danger in making our children take roles on opposite sides of the family room is that the contradictions in their own characters, the things that make humans so interesting, get flattened out and hidden away. The other danger is that they will hate one another.

So far, I think we are doing all right. Certainly there's little 9 hatred, for which I am deeply grateful. But in my attempts to make our chaotic lives orderly, I have to battle constantly against the urge to pigeonhole each of them, to file away the essentials of their personalities as one thing I've finally gotten down, once and for all. I have never said to either, "Why can't you be more like your brother?" I have never compared them aloud. I am always mindful of my mother's will, in which she noted that I was everything she was not; this happened to be true, but since at the time I thought everything she was was wonderful, it left me little doubt about my own inadequacies.

And in truth one boy is not everything the other is not. Both 10 of them are everything—obedient, willful, sensitive, tough, wild, pacific—in different measures. Both look like angels when they are asleep, although neither is anything quite so two-dimensional as angelic. Children are not easy, no matter what mothers sometimes like to think in their attempts to turn all this tortured family calculus into plain arithmetic.

Questions for Study and Discussion

1. In what ways are Quindlen's two children different? How are their sleep patterns a reflection of their individual personalities?

2. Although it is common, and perhaps even understandable, that people compare children from the same family, such comparisons are unfair. What does Quindlen fear will happen when two children are compared?

3. In paragraphs 4 and 5, Quindlen discusses her sensitivity on the subject of comparing children. Why is she so sensitive?

4. How has Quindlen organized her essay? You may find it helpful to make a scratch outline of the essay in answering this question.

5. Quindlen reports that some people say that "the person a second child becomes has more to do with filling in the spaces that haven't been claimed yet than with some innate difference of temperament" (7). How do the examples of her brother and her second son illustrate this theory?

6. What, for Quindlen, are the dangers of making children "take roles on opposite sides of the family room" (8)?

7. In the final analysis, what does Quindlen say about her two sons? What is the meaning of her last line?

Vocabulary

Refer to your dictionary to define the following words as they are used in this selection. Then use each word in a sentence of your own.

miming (1)	malice (6)
futile (2)	innate (7)
foils (3)	languorous (8)
incredulous (4)	pigeonhole (9)
prototypes (6)	pacific (10)

Suggested Writing Assignments

1. Using Quindlen's essay as a model, write an essay in which you compare and/or contrast any one of the following pairs:

the athletic/nonathletic child
the well-adjusted/maladjusted child
the overachieving/underachieving child

the artistic/unartistic child
the handicapped/normal child
the alienated/socially active child
the shy/aggressive child

You should draw on your own experiences as a child or on observations of other children you knew while growing up.

2. Each of us has been compared both favorably and unfavorably to others in our lives—brothers, sisters, cousins, classmates, teammates. Write an essay in which you discuss the nature of the comparisons and the effect(s) that these comparisons had on you. How did you feel when you were compared to someone else?

FABLE FOR TOMORROW

Rachel Carson

Naturalist Rachel Carson (1907–1964) wrote The Sea Around Us *(1951),* Under the Sea Wind *(1952), and* The Edge of the Sea *(1955), sensitive investigations of marine life. But it was* Silent Spring *(1962), her study of herbicides and insecticides, that made Carson a controversial figure. Once denounced as an alarmist, she is now regarded as an early prophet of the ecology movement. In the following fable taken from* Silent Spring, *Carson uses contrast to show her readers the devastating effects of indiscriminate use of pesticides.*

There was once a town in the heart of America where all life   1
seemed to live in harmony with its surroundings. The town lay in the midst of a checkerboard of prosperous farms, with fields of grain and hillsides of orchards where, in spring, white clouds of bloom drifted above the green fields. In autumn, oak and maple and birch set up a blaze of color that flamed and flickered across a backdrop of pines. Then foxes barked in the hills and deer silently crossed the fields, half hidden in the mists of the fall mornings.

Along the roads, laurel, viburnum and alder, great ferns and   2
wildflowers delighted the traveler's eye through much of the year. Even in winter the roadsides were places of beauty, where countless birds came to feed on the berries and on the seed heads of the dried weeds rising above the snow. The countryside was, in fact, famous for the abundance and variety of its bird life, and when the flood of migrants was pouring through in spring and fall people traveled from great distances to observe them. Others came to fish the streams, which flowed clear and cold out of the hills and contained shady pools where trout lay. So it had been from the days many years ago when

the first settlers raised their houses, sank their wells, and built their barns.

Then a strange blight crept over the area and everything be- 3
gan to change. Some evil spell had settled on the community: mysterious maladies swept the flocks of chickens; the cattle and sheep sickened and died. Everywhere was a shadow of death. The farmers spoke of much illness among their families. In the town the doctors had become more and more puzzled by new kinds of sickness appearing among their patients. There had been several sudden and unexplained deaths, not only among adults but even among children, who would be stricken suddenly while at play and die within a few hours.

There was a strange stillness. The birds, for example— 4
where had they gone? Many people spoke of them, puzzled and disturbed. The feeding stations in the backyards were deserted. The few birds seen anywhere were moribund; they trembled violently and could not fly. It was a spring without voices. On the mornings that had once throbbed with the dawn chorus of robins, catbirds, doves, jays, wrens, and scores of other bird voices there was now no sound; only silence lay over the fields and woods and marsh.

On the farms the hens brooded, but no chicks hatched. The 5
farmers complained that they were unable to raise any pigs—the litters were small and the young survived only a few days. The apple trees were coming into bloom but no bees droned among the blossoms, so there was no pollination and there would be no fruit.

The roadsides, once so attractive, were now lined with 6
browned and withered vegetation as though swept by fire. These, too, were silent, deserted by all living things. Even the streams were now lifeless. Anglers no longer visited them, for all the fish had died.

In the gutters under the eaves and between the shingles of 7
the roofs, a white granular powder still showed a few patches; some weeks before it had fallen like snow upon the roofs and the lawns, the fields and streams.

No witchcraft, no enemy action had silenced the rebirth of 8
new life in this stricken world. The people had done it themselves.

This town does not actually exist, but it might easily have a thousand counterparts in America or elsewhere in the world. I know of no community that has experienced all the misfortunes I describe. Yet every one of these disasters has actually happened somewhere, and many real communities have already suffered a substantial number of them. A grim specter has crept upon us almost unnoticed, and this imagined tragedy may easily become a stark reality we all shall know. 9

Questions for Study and Discussion

1. A fable is a short narrative that makes an edifying or cautionary point. What is the point of Carson's fable?
2. How do comparison and contrast help Carson make her point?
3. Does Carson use a point-by-point or a subject-by-subject method of organization in this selection? How is the pattern of organization Carson uses appropriate for her purpose? Be prepared to cite examples from the text.
4. What is the significance of the "white granular powder" that Carson mentions in paragraph 7? Why do you suppose she does not introduce the powder earlier?
5. Carson uses a great number of specific details to enhance her comparison and contrast. Which details had a particularly strong effect on you? Explain why.
6. In the last paragraph Carson tells us that "this town does not actually exist." What effect did this information have on you? Did it lessen the impact of her warning? Did it give you cause for hope?

Vocabulary

Refer to your dictionary to define the following words as they are used in this selection. Then use each word in a sentence of your own.

migrants (2)   moribund (4)
blight (3)   specter (9)
maladies (3)

Suggested Writing Assignments

1. Write an essay modeled after Carson's in which you show how a particular place or area changed character for some reason (for example, as a result of herbicides, gentrification, urbanization, commercialization, strip mining, highway development, hurricane, etc.). Describe the area before and after the change, and be sure to give your reaction to the change either implicitly or explicitly.

2. Using one of the following "before and after" situations, write a short essay of comparison and/or contrast:

   before and after a diet
   before and after urban renewal
   before and after Christmas
   before and after beginning college
   before and after a final exam

17

CAUSE AND EFFECT

Every time you try to answer a question that asks *why*, you engage in the process of *causal analysis*—you attempt to determine a *cause* or series of causes for a particular *effect*. When you try to answer a question that asks *what if*, you attempt to determine what effect will result from a particular cause. You will have frequent opportunity to use cause and effect analysis in the writing that you will do in college. For example, in history you might be asked to determine the causes of the Seven-Day War between Egypt and Israel; in political science you might be asked to determine the reasons why Ronald Reagan won the 1984 presidential election; and, in sociology you might be asked to predict the effect that changes in Social Security legislation would have on senior citizens.

Determining causes and effects is usually thought-provoking and quite complex. One reason for this is that there are two types of causes: *immediate causes*, which are readily apparent because they are closest to the effect, and *ultimate causes*, which, being somewhat removed, are not so apparent and perhaps even hidden. Furthermore, ultimate causes may bring about effects which themselves become immediate causes, thus creating a *causal chain*. For example, consider the following causal chain: Sally, a computer salesperson, prepared extensively for a meeting with an important client (ultimate cause), impressed the client (immediate cause), and made a very large sale (effect). The chain did not stop there: the large sale caused her to be promoted by her employer (effect).

A second reason why causal analysis can be so complex is that an effect may have any number of possible or actual causes, and a cause may have any number of possible or actual effects. An upset stomach may be caused by eating spoiled food, but it may also be caused by overeating, flu, allergy, nervousness, pregnancy, or any combination of factors. Similarly, the high cost of electricity may have multiple effects: higher profits for utility companies, fewer sales of electrical appliances, higher prices for other products, and the development of alternative sources of energy.

Sound reasoning and logic, while present in all good writing, are central to any causal analysis. Writers of believable causal analysis examine their material objectively and develop their essays carefully. They are convinced by their own examination of the material but are not afraid to admit other possible causes and effects. Above all, they do not let their own prejudices interfere with the logic of their analyses and presentations.

Because people are accustomed to thinking of causes with their effects, they sometimes commit an error in logic known as the "after this, therefore because of this" fallacy (in Latin, *post hoc, ergo propter hoc*). This fallacy leads people to believe that because one event occurred after another event the first event somehow caused the second; that is, they sometimes make causal connections that are not proven. For example, if students began to perform better after a free breakfast program was instituted at their school, one could not assume that the improvement was caused by the breakfast program. There could of course be any number of other causes for this effect, and a responsible writer on the subject would analyze and consider them all before suggesting the cause.

NEVER GET SICK IN JULY

Marilyn Machlowitz

Marilyn Machlowitz earned her doctorate in psychology at Yale and is now a management psychologist. She contributes a regular column to Working Woman *magazine, has written* Workaholics *(1980), and is at work on a new book dealing with the consequences of succeeding at an early age. Notice in the following selection, first published in* Esquire *magazine in July 1978, how Machlowitz analyzes why it is a bad idea to get sick in July.*

One Harvard medical school professor warns his students 1 to stay home—as he does—on the Fourth of July. He fears he will become one of the holiday's highway casualties and wind up in an emergency room with an inexperienced intern "practicing" medicine on *him.*

Just the mention of July makes medical students, nurses, in- 2 terns, residents, and "real doctors" roll their eyes. While hospital administrators maintain that nothing is amiss that month, members of the medical profession know what happens when the house staff turns over and the interns take over each July 1.

This July 1, more than 13,000 new doctors will invade over 3 600 hospitals across the country. Within minutes they will be overwhelmed: last July 1, less than a month after finishing medical school, Dr. John Baumann, then twenty-five, walked into Washington, D.C.'s, Walter Reed Army Medical Center, where he was immediately faced with caring for "eighteen of the sickest people I had ever seen."

Pity the patient who serves as guinea pig at ten A.M.—or three 4 A.M.—that first day. Indeed, according to Dr. Russell K. Laros, Jr., professor and vice-chairman of obstetrics, gynecology, and reproductive sciences at the University of California, San Francisco, "There is no question that patients throughout the country are mismanaged during July. Without the most meticulous supervision," he adds, "serious errors can be made."

And they are. Internship provides the first chance to practice one's illegible scrawl on prescription blanks, a golden opportunity to make lots of mistakes. Interns—who are still known to most people by that name, even though they are now officially called first-year residents—have ordered the wrong drug in the wrong dosage to be administered the wrong way at the wrong times to the wrong patient. While minor mistakes are most common, serious errors are the sources of hospital horror stories. One intern prescribed an anti-depressant without knowing that it would inactivate the patient's previously prescribed antihypertensive medication.* The patient then experienced a rapid increase in blood pressure and suffered a stroke.

When interns do not know what to do, when they cannot covertly consult *The Washington Manual* (a handbook of medical therapeutics), they can always order tests. The first time one intern attempted to perform a pleural biopsy—a fairly difficult procedure—he punctured the patient's lung. When an acquaintance of mine entered an emergency room one Friday night in July with what was only an advanced case of the flu, she wound up having a spinal tap. While negative findings are often necessary to rule out alternative diagnoses, some of the tests are really unwarranted. Interns admit that the results are required only so they can cover themselves in case a resident or attending physician decides to give them the third degree.

Interns' hours only increase their inadequacy. Dr. Jay Dobkin, president of the Physicians National Housestaff Association, a Washington-based organization representing 12,000 interns and residents, says that "working conditions . . . directly impact and influence the quality of patient care. After thirty-six hours 'on,' most interns find their abilities compromised." Indeed, their schedules (they average 110 hours a week) and their salaries (last year, they averaged $13,145) make interns the chief source of cheap labor. No other hospital personnel will do as much "scut" work—drawing blood, for

---

*A depressant medicine used to lower high blood pressure.

instance—or dirty work, such as manually disimpacting severely constipated patients.

Even private patients fall prey to interns, because many physicians prefer being affiliated with hospitals that have interns to perform these routine duties around the clock. One way to reduce the likelihood of falling into the hands of an intern is to rely upon a physician in group practice whose partners can provide substitute coverage. Then, too, it probably pays to select a physician who has hospital privileges at the best teaching institution in town. There, at least, you are unlikely to encounter any interns who slept through school, as some medical students admit they do: only the most able students survive the computer-matching process to win the prestigious positions at university hospitals. 8

It may be reassuring to remember that while veteran nurses joke about scheduling their vacations to start July 1, they monitor interns most carefully and manage to catch many mistakes. Residents bear much more responsibility for supervision and surveillance, and Dr. Lawrence Boxt, president of the 5,000-member, Manhattan-based Committee of Interns and Residents and a resident himself, emphasizes that residents are especially vigilant during July. One of the interns he represents agreed: "You're watched like a hawk. You have so much support and backup. They're not going to let you kill anybody." So no one who requires emergency medical attention should hesitate to be hospitalized in July. 9

I asked Dr. Boxt whether he also had any advice for someone about to enter a hospital for elective surgery. 10

"Yes," he said. "Stay away." 11

Questions for Study and Discussion

1. Machlowitz begins her essay with the anecdote of the Harvard medical school professor. Does this brief story effectively introduce her essay? (Glossary: *Beginnings and Endings*) Why, or why not?

2. What, according to Machlowitz, are the immediate causes of the problems many hospitals experience during the month of July?
3. What does she say are the causes of intern inadequacy? Explain how Machlowitz uses examples and quotations from authorities to substantiate the cause and effect relationship.
4. Why, according to Machlowitz, do interns sometimes order unwarranted tests?
5. What suggestions does Machlowitz give for minimizing patient risk during the month of July?
6. How would you interpret Dr. Boxt's answer to the final question Machlowitz asks him?

Vocabulary

Refer to your dictionary to define the following words as they are used in this selection. Then use each word in a sentence of your own.

meticulous (4)	affiliated (8)
diagnoses (6)	prestigious (8)
unwarranted (6)	vigilant (9)
compromised (7)	

Suggested Writing Assignments

1. Write an essay in which you argue for changes in the ways hospitals handle the "July" problem. Make sure your proposals are realistic, clearly stated, and have some chance of producing the desired effects. You may wish to consider some possible objections to your proposals and how they might be overcome.
2. There is often more than one cause for an event. Make a list of at least six possible causes for one of the following:

a quarrel with a friend
an upset victory in a football game

    a well-done exam
    a broken leg
    a change of major

Examine your list, and identify the causes that seem most probable. Which of these are immediate causes and which are ultimate causes? Using this material, write a short cause and effect essay.

WHEN TELEVISION IS A
SCHOOL FOR CRIMINALS

Grant Hendricks

*Grant Hendricks is serving a life sentence
in Michigan's Marquette maximum-security
prison. When he submitted the following article
to* TV Guide *for publication, the editors found
the results of his research so surprising that they
verified the facts for themselves before publishing the article. Hendricks contends that penitentiary inmates watch television not only to pass
the time but also to learn new techniques for
committing yet more crimes—that television
may, in fact, be a school for criminals.*

For years, psychologists and sociologists have tried to find   1
some connection between crime and violence on television
and crime and violence in American society. To date, no one
has been able to prove—or disprove—that link. But perhaps the
scientists, with their academic approaches, have been unable
to mine the mother lode of information on violence, crime and
television available in our prison systems.

I'm not about to dismiss the scientists' findings, but as a pris-   2
oner serving a life sentence in Michigan's Marquette maximum-security prison, I believe I can add a new dimension to
the subject. Cons speak much more openly to one of their own
than to outsiders. And because of this, I spent three weeks last
summer conducting an informal survey of 208 of the 688 inmates here at Marquette, asking them what they felt about the
correlation between the crime and violence they see on television and the crime and violence they have practiced as a way of
life.

Making this survey, I talked to my fellow prisoners in the   3
mess hall, in the prison yard, in the factory and in my cell
block. I asked them, on a confidential basis, whether or not

their criminal activities have ever been influenced by what they see on TV. A surprising 9 out of 10 told me that they have actually learned new tricks and improved their criminal expertise by watching crime programs. Four out of 10 said that they have attempted specific crimes they saw on television crime dramas, although they also admit that only about one-third of these attempts were successful.

Perhaps even more surprising is the fact that here at Marquette, where 459 of us have television sets in our individual cells, hooked up to a cable system, many cons sit and take notes while watching *Baretta, Kojak, Police Woman, Switch* and other TV crime shows. As one of my buddies said recently: "It's like you have a lot of intelligent, creative minds—all those Hollywood writers—working for *you*. They keep coming up with new ideas. They'll lay it all out for you, too: show you the type of evidence the cops look for—how they track you, and so on." 4

What kinds of lessons have been learned by TV-watching criminals? Here are some examples. 5

One of my prison-yard mates told me he "successfully" pulled off several burglaries, all patterned on a caper from *Police Woman.* 6

Another robbed a sporting-goods store by following the *modus operandi** he saw on an *Adam-12* episode. 7

By copying a *Paper Moon* scheme, one con man boasts he pulled off a successful bunco fraud—for which he has never been caught (he's currently serving time for another crime). 8

Of course, television doesn't guarantee that the crime you pull off will be successful. One inmate told me he attempted to rip off a dope house, modeling his plan on a *Baretta* script. But the heroin dealers he tried to rob called the cops and he was caught. Another prison-yard acquaintance mentioned that, using a *Starsky & Hutch* plot, he tried to rob a nightclub. But to his horror, the place was owned by underworld people. "I'm lucky to still be alive," he said. 9

On the question of violence, however, a much smaller number of Marquette inmates feel they were influenced by watching anything on television. Of the 59 men I interviewed who 10

---

*(Latin) *modus operandi,* or method of operation.

have committed rape, only 1 out of 20 said that he felt inspired or motivated to commit rape as a result of something he saw on television. Forty-seven of the 208 men I spoke to said that at one time or another they had killed another person. Of those, 31 are now serving life sentences for either first- or second-degree murder. Of these 31, only 2 said their crimes had been television-influenced. But of the 148 men who admitted to committing assault, about 1 out of 6 indicated that his crime had been inspired or motivated by something he saw on TV.

Still, one prisoner after another will tell you how he has been 11 inspired, motivated and helped by television. And crime shows and TV-movies are not the only sources of information. CBS's *60 Minutes* provides choice viewing for Marquette's criminal population. One con told me: "They recently did a segment on *60 Minutes* on how easy it was to get phony IDs. Just like the hit man in 'Day of the Jackal,' but on *60 Minutes* it wasn't fiction—it was for real. After watching that show, you knew how to go out and score a whole new personality on paper—credit cards, driver's license, everything. It was fantastic."

Sometimes, watching television helps you learn to think on 12 your feet. Like an old friend of mine named Shakey, who once escaped from the North Dakota State Penitentiary. While he hid in the basement of a private residence, they were putting up roadblocks all around the city of Bismarck. But Shakey was smart. He knew that there had to be some way for him to extricate himself from this mess. Then, all of a sudden it occurred to him: Shakey remembered a caper film he'd seen on television once, in which a fugitive had managed to breach several roadblocks by using an emergency vehicle.

With this basic plan in mind, he proceeded to the Bismarck 13 City Hospital and, pretending to be hysterical, he stammered to the first white-coated attendant he met that his brother was lying trapped beneath an overturned farm tractor about 12 miles or so from town. He then climbed into the back of the ambulance, and with red lights blazing and siren screaming, the vehicle drove right through two roadblocks—and safely out of Bismarck.

Two days or so later, Shakey arrived back on the same ranch 14 in Montana where he'd worked before his jail sentence. The foreman even gave him his job again. But Shakey was so proud of what he'd done that he made one big mistake: he boasted about his escape from the North Dakota state prison, and in the end he was turned over to the authorities, who sent him back to North Dakota—and prison. . . .

An 18-year-old inmate told me that while watching an old 15
Adam-12 show, he had learned exactly how to break open pay-phone coin boxes. He thought it seemed like a pretty good idea for picking up a couple of hundred dollars a day, so he gave it a try. To his surprise and consternation, the writers of *Adam-12* had failed to explain that Ma Bell has a silent alarm system built into her pay phones. If you start tampering with one, the operator can notify the police within seconds—even giving them the location of the phone being ripped off. He was arrested on his first attempt and received a one-year sentence.

Another prisoner told me that he had learned to hot-wire cars 16
at the age of 14 by watching one of his favorite TV shows. A week later he stole his first car—his mother's. Five years later he was in Federal prison for transporting stolen vehicles across state lines.

This man, at the age of 34, has spent 15 years behind bars. Ac- 17
cording to him, "TV has taught me how to steal cars, how to break into establishments, how to go about robbing people, even how to roll a drunk. Once, after watching a *Hawaii Five-O*, I robbed a gas station. The show showed me how to do it. Now-adays [he's serving a term for attempted rape] I watch TV in my house [cell] from 4 p.m. until midnight. I just sit back and take notes. I see 'em doing it this way or that way, you know, and I tell myself that I'll do it the same way when I get out. You could probably pick any 10 guys in here and ask 'em and they'd tell you the same thing. Everybody's picking up on what's on the TV." . . .

One of my friends here in Marquette says that TV is just a re- 18
flection of what's happening "out there." According to him, "The only difference is that the people out there haven't been caught—and we have. But our reaction to things is basically the same. Like when they showed the movie 'Death Wish' here, the people reacted the same way they did on the outside—they applauded Charles Bronson when he wasted all the criminals. The crooks applauded Bronson!"

Still, my research—informal though it is—shows that crimi-   19
nals look at television differently than straight people. Outside,
TV is entertainment. Here, it helps the time go by. But it is also
educational. As one con told me, television has been beneficial
to his career in crime by teaching him all the things *not* to do.
Another mentioned that he's learned a lot about how cops think
and work by watching crime-drama shows. In the prison factory, one guy said that he's seen how various alarm systems operate by watching TV; and here in my cell block somebody said
that because of television shows, he's been kept up-to-date on
modern police procedures and equipment.

Another con told me: "In the last five to seven years we've   20
learned that the criminal's worst enemy is the snitch. TV has
built that up. On *Starsky & Hutch* they've even made a sympathetic character out of a snitch. So we react to that in here.
Now the general feeling is that if you use a partner to commit a
crime, you kill him afterwards so there's nobody to snitch on
you."

For most of us cons in Marquette, it would be hard to do time   21
without TV. It's a window on the world for us. We see the news
shows, we watch sports and some of us take great pains to keep
tuned into the crime shows. When I asked one con if he felt that
watching TV crime shows in prison would be beneficial to his
career, he just smiled and said, "Hey, I sit and take notes—do
my homework, you know? No way would I sit in my cell and
waste my time watching comedies for five hours—no way!"

Questions for Study and Discussion

1. Why is Hendricks particularly well suited to write this
   essay?
2. What is Hendricks's purpose in this essay? Where does he
   state his purpose? (Glossary: *Purpose*)
3. What particular cause and effect relationship does the author set out to establish in the essay? Does the essay seem
   sound and logical? Why or why not?
4. For what purpose does Hendricks use examples in this essay? (Glossary: *Example*)

5. What does Hendricks gain by quoting his fellow inmates rather than paraphrasing them? (Glossary: *Dialogue*)
6. In addition to crime shows and TV movies, what other programs did convicts report as useful sources of information?
7. If television is indeed educational for prison inmates, what exactly is it that they learn? Illustrate your answer with references to specific television shows.

Vocabulary

Refer to your dictionary to define the following words as they are used in this selection. Then use each word in a sentence of your own.

correlation (2)   hysterical (13)
extricate (12)   consternation (15)

Suggested Writing Assignments

1. Much attention has been focused on the issue of violence on television. Write a cause and effect essay using the following statement as your thesis:

   Television teaches us that violence is an acceptable way to deal with those who disagree with us or who keep us from having our own way.

2. Write an essay in which you discuss the effects of television on you or on American society. You may wish to focus on the specific influences of one of the following aspects of television:

   advertising
   sports broadcasts
   cultural programming
   talk shows
   national or international news
   children's programming
   educational television
   situation comedies

WHY WE CRAVE HORROR MOVIES

Stephen King

Stephen King's name is synonymous with horror stories. A graduate of the University of Maine in 1970, King had worked in a knitting mill and as a janitor, laundry worker, and high-school English teacher before he struck it big with his writing. Many consider Stephen King the most successful writer of modern horror fiction working in that genre today. His books have sold well over 20 million copies, and several of his novels have been made into popular motion pictures. His books include Carrie *(1974),* Salem's Lot *(1975),* The Shining *(1977),* The Dead Zone *(1979),* Firestarter *(1980),* Christine *(1983),* Pet Sematery *(1983), and* Tommyknockers *(1988). A short story from the collection* Night Shift *(1978) was produced as the movie* Stand by Me. *The widespread popularity of horror books and films attest to the fact that many people share King's fascination with the macabre. In the following selection, King analyzes the reasons we all flock to good horror movies.*

I think that we're all mentally ill; those of us outside the asy-   1
lums only hide it a little better—and maybe not all that much better, after all. We've all known people who talk to themselves, people who sometimes squinch their faces into horrible grimaces when they believe no one is watching, people who have some hysterical fear—of snakes, the dark, the tight place, the long drop . . . and, of course, those final worms and grubs that are waiting so patiently underground.

When we pay our four or five bucks and seat ourselves at   2
tenth-row center in a theater showing a horror movie, we are daring the nightmare.

Why? Some of the reasons are simple and obvious. To show ₃
that we can, that we are not afraid, that we can ride this roller
coaster. Which is not to say that a really good horror movie
may not surprise a scream out of us at some point, the way we
may scream when the roller coaster twists through a complete
360 or plows through a lake at the bottom of the drop. And horror movies, like roller coasters, have always been the special
province of the young; by the time one turns 40 or 50, one's appetite for double twists or 360-degree loops may be considera-
bly depleted.

We also go to re-establish our feelings of essential normality; ₄
the horror movie is innately conservative, even reactionary.
Freda Jackson as the horrible melting woman in *Die, Monster,
Die!* confirms for us that no matter how far we may be removed
from the beauty of a Robert Redford or a Diana Ross, we are
still light-years from true ugliness.

And we go to have fun. ₅

Ah, but this is where the ground starts to slope away, isn't it? ₆
Because this is a very peculiar sort of fun, indeed. The fun
comes from seeing others menaced—sometimes killed. One
critic has suggested that if pro football has become the voy-
eur's version of combat, then the horror film has become the
modern version of the public lynching.

It is true that the mythic, "fairy-tale" horror film intends to ₇
take away the shades of gray. . . . It urges us to put away our
more civilized and adult penchant for analysis and to become
children again, seeing things in pure blacks and whites. It may
be that horror movies provide psychic relief on this level because this invitation to lapse into simplicity, irrationality and
even outright madness is extended so rarely. We are told we
may allow our emotions a free rein . . . or no rein at all.

If we are all insane, then sanity becomes a matter of degree. ₈
If your insanity leads you to carve up women like Jack the Rip-
per or the Cleveland Torso Murderer, we clap you away in the
funny farm (but neither of those two amateur-night surgeons
was ever caught, heh-heh-heh); if, on the other hand, your insanity leads you only to talk to yourself when you're under
stress or to pick your nose on your morning bus, then you are
left alone to go about your business . . . though it is doubtful
that you will ever be invited to the best parties.

The potential lyncher is in almost all of us (excluding saints, 9
past and present; but then, most saints have been crazy in their
own ways), and every now and then, he has to be let loose to
scream and roll around in the grass. Our emotions and our
fears form their own body, and we recognize that it demands
its own exercise to maintain proper muscle tone. Certain of
these emotional muscles are accepted—even exalted—in civilized society; they are, of course, the emotions that tend to
maintain the status quo of civilization itself. Love, friendship,
loyalty, kindness—these are all the emotions that we applaud,
emotions that have been immortalized in the couplets of Hallmark cards and in the verses (I don't dare call it poetry) of
Leonard Nimoy.

When we exhibit these emotions, society showers us with 10
positive reinforcement; we learn this even before we get out of
diapers. When, as children, we hug our rotten little puke of a
sister and give her a kiss, all the aunts and uncles smile and
twit and cry, "Isn't he the sweetest little thing?" Such coveted
treats as chocolate-covered graham crackers often follow. But
if we deliberately slam the rotten little puke of a sister's fingers
in the door, sanctions follow—angry remonstrance from parents, aunts and uncles; instead of a chocolate-covered graham
cracker, a spanking.

But anticivilization emotions don't go away, and they de- 11
mand periodic exercise. We have such "sick" jokes as, "What's
the difference between a truckload of bowling balls and a
truckload of dead babies? (You can't unload a truckload of
bowling balls with a pitchfork . . . a joke, by the way, that I
heard originally from a ten-year-old). Such a joke may surprise
a laugh or a grin out of us even as we recoil, a possibility that
confirms the thesis: If we share a brotherhood of man, then we
also share an insanity of man. None of which is intended as a
defense of either the sick joke or insanity but merely as an explanation of why the best horror films, like the best fairy tales,
manage to be reactionary, anarchistic, and revolutionary all at
the same time.

The mythic horror movie, like the sick joke, has a dirty job to 12
do. It deliberately appeals to all that is worst in us. It is morbid-
ity unchained, our most base instincts let free, our nastiest fan-
tasies realized . . . and it all happens, fittingly enough, in the

dark. For those reasons, good liberals often shy away from horror films. For myself, I like to see the most aggressive of them—*Dawn of the Dead*, for instance—as lifting a trap door in the civilized forebrain and throwing a basket of raw meat to the hungry alligators swimming around in that subterranean river beneath.

Why bother? Because it keeps them from getting out, man. It 13 keeps them down there and me up here. It was Lennon and McCartney who said that all you need is love, and I would agree with that.

As long as you keep the gators fed. 14

Questions for Study and Discussion

1. What, according to King, are several of the reasons people go to horror movies? What other reasons can you add to King's list?

2. Identify the analogy King uses in paragraph 3, and explain how it works. (Glossary: *Analogy*)

3. What does King mean when he says "the horror movie is innately conservative, even reactionary" (4)?

4. What emotions does society applaud? Why? Which ones does King label "anticivilization" emotions?

5. In what ways is a horror movie like a sick joke? What is the "dirty job" that the two have in common (12)?

6. King starts his essay with the attention-grabbing sentence "I think that we're all mentally ill." How does he develop this idea of insanity in his essay? What does King mean when he says "the potential lyncher is in almost all of us" (9)? How does King's last line relate to the theme of mental illness?

7. What is King's tone in this essay? (Glossary: *Tone*) Point to particular words or sentences that led you to this conclusion.

Vocabulary

Refer to your dictionary to define the following words as they are used in this selection. Then use each word in a sentence of your own.

grimaces (1)	puke (10)
hysterical (1)	sanctions (10)
voyeur's (6)	remonstrance (10)
penchant (7)	recoil (11)
rein (7)	anarchistic (11)
exalted (9)	morbidity (12)
status quo (9)	subterranean (12)

Suggested Writing Assignments

1. Write an essay in which you analyze the most significant reason(s) for your going to college. You may wish to discuss such matters as your high-school experiences, people and events that influenced your decision, and your goals in college as well as in later life.

2. Write an essay in which you analyze, in light of Stephen King's remarks, a horror movie you've seen. In what ways did the movie satisfy your "anticivilization" emotions? How did you feel before going to the theater? How did you feel when leaving?

WHO'S AFRAID OF MATH, AND WHY?

Sheila Tobias

*Sheila Tobias served as Associate Provost of
Wesleyan University, where she became interested in the reasons that certain students, nota-
bly women, choose not to pursue careers in math
or math-related fields. On the basis of her research, Tobias, a "mathematics avoider" herself,
founded the Math Clinic at Wesleyan. She is the
author of* Overcoming Math Anxiety *(1978), from
which this essay is taken. As you read the essay,
notice how Tobias systematically analyzes the
possible causes of "math anxiety."*

The first thing people remember about failing at math is
that it felt like sudden death. Whether the incident occurred while learning "word problems" in sixth grade, coping
with equations in high school, or first confronting calculus and
statistics in college, failure came suddenly and in a very frightening way. An idea or a new operation was not just difficult, it
was impossible! And, instead of asking questions or taking the
lesson slowly, most people remember having had the feeling
that they would never go any further in mathematics. If we assume that the curriculum was reasonable, and that the new
idea was but the next in a series of learnable concepts, the feeling of utter defeat was simply not rational; yet "math anxious"
college students and adults have revealed that no matter how
much the teacher reassured them, they could not overcome
that feeling.

A common myth about the nature of mathematical ability
holds that one either has or does not have a mathematical
mind. Mathematical imagination and an intuitive grasp of
mathematical principles may well be needed to do advanced research, but why should people who can do college-level work in
other subjects not be able to do college-level math as well?
Rates of learning may vary. Competency under time pressure

may differ. Certainly low self-esteem will get in the way. But where is the evidence that a student needs a "mathematical mind" in order to succeed at learning math?

Consider the effects of this mythology. Since only a few people are supposed to have this mathematical mind, part of what makes us so passive in the face of our difficulties in learning mathematics is that we suspect all the while we may not be one of "them," and we spend our time waiting to find out when our nonmathematical minds will be exposed. Since our limit will eventually be reached, we see no point in being methodical or in attending to detail. We are grateful when we survive fractions, word problems, or geometry. If that certain moment of failure hasn't struck yet, it is only temporarily postponed.

Parents, especially parents of girls, often expect their children to be nonmathematical. Parents are either poor at math and had their own sudden-death experiences, or, if math came easily for them, they do not know how it feels to be slow. In either case, they unwittingly foster the idea that a mathematical mind is something one either has or does not have.

Mathematics and Sex

Although fear of math is not a purely female phenomenon, girls tend to drop out of math sooner than boys, and adult women experience an aversion to math and math-related activities that is akin to anxiety. A 1972 survey of the amount of high school mathematics taken by incoming freshmen at Berkeley revealed that while 57 percent of the boys had taken four years of high school math, only 8 percent of the girls had had the same amount of preparation. Without four years of high school math, students at Berkeley, and at most other colleges and universities, are ineligible for the calculus sequence, unlikely to attempt chemistry or physics, and inadequately prepared for statistics and economics.

Unable to elect these entry-level courses, the remaining 92 percent of the girls will be limited, presumably, to the career choices that are considered feminine: the humanities, guidance and counseling, elementary school teaching, foreign languages, and the fine arts.

Boys and girls may be born alike with respect to math, but certain sex differences in performance emerge early according to several respected studies, and these differences remain through adulthood. They are:

1. Girls compute better than boys (elementary school and on).
2. Boys solve word problems better than girls (from age thirteen on).
3. Boys take more math than girls (from age sixteen on).
4. Girls learn to hate math sooner and possibly for different reasons.

Why the differences in performance? One reason is the 8 amount of math learned and used at play. Another may be the difference in male-female maturation. If girls do better than boys at all elementary school tasks, then they may compute better for no other reason than that arithmetic is part of the elementary school curriculum. As boys and girls grow older, girls become, under pressure, academically less competitive. Thus, the falling off of girls' math performance between ages ten and fifteen may be because:

1. Math gets harder in each successive year and requires more work and commitment.
2. Both boys and girls are pressured, beginning at age ten, not to excel in areas designated by society to be outside their sex-role domains.
3. Thus girls have a good excuse to avoid the painful struggle with math; boys don't.

Such a model may explain girls' lower achievement in math 9 overall, but why should girls even younger than ten have difficulty in problem-solving? In her review of the research on sex differences, psychologist Eleanor Maccoby noted that girls are generally more conforming, more suggestible, and more dependent upon the opinion of others than boys (all learned, not innate, behaviors). Being so, they may not be as willing to take risks or to think for themselves, two behaviors that are necessary in solving problems. Indeed, in one test of third-graders, girls were found to be not nearly as willing to estimate, to make judgments about "possible right answers," or to work with systems they had never seen before. Their very success at doing what is expected of them up to that time seems to get in the way of their doing something new.

If readiness to do word problems, to take one example, is as much a function of readiness to take risks as it is of "reasoning ability," then mathematics performance certainly requires more than memory, computation, and reasoning. The differences in math performance between boys and girls—no matter how consistently those differences show up— cannot be attributed simply to differences in innate ability. 10

Still, if one were to ask the victims themselves, they would probably disagree: they would say their problems with math have to do with the way they are "wired." They feel they are somehow missing something—one ability or several—that other people have. Although women want to believe they are not mentally inferior to men, many fear that, where math is concerned, they really are. Thus, we have to consider seriously whether mathematical ability has a biological basis, not only because a number of researchers believe this to be so, but because a number of victims agree with them. 11

The Arguments from Biology

The search for some biological basis for math ability or disability is fraught with logical and experimental difficulties. Since not all math under-achievers are women, and not all women are mathematics-avoidant, poor performance in math is unlikely to be due to some genetic or hormonal difference between the sexes. Moreover, no amount of research so far has unearthed a "mathematical competency" in some tangible, measurable substance in the body. Since "masculinity" cannot be injected into women to test whether or not it improves their mathematics, the theories that attribute such ability to genes or hormones must depend for their proof on circumstantial evidence. So long as about 7 percent of the Ph.D.'s in mathematics are earned by women, we have to conclude either that these women have genes, hormones, and brain organization different from those of the rest of us, or that certain positive experiences in their lives have largely undone the negative fact that they are female, or both. 12

Genetically, the only difference between males and females (albeit a significant and pervasive one) is the presence of two chromosomes designated X in every female cell. Normal males exhibit an X-Y combination. Because some kinds of mental re- 13 tardation are associated with sex-chromosomal anomalies, a number of researchers have sought a converse linkage between specific abilities and the presence or absence of the second X. But the linkage between genetics and mathematics is not supported by conclusive evidence.

Since intensified hormonal activity commences at adolescence, a time during which girls seem to lose interest in mathematics, much more has been made of the unequal amounts in females and males of the sex-linked hormones androgen and estrogen. Biological researchers have linked estrogen—the female hormone—with "simple repetitive tasks," and androgen—the male hormone—with "complex restructuring tasks." The assumption here is not only that such specific talents are biologically based (probably undemonstrable) but also that one cannot be good at *both* repetitive and restructuring kinds of assignments.

Sex Roles and Mathematics Competence

The fact that many girls tend to lose interest in math at the age they reach puberty (junior high school) suggests that puberty might in some sense cause girls to fall behind in math. Several explanations come to mind: the influence of hormones, more intensified sex-role socialization, or some extracurricular learning experience exclusive to boys of that age.

One group of seventh-graders in a private school in New England gave a clue as to what children themselves think about all of this. When asked why girls do as well as boys in math until the sixth grade, while sixth-grade boys do better from that point on, the girls responded: "Oh, that's easy. After sixth grade, we have to do real math." The answer to why "real math" should be considered to be "for boys" and not "for girls" can be found not in the realm of biology but only in the realm of ideology of sex differences.

Parents, peers, and teachers forgive a girl when she does badly in math at school, encouraging her to do well in other subjects instead. " 'There, there.' my mother used to say when I failed at math," one woman says. "But I got a talking-to when I did badly in French." Lynn Fox, who directs a program for mathematically gifted junior high boys and girls on the campus of Johns Hopkins University, has trouble recruiting girls and keeping them in her program. Some parents prevent their daughters from participating altogether for fear that excellence in math will make them too different. The girls themselves are often reluctant to continue with mathematics, Fox reports, because they fear social ostracism.

Where do these associations come from? 18

The association of masculinity with mathematics sometimes 19 extends from the discipline to those who practice it. Students, asked on a questionnaire what characteristics they associate with a mathematician (as contrasted with a "writer"), selected terms such as rational, cautious, wise, and responsible. The writer, on the other hand, in addition to being seen as individualistic and independent, was also described as warm, interested in people, and altogether more compatible with a feminine ideal.

As a result of this psychological conditioning, a young 20 woman may consider math and math-related fields to be inimical to femininity. In an interesting study of West German teenagers, Erika Schildkamp-Kuendiger found that girls who identified themselves with the feminine ideal underachieved in mathematics, that is, did less well than would have been expected of them based on general intelligence and performance in other subjects.

Street Mathematics: Things, Motion, Scores

Not all the skills that are necessary for learning mathematics 21 are learned in school. Measuring, computing, and manipulating objects that have dimensions and dynamic properties of their own are part of the everyday life of children. Children who miss out on these experiences may not be well primed for math in school.

Feminists have complained for a long time that playing with 22 dolls is one way of convincing impressionable little girls that they may only be mothers or housewives—or, as in the case of the Barbie doll, "pinup girls"—when they grow up. But dollplaying may have even more serious consequences for little girls than that. Do girls find out about gravity and distance and shapes and sizes playing with dolls? Probably not.

A curious boy, if his parents are tolerant, will have taken 23 apart a number of household and play objects by the time he is ten, and, if his parents are lucky, he may even have put them back together again. In all of this he is learning things that will be useful in physics and math. Taking parts out that have to go back in requires some examination of form. Building something that stays up or at least stays put for some time involves working with structure.

Sports is another source of math-related concepts for chil-   24
dren which tends to favor boys. Getting to first base on a not very well hit grounder is a lesson in time, speed, and distance. Intercepting a football thrown through the air requires some rapid intuitive eye calculations based on the ball's direction, speed, and trajectory. Since physics is partly concerned with velocities, trajectories, and collisions of objects, much of the math taught to prepare a student for physics deals with relationships and formulas that can be used to express motion and acceleration.

What, then, can we conclude about mathematics and sex? If   25
math anxiety is in part the result of math avoidance, why not require girls to take as much math as they can possibly master? If being the only girl in "trig" is the reason so many women drop math at the end of high school, why not provide psychological counseling and support for those young women who wish to go on? Since ability in mathematics is considered by many to be unfeminine, perhaps fear of success, more than any bodily or mental dysfunction, may interfere with girls' ability to learn math.

Questions for Study and Discussion

1. Tobias states that girls suffer more than boys from math anxiety. What does she say causes girls to be more fearful than boys?

2. What evidence does Tobias use to establish the main cause and effect relationship in this essay? Is her evidence sufficient? If not, what else might she have added? (Glossary: *Evidence*)

3. Why does Tobias downplay sex differences as a cause for differences in mathematical performance?

4. Tobias states, "A common myth about the nature of mathematical ability holds that one either has or does not have a mathematical mind" (2). What does she think are the effects of this myth?

5. What is the cause and effect relationship discussed in paragraphs 15–20? What function does paragraph 18 serve in the development of that relationship?

6. What did you learn from Tobias's opening paragraph? Was it an effective introduction for you? (Glossary: *Beginnings and Endings*) Explain why, or why not.

7. What types of support services and requirements does Tobias suggest to help girls overcome math anxiety? What additional suggestions can you offer?

Vocabulary

Refer to your dictionary to define the following words as they are used in this selection. Then use each word in a sentence of your own.

curriculum (1)   innate (9)
myth (2)   commences (14)
intuitive (2)   compatible (19)
unwittingly (4)   inimical (20)
aversion (5)

Suggested Writing Assignments

1. How do you feel about mathematics? Write a short essay discussing the reasons for your attitude. What *caused* you to feel the way that you do?

2. If you were able to find the ideal job after college, what would that job be? Write an essay explaining why you think a particular job would be best for you and, more importantly, explain what forces (causes) in your life have led you to that career choice (effect). For example, you may want to sell automobiles because your uncle is an automobile salesman, or you have spent time in his office and you know what he does, or you enjoy being around cars and working with people.

18

ARGUMENT

Argumentation is the attempt to persuade a reader to accept your point of view, to make a decision, or to pursue a particular course of action. Because the writer of an argument is often interested in explaining a subject, as well as in advocating a particular view, argumentation frequently adopts other rhetorical strategies. Nevertheless, it is the attempt to convince, not to explain, that is most important in an argumentative essay.

There are two basic types of argumentation: logical and persuasive. In *logical argumentation* the writer appeals to the reader's rational or intellectual faculties to convince him of the truth of a particular statement or belief. In *persuasive argumentation*, on the other hand, the writer appeals to the reader's emotions and opinions to move the reader to action. These two types of argumentation are seldom found in their pure forms, and the degree to which one or the other is emphasized in written work depends on the writer's subject, specific purpose, and intended audience. Although you may occasionally need or want to appeal to your readers' emotions, most often in your college work you will need to rely only on the fundamental techniques of logical argumentation.

There are two types of reasoning common to essays of argumentation: induction and deduction. *Inductive reasoning*, the more common type, moves from a set of specific examples to a general statement. In doing so, the writer makes what is known as an *inductive leap* from the evidence to the generalization. For example, after examining enrollment statistics, we can conclude that students do not like to take courses offered early in the morning or late in the afternoon. *Deductive reasoning*, on the other hand, moves from a general statement to a specific conclusion. It works on the model of the *syllogism*, a simple three-part argument that consists of a major premise, a minor premise, and a conclusion, as in the following example:

a. All women are mortal. (major premise)
b. Judy is a woman. (minor premise)
c. Judy is mortal. (conclusion)

A well-constructed argument avoids *logical fallacies,* flaws in the reasoning that will render the argument invalid. Following are some of the most common logical fallacies:

1. *Oversimplification.* The tendency to provide simple solutions to complex problems. "The reason we have low unemployment today is the threat of war in Central America and the Middle East."

2. *Hasty generalization.* A generalization that is based on too little evidence or on evidence that is not representative. "It was the best movie I saw this year, and so it should get an Academy Award."

3. *Post hoc, ergo propter hoc* ("After this, therefore because of this"). Confusing chance or coincidence with causation. Because one event comes after another one, it does not necessarily mean that the first event caused the second. "Ever since I went to the hockey game, I've had a cold." The assumption here is that going to the hockey game had something to do with the speaker's cold when, in fact, there might be one or more different causes for the cold.

4. *Begging the question.* Assuming in a premise that which needs to be proven. "Conservation is the only means of solving the energy problem over the long haul; therefore, we should seek out methods to conserve energy."

5. *False analogy.* Making a misleading analogy between logically unconnected ideas. "Of course he'll make a fine coach. He was an all-star basketball player."

6. *Either/or thinking.* The tendency to see an issue as having only two sides. "Used car salesmen are either honest or crooked."

7. *Non sequitur* ("It does not follow"). An inference or conclusion that does not follow from established premises or evidence. "She is a sincere speaker; she must know what she is talking about."

As you write your argumentative essays, you should keep the following advice in mind. Somewhere near the beginning of your essay, you should identify the issue to be discussed, explain why you think it is important, and point out what interest you and your readers share in the issue. Then, in the body of your essay, you should organize the various points of your argument. You may move from your least important point to your most important point, from the most familiar to the least familiar, from the easiest to accept or comprehend to the most difficult. For each point in your argument, you should provide sufficient appropriate supporting evidence—facts and statistics, illustrative examples and narratives, quotations from authorities. In addition, you should acknowledge the strongest opposing arguments and explain why you believe your position is more valid.

Be sure that you neither overstate nor understate your position. It is always wise to let the evidence convince your reader. Overstatement not only annoys readers but, more importantly, raises serious doubts about your own confidence in the power of your facts and reasoning. At the same time, no writer persuades by excessively understating or qualifying information with words and phrases such as *perhaps, maybe, I think, sometimes, most often, nearly always,* or *in my opinion.* The result sounds not rational and sensible but indecisive and fuzzy.

As They Say, Drugs Kill

Laura Rowley

*Laura Rowley was born in Oak Lawn, Illinois, in
1965 and graduated from the University of Illinois at Champaign—Urbana in 1987 with a degree in journalism. While in college, Rowley was
the city editor for the* Daily Illini. *After graduation she worked at the* United Nations Chronicle
*in New York City. Currently the sales director
for a Manhattan dress company, Rowley continues to work as a free-lance writer and hopes
some day to travel and work in Africa under the
auspices of either the United Nations or the
Peace Corps. In the following essay, which first
appeared in* Newsweek on Campus *in 1987, Rowley argues against substance abuse by recounting a particularly poignant personal experience.
As you read her piece, notice how she attempts to
persuade without preaching.*

The fastest way to end a party is to have someone die in the
middle of it.

At a party last fall I watched a 22-year-old die of cardiac arrest after he had used drugs. It was a painful, undignified way
to die. And I would like to think that anyone who shared the experience would feel his or her ambivalence about substance
abuse dissolving.

This victim won't be singled out like Len Bias as a bitter example for "troubled youth." He was just another ordinary guy
celebrating with friends at a private house party, the kind
where they roll in the keg first thing in the morning and get stu-
pefied while watching the football games on cable all afternoon. The living room was littered with beer cans from last
night's party—along with dirty socks and the stuffing from the
secondhand couch.

And there were drugs, as at so many other college parties.   4
The drug of choice this evening was psilocybin, hallucinogenic
mushrooms. If you're cool you call them "'shrooms."

This wasn't a crowd huddled in the corner of a darkened   5
room with a single red bulb, shooting needles in their arms.
People played darts, made jokes, passed around a joint and listened to the Grateful Dead on the stereo.

Violent fall: Suddenly, a thin, tall, brown-haired young man   6
began to gasp. His eyes rolled back in his head, and he hit the
floor face first with a crash. Someone laughed, not appreciat-
ing the violence of his fall, thinking the afternoon's festivities
had finally caught up with another guest. The laugh lasted only
a second, as the brown-haired guest began to convulse and
choke. The sound of the stereo and laughter evaporated. By-
standers shouted frantic suggestions:

"It's an epileptic fit, put something in his mouth!"   7

Roll him over on his stomach!"   8

"Call an ambulance; God, somebody breathe into his mouth."   9

A girl kneeling next to him began to sob his name, and he   10
seemed to moan.

"Wait, he's semicoherent." Four people grabbed for the tele-   11
phone, to find no dial tone, and ran to use a neighbor's. One
slammed the dead phone against the wall in frustration—and
miraculously produced a dial tone.

But the body was now motionless on the kitchen floor. "He   12
has a pulse, he has a pulse."

"But he's not breathing!"   13

"Well, get away—give him some f———ing air!" The three or   14
four guests gathered around his body unbuttoned his shirt.

"Wait—is he OK? Should I call the damn ambulance?"   15

A chorus of frightened voices shouted, "Yes, yes!"   16

"Come on, come on, breathe again. Breathe!"   17

Over muffled sobs came a sudden grating, desperate breath   18
that passed through bloody lips and echoed through the
kitchen and living room.

"He's had this reaction before—when he did acid at a concert   19
last spring. But he recovered in 15 seconds . . . ," one friend
confided.

The rest of the guests looked uncomfortably at the floor or   20
paced purposelessly around the room. One or two whispered,

"Oh, my God," over and over, like a prayer. A friend stood next to me, eyes fixed on the kitchen floor. He mumbled, just audibly, "I've seen this before. My dad died of a heart attack. He had the same look. . . ." I touched his shoulder and leaned against a wall, repeating reassurances to myself. People don't die at parties. People don't die at parties.

Eventually, no more horrible, gnashing sounds tore their way from the victim's lungs. I pushed my hands deep in my jeans pockets wondering how much it costs to pump a stomach and how someone could be so careless if he had had this reaction with another drug. What would he tell his parents about the hospital bill? 21

Two uniformed paramedics finally arrived, lifted him onto a stretcher and quickly rolled him out. His face was grayish blue, his mouth hung open, rimmed with blood, and his eyes were rolled back with a yellowish color on the rims. 22

The paramedics could be seen moving rhythmically forward and back through the small windows of the ambulance, whose lights threw a red wash over the stunned watchers on the porch. The paramedics' hands were massaging his chest when someone said, "Did you tell them he took psilocybin? Did you tell them." 23

"No, I . . ." 24

"My God, so tell them—do you want him to die?" Two people ran to tell the paramedics the student had eaten mushrooms five minutes before the attack. 25

It seemed irreverent to talk as the ambulance pulled away. My friend, who still saw his father's image, muttered, "That guy's dead." I put my arms around him half to comfort him, half to stop him from saying things I couldn't believe. 26

The next day, when I called someone who lived in the house, I found that my friend was right. 27

My hands began to shake and my eyes filled with tears for someone I didn't know. Weeks later the pain has dulled, but I still can't unravel the knot of emotion that has moved from my stomach to my head. When I told one friend what happened, she shook her head and spoke of the stupidity of filling your body with chemical substances. People who would do drugs after seeing that didn't value their lives too highly, she said. 28

No lessons: But others refused to read any universal lessons 29 from the incident. Many of those I spoke to about the event considered him the victim of a freak accident, randomly struck down by drugs as a pedestrian might be hit by a speeding taxi. They speculated that the student must have had special physical problems; what happened to him could not happen to them.

Couldn't it? Now when I hear people discussing drugs I'm   30
haunted by the image of him lying on the floor, his body straining to rid itself of substances he chose to take. Painful, undignified, unnecessary—like a wartime casualty. But in war, at least, lessons are supposed to be learned, so that old mistakes are not repeated. If this death cannot make people think and change, that will be an even greater tragedy.

Questions for Study and Discussion

1. What is Rowley's purpose in this essay? What does she want us to believe? What does she want us to do? (Glossary: *Purpose*)

2. Rowley uses an extended narrative example to develop her argument. How does she use dialogue, diction choices, and appropriate details to enhance the drama of her story?

3. What does Rowley gain by sharing this powerful experience with her readers? How did Rowley's friend react when she told them her story?

4. Why do you think Rowley chose not to name the young man who died? In what ways is this young man different from Len Bias, the talented basketball player who died of a drug overdose after signing a contract with the Boston Celtics?

5. What in Rowley's tone—her attitude toward her subject and audience—particularly contributes to the persuasiveness of the essay? Cite examples from the selection that support your conclusion. (Glossary: *Tone*)

6. How did Rowley's opening paragraph affect you? What would have been lost had she combined the first two paragraphs? (Glossary: *Beginnings and Endings*)

7. For what audience do you suppose Rowley wrote this essay? In your opinion, would most readers be convinced by

what Rowley says about drugs? Are you convinced? Why, or why not? (Glossary: *Audience*)

Vocabulary

Refer to your dictionary to define the following words as they are used in this selection. Then use each word in a sentence of your own.

ambivalence (2)	gnashing (21)
stupefied (3)	irreverent (26)
convulse (6)	unravel (28)
semicoherent (11)	speculated (29)
audibly (20)	tragedy (30)

Suggested Writing Assignments

1. Write a persuasive essay in which you support or refute the following proposition:

   Television advertising is in large part responsible for Americans' belief that over-the-counter drugs are cure-alls.

   Does such advertising in fact promote drug dependence and/or abuse?

2. Write an essay in which you argue against either drinking or smoking. What would drinkers and smokers claim are the benefits of their habits? What are the key arguments against these types of substance abuse? Use examples from your personal experience or from your reading to document your essay.

3. What is the most effective way to bring about social change and to influence societal attitudes? Concentrating on the sorts of changes you have witnessed over the last ten years, write an essay in which you describe how best to influence public opinion.

WHAT'S WRONG WITH BLACK ENGLISH

Rachel L. Jones

Rachel L. Jones was a sophomore at Southern Illinois University when she published the following essay in Newsweek *in December 1982. Jones argues against the popularly held belief of both her fellow black students and black authorities that speaking "white English" is a betrayal of her blackness.*

William Labov, a noted linguist, once said about the use   1
of black English, "It is the goal of most black Americans to acquire full control of the standard language without giving up their own culture." He also suggested that there are certain advantages to having two ways to express one's feelings. I wonder if the good doctor might also consider the goals of those black Americans who have full control of standard English but who are every now and then troubled by that colorful, grammar-to-the-winds patois that is black English. Case in point—me.

I'm a 21-year-old black born to a family that would probably   2
be considered lower-middle class—which in my mind is a polite way of describing a condition only slightly better than poverty. Let's just say we rarely if ever did the winter-vacation thing in the Caribbean. I've often had to defend my humble beginnings to a most unlikely group of people for an even less likely reason. Because of the way I talk, some of my black peers look at me sideways and ask, "Why do you talk like you're white?"

The first time it happened to me I was nine years old. Cor-   3
nered in the school bathroom by the class bully and her sidekick, I was offered the opportunity to swallow a few of my teeth unless I satisfactorily explained why I always got good grades, why I talked "proper" or "white." I had no ready answer for her, save the fact that my mother had from the time I was old enough to talk stressed the importance of reading and learning, or that L. Frank Baum and Ray Bradbury were my

closest companions. I read all my older brothers' and sisters' literature textbooks more faithfully than they did, and even lightweights like the Bobbsey Twins and Trixie Belden were allowed into my bookish inner circle. I don't remember exactly what I told those girls, but I somehow talked my way out of a beating.

I was reminded once again of my "white pipes" problem 4 while apartment hunting in Evanston, Ill., last winter. I doggedly made out lists of available places and called all around. I would immediately be invited over—and immediately turned down. The thinly concealed looks of shock when the front door opened clued me in, along with the flustered instances of "just getting off the phone with the girl who was ahead of you and she wants the rooms." When I finally found a place to live, my roommate stirred up old memories when she remarked a few months later, "You know, I was surprised when I first saw you. You sounded white over the phone." Tell me another one, sister.

I should've asked her a question I've wanted an answer to for 5 years: how does one "talk white?" The silly side of me pictures a rabid white foam spewing forth when I speak. I don't use Valley Girl jargon, so that's not what's meant in my case. Actually, I've pretty much deduced what people mean when they say that to me, and the implications are really frightening.

It means that I'm articulate and well-versed. It means that I 6 can talk as freely about John Steinbeck as I can about Rick James. It means that "ain't" and "he be" are not staples of my vocabulary and are only used around family and friends. (It is almost Jekyll and Hyde-ish the way I can slip out of academic abstractions into a long, lean, double-negative-filled dialogue, but I've come to terms with that aspect of my personality.) As a child, I found it hard to believe that's what people meant by "talking proper"; that would've meant that good grades and standard English were equated with white skin, and that went against everything I'd ever been taught. Running into the same type of mentality as an adult has confirmed the depressing reality that for many blacks, standard English is not only unfamiliar, it is socially unacceptable.

James Baldwin once defended black English by saying it had 7 added "vitality to the language," and even went so far as to label it a language in its own right, saying, "Language [i.e., black English] is a political instrument" and a "vivid and crucial key to identity." But did Malcolm X urge blacks to take power in this country "any way y'all can"? Did Martin Luther King Jr. say to blacks, "I has been to the mountaintop, and I done seed the Promised Land"? Toni Morrison, Alice Walker and James Baldwin did not achieve their eloquence, grace and stature by using only black English in their writing. Andrew Young, Tom Bradley and Barbara Jordan did not acquire political power by saying, "Y'all crazy if you ain't gon vote for me." They all have full command of standard English, and I don't think that knowledge takes away from their blackness or commitment to black people.

I know from experience that it's important for black people, 8 stripped of culture and heritage, to have something they can point to and say, "This is ours, *we* can comprehend it, *we* alone can speak it with a soulful flourish." I'd be lying if I said that the rhythms of my people caught up in "some serious rap" don't sound natural and right to me sometimes. But how heart-warming is it for those same brothers when they hit the pave-ment searching for employment? Studies have proven that the use of ethnic dialects decreases power in the marketplace. "I be" is acceptable on the corner, but not with the boss.

Am I letting capitalistic, European-oriented thinking fog the 9 issue? Am I selling out blacks to an ideal of assimilating, being as much like white as possible? I have not formed a personal political ideology, but I do know this: it hurts me to hear black children use black English, knowing that they will be at yet an-other disadvantage in an educational system already full of stumbling blocks. It hurts me to sit in lecture halls and hear fel-low black students complain that the professor "be tripping dem out using big words dey can't understand." And what hurts most is to be stripped of my own blackness simply be-cause I know my way around the English language.

I would have to disagree with Labov in one respect. My goal 10 is not so much to acquire full control of both standard and black English, but to one day see more black people less depen-dent on a dialect that excludes them from full participation in the world we live in. I don't think I talk white, I think I talk right.

Questions for Study and Discussion

1. What is Jones's purpose in this essay? (Glossary: *Purpose*) For what is she arguing?
2. What purpose is served by Jones's title? Does the title indicate that she will be arguing for or against black English?
3. What, according to Jones, is the attitude of many blacks toward standard English? What does Jones find wrong with their thinking and the resulting state of affairs?
4. What is black English? Where does Jones provide a definition of the term? (Glossary: *Definition*)
5. What examples does Jones use to argue that a knowledge of standard English does not diminish a person's blackness or commitment to black people? Do you find them convincing?
6. How has Jones used narration to help her case? (Glossary: *Narration*)

Vocabulary

Refer to your dictionary to define the following words as they are used in this selection. Then use each word in a sentence of your own.

linguist (1)	deduced (5)
patois (1)	staples (6)
doggedly (4)	dialect (10)
rabid (5)	

Suggested Writing Assignments

1. Much has been written since the late sixties on how black English should be regarded linguistically, socially, educationally, and personally. The subject is sometimes called bidialectalism or bilingualism. Review some aspect of this controversy as presented in newspapers and popular magazines, and come to some conclusions of your own regarding the issues. You may find it helpful to consult the *Reader's Guide to Periodical Literature* in the reference section of your school library. Finally, write an argument based on

your own views. Be sure to provide as much evidence as possible to support your conclusions.

2. The title of Rachel Jones's essay suggests a formula for other possible arguments. Using the "What's Wrong with _____" as a title, write an argumentative essay on any one of the following topics:

the sale of over-the-counter tranquilizers

U. S. military involvement in Central America

gentrification

the 55-mile-per-hour speed limit

diets

gun control

cheating

salt/sugar

LOTTERIES CHEAT, CORRUPT THE PEOPLE

George F. Will

Born in 1941 in Champaign, Illinois, George F. Will attended Trinity College in Hartford, Connecticut, and Princeton University before going on to teach political science at Michigan State University and the University of Toronto. Will is best known for his syndicated newspaper column and his biweekly column in Newsweek. *He has collected his columns in three books—* The Pursuit of Happiness and Other Sobering Thoughts *(1979),* The Pursuit of Virtue and Other Tory Notions *(1982), and* The Morning After: American Successes and Excesses, 1981– 1986 *(1986). He also has written another book on politics,* Statecraft as Soulcraft: What Government Does *(1983). In the following selection, Will takes issue with government-run lotteries and the delusions they encourage.*

On the outskirts of this city of insurance companies, there is another, less useful, business based on an understanding of probabilities. It is a jai alai fronton, a cavernous court where athletes play a fast game for the entertainment of gamblers and the benefit of, among others, the state treasury.

Half the states have legal betting in casinos, at horse or dog tracks, off-track betting parlors, jai alai frontons, or in state-run lotteries. Only Connecticut has four (the last four) kinds of gambling, and there is talk of promoting the other two.

Not coincidentally, Connecticut is one of just seven states still fiercely determined not to have an income tax. Gambling taxes yielded $76.4 million last year, which is not a large slice of Connecticut's $2.1 billion budget, but it would be missed, and is growing.

Last year Americans legally wagered $15 billion, up 8 per-   4
cent over 1976. Lotteries took in 24 percent more. Stiffening resistance to taxes is encouraging states to seek revenues from
gambling, and thus to encourage gambling. There are three rationalizations for this:

State-run gambling controls illegal gambling.   5
Gambling is a painless way to raise revenues.   6
Gambling is a "victimless" recreation, and thus is a matter of   7
moral indifference.

Actually, there is evidence that legal gambling increases the   8
respectability of gambling, and increases public interest in
gambling. This creates new gamblers, some of whom move on
to illegal gambling, which generally offers better odds. And as
a revenue-raising device, gambling is severely regressive.

Gamblers are drawn disproportionately from minority and   9
poor populations that can ill-afford to gamble, that are especially susceptible to the lure of gambling, and that especially
need a government that will not collaborate with gambling en-
trepreneurs, as in jai alai, and that will not become a gambling
entrepreneur through a state lottery.

A depressing number of gamblers have no margin for eco-   10
nomic losses and little understanding of the probability of
losses. Between 1975 and 1977 there was a 140 percent increase
in spending to advertise lotteries—lotteries in which more than
99.9 percent of all players are losers. Such advertising is apt to
be especially effective, and cruel, among people whose tribula-
tions make them susceptible to dreams of sudden relief.

Grocery money is risked for such relief. Some grocers in   11
Hartford's poorer neighborhoods report that receipts decline
during jai alai season. Aside from the injury gamblers do to
their dependents, there is a more subtle but more comprehensive injury done by gambling. It is the injury done to society's
sense of elemental equities. Gambling blurs the distinction between well-earned and "ill-gotten" gains.

Gambling is debased speculation, a lust for sudden wealth   12
that is not connected with the process of making society more
productive of goods and services. Government support of gambling gives a legitimating imprimatur to the pursuit of wealth
without work.

"It is," said Jefferson, "the manners and spirit of a people which preserves a republic in vigor." Jefferson believed in the virtue-instilling effects of agricultural labor. Andrew Jackson denounced the Bank of the United States as a "monster" because increased credit creation meant increased speculation. Martin Van Buren warned against "a craving desire . . . for sudden wealth." The early nineteenth century belief was that citizens could be distinguished by the moral worth of the way they acquired wealth; and physical labor was considered the most ennobling labor. 13

It is perhaps a bit late to worry about all this: the United States is a developed capitalist society of a sort Jefferson would have feared if he had been able to imagine it. But those who cherish capitalism should note that the moral weakness of capitalism derives, in part, from the belief that too much wealth is allocated in "speculative" ways, capriciously, to people who earn their bread neither by the sweat of their brows nor by wrinkling their brows for socially useful purposes. 14

Of course, any economy produces windfalls. As a town grows, some land values soar. And some investors (like many non-investors) regard stock trading as a form of roulette. 15

But state-sanctioned gambling institutionalizes windfalls, whets the public appetite for them, and encourages the delusion that they are more frequent than they really are. Thus do states simultaneously cheat and corrupt their citizens. 16

Questions for Study and Discussion

1. The city that Will refers to in paragraph 1 is later revealed to be Hartford, Connecticut, long regarded as the nation's insurance capital. Why does Will make this reference to insurance companies? Is buying insurance a form of gambling? Explain.

2. Why does Will state in paragraph 16 that state-run lotteries "cheat and corrupt" society?

3. Where, specifically, has Will answered each of the three "rationalizations" he presents in paragraphs 5–7? On which point does he spend the most time? Why?
4. Do you feel Will's evidence in paragraph 11 is convincing? Why, or why not? (Glossary: *Evidence*)
5. What purpose is served by paragraph 14? Is Will against capitalism because it relies on speculation? Explain.
6. Why do you suppose Will's paragraphs are so short?

Vocabulary

Refer to your dictionary to define the following words as they are used in this selection. Then use each word in a sentence of your own.

probabilities (1)	debased (12)
rationalizations (4)	imprimatur (12)
entrepreneurs (9)	windfalls (15)
tribulations (10)	whets (16)

Suggested Writing Assignments

1. Argue for or against government-run lotteries, bingo, or other form of gambling in your state.
2. Anyone who is against a lottery might feel differently if he or she had bought a $1 ticket and won a million dollars. But should our attitude and actions regarding issues be based on whether or not we stand to gain personally? Make the case for deciding important issues on the basis of principles, however arguable they might be, and not on an individual, case-by-case basis. Think about the possible objections to such a belief and how you might answer these objections in your essay.

THE DECLARATION OF INDEPENDENCE

Thomas Jefferson

*President, governor, statesman, lawyer, archi-
tect, philosopher, and writer, Thomas Jefferson
(1743–1826) was a seminal figure in the early history of our country. In 1776 Jefferson drafted the
Declaration of Independence. Although it was
revised by Benjamin Franklin and other colleagues at the Continental Congress, the document retains in its sound logic and forceful,
direct style the unmistakable qualities of
Jefferson's prose. In 1809, after two terms as
president, Jefferson retired to Monticello, a
home he had designed and helped build. Ten
years later he founded the University of Virginia.
Jefferson died at Monticello on July 4, 1826, the
fiftieth anniversary of the signing of the Declaration of Independence.*

When in the course of human events, it becomes neces-   1
sary for one people to dissolve the political bands
which have connected them with another, and to assume
among the Powers of the earth, the separate and equal station
to which the Laws of Nature and of Nature's God entitle them,
a decent respect to the opinions of mankind requires that they
should declare the causes which impel them to the separation.

We hold these truths to be self-evident, that all men are cre-   2
ated equal, that they are endowed by their Creator with certain
unalienable Rights, that among these are Life, Liberty and the
pursuit of Happiness. That to secure these rights, Governments
are instituted among Men deriving their just powers from the
consent of the governed. That whenever any Form of Government becomes destructive of these ends, it is the Right of the
People to alter or to abolish it, and to institute new Government, laying its foundation on such principles and organizing

its powers in such form, as to them shall seem most likely to effect their Safety and Happiness. Prudence, indeed, will dictate that Governments long established should not be changed for light and transient causes; and accordingly all experience hath shown, that mankind are more disposed to suffer, while evils are sufferable, than to right themselves by abolishing the forms to which they are accustomed. But when a long train of abuses and usurpations pursuing invariably the same Object evinces a design to reduce them under absolute Despotism, it is their right, it is their duty, to throw off such government, and to provide new Guards for their future security. Such has been the patient sufferance of these Colonies; and such is now the necessity which constrains them to alter their former Systems of Government. The history of the present King of Great Britain is a history of repeated injuries and usurpations, all having in direct object the establishment of an absolute Tyranny over these States. To prove this, let Facts be submitted to a candid world.

He has refused his Assent to Laws, the most wholesome and   3
necessary for the public good.

He has forbidden his Governors to pass Laws of immediate   4
and pressing importance, unless suspended in their operation till his Assent should be obtained; and when so suspended, he has utterly neglected to attend to them.

He has refused to pass other Laws for the accommodation of   5
large districts of people, unless those people would relinquish the right of Representation in the Legislature, a right inestimable to them and formidable to tyrants only.

He has called together legislative bodies at places unusual,   6
uncomfortable, and distant from the depository of their Public Records, for the sole purpose of fatiguing them into compliance with his measures.

He has dissolved Representative Houses repeatedly, for op-   7
posing with manly firmness his invasions on the rights of the people.

He has refused for a long time, after such dissolutions, to   8
cause others to be elected; whereby the Legislative Powers, incapable of Annihilation, have returned to the People at large for their exercise; the State remaining in the mean time exposed to all the dangers of invasion from without, and convulsions within.

He has endeavoured to prevent the population of these States; for that purpose obstructing the Laws of Naturalization of Foreigners; refusing to pass others to encourage their migration hither, and raising the conditions of new Appropriations of Lands. 9

He has obstructed the Administration of Justice, by refusing his Assent to Laws for establishing Judiciary Powers. 10

He has made Judges dependent on his Will alone, for the tenure of their offices, and the amount and payment of their salaries. 11

He has erected a multitude of New Offices, and sent hither swarms of Officers to harass our People, and eat out their substance. 12

He has kept among us, in time of peace, Standing Armies without the Consent of our Legislature. 13

He has affected to render the Military independent of and superior to the Civil Power. 14

He has combined with others to subject us to jurisdictions foreign to our constitution, and unacknowledged by our laws; giving his Assent to their acts of pretended Legislation: 15

For quartering large bodies of armed troops among us: 16

For protecting them, by a mock Trial, from Punishment for any Murders which they should commit on the Inhabitants of these States: 17

For cutting off our Trade with all parts of the world: 18

For imposing Taxes on us without our Consent: 19

For depriving us in many cases, of the benefits of Trial by Jury: 20

For transporting us beyond Seas to be tried for pretended offenses: 21

For abolishing the free System of English Laws in a Neighbouring Province, establishing therein an Arbitrary government, and enlarging its boundaries so as to render it at once an example and fit instrument for introducing the same absolute rule into these Colonies: 22

For taking away our Charters, abolishing our most valuable Laws, and altering fundamentally the Forms of our Governments: 23

For suspending our own Legislatures, and declaring themselves invested with Power to legislate for us in all cases whatsoever. 24

He has abdicated Government here, by declaring us out of his   25
Protection and waging War against us.

He has plundered our seas, ravaged our Coasts, burnt our   26
towns and destroyed the Lives of our people.

He is at this time transporting large Armies of foreign Merce-   27
naries to compleat works of death, desolation and tyranny, already begun with circumstances of Cruelty & perfidy scarcely
paralleled in the most barbarous ages, and totally unworthy
the Head of a civilized nation.

He has constrained our fellow Citizens taken Captive on the   28
high Seas to bear Arms against their Country, to become the ex-
ecutioners of their friends and Brethren, or to fall themselves
by their Hands.

He has excited domestic insurrections amongst us, and has   29
endeavoured to bring on the inhabitants of our frontiers, the
merciless Indian Savages, whose known rule of warfare, is an
undistinguished destruction of all ages, sexes and conditions.

In every stage of these Oppressions We Have Petitioned for   30
Redress in the most humble terms: Our repeated petitions have
been answered only by repeated injury. A Prince, whose character is thus marked by every act which may define a Tyrant, is
unfit to be the ruler of a free People.

Nor have We been wanting in attention to our British breth-   31
ren. We have warned them from time to time of attempts by
their legislature to extend an unwarrantable jurisdiction over
us. We have reminded them of the circumstances of our emi-
gration and settlement here. We have appealed to their native
justice and magnanimity and we have conjured them by the ties
of our common kindred to disavow these usurpations, which
would inevitably interrupt our connections and correspondence. They too have been deaf to the voice of justice and of
consanguinity. We must, therefore acquiesce in the necessity,
which denounces our Separation, and hold them, as we hold
the rest of mankind, Enemies in War, in Peace Friends.

We, therefore, the Representatives of the United States of   32
America, in General Congress, Assembled, appealing to the Supreme Judge of the world for the rectitude of our intentions,
do, in the Name, and by Authority of the good People of these
Colonies, solemnly publish and declare, That these United Colonies are, and of Right ought to be Free and Independent

States; that they are Absolved from all Allegiance to the British Crown, and that all political connection between them and the State of Great Britain, is and ought to be totally dissolved; and that as Free and Independent States, they have full power to levy War, conclude Peace, contract Alliances, establish Commerce, and to do all other Acts and Things which Independent States may of right do. And for the support of this Declaration, with a firm reliance on the protection of Divine Providence, we mutually pledge to each other our lives, our Fortunes and our sacred Honor.

Questions for Study and Discussion

1. In paragraph 2, Jefferson presents certain "self-evident" truths. What are these truths, and how are they related to his argument? Do you consider them self-evident?

2. The Declaration of Independence is a deductive argument; it can, therefore, be presented in the form of a syllogism. What are the major premise, the minor premise, and the conclusion of Jefferson's argument? (Glossary: *Syllogism*)

3. The list of charges against the king is given as evidence in support of Jefferson's minor premise. Does he offer any evidence in support of his major premise? (Glossary: *Evidence*)

4. How, specifically, does Jefferson refute the possible charge that the colonists had not tried to solve their problems by less drastic means?

5. Where in the Declaration does Jefferson use parallel structure? What does he achieve by using it? (Glossary: *Parallelism*)

6. While the basic structure of the Declaration reflects sound deductive reasoning, Jefferson's language, particularly when he lists the charges against the king, tends to be emotional. Identify as many examples of this emotional language as you can, and discuss possible reasons why Jefferson uses this kind of language. (Glossary: *Diction*)

7. What, according to the Declaration of Independence, is the purpose of government? In your opinion, are there other legitimate purposes that governments serve? If so, what are they?

Vocabulary

Refer to your dictionary to define the following words as they are used in this selection. Then use each word in a sentence of your own.

prudence (2)   conjured (31)
transient (2)   acquiesce (31)
convulsions (8)   rectitude (32)
abdicated (25)

Suggested Writing Assignments

1. In recent years, the issue of human rights has been much discussed. Review the arguments for and against our country's active and outspoken promotion of the human rights issue as reported in the press. Then write an argument of your own in favor of a continued strong human rights policy on the part of our nation's leaders.

2. Using one of the subjects listed below, develop a thesis, and then write an essay in which you argue in support of that thesis.

the minimum wage
Social Security
capital punishment
the erosion of individual rights
welfare
separation of church and state
First Amendment rights

THE TROUBLE WITH TELEVISION

Robert MacNeil

*Robert MacNeil is best known today as the co-
anchor of the Public Broadcasting Service's
"MacNeil/Lehrer News Hour," a news analysis
program. Born in Montreal, Canada, he is the author of two books. In his first book,* The People
Machine: The Influence of Television on American Politics *(1968), MacNeil launches a criticism
of the broadcast industry's emphasis on the entertainment value of news. In his second book,*
The Right Place at the Right Time *(1982), he recounts his experiences as a journalist. In the following selection, MacNeil warns of TV's adverse
effect on both our culture and our values.*

I t is difficult to escape the influence of television. If you fit   1
the statistical averages, by the age of 20 you will have been
exposed to at least 20,000 hours of television. You can add
10,000 hours for each decade you have lived after the age of 20.
The only things Americans do more than watch television are
work and sleep.

Calculate for a moment what could be done with even a part   2
of those hours. Five thousand hours, I am told, are what a typical college undergraduate spends working on a bachelor's degree. In 10,000 hours you could have learned enough to become
an astronomer or engineer. You could have learned several languages fluently. If it appealed to you, you could be reading
Homer in the original Greek or Dostoyevsky in Russian. If it
didn't, you could have walked around the world and written a
book about it.

The trouble with television is that it discourages concentra-   3
tion. Almost anything interesting and rewarding in life requires some constructive, consistently applied effort. The dull-
est, the least gifted of us can achieve things that seem
miraculous to those who never concentrate on anything. But

television encourages us to apply no effort. It sells us instant gratification. It diverts us only to divert, to make the time pass without pain.

Television's variety becomes a narcotic, not a stimulus. Its   4
serial, kaleidoscopic exposures force us to follow its lead. The viewer is on a perpetual guided tour: 30 minutes at the museum, 30 at the cathedral, 30 for a drink, then back on the bus to the next attraction—except on television, typically, the spans allotted are on the order of minutes or seconds, and the chosen delights are more often car crashes and people killing one another. In short, a lot of television usurps one of the most precious of all human gifts, the ability to focus your attention yourself, rather than just passively surrender it.

Capturing your attention—and holding it—is the prime mo-   5
tive of most television programming and enhances its role as a profitable advertising vehicle. Programmers live in constant fear of losing anyone's attention—anyone's. The surest way to avoid doing so is to keep everything brief, not to strain the attention of anyone but instead to provide constant stimulation through variety, novelty, action and movement. Quite simply, television operates on the appeal to the short attention span.

It is simply the easiest way out. But it has come to be re-   6
garded as a given, as inherent in the medium itself; as an imperative, as though General Sarnoff, or one of the other august pioneers of video, had bequeathed to us tablets of stone commanding that nothing in television shall ever require more than a few moments' concentration.

In its place that is fine. Who can quarrel with a medium that   7
so brilliantly packages escapist entertainment as a mass-marketing tool? But I see its values now pervading this nation and its life. It has become fashionable to think that, like fast food, fast ideas are the way to get to a fast-moving, impatient public.

In the case of news, this practice, in my view, results in ineffi-   8
cient communication. I question how much of television's nightly news effort is really absorbable and understandable. Much of it is what has been aptly described as "machine-gunning with scraps." I think the technique fights coherence. I think it tends to make things ultimately boring and dismissible (unless they are accompanied by horrifying pictures) because

almost anything is boring and dismissible if you know almost nothing about it.

I believe that TV's appeal to the short attention span is not only inefficient communication but decivilizing as well. Consider the casual assumptions that television tends to cultivate: that complexity must be avoided, that visual stimulation is a substitute for thought, that verbal precision is an anachronism. It may be old-fashioned, but I was taught that thought is words, arranged in grammatically precise ways. 9

There is a crisis of literacy in this country. One study estimates that some 30 million adult Americans are "functionally illiterate" and cannot read or write well enough to answer a want ad or understand the instructions on a medicine bottle. 10

Literacy may not be an inalienable human right, but it is one that the highly literate Founding Fathers might not have found unreasonable or even unattainable. We are not only not attaining it as a nation, statistically speaking, but we are falling further and further short of attaining it. And, while I would not be so simplistic as to suggest that television is the cause, I believe it contributes and is an influence. 11

Everything about this nation—the structure of the society, its forms of family organization, its economy, its place in the world—has become more complex, not less. Yet its dominating communications instrument, its principal form of national linkage, is one that sells neat resolutions to human problems that usually have no neat resolutions. It is all symbolized in my mind by the hugely successful art form that television has made central to the culture, the 30-second commercial: the tiny drama of the earnest housewife who finds happiness in choosing the right toothpaste. ·12

When before in human history has so much humanity collectively surrendered so much of its leisure to one toy, one mass diversion? When before has virtually an entire nation surrendered itself wholesale to a medium for selling? 13

Some years ago Yale University law professor Charles L. Black, Jr., wrote: ". . . forced feeding on trivial fare is not itself a trivial matter." I think this society is being force-fed with trivial fare, and I fear that the effects on our habits of mind, our language, our tolerance for effort, and our appetite for complexity are only dimly perceived. If I am wrong, we will 14 have done no harm to look at the issue skeptically and critically, to consider how we should be resisting it. I hope you will join with me in doing so.

Questions for Study and Discussion

1. What is MacNeil's thesis in this essay?
2. In paragraph 2 MacNeil invites us to think about what we might have accomplished with the 5,000 or 10,000 hours we spent watching television. What do you suppose was his intent in having us participate in this exercise? Did it work? Explain.
3. What specific criticisms does he make regarding the way television presents the news?
4. What do television commercials symbolize for MacNeil? (Glossary: *Symbol*)
5. What does MacNeil find wrong with television's appeal to the population's short attention span?
6. What connection does MacNeil see between television and the nation's literacy problem?
7. How would you describe MacNeil's conclusion? What do you think he hopes to accomplish in his conclusion? (Glossary: *Beginnings and Endings*)

Vocabulary

Refer to your dictionary to define the following words as they are used in this selection. Then use each work in a sentence of your own.

dullest (3)	medium (6)
serial (4)	august (6)
kaleidoscopic (4)	anachronism (9)
usurps (4)	skeptically (14)

Suggested Writing Assignments

1. MacNeil's essay is almost totally negative about television's effects on its viewers. Write an essay in which you take the opposing view. Develop a thesis presenting the beneficial effects of television.

2. Write an essay in which you use the following sentence as a thesis statement:

   The best single source for daily news is the (television, radio, newspaper).

THE MIRACLE OF TECHNOFIX

Kirkpatrick Sale

Born in 1937 in Ithaca, New York, Kirkpatrick Sale attended Swarthmore College and graduated from Cornell University in 1958. In the early sixties he served as a foreign correspondent for the San Francisco Chronicle *and* Chicago Tribune *and was a lecturer in history at the University of Ghana. The latter experience resulted in a book* The Land and People of Ghana *(1963). In 1980 he published* Human Scale, *a book in which he presents his solutions to modern society's problems. Here Sale states that "society has grown too large too fast and our bodies and minds can no longer bear the pressures that our fast-paced, over-crowded, technologically-complex lifestyles have placed on them." Sale's solution is for Americans to replace large-scale systems with "smaller, more controllable, more efficient, people-sized units, rooted in local circumstances and guided by local institutions." In the following selection, which first appeared in* Newsweek *in 1980, Sale criticizes our society for becoming too dependent on technology as the answer for all our problems.*

We have tried the future—and it doesn't work. 1

For 30 years now, this nation has been on a relentless 2 and expensive high-technology binge, forging for itself the machines and systems that are supposed to underpin—and to presage—our 21st-century lives. The only trouble is that all this high technology not only doesn't seem to be solving our problems, it actually looks to be compounding them.

Those wonders that were supposed to be brought about 3 through the sophisticated application of modern industrial science—particularly those wonders that would solve such problems as fuel shortages, starvation, poverty, crime and pollution—simply have not materialized. What's more, the attempt to create them has provided us instead with giant systems often beyond human control or guidance (which is why so many "human factor" accidents happen), with enormous capital outlays diverted from more immediate and more down-home solutions, and with a range of life-threatening environmental problems we are only just now beginning to understand.

Somehow this nation has become caught in what I call the mire of "technofix": the belief, reinforced in us by the highest corporate and political forces, that all our current crises can be solved, or at least significantly eased, by the application of modern high technology. In the words of former Atomic Energy Commission chairman Glenn Seaborg: "We must pursue the idea that it is more science, better science, more wisely applied that is going to free us from [our] predicaments."   4

Energy crisis? Try synfuels. Never mind that they will require billions—eventually trillions—of dollars transferred out of the public coffers into the energy companies' pockets, or that nobody has yet fully explored, must less solved, the problems of environmental damage, pollution, hazardous-waste disposal and occupational dangers their production will create. Never mind—it's technofix.   5

Food for the hungry world? Try the "Green Revolution." Never mind that such farming is far more energy- and chemical-intensive than any other method known, and therefore generally too expensive for the poor countries that are supposed to benefit from it, or that its principle of monoculture over crop diversity places whole regions, even whole countries, at the risk of a single breed of disease or pest. Never mind—it's scientific.   6

Diseases? Try wonder drugs. Never mind that few of the thousands of drugs introduced every year have ever been fully tested for long-range effects, or that they are vastly overprescribed and overused, or that nearly half of them prove to be totally ineffective in treating the ailments they are administered for and half of the rest produce unintended side effects. Never mind—it's progress.   7

And progress, God help us all, may be our most important   8
product.

I am not talking about the rare and the outlandish here. I am   9
talking about the commonplace, the very stuff of our daily
lives. The belief in technofix has brought us Valium for anxiety,
nuclear power for electricity, the Law Enforcement Assistance
Administration for crime, Mirex for fire ants, the electronic
battlefield for warfare, SST's for transportation, IUD's for
birth control, MX missiles for defense, Tris for fire protection. . . .

And I'm sure I needn't add that Valium is by all odds the   10
most widely abused drug in America. And that nuclear power,
at enormous financial and social cost so far, with inescapable
risks for the future, provides barely 5 per cent of our energy
supply. And that the LEAA has spent $7 billion while the crime
rate has steadily increased . . . and so on, right down the list.
There are hardly any technofix solutions that do not pose serious threats or place intolerable burdens on the society as a
whole.

Nor is the belief in technofix confined to scientific or merely   11
mechanical matters. This mode of thought has come to characterize the way that we conduct our politics as well.

Examples range from the Green Berets to the Watergate bag   12
jobs, but the starkest instance is that of the hostages in Iran. Do
we contrive human solutions, do we understand, apologize, cooperate, conciliate, negotiate—and free the hostages? No. We
try technofix solutions: international sanctions, naval maneuvers, fomented rebellions and, finally, a rescue mission of such
complexity—based on the same military technology that, you
may recall, brought us such a swift victory the last time out, in
Vietnam—that we are reduced to utter humiliation in the eyes
of the world because a couple of helicopters can't withstand
the very kinds of missions they were (at enormous public expense) designed and built for, and so many machines are mill-
ing around that two of them collide.

Now don't get me wrong. I am not arguing against "prog-   13
ress," provided that it seems to be advancing human welfare in
some truly substantial way without destroying it with what
doctors (the pluperfect technofixers) are pleased to call "side

effects." Only it does strike me that our current version of "progress" is headed more the other way.

We have tried the technofix future, and after 30 years of it I'd ask only: do we seem to be moving toward real and healthy solutions to our nation's crises, does the populace seem safer and healthier and happier with it all, or do we seem, somehow, to have accumulated problems instead of dispelling them and to have created a world of greater anxiety and risk and chaos than we had before? *14*

Solutions, we must remember, are very much like problems: they are rooted in people, not in technology. Schemes that try to devise miracles to bypass people, negate, deny, nullify or minimize people, will not work—or at least they will not work on a planet on which it is people who are expected to live. *15*

Questions for Study and Discussion

1. For the past thirty years this nation has depended on modern industrial science to prepare us for the twenty-first century. Sale contends that it hasn't worked, that expensive high technology has created new problems while trying to solve the problems of energy, food, poverty, crime, and environmental destruction. What are the new problems that high technology has left us?

2. What exactly is the condition or belief that Sale has dubbed "technofix"? What examples does he use to illustrate Americans' reliance on "technofix"?

3. If Sale is "not arguing against 'progress'" (13), what is he arguing for? Where does he state his thesis? (Glossary: *Thesis*) Does he reiterate this point elsewhere in the essay?

4. What is Sale's purpose in writing this essay? What does he want his readers to do after reading it?

5. How does paragraph 11 function in the context of Sale's essay? What is the relationship between paragraphs 11 and 12? What would be gained or lost if these two paragraphs were combined?

6. According to Sale, what kinds of solutions to our nation's crises should we be wary of? Why?

7. What is Sale's tone in this essay? (Glossary: *Tone*) Cite specific sentences and/or paragraphs that led you to this conclusion. What does Sale gain by using the pronoun *we*?

Vocabulary

Refer to your dictionary to define the following words as they are used in this selection. Then use each word in a sentence of your own.

binge (2)	conciliate (12)
synfuels (5)	fomented (12)
coffers (5)	pluperfect (13)
starkest (12)	nullify (15)

Suggested Writing Assignments

1. In *Future Shock* (1970), Alvin Toffler writes: "We cannot and must not turn off the switch of technological progress. Only romantic fools babble about returning to a 'state of nature.'" Is technology really the answer to all our problems? Would it be beneficial to go back in time? In an essay of your own, argue for or against the idea that technology is the solution to our environmental problems.

2. Today many people, especially environmentalists, do not have a favorable opinion of industry and technology. In fact, some have argued that industrial development should be limited. Write an essay in which you discuss the various arguments that can be made in favor of technology.

3. As a library project, do some reading in one of the following subject areas:

   the importation of oil
   relaxation of federal pollution standards
   offshore oil drilling
   strip mining

soil conservation
wilderness areas
endangered species

Develop a position statement based on your research, and write an argumentative essay in which you support your statement.

GLOSSARY OF USEFUL TERMS

Abstract   See *Concrete/Abstract.*

Allusion   An allusion is a passing reference to a familiar person, place, or thing often drawn from history, the Bible, mythology, or literature. An allusion is an economical way for a writer to capture the essence of an idea, atmosphere, emotion, or historical era, as in "The scandal was his Watergate" or "He saw himself as a modern Job" or "The campaign ended not with a bang but a whimper." An allusion should be familiar to the reader; if it is not, it will add nothing to the meaning.

Analogy   Analogy is a special form of comparison in which the writer explains something unfamiliar by comparing it to something familiar: "A transmission line is simply a pipeline for electricity. In the case of a water pipeline, more water will flow through the pipe as water pressure increases. The same is true of electricity in a transmission line."

Anecdote   An anecdote is a short narrative about an amusing or interesting event. Writers often use anecdotes to begin essays as well as to illustrate certain points.

Argumentation   Argumentation is one of the four basic types of prose. (Narration, description, and exposition are the other three.) To argue is to attempt to persuade a reader to agree with a point of view, to make a given decision, or to pursue a particular course of action. There are two basic types of argumentation: logical and persuasive. See the introduction to Chapter 18 (pp. 362–64) for a detailed discussion of argumentation.

Attitude   A writer's attitude reflects his or her opinion of a subject. The writer can think very positively or very negatively about a subject, or somewhere in between. See also *Tone.*

Audience   An audience is the intended readership for a piece of writing. For example, the readers of a national weekly news magazine come from all walks of life and have diverse interests, opinions, and educational backgrounds. In contrast, the readership for an organic chemistry journal is made up of people whose interests and education are quite similar. The essays in *Models for Writers* are intended for general readers, intelligent people who may lack specific information about the subject being discussed.

Beginnings and Endings   A beginning is that sentence, group of sentences, or section that introduces an essay. Good beginnings usually identify the thesis or controlling idea, attempt to interest readers, and establish a tone.

An ending is that sentence or group of sentences that brings an essay to a close. Good endings are purposeful and well planned. They can be a summary, a concluding example, an anecdote, or a quotation. Endings satisfy readers when they are the natural outgrowths of the essays themselves and give the readers a sense of finality or completion. Good essays do not simply stop; they conclude. See the introduction to Chapter 4 (pp. 64–68) for a detailed discussion of *Beginnings and Endings.*

Cause and Effect   Cause and effect analysis is a type of exposition that explains the reasons for an occurrence or the consequences of an action. See the introduction to Chapter 17 (pp. 336–37) for a detailed discussion of cause and effect. See also *Exposition.*

Classification   See *Division and Classification.*

Cliché   A cliché is an expression that has become ineffective through overuse. Expressions such as *quick as a flash, jump for joy,* and *slow as molasses* are clichés. Writers normally avoid such trite expressions and seek instead to express themselves in fresh and forceful language. See also *Diction.*

Coherence   Coherence is a quality of good writing that results when all sentences, paragraphs, and longer divisions of an essay are naturally connected. Coherent writing is achieved through (1) a logical sequence of ideas (arranged in chronological order, spatial order, order of importance, or some other appropriate order), (2) the purposeful repetition of key words and ideas, (3) a pace suitable for your topic and your reader, and (4) the use of transitional words and expressions. Coherence should not be confused with unity. (See *Unity.*) See also *Transitions.*

Colloquial Expressions   A colloquial expression is characteristic of or appropriate to spoken language or to writing that seeks its effect. Colloquial expressions are informal, as *chem, gym, come up with, be at loose ends, won't,* and *photo* illustrate. See also *Diction.* Thus, colloquial expressions are acceptable in formal writing only if they are used purposefully.

Comparison and Contrast Comparison and contrast is a type of exposition in which the writer points out the similarities and differences between two or more subjects in the same class or category. The function of any comparison and contrast is to clarify—to reach some conclusion about the items being compared and contrasted. See the introduction to Chapter 16 (pp. 313–15) for a detailed discussion of comparison and contrast. See also *Exposition.*

Conclusions See *Beginnings and Endings.*

Concrete/Abstract A concrete word names a specific object, person, place, or action that can be directly perceived by the senses: *car, bread, building, book, John F. Kennedy, Chicago,* or *hiking.* An abstract word, in contrast, refers to general qualities, conditions, ideas, actions, or relationships which cannot be directly perceived by the senses: *bravery, dedication, excellence, anxiety, stress, thinking,* or *hatred.* See also the introduction to Chapter 8 (pp. 147–52).

Connotation/Denotation Both connotation and denotation refer to the meanings of words. Denotation is the dictionary meaning of a word, the literal meaning. Connotation, on the other hand, is the implied or suggested meaning of a word. For example, the denotation of *lamb* is "a young sheep." The connotations of *lamb* are numerous: *gentle, docile, weak, peaceful, blessed, sacrificial, blood, spring, frisky, pure, innocent,* and so on. See also the introduction to Chapter 8 (pp. 147–52).

Controlling Idea See *Thesis.*

Coordination Coordination is the joining of grammatical constructions of the same rank (e.g., words, phrases, clauses) to indicate that they are of equal importance. For example, *They ate hotdogs,* and *we ate hamburgers.* See the introduction to Chapter 7 (pp. 124–28). See also *Subordination.*

Deduction Deduction is the process of reasoning from stated premises to a conclusion that follows necessarily. This form of reasoning moves from the general to the specific. See the introduction to Chapter 18 (pp. 362–64) for a discussion of deductive reasoning and its relation to argumentation. See also *Syllogism.*

Definition Definition is one of the types of exposition. Definition is a statement of the meaning of a word. A definition may be either brief or extended, part of an essay or an entire essay itself. See the introduction to Chapter 14 (pp. 276–77) for a detailed discussion of definition. See also *Exposition.*

Denotation   See *Connotation/Denotation.*

Description   Description is one of the four basic types of prose. (Narration, exposition, and argumentation are the other three.) Description tells how a person, place, or thing is perceived by the five senses. See the introduction to Chapter 12 (pp. 236–37) for a detailed discussion of description.

Dialogue   Conversation of two or more people as represented in writing. Dialogue is what people say directly to one another.

Diction   Diction refers to a writer's choice and use of words. Good diction is precise and appropriate—the words mean exactly what the writer intends, and the words are well suited to the writer's subject, intended audience, and purpose in writing. The word-conscious writer knows that there are differences among *aged, old,* and *elderly; blue, navy,* and *azure;* and *disturbed, angry,* and *irritated.* Furthermore, this writer knows in which situation to use each word. See the introduction to Chapter 8 (pp. 147–52) for a detailed discussion of diction. See also *Cliché, Colloquial Expressions, Connotation/Denotation, Jargon, Slang.*

Division and Classification   Division and classification is one of the types of exposition. When dividing and classifying, the writer first establishes categories and then arranges or sorts people, places, or things into these categories according to their different characteristics, thus making them more manageable for the writer and more understandable and meaningful for the reader. See the introduction to Chapter 15 (pp. 290–91) for a detailed discussion of division and classification. See also *Exposition.*

Dominant Impression   A dominant impression is the single mood, atmosphere, or quality a writer emphasizes in a piece of descriptive writing. The dominant impression is created through the careful selection of details and is, of course, influenced by the writer's subject, audience, and purpose. See also the introduction to Chapter 12 (pp. 236–37).

Emphasis   Emphasis is the placement of important ideas and words within sentences and longer units of writing so that they have the greatest impact. In general, what comes at the end has the most impact, and at the beginning nearly as much; what comes in the middle gets the least emphasis.

Endings See *Beginnings and Endings.*

Evaluation An evaluation of a piece of writing is an assessment of its effectiveness or merit. In evaluating a piece of writing, one should ask the following questions: What is the writer's purpose? Is it a worthwhile purpose? Does the writer achieve the purpose? Is the writer's information sufficient and accurate? What are the strengths of the essay? What are its weaknesses? Depending on the type of writing and the purpose, more specific questions can also be asked. For example, with an argument one could ask: Does the writer follow the principles of logical thinking? Is the writer's evidence sufficient and convincing?

Evidence Evidence is the information on which a judgment or argument is based or by which proof or probability is established. Evidence usually takes the form of statistics, facts, names, examples or illustrations, and opinions of authorities.

Example An example illustrates a larger idea or represents something of which it is a part. An example is a basic means of developing or clarifying an idea. Furthermore, examples enable writers to show and not simply to tell readers what they mean. See also the introduction to Chapter 10 (pp. 187–89).

Exposition Exposition is one of the four basic types of prose. (Narration, description, and argumentation are the other three.) The purpose of exposition is to clarify, explain, and inform. The methods of exposition presented in *Models for Writers* are process analysis, definition, illustration, classification, comparison and contrast, and cause and effect. For a detailed discussion of these methods of exposition, see the appropriate section introductions.

Fallacy See *Logical Fallacies.*

Figures of Speech Figures of speech are brief, imaginative comparisons that highlight the similarities between things that are basically dissimilar. They make writing vivid, interesting, and memorable. The most common figures of speech are:

Simile: An explicit comparison introduced by *like* or *as.* "The fighter's hands were like stone."

Metaphor: An implied comparison that makes one thing the equivalent of another. "All the world's a stage."

Personification: A special kind of simile or metaphor in which human traits are assigned to an inanimate object. "The engine coughed and then stopped."

See the introduction to Chapter 9 (pp. 172–73) for a detailed discussion of figurative language.

Focus   Focus is the limitation that a writer gives his or her subject. The writer's task is to select a manageable topic given the constraints of time, space, and purpose. For example, within the general subject of sports, a writer could focus on government support of amateur athletes or narrow the focus further to government support of Olympic athletes.

General   See *Specific/General.*

Idiom   An idiom is a word or phrase that is used habitually with special meaning. The meaning of an idiom is not always readily apparent to nonnative speakers of that language. For example, *catch cold, hold a job, make up your mind,* and *give them a hand* are all idioms in English.

Illustration   Illustration is the use of examples to explain, elucidate, or corroborate. Writers rely heavily on illustration to make their ideas both clear and concrete. See the introduction to Chapter 10 (pp. 187–89) for a detailed discussion of illustration.

Induction   Induction is the process of reasoning to a conclusion about all members of a class through an examination of only a few members of the class. This form of reasoning moves from the particular to the general. See the introduction to Chapter 18 (pp. 362–64) for a discussion of inductive reasoning and its relation to argumentation.

Inductive Leap   An inductive leap is the point at which a writer of an argument, having presented sufficient evidence, moves to a generalization or conclusion. See also *Induction.*

Introductions   See *Beginnings and Endings.*

Irony   The use of words to suggest something different from their literal meaning. For example, when Jonathan Swift proposes in *A Modest Proposal* that Ireland's problems could be solved if the people of Ireland fattened their babies and sold them to the English landlords for food, he meant that almost any other solution would be preferable. A writer can use irony to establish a special relationship with the reader and to add an extra dimension or twist to the meaning. See also the introduction to Chapter 8 (pp. 142–57).

Jargon   Jargon, or technical language, is the special vocabulary of a trade, profession, or group. Doctors, construction workers, lawyers, and teachers, for example, all have a specialized vocabulary that they use "on the job." See also *Diction*.

Logical Fallacies   A logical fallacy is an error in reasoning that renders an argument invalid. See the introduction to Chapter 18 (pp. 362–64) for a discussion of the more common logical fallacies.

Metaphor   See *Figures of Speech*.

Narration   One of the four basic types of prose. (Description, exposition, and argumentation are the other three.) To narrate is to tell a story, to tell what happened. While narration is most often used in fiction, it is also important in expository writing, either by itself or in conjunction with other types of prose. See the introduction to Chapter 11 (pp. 209–11) for a detailed discussion of narration.

Opinion   An opinion is a belief or conclusion, which may or may not be substantiated by positive knowledge or proof. (If not substantiated, an opinion is a prejudice.) Even when based on evidence and sound reasoning, an opinion is personal and can be changed, and is therefore less persuasive than facts and arguments.

Organization   Organization is the pattern of order that the writer imposes on his or her material. Some often used patterns of organization include time order, space order, and order of importance. See the introduction to Chapter 3 (pp. 49–50) for a more detailed discussion of organization.

Paradox   A paradox is a seemingly contradictory statement that is nonetheless true. For example, "We little know what we have until we lose it" is a paradoxical statement.

Paragraph   The paragraph, the single most important unit of thought in an essay, is a series of closely related sentences. These sentences adequately develop the central or controlling idea of the paragraph. This central or controlling idea, usually stated in a topic sentence, is necessarily related to the purpose of the whole composition. A well-written paragraph has several distinguishing characteristics: a clearly stated or implied topic sentence, adequate development, unity, coherence, and an appropriate organizational strategy. See the introduction to Chapter 5 (pp. 87–89) for a detailed discussion of paragraphs.

Parallelism   Parallel structure is the repetition of word order or grammatical form either within a single sentence or in several sentences that develop the same central idea. As a rhetorical device, parallelism can aid coherence and add emphasis. Franklin Roosevelt's statement, "I see one third of the nation ill-housed, ill-clad, and ill-nourished," illustrates effective parallelism.

Personification   See *Figures of Speech.*

Point of View   Point of view refers to the grammatical person in an essay. For example, first-person point of view uses the pronoun *I* and is commonly found in autobiography and the personal essay; third-person point of view uses the pronouns *he, she,* or *it* and is commonly found in objective writing. See the introduction to Chapter 11 (pp. 209–211) for a discussion of point of view in narration.

Process Analysis   Process analysis is a type of exposition. Process analysis answers the question *how* and explains how something works or gives step-by-step directions for doing something. See the introduction to Chapter 13 (pp. 258–59) for a detailed discussion of process analysis. See also *Exposition.*

Purpose   Purpose is what the writer wants to accomplish in a particular piece of writing. Purposeful writing seeks to *relate* (narration), to *describe* (description), to *explain* (process analysis, definition, classification, comparison and contrast, and cause and effect), or to *convince* (argumentation).

Rhetorical Question   A rhetorical question is asked but requires no answer from the reader. "When will nuclear proliferation end?" is such a question. Writers use rhetorical questions to introduce topics they plan to discuss or to emphasize important points.

Sentence   A sentence is a grammatical unit that expresses a complete thought. It consists of at least a subject (a noun) and a predicate (a verb). See the introduction to Chapter 7 (pp. 124–128) for a discussion of effective sentences.

Simile   See *Figures of Speech.*

Slang   Slang is the unconventional, very informal language of particular subgroups in our culture. Slang, such as *zonk, coke, split, rap, dude,* and *stoned,* is acceptable in formal writing only if it is used selectively for specific purposes.

Specific/General   General words name groups or classes of objects, qualities, or actions. Specific words, on the other hand, name individual objects, qualities, or actions within a class or group. To some extent the terms *general* and *specific* are relative. For example, *clothing* is a class of things. *Shirt,* however, is more specific than *clothing* but more general than *T-shirt.* See also *Diction.*

Strategy   A strategy is a means by which a writer achieves his or her purpose. Strategy includes the many rhetorical decisions that the writer makes about organization, paragraph structure, sentence structure, and diction. In terms of the whole essay, strategy refers to the principal rhetorical mode that a writer uses. If, for example, a writer wishes to show how to make chocolate chip cookies, the most effective strategy would be process analysis. If it is the writer's purpose to show why sales of American cars have declined in recent years, the most effective strategy would be cause and effect analysis.

Style   Style is the individual manner in which a writer expresses his or her ideas. Style is created by the author's particular choice of words, construction of sentences, and arrangement of ideas.

Subordination   Subordination is the use of grammatical constructions to make one part in a sentence dependent on rather than equal to another. For example, the italicized clause in the following sentence is subordinate: They all cheered *when I finished the race.* See the introduction to Chapter 7 (pp. 124–28). See also *Coordination.*

Supporting Evidence   See *Evidence.*

Syllogism   A syllogism is an argument that utilizes deductive reasoning and consists of a major premise, a minor premise, and a conclusion. For example,

All trees that lose leaves are deciduous. (major premise)
Maple trees lose their leaves. (minor premise)
Therefore, maple trees are deciduous. (conclusion)

See also *Deduction.*

Symbol   A symbol is a person, place, or thing that represents something beyond itself. For example, the eagle is a symbol of the United States, and the maple leaf, a symbol of Canada.

Syntax   Syntax refers to the way in which words are arranged to form phrases, clauses, and sentences, as well as to the grammatical relationship among the words themselves.

Technical Language   See *Jargon.*

Thesis   A thesis is the main idea of an essay, also known as the controlling idea. A thesis may sometimes be implied rather than stated directly in a thesis statement. See the introduction to Chapter 1 (pp. 15–16) for a detailed discussion of thesis.

Title   A title is a word or phrase set off at the beginning of an essay to identify the subject, to state the main idea of the essay, or to attract the reader's attention. A title may be explicit or suggestive. A subtitle, when used, explains or restricts the meaning of the main title.

Tone   Tone is the manner in which a writer relates to an audience, the "tone of voice" used to address readers. Tone may be friendly, serious, distant, angry, cheerful, bitter, cynical, enthusiastic, morbid, resentful, warm, playful, and so forth. A particular tone results from a writer's diction, sentence structure, purpose, and attitude toward the subject. See the introduction to Chapter 8 (pp. 147–52) for several examples that display different tones.

Topic Sentence   The topic sentence states the central idea of a paragraph and thus limits the content of the paragraph. Although the topic sentence normally appears at the beginning of the paragraph, it may appear at any other point, particularly if the writer is trying to create a special effect. Not all paragraphs contain topic sentences. See also *Paragraph.*

Transitions   Transitions are words or phrases that link sentences, paragraphs, and larger units of a composition in order to achieve coherence. These devices include parallelism, pronoun references, conjunctions, and the repetition of key ideas, as well as the many conventional transitional expressions such as *moreover, on the other hand, in addition, in contrast,* and *therefore.* See the introduction to Chapter 6 (pp. 105–107) for a detailed discussion of transitions. See also *Coherence.*

Unity   Unity is that quality of oneness in an essay that results when all the words, sentences, and paragraphs contribute to the thesis. The elements of a unified essay do not distract the reader. Instead, they all harmoniously support a single idea or purpose. See the introduction to Chapter 2 (pp. 32–33) for a detailed discussion of unity.

Verb Verbs can be classified as either strong verbs (*scream, pierce, gush, ravage,* and *amble*) or weak verbs (*be, has, get,* and *do*). Writers often prefer to use strong verbs in order to make writing more specific or more descriptive.

Voice Verbs can be classified as being in either the active or the passive voice. In the active voice the doer of the action is the subject. In the passive voice the receiver of the action is the grammatical subject:

Active: Glenda questioned all of the children.
Passive: All of the children were questioned by Glenda.

Acknowledgments (continued from copyright page)

2. Unity
Page 34, "Modern Courtesy" by Lore Segal. Copyright © 1987 by The New York Times Company. Reprinted by permission.
Page 38, "Be Kind to Commuters" by Christopher M. Bellitto. From *Newsweek*, October 1986. © 1986, Newsweek Inc. All rights reserved. Printed by permission.
Page 43, "Don't Let Stereotypes Warp Your Judgments" by Robert L. Heilbroner, Professor of Economics, New School for Social Research. Reprinted by permission of the author.

3. Organization
Page 51, "Reach Out and Write Someone" by Lynn Wenzel. Reprinted by permission of the author.
Page 55, "Permanent Record" by Bob Greene. Copyright © 1985, John Deadline Enterprises, Inc. Reprinted by permission of Atheneum Publishers, an imprint of Macmillan Publishing Company.
Page 60, "The Corner Store" by Eudora Welty. From "The Little Store," copyright © 1975 by Eudora Welty. Reprinted from *The Eye of the Story: Selected Essays and Reviews* by Eudora Welty, by permission of Random House, Inc.

4. Beginnings and Endings
Page 64, "What Is Freedom?" by Jerald M. Jellison and John H. Harvey. Reprinted from *Psychology Today* by permission of APA.
Page 72, "You Are How You Eat" by Enid Nemy. Copyright © 1987 by The New York Times Company. Reprinted by permission.
Page 76, "How to Take a Job Interview" by Kirby W. Stanat. © 1977, Raintree Publishers Inc. 310 West Wisconsin Avenue, Milwaukee, Wisconsin 53203.
Page 82, "Hugh Troy: Practical Joker" from *The People's Almanac #2* by David Wallechinsky, Irving Wallace, Alfred Rosa, and Paul Eschholz. Copyright © 1978 by David Wallechinsky and Irving Wallace. Reprinted by permission of William Morrow & Company.

5. Paragraphs
Page 90, "Claude Fetridge's Infuriating Law" by H. Allen Smith. Reprinted with permission from the June 1963 *Reader's Digest*. Copyright © 1963 by The Reader's Digest Assn., Inc.
Page 93, "Simplicity" by William Zinsser. From *On Writing Well*, 2d ed. by William Zinsser, (1980), Harper & Row. Copyright © 1980 by William Zinsser. Reprinted by permission of the author.
Page 100, "Old at Seventeen" by David Vecsey. Copyright © 1987 by The New York Times Company. Reprinted by permission.

6. Transitions
Page 108, "Why I Want to Have a Family" by Lisa Brown. From *Newsweek*, October 1984. © 1984, Newsweek Inc. All rights reserved. Printed by permission.
Page 113, "Auto Suggestion" by Russell Baker. Copyright © 1979 by The New York Times Company. Reprinted by permission.
Page 117, "How I Got Smart" by Steve Brody. Copyright © 1986 by The New York Times Company. Reprinted by permission.

7. Effective Sentences
Page 133, "Terror at Tinker Creek" by Annie Dillard. Excerpted from *Pilgrim at Tinker Creek* by Annie Dillard. Copyright © 1974 by Annie Dillard. Reprinted by permission of Harper & Row, Publishers, Inc.

Page 137, "Boy Meets Bear" by Stephen W. Hyde. Originally published in *Yankee*, November 1987. Reprinted by permission of the author.

Page 141, "Salvation" by Langston Hughes. From *The Big Sea* by Langston Hughes. Copyright 1940 by Langston Hughes, renewed © 1968 by Arna Bontemps and George Houston Bass. Reprinted by permission of Hill & Wang, a division of Farrar, Straus & Giroux, Inc.

II. The Language of the Essay

8. Diction and Tone

Page 153, "On Being 17, Bright, and Unable to Read" by David Raymond. Copyright © 1976 by The New York Times Company. Reprinted by permission.

Page 158, "The Flight of the Eagles" by N. Scott Momaday. Excerpts from *House Made of Dawn* by N. Scott Momaday. Copyright © 1966, 1967, 1968 by N. Scott Momaday. Reprinted by permission of Harper & Row, Publishers, Inc.

Page 161, "The Pond" by Ellen Gilchrist. Excerpt from *Falling Through Space: The Journals of Ellen Gilchrist* by Ellen Gilchrist. Copyright © 1987 by Ellen Gilchrist. Reprinted by permission of Little, Brown and Company.

Page 164, "Nameless, Tennessee" by William Least Heat Moon. From *Blue Highways: A Journey into America* by William Least Heat Moon. Copyright © 1982 by William Least Heat Moon. Reprinted by permission of Little, Brown and Company.

9. Figurative Language

Page 178, "Bullish on Baseball Cards" by Henry Petroski. From *Beyond Engineering* by Henry Petroski. Copyright © 1986 by Henry Petroski. Reprinted by permission of St. Martin's Press, New York.

Page 182, "The Death of Benny Paret" by Norman Mailer. Reprinted by permission of the author and the author's agent, Scott Meredith Literary Agency, Inc., 845 Third Avenue, New York, New York 10022.

III. Types of Essays

10. Illustrations

Page 190, "Brotherhood of the Inept" by David Binder from "About Men." Copyright © 1987 by The New York Times Syndicate Sales Corporation. Reprinted by permission of Poseidon Press, a division of Simon & Schuster, Inc.

Page 195, "One Environment, Many Worlds" by Judith and Herbert Kohl. From *The View from the Oak* by Judith and Herbert Kohl; illustrated by Roger Bayless. Copyright © 1977 by Judith and Herbert Kohl. Reprinted by permission of Little, Brown and Company.

Page 199, "What Makes a Leader?" by Michael Korda. © 1981 by Michael Korda. Reprinted by permission of the author.

Page 204, "Let's Hear It for Losers!" by Michael J. O'Neill. From *Newsweek*, November 2, 1987. © 1987, Newsweek Inc. All rights reserved. Printed by permission.

11. Narration

Page 212, "Shame" by Dick Gregory. From *Nigger: An Autobiography* by Dick Gregory with Robert Lipsyte. Copyright © 1964 by Dick Gregory Enterprises, Inc. Reprinted by permission of E. P. Dutton, a division of NAL Penguin, Inc.

Page 217, "38 Who Saw Murder Didn't Call the Police" by Martin Gainsburg. Copyright © 1964 by The New York Times Company. Reprinted by permission.

Page 223, "The Dare" by Roger Hoffman from "About Men." Copyright © 1987 by The New York Times Syndicate Sales Corporation. Reprinted by permission of Poseidon Press, a division of Simon & Schuster, Inc.

Page 228, "Momma, the Dentist, and Me" by Maya Angelou. From *I Know Why the Caged Bird Sings* by Maya Angelou. Copyright © 1969 by Maya Angelou. Reprinted by permission of Random House, Inc.

12. Description
Page 238, "Subway Station" by Gilbert Highet. Reprinted by permission of Curtis Brown, Ltd. Copyright © 1957 by Gilbert Highet.

Page 241, "The Sounds of the City" by James Tuite. Copyright © 1966 by The New York Times Company. Reprinted by permission.

Page 245, "Unforgettable Miss Bessie" by Carl T. Rowan. Reprinted with permission from the March 1985 *Reader's Digest*. Copyright © 1985 by The Reader's Digest Assn., Inc.

Page 251, "My Friend, Albert Einstein" by Banesh Hoffmann. Reprinted with permission from the January 1968 *Reader's Digest*. Copyright © 1968 by The Reader's Digest Assn., Inc.

13. Process Analysis
Page 260, "How to Write a Personal Letter" by Garrison Keillor. From International Paper's "Power of the Printed Word" series. Reprinted by permission of International Paper.

Page 265, "How to Survive a Hotel Fire" by R. H. Kauffman. Copyright © 1976 and 1981 by Jazerant Corporation, 31 Tallman Place, Nyack, New York 10960.

Page 271, "Beauty and the Beef" by Joey Green. Reprinted by permission of United Features Syndicate, Inc.

14. Definition
Page 278, "A Jerk" by Sydney J. Harris. From "Strictly Personal" by Sydney J. Harris. Copyright © News American Syndicate. Reprinted by permission of King Features, a division of Hearst Corporation.

Page 281, "Cholesterol" by Isaac Asimov. Copyright © 1986, reprinted by permission of Los Angeles Times Syndicate.

Page 286, "Breaking the Hungry Teen Code" by Ellen Goodman. Copyright © 1988, The Boston Globe Newspaper Company/Washington Post Writers Group. Reprinted by permission.

15. Division and Classification
Page 292, "Children's Insults" by Peter Farb. From *Word Play: What Happens When People Talk* by Peter Farb. Copyright © 1973 by Peter Farb. Reprinted by permission of Alfred A. Knopf, Inc.

Page 295, "Hot Boxes for Ex-Smokers" by Franklin Zimring. From *Newsweek*, April 20, 1987. Copyright © 1987, Newsweek Inc. All rights reserved. Printed by permission.

Page 300, "The Ways of Meeting Oppression" by Martin Luther King, Jr. Excerpt from *Stride Toward Freedom* by Martin Luther King, Jr. Copyright © 1958 by Martin Luther King, Jr. Reprinted by permission of Harper and Row, Publishers.

Page 305, "Friends, Good Friends—and Such Good Friends" by Judith Viorst. Copyright © 1977 by Judith Viorst. Originally appeared in *Redbook*.

16. Comparison and Contrast
Page 316, "That Lean and Hungry Look" by Suzanne Britt. Reprinted by permission of the author.

Page 321, "Grant and Lee: A Study in Contrasts" by Bruce Catton. Copyright U.S. Capitol Historical Society. Reprinted by permission.

Page 327, "The Knight and the Jester" by Anna Quindlen. Copyright © 1988 by The New York Times Company. Reprinted by permission.

Page 332, "Fable for Tomorrow" by Rachel Carson. From *Silent Spring* by Rachel Carson. Copyright © 1962 by Rachel L. Carson. Reprinted by permission of Houghton Mifflin Company.

17. Cause and Effect

Page 338, "Never Get Sick in July" by Marilyn Machlowitz. Reprinted by permission of the author.

Page 343, "When Television Is a School for Criminals" by Grant Hendricks. Reprinted with permission from *TV Guide®* Magazine. Copyright © 1977 by Triangle Publications, Inc., Randor, Pennsylvania.

Page 349, "Why We Crave Horror Movies" by Stephen King. Reprinted by permission of the author's agent Kirby McCauley Ltd. Originally appeared in *Playboy* magazine: Copyright © 1982 by *Playboy*.

Page 354, "Who's Afraid of Math, and Why?" by Sheila Tobias. Reprinted from *Overcoming Math Anxiety* by Sheila Tobias, with the permission of W. W. Norton & Company, Inc. Copyright © 1978 by Sheila Tobias.

18. Argument

Page 365, "As They Say, Drugs Kill" by Laura Rowley. From *Newsweek*, February 1987. Copyright © 1987, Newsweek Inc. All rights reserved. Printed by permission.

Page 370, "What's Wrong with Black English" by Rachel L. Jones. Reprinted by permission of the author.

Page 375, "Lotteries Cheat, Corrupt the People" by George F. Will. Copyright © 1984, Washington Post Writers Group. Reprinted with permission.

Page 385, "The Trouble with Television" by Robert MacNeil. Reprinted by permission of the author and *Reader's Digest* from the March 1985 *Reader's Digest*. Copyright © 1985 by Robert MacNeil. From speech delivered November 13, 1984, at the President's Leadership Forum, State University of New York at Purchase.

Page 390, "The Miracle of Technofix" by Kirkpatrick Sale. Reprinted by permission of the author.

INDEX